THE KNIGHT'S SQUIRE

THE KNIGHT'S SQUIRE

A SQUIRE FOR THE REALM

JOHN J. CURTA

ISBN: 979-8-9959089-1-3
Library of Congress Control Number: 2026911093

For Cinco, the best squire a knight ever had.

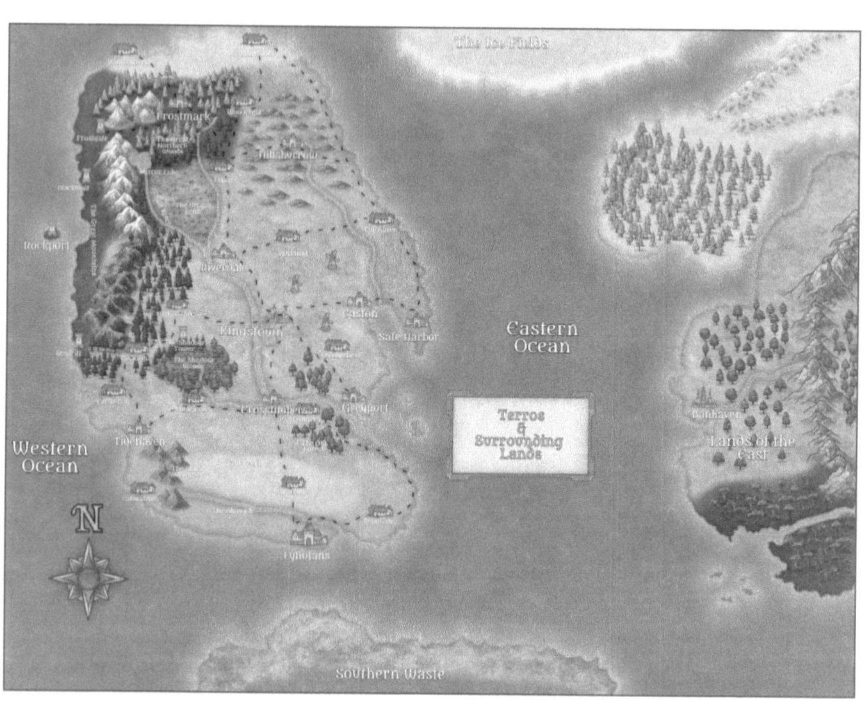
The Ice Fields
Frostmark
Frostgate
The Great Northern Woods
Hillshotrow
Crue Lake
The Dragon's Teeth
Riverdale
Rockport
Blackwall
Kingstown
The Great Mountains
The Shadow Woods
Eastern Ocean
Easten
Safe Harbor
Crosstimbers
Greyport
Tidehaven
Fyliolans
Western Ocean
Banhaven
Lands of the East
Southern Waste
N
Terros
&
Surrounding
Lands

Western Ocean
N
Whitehaven
Summerport
Frostmark
Woodcrest
Frostgate
The Great Northern Woods
Hillsburrow
Blackwall
Mirror Lake
Felfire
The Brown Fenn
White River
Rockport
The Great Mountains
Fairhaven
Duskfield
Riverdale
Caston
High Meadow
Kingstown
Safe Harbor
The Shadow Tower
Amberfield
Seadrift
Buckton
The Shadow Woods
Green River
Turtle Bay
Pebble Creek
Crosstimbers
Greyport
Tidehaven
Duxbury
The Old Forest
The Shield Mountains
The Stills
Tarringtum
The Notonoch
Dockwood
Wytefam
Fynorans

PROLOGUE

The citadel's bell rang out in a low somber tone, one toll for each year of King Edward's reign.

Helena Phoca watched from her bedroom window as the stableman unhitched the horses from her carriage. She counted the tolls of the bell and sighed, thinking her trip would have to be delayed. A knock on the chamber door caused the minister to lose her toll count at twenty-two.

"You may enter," she called from the window.

A servant entered carrying a silver tray with bread and fruits and set it on a table near the window. "Your breakfast, Minister. Your baggage is being unloaded and will be brought back to your room."

"Very good, Sarah. The trip to Amberfield for my great-great-grandchild's naming day will have to be delayed. With the king's passing, I need to remain in the capital. Let me know immediately if any messages come from the other council members, would you," Helena said as she turned to the table.

Helena sat and spread a cloth napkin over her lap. She stabbed a strawberry with a silver knife and took a small bite. The death bell continued to toll.

Helena gazed out her window at the city of Kingstown. To the north, the citadel's stone walls gave off a pinkish-gray color with the rising of a new yellow sun. The Holy Temple of the Four dominated the western part of the city with its ivy-covered pillars and cracking stone facade. Helena's building, the Ministry of Law, stood opposite the temple to the east. The white marble building gleamed in the early morning light.

As the bell continued to ring, the Grand Minister of Laws thought about her fifty-two years of service for two kings. Over those years she trained and appointed judges and worked to make sure the law of the land was enforced equally for all the people. It occurred to her that this would be a suitable time to retire. Get out of the city with all its daily problems and move back to a small farm in Amberfield to live out her remaining years closer to family. Maybe even have some chickens or ducks in the yard.

Another knock on her door brought Helena out of her thoughts.

"I am still eating, Sarah."

The door opened and a coldness engulfed the room. Helena glanced out the window to see if clouds were gathering, but the sky remained clear. She turned back to the door and a hooded figure entered and walked toward her.

"What is the meaning of this intrusion? Who are you?"

"It is time for a new order, Minister Phoca," the unknown man replied.

He stopped next to the table. His face was covered in dark rags wrapped around his head. All Helena could make out were his dark eyes.

The intruder produced a cruel-looking dagger with a curved black blade. Helena sat upright. Her eyes opened wider in panic as the tales from her youth came back to her.

A Summoner.

She thrust her hand holding the knife at the Summoner. He easily grabbed her wrist, and the knife fell to the floor. The Summoner held out his hand, pointing his long fingers toward Helena's head. A thin, ghostly vapor emitted from her. She rose from her chair as if she were a puppet on strings. The vapor curled around the Summoner's fingers and the blade of the dagger began to emit a bluish glow. Helena's breath stopped, and her lifeless body slumped back into the chair.

The death bell continued to toll.

Lord Jens Bowen sat impatiently at his table. His head hurt from looking over the ledgers. The numbers were poorly written across every page. The incessant tolling of the bells across Kingstown added to his discomfort.

Imbeciles. Incompetents. Northerners.

"Klaus! Get in here!" he yelled at his office door.

A young man opened the door and nervously stepped in. Lord Bowen noted the clerks outside his office were all standing at their desks, not working.

"Yes, Lord Minister?"

"These accounts you recorded need to all be transcribed again. I cannot read them. It needs to be done today. You and the other dolts you work with need to redo it. The king's passing is not a holiday."

He pushed the book across his table to the clerk.

"Yes, Lord Minister, right away."

The clerk took the book and closed the door to the Grand Minister of Coin's office. Lord Bowen settled behind his desk and began to open another account book when the sound of cracking wood and furniture being tossed about came from outside his door.

What now? What are those simpletons up to out there?

The minister's door burst open with a gust of wind. His clerk lay outside his door on the floor as papers floated and swirled about in the wind that blew through the office.

A hooded figure strode through the outer office as the other clerks took shelter under their desks. Bowen rushed to the door to try to close it, but the hooded figure raised a hand, and the wind grew in force.

The hooded figure stepped over the frightened clerk and into Bowen's office. The door slammed behind him. The visitor lowered its hood to reveal the face of a young man with light-brown skin. His black hair was done in braided rows ending in beads that swirled about him in the wind.

"What is the meaning of this?" Bowen demanded.

No reply came as the mysterious man silently picked up a stack of coins from the table and narrowed his eyes at Bowen.

"Guards! Guards!" Bowen called.

The man tossed the coins up in front of him with one hand and with the other thrust his fist into the air. The coins shot toward Bowen, slicing into his face. The man pulled a wooden staff from behind his back, spun it around in his hands, and cracked Bowen on the side of the head with it. Minister Bowen fell to the ground dead.

Merens Hiam labored up the carved steps to the Temple of the Four. His feet scraped on the loose pebbles that gathered in the cracks of the ancient stairs. The night air chilled him to the bone, but at least it was quiet now.

Too quiet, maybe.

He looked over his shoulder again to make sure no one was following. He clutched at the secret hidden in the sleeve of his robes to make sure it was still there, safe.

An acolyte met him at the Grand Sept and in silence led him deeper into the temple. He was left alone outside the chamber door of the high priestess. His hand shook before he gathered the strength to knock on the door.

"You may enter, Grand Minister," she called from the other side of the door.

Grand Minister Hiam found the high priestess sitting in a straight-backed wooden chair staring into a low fire that burned in the fireplace of her receiving room, which was dark and sparsely decorated.

"Do you have the scroll?" the high priestess asked. "Is it still sealed?"

"Yes, Your Holiness. It is my duty as the Minister of the Word to keep track of the king's last will and testament."

Hiam produced a scroll tied with three ribbons and three seals on it from inside the sleeve of his baggy robe.

"You do not know what the king decreed inside that scroll? Only the other three ministers were present for its signing?" the priestess asked.

"Yes, it is assumed that the crown will pass to his nephew, James."

"The nephew is of royal blood, but so is King Edward's cousin, Lord Russ. We should remind Russ—and more importantly, his wife—of that fact. A claimant from the West versus one from the East. Who will the people support? On which side will the lords of the North and South fall?"

"Shall I break the seals to read the king's final commands?"

"No...I think not."

The priestess strolled over to the minister and took the scroll from his hands.

"It is time that the people remember their faith. The faithful are the ones who ended the days of darkness and magic. The faithful are the ones who protected the people and their towns from the dragon." She examined the unopened scroll along with the three seals and ribbons of the ministers who witnessed the king's signing. "Our duty, as descendants of the faithful, is to bring the faith back to the fore and our temples back to their former power. There are embers out there waiting to be stoked. All we need to do is supply those small fires with some fuel."

Abruptly, she threw the unopened scroll into the fire.

Hiam looked up at the domed ceiling with frescoes of the Four Gods of the Faith battling dragons and the forces of evil painted on it. A black dragon reminded him of the priestess.

"Have you heard any word from the other grand ministers?" the priestess asked.

"No, Your Holiness. It seems Minister Phoca passed in her sleep, not a surprise at her age. Minister Bowen was murdered this morning in a robbery at the Ministry of Coin. And no one has been able to locate the Minister of War. It seems the king's passing has unleashed a rash of lawlessness and banditry in the city." Hiam wrung his hands nervously as he recounted the deaths and disappearance of the other Grand Council members.

"Fear not, Minister Hiam. You are safe in the protection of the temple. You have always been a loyal servant. I do have one other task for you, however. Before you leave, go down into the temple's dungeon. See if there is anyone in the cells we could...use to further our goals. Look for someone who would be willing to provide us with information on our would-be king, someone who is hungry for their freedom."

1
JORY I

The knight serves his lord with honor and courage...
The squire serves his knight with obedience, respect, and humility.
The squire stands in vigilance to defend his knight...

—The Book of Chivalry

The first lesson of being a squire repeated in Jory's head as he ran into the tent and flung the lid to the food basket open.

"It has to be here," he said out loud to himself.

He rummaged through the apples and carrots and tossed an onion to the ground. The lemon was gone.

Where is it? Sir Cley always has it for the finals.

Jory turned back to the camp table—nothing but plates and cutlery from the morning's breakfast. He dumped the food sacks on the floor—salted beef, flour, and a few turnips. No lemon.

A loud roar came up from the arena.

I'm missing it.

Jory bit his lower lip and took a deep breath. He grabbed the waterskin off the center pole and ran out of the tent toward the tournament grounds.

People, carts, and horses packed the entrance to the arena. Commoners trying to get a look, knights waiting for their events along with their squires, and groomsmen caring for the horses. Jory dodged through the crowd. He ran around an unruly black stallion and crashed into a knight walking on foot from the jousting grounds. Jory bounced off the knight's armor and fell to the ground.

"Watch where you're going, boy," the knight growled.

"S-sorry, Sir," Jory replied. The knight wore a doublet with a silver tower on a blue field sewn on it, as did the squire who followed him.

A knight from the West, from Tidehaven. And he is without his horse, which means he lost.

Jory sprang up from the ground and started for the gate to the contestants' entrance when the knight grabbed him by the back of his neck. His skin crawled at the feel of the knight's grasp.

"Where do you think you are going? Commoners watch from the rails."

"I-I am a squire, Sir," Jory stuttered. He squirmed loose only to bump into the knight's squire behind him.

"He's not even big enough to lift a lance," the squire said, standing almost a full head taller than Jory.

"Who do you squire for, boy?" the knight asked with a smirk.

"Sir Cley, S-Sir," Jory answered.

"I am Sir Tristan Harroldson, heir to Tidehaven. You will address me as My Lord," Sir Tristan scolded. "Sir Cley is already jousting, fool. Where are you from? The truth this time."

Another roar came from the crowd as the joust continued inside the arena.

Jory clenched his fists together and narrowed his eyes at the knight who was delaying him.

"I-I'm from Seadrift, My Lord," Jory answered.

"A bay rat? I didn't know anyone ever left that pile of rocks," the knight scoffed.

"He tells it true." A knight in all-white armor and doublet leaned down from his horse and spoke to Jory. "Sir Cley has been asking for you. You had better hurry to him."

"Let him pass, Theo. The sooner we are gone from this dusty village, the better," the knight in blue said.

"See you...bay rat," the squire named Theo scoffed, stepping out of Jory's path.

Jory nodded to the knight in white and raced through the contestants' entrance to the arena. Along the wall under the stands set up for the nobles he found the other squires lined up, ready to assist the knights on the jousting field. Jory squeezed in between two taller squires and tried to catch his breath. He looked to the north end of the rail and found his knight, Sir Cley, clad in green, sitting atop his charger, Thunder. On the other end of the rail awaited a knight with a golden boar painted on his blue shield.

The judge moved to the middle of the field and held his flag high for all to see. Every muscle in Jory's body tensed and he held his breath.

The flag dropped.

"Hup!" the green knight called, and Thunder burst into full charge within two strides.

The wooden wall behind Jory shook as the nobles jumped to their feet to get a better view. Jory covered his ears as the crowd roared.

The knight in green charged toward the knight in blue. As the two knights converged, the green knight leaned forward with his lance, holding it level and straight until it struck the center of his opponent's shield. The sound of metal striking metal and the crack of wood rang out. Wooden splinters filled the air and clattered off the knights' armor.

Thunder slowed to a trot as they reached the end of the rail. The green knight tossed his shattered lance to the side. The blue knight's lance remained intact, having missed its mark. The judge held up a green flag. Another lance for the green knight. He led four to two.

Jory ran out to Sir Cley carrying the waterskin.

"W-well done, Sir," Jory called. "One more lance and y-you're the champion."

Jory patted Thunder on the neck and handed Sir Cley the waterskin. The knight raised his visor and squeezed the waterskin, taking a long drink.

"Where have you been?" Sir Cley asked. "You almost missed the championship."

"I had to get a...more water."

Sir Cley checked his armor and shield. A long scratch ran through the white tree painted on his green shield.

"This shield is going to need a fresh paint job," Cley said, handing the waterskin back to his squire.

"Y-yes, Sir."

Two large boys ran out and lifted a new lance up to Sir Cley, and the knight moved to the beginning of the lists for the next tilt. Jory ran back to the side of the arena and found his spot alongside the other squires. Wearing a green doublet two sizes too big, Jory puffed his chest out and tried to stand taller next to them.

"Come on now, Cley!" someone yelled from the viewing stands.

The commoners surrounding the arena stood ten deep, nudging and pressing against each other to get a better look. Fathers held their children up on their shoulders so they could see Sir Cley, who lowered the visor on his helmet and waited for the flag to drop. Thunder snorted and pawed at the chewed-up turf. The middle judge moved into position and dropped his flag, and the green and blue knights charged back at one another again. With a crash, the blue knight was jolted from his saddle, and the crowd roared with approval.

Jory let go of the breath he had been holding as Sir Cley dropped his shattered lance and rode back to where the blue knight had fallen on the turf. Sir Cley dismounted and helped his opponent to his feet. Jory ran out to grab Thunder's reins and walked the horse behind his knight.

The crowd cheered for both knights as they walked to the viewing stands and received their laurels from the Lord of Duskfield and his eldest daughter.

"The champion, The Knight of the Tall Tree, Sir Cley Woods," called a herald to the crowd.

Jory watched the lord's daughter drape the champion's laurels over Sir Cley. The tall, young knight bent down to kiss her on the cheek. She smiled shyly, revealing crooked teeth.

I would kiss a strange girl if it meant I could be champion. Knights do those kinds of things.

Jory waited behind Sir Cley, holding Thunder's reins in one hand and a small bag in the other. Sir Cley returned to him after the ceremony and took the reins and bag from him, then climbed back on top of his charger. He rode to the crowd of commoners pressed in to see him, then reached into the small bag and retrieved a handful of copper coins, tossing them to the cheering commoners, who threw flowers back as they called his name.

Another tournament, another championship, another kiss from some maiden or lady.

The knight and his squire sat outside their green and white pavilion as the sun descended behind the tower of the keep at Duskfield. The smell of cookfires and horses hung in the early-spring air over the small camp of tournament knights. Jory struck at his flint for the seventh time, producing a spark that bounced off the dry leaves and tinder. Frustrated, he struck the flint harder.

"Relax, Jory. Strike the flint calmly. Hitting it harder won't make it catch," Sir Cley instructed from his camp chair.

Sir Cley continued rubbing down his shield arm with balm. Jory went back to striking the flint with his knife. The boy sat back limply after a few fruitless strikes.

"I sh-should go collect Sir Preston's horse," Jory said.

"We will not be collecting Preston's horse. He already paid its ransom. He was unhorsed honorably. No need to shame him by claiming his charger," Sir Cley replied.

"I c-could go to Sir Thurmond's camp and get some fire."

"You could, but that wouldn't improve your fire-building skills, would it?"

"No, but it would be faster."

"Strike the flint like you are peeling a potato or sharpening a stick...and relax," Cley instructed.

On the fourteenth strike, a spark jumped into the tinder and caught. Jory fed the small flame with dry straw patiently, and it grew.

"I think maybe it's time you should start training for the joust," Sir Cley announced.

"The joust?" Jory jumped to his feet, forgetting the fire.

"We will need to get you a proper horse to train with first, but I think it is time. You have been training for over two years now. You're almost twelve and can start competing in the squires' games. You have archery down and are pretty good with the sword for your age. The joust is the next skill."

The muscles in Jory's face hurt from smiling.

"You're ready. Your father started me on the joust

when I turned thirteen. You are a full year ahead," Sir Cley continued. "Right now, you need to get back to tending our fire."

Jory knelt back down to feed the small flames. He tried to picture his father. The vague memory of a tall man handing him a puppy before he rode off to war was all he could conjure now. A greater knight than his father did not exist in all of Terros. The stories and songs all said so.

"Be a good boy, Jory. Obey your mother and protect your sister," his father had said.

Bong! Bong!

The tolling of the keep's bell broke through the sleepy camp. The sound drew the assembled knights from their tents and pavilions, wondering what it could mean. A rider came galloping from the small keep.

"The king is dead! King Edward is dead!" the rider yelled as he rode between the tents.

Jory peered up at Cley from the growing fire.

"What does that mean? Who will be k-king now?" Jory asked as he stood.

"I'm not sure. The lords will summon their knights. Lord Buckhorn will be expecting me. We will need to travel to the West."

"W-we are going to Buckton?" Jory asked. His throat tightened thinking of traveling back to the West.

"Maybe not... We will see." Cley put his hand on his squire's shoulder. Jory's muscles tensed at his touch. Cley removed his hand.

"Will...he be there?"

Cley knelt in front of Jory at eye level. Jory bit his lower lip and narrowed his eyes.

"It will be okay. It's been over two years, and you are my squire. Nothing is going to separate us."

Sir Cley went inside their pavilion, leaving Jory outside listening to the bell and staring at the setting sun in the west.

My home is there, and so is the man who lives there now.

Jory shuddered at the thought of his stepfather.

2

THE GOLDEN KNIGHT I

"Stay close to me. Do not wander off. And remember, if he asks you any questions, answer 'Yes, My Lord,' and 'No, My Lord.'" Sir Cley looked down at his squire. The boy nodded.

The Crow's Nest had to be one of the most out-of-the-way taverns in Tidehaven. Cley pulled open the tavern's iron-studded door, and the sounds from inside rushed out into the night air. The smell of people, smoke, and ale entwined, making Cley's eyes water.

Cley cleared his throat and ushered Jory through the door and toward the bar.

"One ale and one water, good sir," Cley called to the barkeep as he set a copper down on the worn-wood counter. He scanned the tables and booths along the edge of the tavern. A table of soldiers playing cards drew his attention with their catcalls to the serving girls and raucous behavior. A man played a fiddle near the hearth with his hat turned over on the table collecting coins. No one seemed to be paying attention to his playing. In a dark corner to the left of the hearth, a man reclined in a chair. His face was covered in shadow, but the shiny hilt of the dagger in his boot glittered in the firelight. Cley pulled Jory by his shoulder to stand closer to him.

"Here ya go," the barkeep said as he set two tankards down in front of Cley.

The tankards were greasy, and Cley grasped them tightly. The ale smelled like honey, and the water smelled like fish. Cley looked across the tavern and spotted what he was looking for.

"Follow me," Cley said to Jory as he headed to the back of the tavern, away from the drunken soldiers and fiddle playing. He stopped at a booth with a lit candle on the edge of the table. An old man with gray hair and a matching beard sat inside on one of the benches. He was dressed in traveling attire with a dark cloak pulled over a leather jerkin. The old man looked up at Cley and Jory, and his eyes sparkled. A smile came to his face.

"Sit down," the man said. He rubbed his hands together and sat up straight.

Cley gestured for Jory to enter the booth across from the man. The boy slid across the bench to the tavern wall, and Cley sat next to him. He set the tankard of ale in front of the older man and the tankard of water in front of himself.

"It's good to see you, Cley," the old man began. He took a deep drink from the tankard and set it down. "Let's have a better look at you, boy." He slid the candle across the table so that it was now in front of Jory. Reaching across the table, he lightly brushed the long blond hair away from Jory's eyes to reveal the scar through his eyebrow. Jory pulled away quickly.

"This is Lord Buckhorn," Cley said to Jory. "He knew your father."

"Has this one been good to you?" Lord Buckhorn asked, nodding at Cley. "Are you keeping him out of trouble?"

"Y-yes, My Lord," Jory replied.

"That's good. Are you hungry?"

"Yes, My Lord."

Lord Buckhorn reached into his cloak and pulled out three copper coins. He summoned one of the serving girls to the table and pressed the coins into her hand.

"Take the boy back into the kitchen and let him have whatever he wants," he told her.

Jory climbed across Cley to get out of the booth and followed the girl back to the kitchen.

"He looks like his father," Lord Buckhorn said.

"I know. He's starting to sound like him too," Cley replied.

"Who knows?"

"No one really. A small squire gets little notice out east or in the South. He has been mistaken for an urchin more than once. Will his presence be a problem?"

"No, I took care of that. I did not send for Sir Wells. I knew you would come. There is no need to keep the boy's identity secret. There are plenty of rumors as to what happened to him. Some say he drowned in the surf. Others that he fell from the Broken Tower. It is high time those stories were corrected. Tomorrow, you and Jory will join my ranks. You will ride with me as a knight of my household to Pebble Creek for the prince's engagement."

"And how is our prince?"

"A little unprepared and probably a little fearful, but that is what we are for," Lord Buckhorn said before he took another long drink and then smiled broadly at Cley. He clasped a weathered and calloused hand over Cley's arm. "It is good to see you, Cley. You have been gone too long. How are you?"

"I am fine. The travel and tournaments keep me busy, as

does the boy. My mind has little time to wander." Cley swallowed hard. "His mother... How is she? And the girl?"

"They are well. The boy's mother writes constantly for any news. I send her what I can."

Cley leaned back on the bench and with effort returned Lord Buckhorn's smile. Jory presented himself back at the booth holding a turkey leg.

"At Pebble Creek, there will be a tournament. Cley, I expect you to represent Buckton," Lord Buckhorn said. "And there will be squires' games. Each lord will enter a squire to participate. My squire is too old to enter the melee as it is for the younger squires. Maybe Jory would like to enter."

Jory's eyes widened, and Cley could see the wheels spinning in the boy's head.

"I don't know. He is only eleven," Cley said. "The other squires will be a year or two older than him."

"Can you swing a sword, boy? Can you hold a shield?" Lord Buckhorn asked Jory.

"Y-yes, My Lord," Jory replied, hopping from one foot to the other.

"Then you are probably more prepared than some of those lads from their fancy castles." Lord Buckhorn smiled.

Cley looked from Jory to Lord Buckhorn, who gave him a nod.

"I'll have to think on it," Cley finally said.

3

JORY II

The green and purple knights charged at each other. Their lances cracked and shattered. The crowd in the arena at Pebble Creek cheered. Jory ran to Sir Cley at the end of the list to hand him a waterskin. Thunder snorted angrily, glaring down the jousting field at the opposing knight.

"Y-you are way ahead. Four lances to one... Sir Blake cannot hope to win," Jory called up to Sir Cley.

"Remember, the joust is never over until the final tilt. Honor in victory and defeat always, no matter what," Sir Cley said, looking down the field.

"Yes, Sir."

Sir Cley moved back to the beginning of the rail for the next tilt. The visiting lords and ladies sat in their finery on raised benches and politely clapped for the knights. The platform holding Prince James Tolar and Princess Rebecca Fowler rose up behind them. Their host, Lord Guy Pontifer of Pebble Creek, sat quietly to the side of the newly engaged couple.

The commoners gathered around the arena had been rowdy for the entire tournament, but their cheers were the loudest for Sir Cley, even in this joust with Sir Blake, the son of Lord Pontifer.

At the other end of the rail, Sir Blake struggled to get his horse in line. The black charger shook its head stubbornly and gnashed at the bit in its mouth. Sir Blake kicked and spurred his horse into position along the rail for the next tilt.

Sir Cley lowered the visor on his helmet, waiting for the flag to drop. He leaned forward, whispering into Thunder's ear. The flag dropped, and the knight in green and the knight in purple charged at one another again. Thunder's hooves churned up the turf as Sir Cley couched his lance. As the two knights clashed, Sir Cley's lance lowered and struck the bottom quarter of Sir Blake's shield. Sir Blake's lance delivered a glancing blow to the top of Sir Cley's shield. Sir Cley rolled back onto his saddle. With a sickening crash, the green knight fell from his horse, and the crowd dropped into silent disbelief. Sir Cley Woods was on the ground, defeated.

Sir Cley kept still on his back for a moment as Jory rushed to his side.

"Are you alright, Sir?" Jory said.

"Yes...yes, only a fall. No harm done," Sir Cley said, sitting up.

Jory helped the armored knight to his feet, and Sir Cley removed his helmet.

"Go fetch Thunder for me."

Jory quickly brought the charger back, and Sir Cley remounted his horse. He rode to the middle of the arena, joining Sir Blake. The two knights bowed in their saddles to the prince and princess. Sir Blake was proclaimed the victor at five lances to four by virtue of unseating his opponent. His father, Lord Pontifer, stood and clapped madly for his son. The rest of the crowd cheered with less enthusiasm.

Sir Cley took Sir Blake's hand and raised it in victory. He then led the victor in a lap around the arena slowing near the commoners to allow the people to yell and chant their names. Jory was not sure if the people were cheering for the champion.

Outside the jousting arena, a boy dressed in a doublet of Sir Blake's colors approached Sir Cley sheepishly.

"I...I have come for the horse," the boy said. "I am Sir Blake's squire."

"No reason to be ashamed of it, lad. Your knight was the winner," Sir Cley said. "Jory, hand over Thunder's reins."

Jory led the charger over to the other boy. He patted Thunder on the neck.

"T-take good care of him," Jory said to the other squire.

"We will...bay rat," the squire whispered back.

The squire took Thunder and walked off toward the castle's stables. Jory stood there quietly and watched. He did not want to turn around to let Sir Cley see his eyes had gone red and watery.

"We'll get Thunder back tomorrow. It's a small ransom," Sir Cley said. "You know the rules. They will take care of him, and he will get a good night's rest inside the castle's stable. Speaking of a good night's rest, that's what you will be needing for your big melee tomorrow."

Jory sat atop Thunder, clad in the black and blue colors of his father and holding a shield emblazoned with a broken gray tower struck by a white lightning bolt. He glanced at the prince and princess in the royal box, then honed his focus on the end of the lists. There, the Black Knight paced back and forth on his snorting steed.

Jory spurred Thunder forward to meet the Black Knight. The crowd picked up a cheer. A roar arose as if a wave of sound that he rode upon. He leveled his lance at the Black Knight.

The Black Knight's cruel and heavy lance dipped as the knights clashed together. The black lance tip glanced against the painted tower on the shield. Jory's own lance found its mark on the shield of the Black Knight. The tournament lance broke with splinters flying. The Black Knight was thrown off his horse, landing on his back on the churned-up turf.

The crowd roared approval. Roses were thrown onto the field. The prince and princess stood and cheered. The commoners in the stands chanted his name, and it boomed and echoed in the arena.

"Jory...Jory...Jory..." they chanted.

"Jory...Jory...Boy...Boy!"

He was sure he heard it that time. Jory opened his eyes. The sun's rays streamed through the pavilion's entrance flaps.

"Boy...it is time you woke." Sir Cley's foot nudged Jory. "Come on, sleepyhead. I said you could sleep late today, not the entire morning."

Jory sat up on his bedroll, yawning and stretching with Sir Cley squatting beside him.

"Good morning... Get up and wash your face. Breakfast is ready. Bacon and eggs. Your favorite." Sir Cley ruffled Jory's hair into more of a mess than it already was.

The smell of bacon filled the tent. Jory stood and walked to the water basin. He washed his face with his hands in the cool water he had fetched from the creek last night, then wetted and slicked back the hair that had fallen over his eyes. In the two years he had been with Sir Cley, he had let his hair grow. It now reached his collar and would curl up at the back and around his ears.

Jory untangled the shark tooth necklace that had wrapped itself around his neck during his sleep. A large white tooth carved into a hook on a simple string, it had been one of the last things his father gave to him before he went off to war.

Father said it would bring me good luck. I am going to need that luck today.

Jory returned to his bedroll area. He dug through a pile of clothes and found a tunic to pull over his head. It was too big for him, but finding squire's clothes that fit him was always a problem.

"A good knight wears proper attire to sit at a table and eat," Sir Cley always reminded him.

The baggy tunic hung like a dress on Jory, but it covered his underclothes, and that was good enough for breakfast in Sir Cley's pavilion. He joined Sir Cley at the table and began to eat.

"So, are you ready for today?" Sir Cley asked while biting into a strip of bacon.

Jory swallowed what he was chewing.

"Yes, I c-cannot wait," Jory replied.

Slow down. You stutter less when you slow down, Jory reminded himself.

Jory stabbed the fried egg on his wooden plate with a knife and began to dip a strip of bacon into the runny yolk. He thought of his first melee. It would be one of his first steps to knighthood. In his mind, Jory knew he would perform some act of bravery and take his knightly vows by the time he was fifteen. He would be the youngest knight ever.

When I get my knighthood, I will be famous like my father and Sir Cley. I will return home to my mother and sister and get...

"I heard that the princess will be there with all her ladies-in-waiting," Sir Cley added.

"What about the k-king? Will he be attending?"

"You mean prince. Prince James will be declared king when we reach Kingstown," Sir Cley reminded Jory.

"The prince might be there, but I doubt it. A prince has more important matters to deal with than to cheer at a squire's melee. Two more lords from the coast and the wilderness arrived last night with their levy of knights. Prince James will need to meet with them to discuss the marching order. I heard that Lord Buckhorn has the honor of leading the procession, which means we will be in front as we enter the gates of Kingstown. Of course, the prince will ride with the men from Tidehaven and Lord Harroldson. The knights from Greyport and Lord Fowler will follow with his daughter, the princess. No one wants to ride in the rear guard. The crowds will be tired of cheering. The pretty girls will have thrown all the flowers, and those in the rear will be marching in streets already filled with horse dung."

Sir Cley pinched his nose to illustrate. Jory laughed at Sir Cley's antics.

"Give me your plate and knife. I will clean up the dishes," Sir Cley said. "Find your breeches and get your boots on. I will help you with your practice armor when I get back from the creek. You must look your best for your first tournament."

Sir Cley stacked their plates and left the pavilion. The sounds of a bustling camp outside poured in. Jory got off his stool, walked to his pile of clothes, and found the breeches he normally wore when training with Sir Cley.

Jory pulled his breeches on and laced them at the top. They were the smallest pair they could find in Tidehaven, but they were still baggy on him. He normally would tie a rope around his waist to hold them up, but today he did not want to look like some country boy in front of the other knights and lords of the West, and especially the princess.

Jory undid the knot in his strings and pulled them tighter. The only thing worse than having to wear a rope for a belt would be for his breeches to drop in front of everyone. He had seen that happen to a knight over a year ago at the Winter's End Tournament. That knight had been laughed at and jeered by even the commoners. Jory had not seen that knight in any town or tournament since.

Sir Cley re-entered the pavilion whistling a happy tune. Jory stood in his baggy tunic and breeches in front of the looking glass they kept by the water basin.

"I thought I told you to find your clothes."

"These are my c-clothes," Jory replied, turning to face Sir Cley.

"The king's grief," Sir Cley said and put his hands on his hips. "If you don't want to be in the melee, you don't have to. You are going to be the youngest by far. Some of the other squires will tower over you and will be stronger too."

"I'm almost tw-twelve," Jory protested softly. "I want to be in the melee."

"Okay, but the squire of Sir Cley Woods cannot show up looking like some peasant boy. I figured you would have found the package by now."

Sir Cley walked over to his sleeping area. He dug under a few of the pillows and produced a package. He untied the string holding it and unfolded a small white tunic with long sleeves, and a pair of small black cloth breeches with brown leather patches on the thighs along with a black leather belt.

"Now a stable boy could win a melee in these clothes alone. I expect no less from you." Smiling, Sir Cley handed the new clothes over to Jory, whose eyes widened with excitement seeing his new gear. He pulled off the tunic he wore and let the breeches drop to his ankles, wiggling his feet out of them. After putting on the new clothes, Jory looked at his reflection in the looking glass. The pants and shirt fit him. He could have been the son of a great lord. The sunlight coming into the pavilion shone on his light-blond hair and made the new white tunic he wore glow. The only blemish he could see was the scar above his left eye running through his eyebrow. Jory played with his hair in the front so that it would cover his defect.

"Alright, little lordling, if you can pull yourself away from the looking glass, I will help you into your armor," Sir Cley teased.

"You're one to t-talk. You tied and re-tied your hair three times before you were happy yesterday. You changed your riding pants twice. You almost missed your joust."

"The fair ladies and maidens expect my best young squire," Sir Cley responded with his fake proper accent. "And I will not disappoint. The Knight of the Tall Tree has a reputation to uphold. You will learn. Being a crowd favorite has its advantages, but it takes work."

Sir Cley was a crowd favorite and he normally won. What will happen if I lose?

The thought of losing quickly left his mind as Sir Cley helped Jory into his gear. It was not real armor that knights would wear, instead padding used for training that would cover Jory's chest, back, and groin.

The Squires' Melee was for the new squires, normally thirteen- and fourteen-year-olds. The older squires would be in the joust. The fact that Jory was not even twelve yet did not concern him. He had been Sir Cley's squire for two years now and would be twelve in sixteen days. He was strong and skilled in his training. Although shorter than the other squires, he was tall for his age and knew he could hold his own. While these other boys were living in castles and manses, pampered by servants, Jory had been working, learning, and training.

Sir Cley handed Jory his helmet. He had added more

padding inside so it would fit better and stop sliding forward to obstruct Jory's vision. Jory began to put it on.

"Don't put the helmet on yet. You carry it to the ring. Oh, and one more thing..." Sir Cley reached forward and pulled Jory's hair back away from his face and tied it in a knot in the back of his head with a leather string. "There, let the people see your face so they will remember you and your name for the next time."

Sir Cley grabbed Jory's wooden tournament sword and shield before Jory could even reach for them, then left the pavilion with Jory following close behind. The camp outside buzzed alive with servants, washerwomen, and knights and squires all about their business in the morning hours. The blacksmith's tent rang with the song of hammers repairing weapons and armor from the previous days of the tournament.

Jory tried to keep up with Sir Cley as he stepped around pits and ruts in the ground from the horses and carts, as well as avoided the occasional pile of horse dung. The Buckton camp was organized efficiently. Lord Buckhorn had taken a spot along the creek with a grove of trees for shade. Sir Cley found a flat spot that was on a gentle rise for his pavilion, and it was the farthest tent upstream too, which guaranteed clean water.

Lords from the West and East also made camp at Pebble Creek. They gathered in a show of support for Prince James, who was engaged to Princess Rebecca of Greyport. Brightly colored tents and pavilions filled the camp. Jory counted and named the banners of the different lords and knights as they fluttered in the wind. The town and castle displayed the white feather on purple of Lord Pontifer, while Tidehaven's silver tower on a field of blue prevailed in the camps. Single banners with images of a red mustang, blue bull's head, golden hawk, and white owl announced the presence of traveling knights. The gray eagle on red surrounded the castle as the Fowlers of Greyport made camp there. Lord Buckhorn's brown antlers on a green field marked the Buckton camp where Sir Cley and Jory were settled.

Knights from other towns and places called to Sir Cley as he walked by, and some wished Jory good luck in his first melee. Sir Cley waved and shouted back to the other knights, complimenting them on their performance and bravery in the tournament or joking about their poor dancing at the gatherings held at night.

A huge burly knight with a long black beard and large belly stepped out in front of Sir Cley, blocking his path. "Well, the Knight of the Tall Tree is out playing squire again, I see."

Jory recognized the large man as Sir Torrent, one of Lord Buckhorn's men. The knight had a reputation as one of the strongest and toughest knights from Buckton. The brute scowled at Sir Cley and then began a laugh that boomed in Jory's ears.

"The Great Tor. You honor me, sir." Sir Cley bent himself at the waist in an exaggerated bow. "Now tell me, did you fall faster from your horse in your tilt with the White Owl on day one of the joust, or was it when you fell from the dining hall bench on the fourth night of drinking too much ale?"

The two men clasped arms, and Sir Torrent pulled Sir Cley into a bear hug. Sir Torrent spotted Jory trailing Sir Cley and pushed the young knight out of his way. He knelt before Jory and grabbed him by the shoulders roughly.

"Good luck to you, boy. Watch out for those twins, and keep your shield up," Sir Torrent said. "Your father was a great fighter, you know. Taught Cley here everything he knows. You come from good stock. Us Buckton men will be there for ya."

Jory froze in the large man's grasp, noting that his breath smelled of stale ale and onions. Jory felt like worms were wriggling under his skin, trying to break free. He nodded and tried to smile but only wanted to be let go. Jory's breakfast churned in his stomach when Sir Torrent suddenly released him.

"Come on, Jory. We don't want to be late." Sir Cley's voice made Jory jump.

The tournament grounds were not much farther. The ring and smaller stands for the melee arena appeared before them. A crowd was gathering. Commoners and soldiers stood around the ring, while the seats in the stands were reserved for the nobles. A raised platform for the prince and princess to view from sat in between the stands. Jory's stomach tightened, and he suddenly had the urge to pee.

When they reached the ring's gates, Sir Cley bent down to Jory's ear and asked, "You're awfully quiet. Do you have to visit a tree?"

"Yes," Jory answered in relief, and he ran off to a small clump of trees away from the crowd.

How did Sir Cley know I needed to pee?

When he finished, Jory tied his breeches up and headed back to Sir Cley at the gates. On his way, he spotted the armed guards of House Fowler escorting Princess Rebecca to the raised platform so she could watch her brothers compete in the melee. Along with her were four of her maidens-in-waiting.

Jory had seen the princess from afar, but now she was much closer. She was the most beautiful girl he had ever seen before, more beautiful than he remembered his own mother. Her dress matched the blue flowers wrapped around her head. Her long chestnut-brown hair framed her face, and she had large brown eyes with long eyelashes. Her maids wore matching gowns of lighter blue with white flowers adorning their hair.

When Jory found Sir Cley, they went through the gates and into the ring where there were ten or twelve other boys with wooden tournament swords and shields. They were attended to by servants or older masters-at-arms of their houses. Each boy wore a helmet adorned with ribbons in the colors of their house or the knight the boy squired for.

Sir Cley pulled out two ribbons, one green and one white, and tied them around Jory's helmet. Upon seeing him, the commoners cheered and called Sir Cley's name.

"Remember, if you fall to your knees or fall to your back, you are out," Sir Cley reminded Jory while ignoring the people calling out his name. "Obey the commands of the judge. Keep your feet spread shoulder width apart with your knees bent and ready. Look side to side. Most importantly, remember to keep your shield up."

"Y-yes, Sir. I'll remember," Jory replied, reverting to how he spoke with Sir Cley in training and formal occasions.

"Oh, I have one more thing for you. I almost forgot."

Sir Cley dug into his belt. He produced a piece of cloth the size of a scarf and tied it around Jory's sword arm, pulling the cloth wider to show its colors and design. Jory's lips burst into a broad smile as a surge of energy tingled across his skin. The cloth of the armband was striped, black on top and blue underneath. In the middle was a design that had been sewn on it, a broken gray tower being struck with a white bolt of lightning.

4

THE PRINCE I

James squirmed in his chair. The silver circlet they fashioned for him to wear as crown prince squeezed his
head from both sides like a grape between two fingers.
However, it was the debate between his father's advisors and
his mother that produced his true headache.

"You mean to tell me that Ivan has claimed the throne?"
she yelled.

His mother stood at the head of the table, railing at the
men seated around it. Lady Tolar was an imposing woman,
tall with high cheek bones and an angular nose. Her long
black hair was held up in a style that was popular with the
women of the West. She was dressed in all black, as she had
been for the last two years since the death of her husband.

"How can this be? Ivan is only a cousin to King Edward.
James is a nephew. We have the better claim." Lady Tolar
pounded her fist onto the long table before her.

"My lady, I assure you our agents do not lie. Lord Ivan
Russ arrived in Kingstown a week ago with his family and
knights of his household. He declared himself the rightful
heir three days later. The high priestess herself crowned him.
The commanders of the royal army and navy stand behind

him," stated an old man who had been an advisor to James's father.

James thought back to his uncle, King Edward the Fifth. James had met him several times when he had traveled with his family to the capital or when the King himself had made a visit to Tidehaven. He was already being referred to as Edward the Great by some, and he had died less than two months ago.

Edward was king at age thirteen and led his armies. And here I sit at sixteen like a boy being lectured by his tutor.

"As to who has a better claim to the throne, well, it is unprecedented to be sure," another of the old, white-bearded men stated. "My Lady, I agree with you that a nephew would be closer in blood than a cousin, but there are no writings or laws to confirm this. Edward named no heir. Ivan has taken the throne and the capital."

"What of the Grand Council? Where do their loyalties lie?" Lady Tolar asked.

"Lord Russ has appointed two of his own supporters to the vacant positions on the council."

"How could you doddering fools have allowed this to happen?" James's mother screeched. "Ivan was supposed to have gone to the capital to get everything prepared for my son's arrival. How could you have trusted him? James and Lord Fowler's daughter were to be married and crowned as king and queen on the same day. How could that man suddenly decide that he should be king?"

"My Lady, if you will, one of our agents at the capital says it is Lord Russ's wife, Lady Sinessa, who is behind this treachery," another old man stated calmly. "She is trying to put one of his sons on the throne."

"Oh, yes, I know the boys. The two oldest, a coward and a drunkard. The youngest is not even of an age when he could take the crown. Each would make a worse king than their father." Lady Tolar looked down the table at Lord Fowler, who sat gravely silent at the far end. "Lord Fowler, our children are engaged to one another. Do you still support my son's claim to the throne?"

James looked to the far end of the table at Lord Fowler, who was not a handsome man. His nose turned up like a pig's snout, and his eyes were a dull black color. There was never a smile or a frown, only a constant look, like he was observing, calculating everything being said.

"Lady Tolar...my support for Prince James is unwavering. For this land to be ruled by Lord Russ or any of his sons would be a catastrophe," Lord Fowler said slowly, as if every word were of grave importance. "We must march on Kingstown now, before Lord Russ finds more allies. With the Army of the West, my forces from the East, and the Army of the South coming to join us at Crosstimbers, we will outnumber any army Lord Russ can put together three to one. When the royal commanders see our numbers, they will abandon this pretender, and Russ will slink back to Easton and wish he had never thought of this folly."

"What of the lords of the North? Has anyone heard from them?" Lady Tolar asked.

James watched the old men that his father once had relied on as they diverted their eyes to their hands or beards and tried to avoid the gaze of his mother.

"Well...don't sit there like imbeciles. What reports come from the North?" Lady Tolar screamed.

"My Lady, the only word that we have heard from the North is that they are calling for a Council of Lords," one old man replied reluctantly. "A council of all the lords of Terros to sit and decide on who should be king."

"And, My Lady, there are rumors of fighting in

Summerport," said a man with watery eyes. "My informants have told me that immigrants, the elves, desecrated one of the Temples of the Four there. Rogue bands of Northerners are going about, burning elven settlements in retaliation. The Lord of Summerport sits and takes no action to restore the peace, while hordes of elves arrive daily by ship from the lands of the East."

"No doubt the North would drag out every lord they could find up in those mountains and forests and have one of their own chosen," Lady Tolar scoffed. "As long as the North is not allied with Lord Russ, let them demand their council. They will accept James as their king once he is on the throne. The northern lords will go back to their own problems. Now, if there is nothing else, we must all agree that this information is not to be told to anyone else tonight. We do not want to spoil the engagement banquet. Agreed?"

The old men nodded in agreement and stood to leave the room, each bowing to James before they walked out. James watched as they all filed out of the small chamber Lord Pontifer allowed him to use as his own council room.

Lord Fowler paused at the door. "You have my undying support, My Prince and Lady Tolar," he said as he bowed and left the room.

James wished he was leaving the room with Lord Fowler. He felt tired and had not been sleeping well since it was decided he should be king. The meetings and planning sessions weighed on him.

Is this what it is like to be king?

"James, pay attention to what I am saying to you right now. You need to find your own men, younger men than these fools. You need to surround yourself with men who will be loyal to you and you alone. Your father's advisors were loyal to him, but they are old now and too comfortable in their own lives and wealth. You need men who are ambitious and willing to serve you without question."

"What about Lord Fowler and Lord Harroldson?"

Lady Tolar leaned in close to James.

"I said men who will be loyal, my boy. Fowler and Harroldson are both lords of great cities, but they are not to be trusted. You have nothing to give them that they do not already have. We will keep them close as we depend on them for their armies. When you marry Rebecca, she will be queen and Fowler's grandchildren will be heirs to the throne. That should be reward enough for him and keep the East on our side. As for Harroldson, you can grant his son—umm, what's his name?—some title or position that will flatter his father."

"You mean Tristan?" James sighed. "Father always spoke favorably about Lord Buckhorn. What about him?"

"An old man from a backwoods village? I think not. The Buckhorns do not even have a proper castle. The men of Buckton are simple warriors. No, what you need are capable men who will be loyal to you. I will start to make a list of who I think will be suitable."

Lady Tolar straightened herself and smoothed out her black dress. "Right now, you need to clean up for the banquet tonight. Be sure to wear that dark-red robe I had made for you, as the princess will be wearing a dress to match."

Lady Tolar left the room without bowing to her son. James slouched in his chair and took a relaxed breath. He removed the silver circlet off his head and tossed it on the table in front of him, then bowed his head and rubbed his temples with his fingers.

5

JORY III

"My Lords and Ladies...dear Princess...and good people of Pebble Creek..." A herald in brightly colored clothes spun around as he spoke to the crowd of people.

The arena was not as full as it had been for the Knights' Melee the day before, but it was still a good gathering. It was an opportunity for some entertainment for the common folk and soldiers. For the nobles, it was an opportunity to show off their sons and to display the strength of their houses. Of course, it was also a chance to place a wager or two on who might win or who would be the first to lose.

"I introduce to you Lord Fowler's own noble sons, Jaxian and Daxian." The herald finished his introduction with a flourish of hand gestures, a turn, and a low bow to the two squires behind him. The crowd cheered. They were loudest where the soldiers of Greyport gathered to see the twin boys of their lord. The princess and her maids stood clapping excitedly.

The twins looked formidable in their padded armor. They were good-sized boys, both with red and gray ribbons waving in the air from their helmets. Which one was Jax and which one was Dax, Jory had no idea. Another squire told him that the twins were fifteen, too old for the melee.

Another man stepped up and spoke for some boy from the West. Jory did not know him but had seen him before when he and Sir Cley were in Tidehaven. He was a friend of Theo Harroldson. That fact alone gave Jory reason to dislike him. The huge boy wore gold and black streamers around his helmet. Jory guessed he had to be at least six feet tall and heavier than himself by a hundred pounds.

The big squire drew a few cheers. Jory could hear soldiers behind him, beyond the ring's barrier, betting on "the big one" to win it all.

One of the squires who stood in the ring was alone. No servants, master-at-arms, or even the knight he served were to be seen. He stepped out to the middle of the ring and shouted through the grated visor of his helmet.

"I am Aiden of Two Towers," he announced in a serious voice that sounded like he was trying to make it lower, more important. His red, black, and white ribbons flowed in the breeze as he walked to the viewing stand and bowed before the princess. His stride was confident and sure-footed.

Sir Cley nudged Jory with his elbow, whispering to him, "That was a nice touch. Remember that."

Jory had never seen this boy before, and he had no idea where Two Towers was located.

It must be in the North somewhere.

Aiden appeared tall and strong by the way he carried his sword and shield, but his padded armor was poor. Instead of wearing leather boots like the other squires, he wore leather straps tied around his feet and legs.

Another herald stepped forward to introduce a boy from Tidehaven. "This is Theo, squire and son to Lord Harroldson of Tidehaven."

Jory rolled his eyes as the herald went on for ages about the son of Lord Harroldson. He recalled the first time they had met when Jory had bumped into him and his brother at a tournament. Theo was an average-sized boy for a fourteen-year-old, strong and athletic. Jory had met him again on the march from Tidehaven but was not impressed.

Theo is a loudmouth.

Amongst the other squires, Theo bragged about how important his father Lord Harroldson was and how his older brother, Sir Tristan, was best friends with Prince James growing up. He was even predicting how someday he would be picked to serve as one of the king's guards when he became a knight. But what bugged him the most was when Theo reminded Jory whenever the two crossed paths that Jory was from the fishing village of Seadrift by calling him "bay rat." The other squires had taken to calling Jory that too on the march from Tidehaven. Of course, it was always out of earshot of Sir Cley and the other knights.

Lord Harroldson's servant finally finished introducing Theo to some light applause from the crowd, mainly from the knights and people there from Tidehaven.

Sir Cley pushed Jory forward in front of him, jolting him from his thoughts about Theo. The crowd cheered immediately, seeing the Knight of the Tall Tree. Women threw flowers into the ring near Sir Cley and Jory.

"My friends...my friends...Lords and Ladies..." Sir Cley began, using his outstretched hands to quiet the crowd and giving a sly grin to the women around the ring, "I bring to you today, with the greatest of honor, in his first ever tournament..."

Jory stepped forward to nod to the crowd, but Sir Cley grabbed his shoulder, holding him back as he continued his introduction. Jory exhaled nervously. Once Sir Cley would start to speak in front of a crowd, it could take forever. He once witnessed him give a toast at a banquet that had the women in tears, and a few men too. People would stop whatever they were doing to hear him speak or recite some line of poetry.

I wish I could talk as smoothly as Sir Cley.

"He is the son of one of our land's greatest heroes." A hush grew over the crowd as Sir Cley paused for dramatic effect. "The only son of the Hero Knight, the Sword of the West, the Knight of the Broken Tower, Sir Jonas Turner."

Jory thought he heard someone gasp in the crowd, but that could have been him trying to breathe and swallow as a lump grew in his stomach like he was going to throw up.

"I present to you my eleven-year-old squire, Jory Turner."

Sir Cley stepped back from the middle of the ring, leaving Jory alone in the wash of cheers from the spectators. Jory froze, not sure what to do. He raised his hand, waving bashfully to the crowd, then remembered something he had seen Sir Cley do once. He knelt and picked up a pink flower and walked the flower over to the viewing stand to give to the princess. When he got to the royal viewing box, he realized it was too high for him to reach up to hand the flower to her, and he did not want to toss it. One of the princess's maids noticed Jory's dilemma and stepped forward to reach down and take the flower from him. She turned and gave the small flower to the future queen.

"F-for you, My Princess," Jory said loudly so all could hear. The crowd cheered with approval.

"Thank you, dear Squire. May you fight your best."

Her voice was a gentle, cool breeze. The princess tucked the flower in her hair, and Jory felt sweat drip down his back.

Jory walked back to where Sir Cley was waiting with his gear. Sir Cley knelt and smiled at him broadly as he buckled Jory's helmet down and strapped his shield onto his left arm.

"Nicely done, boy. You have been paying attention. Let's hope you learned your lessons with the sword and shield as well. Try to stay on the opposite end of the ring from the Fowler twins. They will fight together. Avoid the big boy till later if you can. He will tire out. Find someone your size. Use your speed and..."

"Keep my shield up," Jory finished with him. Sir Cley clapped Jory on the shoulder and hopped over the rail into the crowd with the commoners to watch.

An older master-at-arms stood in the middle of the ring explaining the rules.

"It is better to say, 'I submit,' than to take a serious injury," he reminded the boys.

I would rather break a leg than cry out "I submit" in front of this crowd and the princess.

The Fowler twins stood opposite Jory in the ring, and the big squire stood three boys to his left. He noticed a squire wearing orange and black ribbons inching his way closer to his position. Eventually, the boy in orange and black switched spots with the boy called Aiden so that now he was right next to Jory in the ring.

Why did Sir Cley have to announce that I was only eleven? These boys will be lining up to have an easy bout with me.

"Good. Fight with honor. Begin!" the man-at-arms commanded.

The boy wearing orange and black turned immediately and made a wild cut at Jory's head. Jory's training kicked in, and he raised his shield while ducking. The blow glanced off his shield harmlessly. The boy chopped downward at Jory with his sword. Jory dodged to the left, avoiding the blow, while with his own sword he hit the boy on the side above the hip. The squire swung again at Jory so hard his helmet spun. The boy then stumbled, and Jory took his opportunity. He moved to the side of the stumbling boy, cutting down hard with his sword at the back of the boy's knee. It was not a killing blow, but Sir Cley taught him that you didn't have to always make a killing blow, just one good enough to take another knight out. The squire's leg buckled, and his knee hit the ground.

"You there, in orange and black. Outta the ring!" one of the judges barked. The crowd cheered. Jory made the first elimination.

I beat him...I beat him! That was easy, and I was not the first to get knocked out!

Jory's heart raced. Hidden under his helmet a smile sprouted on his face.

He took a deep breath. It was hard to see out of the visor of his helmet, and it was even more difficult to breathe. Only seven other boys were left in the ring. The weaker, less prepared boys were all easily beaten by the bigger or more skilled squires. The big squire in black and gold was facing off with the twins at one end of the ring. The boy in red, black, and white was matched up with another boy to Jory's right. Jory stepped forward to go after one of the twins. That was when Theo Harroldson stepped into Jory's line of sight.

"It looks like I will have the pleasure of dueling the bay rat." Theo leveled his sword at Jory and raised his shield.

Seeing Theo's shield raised, Jory went through the basic steps of Form One in his head.

Shield, parry, shield, thrust.

He knew the progression and the steps to this dance. Theo clashed his shield against Jory's, then made a cut with his sword that Jory deflected with his shield. Theo used his shield to try to knock Jory's shield away while thrusting his sword forward. Jory braced himself, bending his knees to keep his balance. Jory played defense with his sword as it caught each incoming stroke.

Theo's swings became wider and wilder as Jory's defensive style frustrated him. Theo grew impatient. Jory darted to Theo's right as Theo swung down with an overhead cut. Jory spotted an opening and sharply struck Theo on his hand, causing him to drop his sword.

Theo was lost without his sword, so he circled Jory, looking for an opportunity to retrieve his weapon from the ground. Jory finally stepped back from the sword. It was something he had seen Sir Cley do in a knights' melee. It was an honorable gesture to let your opponent retrieve his weapon. The crowd cheered. Jory was not certain if the cheer was for someone getting an elimination or if it was for his own act of honor. Theo picked up his sword and bowed to Jory, then took a knee in front of him, holding out the hilt of his sword.

"That blow would have taken off my hand if these were real blades. A lucky blow, but I am beaten...this time," Theo said. He stood and walked to the gate. Jory heard knights and soldiers in the crowd congratulating Theo for his own act of honor.

Jory had enough time to survey the ring while catching his breath. On one side, the Fowler twins and the big squire were bent over, panting. They were so close they could have easily pushed each other over. To his right, Jory spotted the squire with red, black, and white streamers coming toward him.

"It appears the other three are too tired to fight. Shall we show them how it's done?" Aiden asked.

Jory raised his sword and shield again. His sword arm was tired now. It was hot inside the helmet, and there was no way to wipe away the sweat that stung his eyes.

Aiden stepped forward and made his first cut. The blow shook Jory. Aiden feigned as if he were going to make a cut toward the head but brought the sword below Jory's shield. It was a clean slash to Jory's ribs. Aiden's reach and longer legs gave him an advantage. Jory found Aiden was quick too. If Jory jumped to the side, Aiden matched him and would deliver another blow to his ribs.

This boy is not using the usual training steps.

Aiden did not make wild attacks either. He was patient and used his feet and shield to set up short, quick cuts with his sword. Jory could feel the sting to his sides each time Aiden found a gap in his defenses, and it was becoming more difficult to take a full breath. Aiden feigned a lunge to the left but moved to his right, delivering another strike. Jory lowered his shield to catch the blow this time, but Aiden reloaded, spun in a full turn, and on his backswing landed a blow to Jory's helmet that left his head ringing like a bell. Jory staggered back in a daze. His vision blurred as Aiden stepped toward him. Jory's legs wobbled, and his knees began to buckle.

I will not take a knee and submit.

Jory's head was in a fog, and everything around him moved slower. His arms lost their strength, and his sword and shield rested uselessly at his sides. Aiden moved in to put him on his back with his sword ready to swing.

"Finish him!" someone in the crowd yelled.

Jory instinctively tried to raise his shield but knew it would be too late. Aiden was already within striking distance. He closed his eyes, bracing himself for the hit.

Jory heard a crash, then a cheer from a group of soldiers in the crowd. Jory opened his eyes to see Aiden sprawled out on the ground to his right with the big squire in black and gold standing over him.

"Like a bull, that one!" someone yelled.

"Bulled that boy over, right good," another said.

"Got him from his blindside, he did. Thataway, Bull. I want two more coppers on the Bull to win!" shouted a man in the crowd.

The crowd chanted, "Bull...Bull...Bull..."

The Bull reached down and pulled Aiden's ribbons off his helmet. He wrapped them around his sword hand and kicked Aiden in the stomach as the boy tried to get up. The Bull turned to face Jory, who took a step back and stumbled into the rail that encircled the arena. It was right behind him. There would be no room for retreat.

"Want to play with the big boys, do ya? Little bay rat. I will crush you."

The Bull raised his shield and charged right into Jory, crushing him against the rail. Jory's shield arm ended up pinned against the wood, and flames of pain spread from his shoulder. If not for the rail holding him up, Jory would have been trampled.

The Bull backed up to get ready for another charge.

He heard Sir Cley's voice in his head as he drilled him on defense: "Stay away. Use your opponent's aggression against him."

Jory jumped to the side when the Bull made his second charge, and the Bull crashed into the rail, shield first, with a cracking of wood on wood.

Stay away long enough to clear my head.

The Bull made another, more desperate charge. Jory easily jumped out of the way again at the last second. The Bull was breathing hard now, so he came after Jory, swinging his sword. Jory dodged most of his blows but caught one on his shield. The force was heavy, making Jory's shoulder ache. The Bull rained down another blow, but this one Jory ducked to avoid. He circled around behind the big squire. The Bull spun and swung his sword at Jory's head three times in a row, each cut met by Jory's sword. The Bull made a low cut at his legs, which Jory jumped over.

Then the Bull raised his sword and cut down from above. Jory sidestepped the blow as the sword hit the ground, and the Bull stumbled forward. Jory noticed the ribbons wrapped around his sword hand were touching the ground, so Jory moved close to the Bull and stepped on the ribbons.

The Bull tried to raise his sword, but his arm was now held still by the ribbons trapped under Jory's foot. Jory hit the Bull flush in the helmet with his sword. The Bull swung up with his shield violently to push Jory down, but Jory stepped off the ribbons as the Bull flailed, trying to regain his footing.

Jory delivered another ringing blow to the Bull's helmet. The big squire reeled backward in a stupor and went to one knee on the ground. Jory went to the dazed boy's side and unwrapped the red, black, and white ribbons from the Bull's arm, then tossed them on the ground.

Cheers came from the crowd, as well as some groans from those who had bet on the Bull to win. Jory listened to the cheers, hearing one voice above them all.

"Keep them both in front of you. Put your back to the rail." The voice was Sir Cley shouting strategy to him. That was when Jory remembered the Fowler twins. It was too late for him to maneuver his back to the rail of the ring. During his fight with the Bull, the twins had moved into position with one on each side.

Jory tried to catch his breath. His heart thumped in his chest. His tunic and breeches stuck to his skin, wet with sweat. He was still dizzy from Aiden's blow, and the hand of his shield arm tingled with pinpricks.

One of the twins moved in front of Jory, the other slipping behind him. He tried to remember what Sir Cley had taught him about fighting two against one: "Attack what you see in front of you. Defend what you can from behind."

Sir Cley's instructions came to him as the crowd roared for the brothers of the future queen.

Most of the crowd was now chanting "Fowler" or "Greyport." Another group was yelling "End it!" or "Finish him!" but Jory also heard "For Buckton" and "For the West," although not as loudly.

Jory noticed that the twin in front of him was in an area where the ground was pocked and chewed up by the heavy boots of the knights who had their melee the day before. Sir Cley taught him to use his surroundings as an advantage when he could, so Jory charged ahead, attacking the twin in front of him.

The twin stepped into one of the holes in the turf as he tried to avoid Jory's rush and looked down to find better footing. Jory hit the boy in the ribs below his raised shield. In rapid succession, Jory dealt a stinging blow to the boy's shoulder as he lowered his shield to cover his ribs. Jory took the opportunity to deliver another blow to the boy's head.

The twin to Jory's rear was slow to react. Jory struck another blow to the twin in front of him. This time, Jory crouched and went low, finding the mark on the boy's right side. As Jory swung, he found the strength to hold up his own shield to cover his back, catching a blow that was aimed at his head from behind by the other twin. The blow stung Jory's arm, and it went numb.

Jory swung his sword at the boy behind him as he spun around to face his attacker and caught him in the ribs. The twin took three steps back from him. Jory spun again, then returned his efforts to the boy who had been in front of him, delivering a cut to the boy's midsection. The twin dropped to both knees on the ground, wheezing to catch his breath. The knights and people from the West cheered for Jory.

Jory turned around. The other twin kept his distance and assumed a defensive stance. Jory took a brief glimpse up at the viewing stand. The princess stood with her hand covering her mouth as if she were viewing some horror in the ring.

He turned back to the twin who charged forward with his shield raised. As Jory took a tiny step backward to brace himself, something pressed up against the back of his legs. The twin charged into Jory with his shield clashing against Jory's. The force sent Jory flipping backward over the defeated twin who had snuck up behind him and kneeled on all fours.

The melee was over. The victorious twin removed his helmet.

Daxian Fowler, champion of the Squires' Melee, basked in the cheers of the men and women from Greyport for their favorite son, as Jory, the bay rat, squirmed in the dirt and mud, defeated.

6

THE GOLDEN KNIGHT II

Sir Cley jumped over the rail surrounding the ring and ran to Jory's side as he was on the ground.

"Well done, Jory. Can you sit up?" Cley asked.

Jory nodded. Cley took the boy's helmet off. Streaks of sweat and dirt ran down his squire's face, and tears welled up in his eyes.

"But I lost. An-and I let you and the people from Buckton down," Jory said in a breathless sob as he sat up.

"You let no one down, boy. You fought well. The Fowlers fought dirty," Cley whispered while he unstrapped the shield from his arm. He handed a small cloth to Jory. "Wipe your face and eyes. No crying. A true knight does not cry if he loses."

Jory wiped his nose and eyes as well as his cheeks and his forehead.

"Take a few deep breaths. I am going to help you stand up, then we are going to walk over to the viewing stand. Bow before the princess and shake that Fowler boy's hand. No tears, right?"

Jory nodded.

"I am proud of you," Cley said as he pulled his squire

onto his feet and led the wobbly boy over to the viewing stand. An older knight from Greyport was also in the ring, patting Daxian on the shoulder as the Greyport people cheered for him. With Daxian's helmet off, Cley guessed that the princess must have taken all the good looks in the Fowler family. The boy was of course dirty and sweaty, but Cley noted he had an upturned, piggish nose like his father. His eyes were a dull brown, almost black color and set close to each other. His face was spotted with pimples, and his teeth were crooked as he turned and smiled at Jory.

Jory walked up to Daxian, bowing to the winner and offering his hand. The whole crowd cheered the two boys as Daxian accepted his hand. Cley could not help but notice that the other twin, Jaxian, stood alone to the side, pressed up against the rail with his helmet off. The blond-haired boy glared at his twin with eyes burning in pure envy.

Cley turned back to Jory, who was approaching the viewing stand to bow to the princess. Jory veered to the side of the ring where he bent down to pick up three ribbons from the ground, which he tucked into his belt, then he walked over before the princess and went to one knee.

"My Pr-princess, to you I pledge my s-sword and my life," Jory said in a loud voice.

Cley walked over and took a knee next to his squire. "And I pledge my sword and life as well." The crowd reacted predictably and applauded with approval.

The boy has been paying attention to my lessons. Not only was he quick with the sword and his feet, but he had a flare for the theatrics too. His speaking is getting better in public. His father would have been proud.

Cley noticed the princess looking for a way to get down into the ring. He decided this was a suitable time to get Jory out of the crush of people forming around them.

"Let's go. Let the Fowlers enjoy their victory. Do you think you can walk back to camp?"

Tears were gathering in Jory's eyes again.

"It's my shoulder. It hurts so bad. It f-feels like it's on fire."

"Climb on my shoulders. I will give you a champion's ride back to the Buckton camp."

Jory stood and straddled his legs over Cley's shoulders. Cley stood, balancing the weight of the boy on his shoulders, and made for the open gate to the ring. As he walked out of the gate and into the commoners who crowded around that part of the ring, he spotted a lad from Buckton he recognized.

"You, boy, go into the ring and fetch my squire's helmet, shield, and sword. Bring them to my pavilion by midday, and I will pay you a silver," Cley said. The boy did not hesitate and ran into the ring to gather Jory's equipment.

As Cley made his way through the crowd, the commoners all greeted him and called up to his squire.

"Well done, lad."

"You were the true champion, boy."

"The Fowlers cheated you."

Many of the people surrounding them agreed. Anger was building in the crowd.

"Smile and wave. Say nothing but thank you," Cley called up to Jory.

Cley made his way toward the area where the Buckton men were gathered. The crowd of commoners followed him. The people pushed up against Cley and reached up to touch Jory's leg or arm.

"How about we have a little melee of our own? Buckton versus Greyport!" one Buckton man called out.

Back at the ring, some of the armed guards with the

princess had their hands on the hilts of their swords. The men from Greyport stopped cheering their champion.

This is dangerous.

"My friends," Cley called out to the mob surrounding him, "to honor my squire, you are all invited back to the Buckton camp. I will buy the drink. You will provide the music and songs. We will drink to my squire's deeds and to the health of our future king and queen."

The crowd cheered raucously. Cley hurried off in the direction of the Buckton camp with his squire seated upon his shoulders like a rag doll, a crowd of people following him.

Cley made his way toward the tent that was set up as a tavern. As he approached, he noted some of the crowd was drifting away, seeing that there would be no fight between the men of the West and the men of the East. Many had chores or tasks to do for their lords, and were wary of being seen as lazy or disobedient.

All the better. This may not end up costing me as much as I thought.

He stopped outside the tent, bending to one knee so Jory could climb off his shoulders.

"My friends, I have some gold, and I want to celebrate the performance of my young squire here," Cley exclaimed as he entered the tent. The serving women and ale master were sitting at the drinking tables, bored in the late-morning hours. The only other people in the tent were the group of knights Cley liked to refer to as the Knights of the Barrel. The group attended every tournament. They rarely participated in the contests, but they could forever be found at the ale tents or local taverns drinking, laughing, and telling stories.

The serving staff scrambled to their feet as the benches filled up with the small crowd that followed Cley and Jory. The ale tent's owner walked over to where Cley claimed a bench. Cley counted out five gold pieces on the table for him.

"Here, good man. This should be enough to keep this lot happy for an hour or two." The owner nodded, scooping the coins into his own money pouch. "My squire and I will have lemon water, if you have it," Cley said in a lower voice.

Cley spotted Sir Torrent entering the tent. "Ah-ha. I knew the Great Tor would not be too far away from a free tankard of ale. Come over here, Torrent," Cley called across the benches. Sir Torrent made his way over to Cley and Jory, forcing himself between people with his ample girth.

"That was some good work you put in today, boy," Sir Torrent said as he plopped onto the bench near Jory and thumped his huge fist on Jory's thigh. "Those Fowlers are a disgrace. To cheat like that and claim a victory is an embarrassment. You were the real winner, boy. Everyone knows it."

Cley sat down next to Sir Torrent with Jory.

"Do you think you can entertain this crowd while I take him over to the healer's tent to have her see to his shoulder?" Cley asked.

Sir Torrent stood, raising his tankard of ale in the air.

"My friends, a salute to young Jory here after his first melee, a salute to the future king, Prince James, and his beautiful future queen..."

The crowd sat quietly at the mention of the Fowler girl. Sir Torrent surveyed the crowd.

"And finally, a salute to the men of the West."

The tent erupted into cheers and loud chatter.

Cley took a long drink from his tankard and nodded his appreciation to Sir Torrent, then he took Jory by his good arm and led him out the back of the tent.

"How do you feel now?" Cley asked Jory as they walked away from the noisy ale tent.

"I feel a little better now. My head feels cl-clearer…but my shoulder still hurts."

"Let's walk over to the healer's and let her have a look at you. Plus, you still have chores, and I cannot have my squire staggering around all day."

Cley grinned, coaxing a smile from the boy.

Cley prodded Jory ahead of him as they entered the healer's tent. Tables and cots were set up for men who suffered the injuries that were bound to happen at any tournament. No injured knights were inside the tent today, as the jousting and melees for the men were already over. The two women and the girl who worked the tent were sitting, busily rolling bandages and preparing for the Squires' Joust that day. There would certainly be injuries during that event. There always were. Jousting could be dangerous, even if it were squires using short tournament lances. The old healer from Buckton, Maggy, had seen Cley himself a few times when he was younger. Nothing serious, usually a scratch or bruise for her to put one of her ointments on.

Cley hoped the younger woman, Alyss, would not be there, but it was not his lucky day.

"What do we have here? The Knight of the Tall Tree comes to visit old Maggy—and look, he brings in his little sapling," the old woman said when Cley stepped into the tent with Jory. "He didn't break a branch, did he?" She smiled at her own joke, showing her missing teeth.

"No broken bones, Maggy. I think. But the boy says his shoulder hurts, and he got his bell rung a couple of times."

Cley nudged Jory toward the old healer. "Anyway, I figured you good ladies could work your magic on him and get him back to as good as new."

Cley found an apple in a bowl on a nearby table and shined it on his tunic while he tried to avoid making eye contact with the younger healer.

"Alyss, get the boy up on the table. Get his tunic off so you can have a look. Emm, go outside and get some of the cloth off the line to make a sling," the healer ordered, straightening herself up from her camp chair.

"Magic is dead, Sir Cley, and has been for over a hundred years. What we do here is knowledge and skill," said Alyss.

She stood up, walked over to Jory, and led the boy over to a long narrow table the healer used to work on injured men or knights. The girl, Emily, sprang up, and ran out of the tent.

"How did he get hit in the head?" Alyss asked as she untied the laces on Jory's new and now dirty tunic. She pulled the armband Cley had given him off his right arm, setting it beside the boy on the table. Jory winced as he raised his left arm up to let the tunic be pulled over his head.

"A few blows to the head during the Squires' Melee." Cley took a large bite of the apple.

Alyss turned and gave Cley a look that would have many men ducking for cover.

"Hey...it's not my fault, if that's what you think. I told the boy to keep his shield up, but what can you do? A squire sometimes learns that lesson the hard way." Cley hopped up onto a table across from Alyss and Jory, then took another bite from the apple. Maggy busied herself at a table with bottles and vials, mixing the different liquids contained in them into a bowl.

Cley watched Alyss work and thought about how he had

known her since he was a squire and she was only a girl. Her black hair and green eyes highlighted her smooth skin and small nose.

Alyss is pretty in a common way, almost beautiful. Some common man will be lucky to wed her someday.

"You let him join in the melee?" Alyss kept her hot glare on Cley while she continued to examine Jory. "He does not even look old enough to be a squire yet."

She began to wiggle Jory's arm around with one hand and prodded around his shoulder joint with the other. Jory winced in pain again.

"He was good though. You should have seen him out there in the ring. It took two of them cheating together to get him out."

"I am old enough to be a s-squire," Jory chimed in. "I will be tw-twelve in sixteen more days."

Alyss glanced back at Jory and rolled her eyes at his defense. She put her hand in the middle of his chest and pushed him back flat on the table.

"Hush, boy, you're in good hands now."

She pulled his left arm out to his side and slowly twisted it. Jory's eyes bulged as if in pain until a look of relief crept across his face.

Cley reclined back on his left elbow. He brought his right leg up, placing his boot on the table.

"The boy begged me to enter him in the melee. He is very persistent, you know," Cley said with a mouthful of half-chewed apple.

"If he begged you to let him jump off a cliff, would you let him?" Alyss shot back. "And get your dirty boot off the table!"

Cley absently took another bite of the apple. "How high is the cliff?"

"Ugh! You are impossible. Whoever thought it was a good idea to let you have a young boy for a squire should be put in the stocks for a week."

Alyss jerked Jory back up into a sitting position on the table by the arm she had been working on. She ran her fingers through his hair and pressed against his skull. "I mean, what kind of mother would let her child go off with some wandering knight who can barely take care of himself?"

Cley glanced over at Maggy. The two exchanged knowing looks. At that moment, the apprentice returned with a long piece of cloth. The girl stopped at the tent's entrance, held in place by the heavy silence.

"Is the boy alright, Alyss?" Maggy asked in earnest. "Did you check his ribs?" She shuffled over to where Alyss was torturing Jory.

Alyss poked around his ribs and stomach. "No broken bones in his arm. Simply a bruised shoulder," she answered as she turned her full attention to Jory. "His skull feels fine. None of his ribs are broken...luckily." She glared at Cley.

"Here, boy, drink this for your head," Maggy said, handing a small wooden bowl to Jory. "When you're done, hop off the table and go sit on the chair over there so Emm can wrap your shoulder in some cloth."

Cley watched Jory gag as he swallowed the healing potion Maggy gave to him. The boy leaped off the table to remove himself from Alyss and sat in the lower chair.

The girl, Emm, gently began to wrap a cloth around Jory's arm and shoulder. Cley thought he noticed Jory blushing as the pretty girl touched him.

"Well...I can see Jory is in good hands now," Cley said sarcastically toward Alyss as he hopped off the table. "Jory, I will meet you back at our camp. I need to get back to the ale tent and make sure no riot has broken out. Oh, and I guess I can pick up my clean clothes from the laundresses, so you don't have to. Gotta look good for the royal banquet tonight."

Cley walked to the tent's entrance. "Maggy, thank you so much for the care you have given my squire. Ladies..." Cley spotted a basket in a corner on the other side of the tent filled with garbage from the day before and tossed the apple core into it. With a slight bow to the women and a wink to Jory, Sir Cley backed out of the tent.

7
EMILY I

Emily continued to wrap the cloth around the boy sitting in front of her. The wrapping of a knight's arm or leg was something Emily had done many times before. Making a sling was an easy task.

The cloth is too long for this boy. I will need to tie off the loose end so it is not hanging off him.

"My name is Emily, or Emm for short if you like," she said to the boy squire. "I have been Maggy's apprentice for two years now. I can name most herbs and plants used for healing."

The squire smiled back at her but remained silent as she finished looping the cloth around his arm and over his shoulder. He was avoiding eye contact with her. She could sense the boy was nervous, but there was something else about him too.

Emily maneuvered the cloth up under his arm, looping it back around his shoulder. She noted the shark tooth necklace that hung loosely around his neck. It was a crude piece of art, an actual shark's tooth carved into a hook shape. The thong that wrapped around his neck was a string used in fishing nets.

The squire is cute in a puppy-dog kind of way.

He had a nice smile, and blue eyes much like the knight he squired for. His blond hair was pulled back from his face, revealing a nasty scar that ran through his left eyebrow. He was boyishly cute, but he was not like the older squires Emily was interested in. He was still a boy—no muscles, or at least not like the ones on Theo.

Theo Harroldson—now, he is handsome.

Emily recalled slipping off to the Squires' Melee to watch the boy from Tidehaven. Theo looked so gallant in his helmet, holding his sword and shield. The silver and blue ribbons that were the colors of his house suited him perfectly.

Her first glimpse of Theo happened as he rode through the Buckton camp in his squire's attire with a silken gray tunic and a blue cape wrapped over him. Since that day, she tried to see more of him. Emily accidentally came upon him in the creek, splashing around with some other boys without his tunic on. She found out he was even the same age as she was, fourteen years old. But Theo was nobility, the son of a great lord of a major city. The idea of him being interested in her, an apprentice girl, was a silly dream.

"Emm, finish up that sling on the boy and be sure to tie a good knot to hold it," Maggy instructed her. "Boy, you need to soak that shoulder in the creek when you can. It might bruise some, but you will be fine. Alyss, can you help me dump this water outside the tent?"

Maggy grabbed hold of the water bucket and struggled with it until Alyss came over to help her carry it outside. Emily knew this was an excuse the old healer often used to talk to Alyss in private. She stood up from knotting the sling for the boy and moved over to the side of the tent where she could hear Maggy and Alyss speaking outside.

"I know, Maggy, but Cley infuriates me. The boy had no business being in that melee with those older, bigger squires,"

Alyss said. "He clearly got hurt, and it could have been worse. Cley didn't even stay to walk him back to his camp. He dumped the boy off with us and headed back to the ale tent and his drinking buddies. There is no telling what other injuries that boy has suffered while training at such an early age. Like that old scar through the boy's eyebrow, how did that get there?"

"Now, Alyss," Maggy responded in a calm voice, "the training of squires involves injuries every now and then. All squires go through it. Injuries are bound to happen. A knight must know he can trust that his squire will be there for him in battle to watch his back."

"A boy his age should still be at home with a mother, not out roaming around the countryside from camp to camp and tournament to tournament. What kind of life is that? And what of the drinking and gambling that Cley does all night? Not to mention the women coming in and out of his tent. You've heard the stories around camp. There is no telling what that boy has seen since he has been with him."

"Alyss, I have known Cley since he was a boy himself. He was young for his age as a squire too. He would not endanger the boy or lead him down a path away from the Four. You have known Cley for almost as long as I have. Camp gossip is all that is. Are you more concerned about the boy or with the rumors about Cley?"

Emily heard nothing but silence on the other side of the tent for a moment until Alyss spoke again.

"And what kind of mother would allow her own child to be sold for a workhorse and some coins?"

Emily looked over at the boy, who was sitting there quietly with his back turned to her. She counted four old scars across his back that she had not noticed earlier. She wondered how he might have received those and began to feel sorry for the boy.

"We cannot solve everyone's problems, Alyss. What's done is done. We cannot change the past. As a healer, we can only patch up the ones who come to us injured. There are some wounds that cannot be healed by our hands."

Emily went back over to where the squire was sitting.

"I am all done here," she said, finishing the knot in the sling. "Let me help you back into your tunic." She picked up the squire's tunic off the table and noticed it was stained with mud.

"Oh, umm, I can w-walk back to camp like this," the boy stuttered in reply. "Plus, I won't be able to get my arm through it with the sling on."

"Let me wash the tunic for you at least. I have a lot of washing I must do for Maggy today, and I have something I can put on it that will get the mud stain out for you. It will be like new."

The boy's smile told her that the idea of getting a clean tunic with no stain was something he wanted. She noted again the jagged scar above his left eye that ran through his eyebrow, dividing it into two unequal parts.

The boy certainly did not see Maggy when this happened. She would never have left a scar like that.

"After I finish washing your tunic, I will bring it to your campsite," she offered.

"Oh, okay, I guess that will be al-alright. We are on the far end of camp, right next to the creek, in the green pavilion."

"Don't worry. Everyone knows where Sir Cley is camped."

The boy stood and turned to leave but ran back to the table to grab his armband. He smiled at Emily and ran from the tent.

When Maggy and Alyss came back in, there was still tension between them.

"I am going to take these bandages down to the creek and wash them," Emily said. "I will be back before lunch." She tossed the squire's tunic into a small basket with a few bandages that had been washed the day before but not rolled up. She grabbed a bottle of liquid she used to get blood stains out of bandages and hurried out of the tent before Maggy or Alyss could give her some other chore to do.

As Emily approached the washing area near the creek, she spotted a couple of the washerwomen busy at work near the large kettles they used to boil the water for the laundry. She recognized Betha, an older woman from Buckton, scrubbing some pants. The other was Saph, a girl from Tidehaven.

"Hi, Emm. I see Maggy has you busy washing more bandages for her," Saph said, looking up from her work.

Emily pulled the squire's tunic out of the basket and put it in the water. "Yes, we went through three baskets of bandages yesterday after the Knights' Melee."

"I went and watched that Squires' Melee this morning," Betha spoke up. "I even made a silver when that big one they called the Bull went down. I had a feeling that squire with Sir Cley was going to wear him out, running and darting around like a water bug."

"Yes, I saw that," Emily replied, remembering the boy jumping over and ducking the wild swings from the Bull. "It was very exciting."

"I would have made another silver if not for those cheating Fowler boys," Betha added.

"Did you see Theo Harroldson? He was so honorable when he took the knee. Everyone said he could have gone on fighting, but he was so gallant," Saph gushed. "He is so handsome too. Did you see him when he took his helmet off?"

"No, I lost sight of him when he left the ring," Emily replied.

"Oh, well his black curls were pressed against his forehead and neck with sweat. His face was flushed with a beautiful rose color. He looked like a painting of a young knight after battle," Saph recalled breathlessly.

Emily held up the squire's tunic and began to wring the water out of it. She rubbed the stain with some of the cleaning liquid she brought with her and plunged the tunic back into the water to scrub.

"That cloth there looks too nice to be a bandage and too small for you to wear, Emm," commented Betha.

"Oh, this shirt is from Sir Cley's squire. He had to visit Maggy because his shoulder was hurting."

Emily continued to scrub, though most of the stains were already gone.

"Sir Cley is so handsome. If only I were older, he would notice me. His squire is kind of cute too, but it's sad what happened to him," Saph said and sighed.

"Why? What happened to his squire?" Emily asked.

Saph lowered her voice. "I heard some women at the melee say the squire's mother married a man named Lord Wells after his natural father, Lord Turner, died in battle. A year later, she gave birth to a boy. When that baby got old enough, Lord Wells sold the older boy to Sir Cley to serve as a squire, all for the price of three milk cows and thirty gold pieces. And the mother agreed to it! Can you imagine that?"

Emily's jaw dropped. The story she heard Alyss tell back at the tent was true, if not distorted.

Emily turned to Betha to see if she would give any indication if this was the truth. If anyone knew, it would be Betha, who had lived her whole life around Buckton and served as a washerwoman in Lord Buckhorn's house.

Betha shook her head. "That wasn't the way of it," she began.

Emily breathed a sigh of relief.

"The way it happened is right, but those women got the facts wrong. First, Turner and Wells aren't lords. They are landed knights. Lord Buckhorn gave Sir Jonas the Broken Tower and its lands, such as they are, as reward for his service in the Second Northern Rebellion. Now, Wells was given the Broken Tower by King Edward himself after Sir Jonas died at Falling Stone, like you said," Betha explained to the younger girls.

"Wells took Turner's wife as his own and had a baby boy with her. When that boy turned three, Wells knew he was strong enough to get on, and an older boy by another man might stand in his son's way of inheriting the tower and its lands someday. So Wells decided to sell him off as a squire. As it happened, Sir Cley was a newly made knight, who did not have a squire yet, and he was close by in Buckton serving Lord Buckhorn."

Emily stared in disbelief down into the kettle where she was stirring the boy's tunic.

"Oh, and you heard wrong about the price too. It was not three cows. It was a strong draft horse from Lord Buckhorn's own stable. And it was thirty pieces of copper, not gold. But I think Sir Cley got the best of the deal. He not only took the boy but claimed Sir Jonas's sword as well. He left the Broken Tower with the boy riding in front of him and the sword strapped to his back."

Emily sat quietly, feeling sad for the boy who owned the tunic she was scrubbing.

"How could his mother let that happen?" Saph asked what Emily was thinking.

"It's those nobles' way of doing things," Betha replied. "The boy's mother had no choice in the matter. We look at them highborn as our betters and envy them for their pretty hair and fancy dresses, but in many ways we have it better. I was never traded for some land. I married the man I loved, and no one ever took any of my children away."

The younger girls sat and listened in silence.

"The boy got himself a fine knight," Betha went on with a little more cheer. "You couldn't ask for better. Sir Cley served as squire to the boy's father when he was almost the same age. Sir Jonas found him as an orphan in some city up in the North, as the rumors go, so I dare say the boy would have ended up with Sir Cley even if Turner still lived."

Saph nodded in agreement. Emily thought about the squire.

It's still sad.

Emily sat with the boy's tunic in her hand. It was clean now, but as she examined it closely, she could make out the shadow of a stain that could not be washed away.

8
JORY IV

As soon as he was far enough away from the healer's tent, Jory pulled the sling off and unwrapped his left arm. The searing pain in his shoulder was gone. Jory tossed the wrappings into a campfire outside some knight's pavilion.

The camp was eerily silent. Most were off to watch the older squires' joust. After the last joust, the camp would become a beehive of activity as people prepared for the last banquet tonight and the start of the march to Crosstimbers the next morning.

Jory thought about going back to his tent to get another tunic to wear so he could go watch the joust. As he was thinking, he found himself pulled toward the creek near the campsite Sir Cley had picked out for them.

The murmuring sound of the slow-moving water called to Jory. He decided to skip the joust and jump in the creek to get himself a quick wash while no one else was around. Jory kicked his boots off, set them beside the tent, and walked barefoot down the sloped incline that led to the creek.

A horse's snort brought Jory's attention to the opposite bank. Across the creek, someone had set up camp.

Must be some late-arriving soldier hoping to find a lord to work for.

Jory spotted a huge black charger next to a tree, untied and eating some of the long grass shoots that grew by the creek. There was a small campfire burning that was giving off a little smoke. The fire was set up in front of a ragged-looking black tent that had several patches of different dark colors sewn onto it. There was an old leather saddle tossed on the ground along with a few sacks of what was probably food.

Whoever lives at that camp needs a better squire.

Jory decided to walk farther downstream in case someone was still about. He walked down the creek until he found a bend in its path well out of sight of anyone. Standing on a large rock looking over the slow-moving water, the sun warmed the bare skin on his upper body. Jory stepped down into the creek, feeling the chilly water covering his feet and ankles. His mind drifted. Memories slowly flowed into his head of playing in the surf with his friends on the beaches back home as a little boy. Running on the beach, jumping into the foamy surf, and riding the waves came back to him in ripples. Jory could picture the boys he used to play with. He could smell the salty air and hear the roar as breakers rolled in and smashed against the sea rocks and cliffs.

Jory turned his back to the creek and lowered his new breeches, being careful not to let his armband or the ribbons he had picked up back at the ring fall into the creek. He was about to take off his underclothes when he heard a splash behind him. He turned around and a boy stood with his back to him, waist-deep in the middle of the creek. The boy slicked back his wet hair and rubbed the water from his face. Jory froze for a second, noticing the scars scattered across the boy's back that ran down from his shoulder blades to his lower back then disappeared under the water.

Whip marks.

Jory turned away to pick up his breeches, thinking he would come back later.

"Hey, where are you going?" the boy called.

Jory turned back around to see the boy was now facing him. He had long blond hair only at the top of his head, and his small ears stuck out a bit from the shaved sides.

"Umm, I was gonna wash myself...I'll c-come back later," Jory said as he reached down to gather his clothes.

"You got my colors," the boy called back to Jory.

Jory stood holding the red, black, and white ribbons. He thought for a moment and matched the boy's voice with the squire he had faced in the ring.

"Yeah, those are my ribbons. I'm Aiden," the boy said. "Look, you don't have to go. The creek is big enough for the both of us, and the water feels good."

Jory set his things back down and slowly re-entered the water, walking out until he was in the middle, a few feet away from Aiden. The water came up to his chest, and it did feel good, but it was cold, and goosebumps popped up on Jory's skin. The waters running through Pebble Creek had yet to warm up with the beginning of summer.

"I'm Jory. I think you were about to b-best me in the ring today."

"Nah, you fought well, better than any of the other squires in there. Thanks for saving my colors," Aiden said. "Do you always wash yourself in your underclothes?"

"Oh, yeah...I-I mean, no, I don't. I guess I forgot I still had them on. You surprised me."

Jory could make out in the water that Aiden was not wearing anything. He reached under the water, undid the knots that held his underclothes together, and threw the cloth back over to the rock where his breeches were. The cold water surrounded him now as it ran around and between his legs. He dug his feet into the creek bed, finding smooth pebbles and sand that squished between his toes.

"I like your necklace. What's it made of? Whale bone?" Aiden asked.

"It's a shark tooth," Jory replied. "It's supposed to bring me g-good luck. I guess it doesn't really work."

"Yes, but you fought well in the ring." Aiden lowered himself so that the water was to his chin. "I heard some of the men say that the Fowler twins and that one they called the Bull were too old to be in the melee. Someone told me they were fifteen."

"Yeah, I h-heard that too. How old are you?" Jory asked.

"I turned fourteen about a month ago, I think."

"You're not sure if you are fourteen?"

"No. I mean, I know I am fourteen but not sure of the exact day," Aiden tried to explain. "I know it's always on the first full moon after the spring solstice. I'm not big on dates or numbers. Anyway, you're only eleven. You almost won."

"I will be tw-twelve soon."

"You are lucky to have the Knight of the Tall Tree to squire for. I bet you know all kinds of tricks with your sword. How long have you been with him?" Aiden asked.

"Since I was nine." Jory did not like to remember the day Sir Cley came to get him. "I don't know any tricks. Sir Cley calls it strategy and knowing your opponent's weaknesses."

"What did you think my weakness was?"

"Umm, none to be honest. You were good. You never reached too far or lost your balance. You were about to beat me until the Bull rushed you from your blindside." Jory noticed he did not feel as tongue-tied talking about the melee.

"The knight you squire for trained you well. Who is he?

He must be a great fighter. I bet I have seen him at one of the other tournaments."

"Probably not. He's not much for tournaments."

Aiden's smile disappeared at the mention of his knight, and he sank farther under the water so that he was completely submerged. Jory remembered the scars on Aiden's back. He knew that some knights would punish their squires by whipping or beating them. Sir Cley sometimes said that he would "whump" Jory if he did not get out of bed or was lazy with his chores or training. But the knight never hit him.

Aiden resurfaced on Jory's left.

"Hey, I forgot to warn you about the green river turtles in the creek," Aiden said in a serious tone.

"Green river turtles?" Jory repeated.

"Yeah, the turtles that live in this creek love to bite worms or fingers."

Aiden pointed excitedly behind Jory.

"Oh, there's one right behind you!"

Jory's hands shot down between his legs to protect himself. He turned around to find the turtle when Aiden's hands grabbed his shoulders, pushed him down, and dunked him under the water. Jory thrashed in a panic with his head forced under the water, but Aiden released his grasp.

Jory rubbed the water out of his face as he resurfaced.

"Hey, no fair," Jory protested.

"Everything is fair in a water battle," Aiden said and laughed. He sliced his hand into the water, causing a splash to hit Jory in the face.

Jory began to fight back, splashing at Aiden. After spending time swimming, splashing, and trying to dunk each other under the water, the two boys climbed up on the rock overlooking the creek and dried themselves in the sun, with only the sound of the breeze and flowing water. Jory liked the company. He never had a friend close to his age after Sir Cley had come for him, as they never stayed in one place long enough for him to make any.

"Why did you come all the way down here to bathe? Your camp is back around the bend," Aiden asked, breaking the silence between them.

"Someone set up camp across the creek from us. I wanted to relax and be away from everyone, so I came this way, but I am glad you were here. Now I can give you back your colors."

"Who's camping across from you?" Aiden asked.

"I don't know. Some soldier or poor knight with a horrible squire. His tent was full of patches. His charger wasn't even tied up, and there were sacks of food lying on the ground."

"The charger, was it a huge black one?"

Jory nodded.

"I bet that's the Dark Sorrow. I heard he rode in late last night."

"The Dark Sorrow?"

"I don't know his full name, but I think it's Sir Crowe or something like that."

"Why is he called the Dark Sorrow?"

"He travels Terros by himself. They say he kills men for money. If a lord has an outlaw on his lands or needs a knight removed from his holdings, they pay Sir Crowe to do it. He has killed over thirty knights. On the battlefield, I heard he kills anyone who dares stand before him, including lords. He takes no prisoners or hostages, and takes no ransoms."

"Well, I have never heard of him, and Sir Cley and I have been to almost every city in Terros except for the ones in the North."

"I heard he was put in prison for some crime. Maybe he got out."

Jory puzzled over Sir Crowe.

How can he be a knight when he is not doing something honorable?

He knew there were men who worked as bounty hunters, but they were not knights. Bounty hunting was not acceptable work for knights. On the battlefield, if your opponent yielded to you, a true knight would accept your surrender, holding you as prisoner until a ransom was paid. Deaths occurred on the battlefield, but mostly amongst the ranks of the common soldiers.

After a few more minutes, Aiden sat up and left the rock they were sunning on and went down to some bushes that lined the creek, pulling some clothes out from under them. Jory sat up and watched Aiden put his clothes on, noting his tunic and breeches were poor and had holes.

"I have to go. Chores, ya know." Aiden pulled his tunic down over his head. "Maybe we will meet again on the road to Crosstimbers."

"Yeah, it was fun. Maybe you and your knight can travel next to Sir Cley and me on the way there."

"Maybe. I will see what I can do." Aiden hopped across some rocks to the other side of the creek and climbed the bank. Jory was about to call out to Aiden that he had forgotten to take his ribbons, but the boy had already disappeared into the woods.

9
THE GOLDEN KNIGHT III

Three years in the past...

The frigid winter rain continued to come down at a steady pace as the young knight made his way along the path that led to the fishing village of Seadrift. It had been raining on and off for the past three days, and the canopy of tall redwoods had not kept the knight dry. In the knight's mind, it had never stopped raining on him since Falling Stone.

The knight pulled his wet cloak tighter around himself to keep the rain out of his face and eyes, but the cold dampness seeped through to his skin. He was thoroughly drenched despite all his rain gear. Everything he owned was soaked through, but he was not cold. The rage that burned inside him made sure of that.

The rough path people called a road was swamped as the knight's horse splashed through the growing puddles. The knight had tried to guide the horse carefully between them at first, but by the third day of this journey he was tired, and the path was one great big puddle anyway. The knight had encountered no one since he had left Buckton. No travelers, not to Seadrift. There was no reason for anyone to visit

Seadrift, ever. Seadrift had no desire for outsiders either. The villagers of Seadrift were of the sea. They were born by the sea. They scratched out a living on the sea. And when they died, they were returned to the sea. The rest of Terros could have been on another continent, for all the local people cared. But if the Lord of Buckton summoned his swords, the men of Seadrift would do their duty, if begrudgingly.

The smell of salt in the air and the roar of the breakers in the distance told him he was close. The knight emerged from the woods at what he thought was dusk. Before him stretched the familiar rocky shore. Twenty or more houses made of dark, warped wood and scavenged hulls from lost ships were scattered about the rocks where level land could be found. He could see small fishing boats tied up, bobbing in the waves not far out from the crushed-shell beach. Fisher folk trudged back and forth in the surf between their boats to their carts on shore, bringing in their catch for the day. The knight pulled his hood lower over his face. The people here would probably not recognize him, but he was not going to give them a chance.

The knight rode to the edge of the village but veered his horse to the right as the path split, heading up to higher ground. As he turned, he spotted a house above the small fishing village—the manor house, home of the Knight of the Broken Tower. He gritted his teeth and clenched his fists around his horse's reins. He had promised Lord Buckhorn there would be no bloodshed, and he would honor his word for as long as he could.

A single candle lit up one window of the manor. It was the local custom for helping villagers find their way home on stormy nights or in dense fog. The glow of the candle revealed the shape of a woman in the window.

This is not my home. How could it ever be again?

The knight did not remember many of the details in the letter that had arrived in Buckton three days past. He had lost his senses as Lord Buckhorn had read it to him, and his anger still boiled.

The boy is hurt. The boy is missing. The rest of the letter does not matter.

The knight rode past the broken gates of the manor and continued up the path that sharply inclined to the top of a cliff overlooking the sea, the village, and the manor. That was when he saw it in the wet gloom. The Broken Tower loomed above him.

The tower had been there for centuries, and for all anyone knew, it had always been broken. For what reason a fortress had been built here on top of the cliff, no one remembered. Seadrift was a poor fishing village surrounded by mountains to the north and the dense Misty Woods to the east. The sea was rough here, with massive waves that rolled in and crushed larger ships against the jagged sea rocks that littered the shore. Farther south was the port city of Turtle Bay. Its deep harbor had made the city wealthy, but the old fortress and tower were here in Seadrift.

The circular tower was all that remained of the small fortress. Made of sea rock and black basalt, the tower was mostly intact, but the side facing the sea had an open gash in the wall caused by what most locals believed to be lightning from the gods who had been angry at the villagers or the lord who had lived there.

The summit was littered with the shattered rock that used to make up the outer wall and the other buildings of the fortress. The knight had always wondered how people had hauled these huge stones up the cliff. Old fishwives told tales of giants carrying the stones upon their backs and building the tower. That was when the dragons had come, using their fiery breath to smooth the stone. But those were stories for children.

Outside the tower, the knight dismounted and pulled a bundle off the saddle. He walked up some stone steps and squeezed through a small passage through the rubble that blocked the entrance to the tower. It was the perfect hiding place.

As a boy, the knight had explored this place. He had commanded battles from the top of the tower against giants, dragons, and the armies of darkness. He had defended the entryway from all sorts of enemies. He had tied up evildoers in the dungeon. He had even received his first real kiss from a fair maiden on top of the tower as the sun had set over the Western Ocean.

The knight opened the bundle he carried with him. He struck his flint, and after a few attempts and a few curses, a spark ignited a small torch, which gave off enough light to see the floor of the tower as well as the broken stone steps that ascended to the top. The holes in the rotten wooden floors above him let in rain but not much light.

The knight made his way to the back of the main chamber and found the side room. What this room had been used for, he had no idea. He used it as a privy once when he was a boy. That was when he discovered there was a secret door in the floor that opened to a small tunnel he used to pretend was his dungeon. It had probably been designed to be a hiding spot or even an escape route at one time.

The knight found the large stone on the floor. It was still loose. It was harder trying to get a grip on it now with his larger fingers, but eventually he pulled the stone up. The hole and tunnel beneath were dark, though he heard something scrape on the floor below.

"Jory...is that you?" The knight was on the floor, holding

his torch lower. The light barely illuminated the darkness. Again, he heard a shuffle of bare feet on the tunnel floor.

"Jory, come out. It's safe. I'm here now. It's me, Cley."

Sir Cley saw the small boy crawl to the tunnel entrance. Cley dropped his torch and grabbed the boy under his arms, lifting him up into the side room with him. The boy was dressed in a torn undertunic and soiled underclothes. By the light of his torch, Cley could see the boy's face. His left eye was swollen shut, and there was a festering gash above it. His lower lip had been split, and the right side of his jaw was swollen and turning a purplish color. He hugged the boy tight, but the boy stood there limply.

Cley picked up Jory and carried him into the main chamber of the tower. He found the dry cloak he brought in his bundle and wrapped the boy in it, pulling the hood down over his face. The boy stood, stoically gazing past Cley toward the hole in the tower wall that looked out to the ocean.

Cley scooped the boy up and carried him over his shoulder to the entryway of the tower. Slowly, he picked his way through the rubble and was back outside where he set the boy on his horse. Cley remounted behind the boy, wrapping his arms around him as he took the reins.

The descent down the cliff path passed by in a blur as thoughts raced through his head, and Cley found himself at the broken gates that led to the manor house. On the stairs, the woman stood wrapped in a blanket, holding a small child to her chest. A little girl stood below the woman, holding her hand. Cley jumped off his horse and stormed up the path to the stairs.

I will not look at her. I will not meet her eyes.

Walking past her, he pushed open the door and went inside.

In the warm main room of the manor, mounted above

the hearth, was the sword of Sir Jonas Turner. It hung there proudly, as if the new owner had the strength or honor to wield it. Cley went to the mantle and pulled the sword off the wall. When he turned back to the door, he saw him...Sir Raymond Wells.

Cley was on him before Sir Raymond could speak. Cley had him on his back pinned to the floor with his hands around his neck.

"I promised there would be no blood, but I swear to the Four that if I hear of you ever touching the woman or the girl, I will come back, and no oaths or pledges will save you."

Cley let go of Sir Wells, stood back up, and left the manor. At the stairs, the woman stood waiting.

Do not look at her.

Do not meet her eyes.

Just walk past her.

Sir Cley Woods, the Knight of the Tall Tree, slung the sword of Sir Jonas Turner across his back. He walked down the path to the broken gates where he had left the boy on his horse, then climbed back up onto the saddle behind Sir Jonas's son and rode off into the cold rainy night having kept at least one promise.

10
EMILY II

Maggy and Alyss were still not speaking to each other, though it was more so Alyss not speaking. Maggy was a kind old woman, wise with years of knowledge and experience. Alyss, on the other hand, was barely twenty, but she knew almost as much about caring for the injured and sick as Maggy did.

Emily was tired of the uneasy silence in the tent.

"I am going to go down to the joust to have a look," she announced.

"That's a clever idea, girl. Go see some of those young squires. Alyss, you should go with her," Maggy suggested.

No, that's not what I want. I don't need a moody Alyss bossing me around.

Alyss tried to look busy stirring a boiling pot of something that smelled noxious.

"I have no interest in seeing any more boys being injured today."

"Suit yourself," Emily said, then rushed out of the healer's tent, stopping to grab the squire's tunic off the drying line. She headed in the direction of Sir Cley's pavilion, running between some tents and out to the main lane that divided the camps of Buckton and Tidehaven.

"Whoa, there. Where are you going in such a hurry?" a voice called out.

Emily stopped and turned toward the voice to see if someone was talking to her. She spotted Theo Harroldson sitting on a camp chair next to another boy. He was looking at her.

"Yes, you. Where are you running to? If someone is hurt, you are going the wrong way. The jousting arena is back that way." He pointed with a stick.

"Oh, I wasn't...I mean, I was sent on an errand by the healer...to get water at the creek."

The two boys stood from the camp chairs and walked over to her. The bigger boy, she guessed, must be the squire they called the Bull.

"I am Theo Harroldson, and this is my friend Draven. He serves as squire for Sir Lennon Wooten."

Theo is so handsome.

His curly black hair came down to his ears on the sides and fell on his forehead below his light-brown eyes, framing them. His olive-colored skin was smooth and flawless, and as he flashed a sly smile, he revealed straight white teeth. Draven looked like he could stand to wash his face and push himself away from the table occasionally. Unlike Theo, Draven had the beginnings of a mustache above his lip and darker hairs growing down the sides of his face.

"Might I ask your name, My Lady?" Theo asked with court-like courtesy, giving her a bow.

Emily blushed at being addressed as "My Lady."

"My name is Emily. I am the healer's apprentice," she said with a curtsy.

"I have seen you around camp," Theo said.

"Yes...we traveled from Buckton to Tidehaven to join the wedding procession to the capital."

Theo noticed me. Stay calm and don't act like some silly lovesick girl.

"Well, it was nice meeting you. I must get going." Emily turned to walk away.

"Let us help you. We were going down to the creek too," Theo said.

"No, that's okay. I can manage."

"You are not going to carry much water from the creek with that tunic in your hand. Where's your bucket?"

"Oh...Maggy told me to drop this tunic off at Sir Cley's tent. They left his squire's tunic behind after they came to see her."

"In that case, we will come with you. Sir Cley's squire is one of our good friends. Isn't he, Draven? We should check on him to make sure he is feeling better."

"Yeah, and I need to talk to him about something he has of mine," the bigger boy added.

"Ladies first." Theo stepped next to Emily and let her lead the way to Sir Cley's tent.

"You know after you drop off the tunic, maybe we could go down to the creek for a swim," Theo suggested, walking in step with Emily. "I am feeling kind of hot in all these clothes."

This boy must think I am stupid. He might be the son of a great lord, but I am not about to go swimming with him and his friend. He is like any other boy, nobility or not. He will try to steal a kiss or touch me, and brag about how he did much more than that to the other squires.

"Oh no, I couldn't. Maggy needs me back at the tent in case an older boy gets hurt in the joust. Those older squires are so gallant."

"Well, maybe after the banquet tonight you and one of your friends would like to come with us to see the woods witch," Theo persisted.

"Woods witch?" Emily arched her eyebrow with interest.

"Yes, an old witch has set up her wagon in the forest not far from camp." The pitch in Theo's voice rose in excitement when he saw Emily was curious. "My brother went to see her last night to get his fortune told. We could all walk there after the banquet. If you know a friend—you know, another girl to come along—it would be fun for all of us. We could get our fortunes told."

"Maybe I could. I would have to ask Maggy if it's alright."

The three teens walked around the corner and spotted Sir Cley's pavilion near the creek, away from the other tents in the camp. It appeared to be empty. They approached the tent and did not find anyone moving around inside.

The sound of humming brought Emily's attention to the creek bed below her. She spotted the squire boy walking along the creek, humming a tune while poking the water with a long thin branch. He was shirtless and had taken off the sling she had so carefully fashioned for him. He was holding up his sagging breeches with his left hand with the belt draped over his shoulder along with three ribbons. The legs of his breeches were rolled up above his knees, and at every other step he would kick his right foot into the water with a loud splash. The boy was completely unaware he was being watched.

Emily walked to the edge of the creek bank and asked sharply, "Where's that sling I made for you?"

Jory's head snapped up to the top of the bank where Emily stood, his eyes widening in surprise. His expression then changed to a blush of embarrassment at being barely dressed in front of the girl.

"See? Look, you can't keep a bay rat out of the water," Theo said, looking down on Jory. "This is probably the only bath in clean water you get, isn't it, bay rat?"

Emily watched as Jory turned away from them to tie up the laces on his breeches. When he finished, he pulled himself up the bank using the long water grass to reach the others.

Emily handed the tunic to Jory.

"Here is the tunic you forgot at the healer's tent."

"Oh, yeah. Umm, thanks for br-bringing it to me."

The Bull walked up to Jory and pointed at the red, black, and white ribbons hanging over his shoulder.

"Those are my ribbons."

Jory stepped back from the larger boy.

"Are not. These are A-Aiden's c-colors. You stole them."

"I beat him fair, and I get to keep them." The Bull stepped closer to Jory. "I would have guessed that taking a blow to the head would have stopped your stuttering, bay rat."

"You hit him from his blindside. That was ch-cheap." Jory took another step back.

"It's not my fault he didn't see me. Now gimme those ribbons back. They're mine."

"Well, I beat you and t-took them from you, so that means they're mine now."

"He has a point, Draven." Theo stepped in between the two boys. "Let him keep them. I'm sure he will use them to line his rat's nest." Theo pushed the two boys farther apart with his hands and stepped from between them to walk over to Sir Cley's tent.

"This is the pavilion of Sir Cley Woods? I thought it would be bigger. Where's his charger at? It's a beautiful horse."

"I had to give it to Sir Blake, y-yesterday," Jory mumbled.

"That's right. The Knight of the Tall Tree lost in the final tilt, didn't he? A pity. He could have used the prize money to buy a smaller tent for you to sleep in, instead of you having to sleep out in the open when he is entertaining one of the...local women."

Draven followed Theo over to Sir Cley's tent to have a look around as well, then turned back to look at Jory after Theo's comments.

"Nah, bay rats like sleeping outside, I heard," Draven said and laughed.

Emily noticed Jory's fists clenching. His eyes narrowed and darkness seemed to radiate from him. She stepped in front of him.

"Your name is Jory, right?"

Jory nodded and tried to look around Emily to see what the other two boys were doing.

"Tonight, after the banquet, we are going to visit the woods witch. Would you like to come with us?"

"Me? You w-want me to come with you?"

Jory's expression changed, and whatever darkness was there in his eyes passed.

"Yes, the four of us will go. I have a friend, Saph, whom I will ask also. She loves witches. That will make five of us. Five is a lucky number, right, Theo?"

"Umm, yeah. I guess." Theo shrugged.

"After the banquet, come by the healer's tent. Saph and I will be waiting for you." Emily paused and turned back to the two older boys. "Oh, Theo, I remember now. I wasn't supposed to be getting water from the creek. I was coming here to gather firewood. I am so forgetful. Would you and Draven gather some wood and carry it for me?"

<h1 style="text-align:center">11</h1>

THE GOLDEN KNIGHT IV

The rain would not let up, and after two days of riding in it, Sir Cley shivered uncontrollably and the boy shook violently. Cley tried to find shelter or some high ground where they could get away from the rain, but there was none to be found. They kept on riding to put Seadrift behind them.

Cley stopped before dusk at a small hill covered with cedar trees. The ground was dry under the thick canopy, and he found some dry wood for a small fire. The boy drank some water and ate some soggy bread. Cley recognized the look of pain on his face when he tried to open his mouth or chew.

We can make it to Maggy's before nightfall if we set off early tomorrow.

The boy still had not spoken. Cley tried to talk to him about what happened. He asked if the boy was warm enough or dry enough. He asked if the boy was tired of riding. He even asked what his favorite foods were. But all he got was silence. The boy never made eye contact with him, and he had a look on his face that said his spirit had gone to another place.

Sleep came quickly to Cley that night, but after one of his dreams of Falling Stone, he awoke to chills shaking his body.

Next to him, he heard the boy wheezing as he slept. Cley put his hand under the boy's tunic and felt his chest rattling as he tried to breathe. His skin burned with fever. Cley rose from his damp bedroll, not bothering to wake the boy. He saddled his horse, set the boy up on it, and climbed up behind him. He had to make it to Maggy's that night.

In the gloom of the forest, Cley spotted a light coming from the small house. He tied his horse to a tree some distance away and hauled the boy down. The boy was unconscious, barely breathing. He threw him over one shoulder and walked through the puddles and mud to the door.

I could leave him here. Maggy will take care of him. One day the boy could go to Buckton, and Lord Buckhorn will find a place for him in his house, maybe even make him a squire.

Cley rapped on the door. He heard footsteps approaching and thought about running back to his horse, but the footsteps sounded slow. It had to be Maggy. He prayed it was Maggy. Cley waited. The door opened, and the old healer stood behind it.

"Come in, come in... Don't let that chill in," she said.

"Maggy, it's the boy. He is hurt and sick." Coughing, Cley found his own breathing was labored.

"Set him down over there on the floor by the hearth," she said as she made her way to the fire and pushed a pot of something over it.

Cley laid the boy on the floor, stood back up, and walked back to the door to leave.

The boy is safe now. Maggy will tend to his wounds, and I can ride off. But where to?

"Bring me those two blankets over there. Take a seat by

the fire. I might need your help." Maggy knelt next to the boy and pulled off his rain-soaked cloak.

Cley handed Maggy the two blankets.

"Take those wet clothes and boots off and pull this blanket around you. Sit down before you fall," Maggy ordered.

Cley did as he was told. As he sat down, he realized how tired he was. His muscles and back ached terribly.

Maggy pulled the wet undertunic off the boy. His shark tooth necklace stuck to his damp, bruised skin. The bruises were mostly purple, though a few had turned yellow. They ran up and down the boy's ribs and around his back.

Maggy leaned the boy forward to look at his back, where she noticed old welt marks and scars, as well as a trail of blood that ran from the back of his head. She wrapped the boy tightly in the other blanket and got up to shuffle over to the hearth. She produced two cups and ladled out a steaming liquid from a pot she kept over the smoldering coal. Maggy handed one of the cups to Cley.

"Drink this."

With the other cup, she knelt back down onto the floor and pulled a cloth out of one of the pockets in her apron. She dipped the cloth in the warm liquid and put it to the boy's lips. After a moment, the boy's mouth began to move.

"You'll stay here for a few days. There's a spare room in the back."

Maggy dipped the cloth again and held it to the boy's lips once more. Before Cley could protest, she spoke.

"She's not here—Alyss. She went to High Meadow to see old Lord Day. His days are numbered, I'm afraid. Won't be much she can do for him, but she'll be gone for five or six days, maybe more. No one comes out this way. No one will know you two are here. No one will know what has been done."

Cley took another drink of the warm liquid, which smelled of mint. Warmth coursed through his limbs, and his eyelids closed.

Cley woke with a start from another of his dreams of Falling Stone. In the dark, he could see he was in a different room in a bed with large blankets covering him. He was burning up and shivering at the same time. The old healer hovered over him and handed him a small bowl.

"Drink this."

A thick liquid rolled over his tongue, and Cley gagged at its taste.

"The boy?" Cley said in a sickly voice he did not recognize.

"On the bed behind me. Safe. Go back to sleep."

Cley awoke and sat up in bed. He was no longer shivering but had a terrible taste in his mouth as if he had been sleeping with a copper coin in it. His eyes adjusted to the darkness and he could see the bed opposite him was empty. Dry clothes hung from hooks over his bed. Cley pulled his breeches on, yanked his tunic over his head, and stood up. He staggered and had to put his hand on the wall to steady himself as he walked over to the door and opened it. The sunlight coming in from the single window in the house blinded him. Cley tried to remember the last time he had seen sunlight.

The door to the house opened, and Maggy walked in.

"Oh, you're up. Good, good. Come out here and sit in the sun."

She motioned Cley to the door, and he walked outside.

"How long have I been asleep?"

The sound of his own voice, scratchy with disuse, surprised Cley.

"It's been a few days. Not to worry, I have sent Alyss off on another errand that will take some time. You and the boy are safe here."

Sunlight drifted down to the house between the limbs and leaves of the trees overhead. The air was cool and crisp, and the woods had a freshly washed smell to them.

"There's a bench over there in a nice patch of sunlight. Go sit with the boy. I will bring you a bowl of soup."

Cley walked over to the bench next to Jory. The boy wore a cloak wrapped tightly around him with the hood pulled over the top of his head. The bruises over the boy's jaw and on his eye were now greenish yellow and fading. Stitches zigzagged over his left eye.

Cley sat down next to him and sighed.

"Jory, are you feeling better?"

The boy sat in silence on the bench, staring blankly at the small bowl of uneaten soup in his hands.

Cley chose back trails that led to Buckton where there would be few if any travelers. The days grew colder as winter deepened. The boy was walking and eating now, but he still had not spoken. Maggy had not been able to explain why.

"I suppose he'll speak when he's ready. The boy's body will mend itself," she said when they left her. "But some hurts will not go away. Sometimes those who are hurting are good for each other."

Cley decided to make camp for the night in a hollow he

found off the path. It was getting dark, and they were still half a day's ride from Buckton.

Cley unpacked his horse and tied up the brown mare so that it could eat the grass that stuck out between the fallen leaves. Jory slowly walked with his head down, scanning the ground for fallen branches and sticks for the fire they would need. He kept his hood pulled down over his head.

The boy is probably cold with his head shaved.

Maggy had found two large cuts—one above his hairline in the front and another on the back. Both needed stitches. Cley had only seen the boy once with his hood pulled back. His ears stuck out from his head like handles on a cup.

The hair will grow back. The boy will be fine.

Cley finished the bread and cheese that Maggy had packed for them and reclined on his bedroll.

"We will be in Buckton tomorrow night and see Lord Buckhorn. Let's find you some clothes that fit and maybe some boots too. Would you like that?"

The boy stared blankly into the night. Sir Cley sat back up, looking at the emotionless boy.

"No! You know what? I'm tired of you not talking. I don't know how to help you, Jory."

On his bedroll, the boy rolled over on his side, facing away from Sir Cley.

"I don't know what to do with you. I'm a knight, not a healer. I can't go around playing wet nurse to some boy. To-morrow when we get to Buckton, I am going to leave you with Lord Buckhorn. You can live there, or maybe there is someone in town who needs an apprentice. You can learn a trade or something."

Sir Cley closed his eyes. The small campfire crackled, and after a moment he heard faint sniffling from where the boy was lying. He turned his head and saw the boy sitting up facing the darkness of the woods. By the light of the small fire, Cley could see the small boy's shoulders shaking as he cried.

"It'll be for the best, Jory. You will have a better life." Cley rolled to his side toward the boy.

"W-why didn't you come back?"

The boy's soft voice bit hard into Cley.

"What? I came as soon as Lord Buckhorn told me. I rode three days straight, in the rain."

"After the w-war, I mean. You and F-Father said you would be back."

Cley's shoulders slumped, and he lowered his head.

"Jory, your father died in battle."

"I know, but you didn't c-come back either, and you could have."

"It's complicated, Jory. I wanted to but couldn't."

A deep pain in his stomach flared.

Cley crawled over to where Jory was sitting and tried to put his arm and blanket around the sobbing boy. Jory flinched, jerking his body away as the knight touched him. Cley wrapped his blanket around Jory and sat next to the boy.

It had been so long since he had heard the boy speak. It was not the same voice as that of the six-year-old boy who had laughed as he played in the waves or sang songs with his mother. It was not the same voice as that of the boy who had cried when Cley and the boy's father left Seadrift three years earlier. Cley searched his memory. He did not remember the boy stuttering before.

"I'm here now. Tell me what you want."

"I w-want things to go back like before you and Father went away, but I know that c-can't happen. I prayed to the gods that you and Father would return. We heard F-Father had fallen. I prayed the gods would bring you back, and I put the c-candle in the window for you, but all they sent was...*him*."

Sir Cley was speechless. He did not know how to explain himself or make the boy feel better.

"Let's start with an easier question: Where do you want to live? In Buckton? You can stay with Lord Buckhorn, or we can find somewhere else for you."

Jory was silent for a long moment.

"I want to stay with you."

It was dark when Cley approached the wooden gates to the keep that was in the middle of Buckton. The town of mostly single-story wooden buildings and homes had grown up around the stone keep and now surrounded it. The guard on duty at the gate recognized Sir Cley and let him through to the inner courtyard. A guard there went inside to find the lord.

Lord Buckhorn was nearly sixty years old but could still ride a horse into battle. He burst out of the main doors and walked over to the knight. Cley dismounted and bowed his head to the man.

"Cley, I received your message and gathered what I could for you. The lances and armor will take longer, but I will have them made along with a banner for you. Also, a custom pavilion in your colors would be appropriate. I think green and white. Green for your name, Woods, and white for your birthplace in the North. I cannot recall any other knight with those colors in the West." Lord Buckhorn handed Cley a large saddle bag that made a metallic clinking sound as Cley tossed it over his shoulder. "How is the boy?"

"The bruises are fading. His ribs and jaw are mending. His hair is already starting to grow back from the shearing Maggy had to give to him. He speaks some, but not of what happened. I snuck him into one of the inns outside of town where few questions are asked. I should get back to him."

Lord Buckhorn lowered his voice. "Cley, the boy cannot be seen while he is still bruised and battered looking. My hands are tied in this matter. If the common folk saw the boy, and recognized him as Sir Jonas's son, they would cry out for justice. Of all the places in Terros, the king had to saddle me with his good friend, Raymond Wells. The fool may send someone after the boy."

Cley nodded and bit his tongue. "I understand, My Lord."

"Ride to Shadow Woods. There is an old keep on the northern stretches of it. It is still part of my lands, but it was abandoned after the knight there died. None of my household knights want it. They think it is cursed. I will send the rest of what you requested plus food and supplies to get you through the winter. If you want the keep for yourself, you are more than welcome to take it."

"No, I cannot see myself as a landed knight. I am too young, and I know nothing of growing crops or counting cords of wood or heads of sheep."

"The life of a traveling knight is not much better. The road is hard. There are bandits and outlaw knights, harsh weather, and bad luck. It won't be easy with a young boy tagging along."

"No, but Sir Jonas taught me what I needed to know. He taught me how to survive. I will teach his son. I owe it to him."

A stable boy led three horses out into the courtyard. One was a gray pack horse with three bundles tied to it. A large white charger snorted as it walked along next to a smaller horse, which was chestnut brown with a thin white streak above its nostrils that ran up its nose to its eyes. The brown horse had a small riding saddle on it.

Cley took the reins from the boy and turned to climb back up onto his riding horse, but Lord Buckhorn stood right in front of him.

"There's food and a tent in the packs, plus clothes and blankets for you and the boy." Lord Buckhorn surprised Cley and embraced him in a hug. "Cley, you are always welcome in Buckton as long as a Buckhorn is in this keep. A knight must find a home sometime, and this is as good a home as any."

Cley returned the man's embrace. After the hug, he climbed back up onto his horse.

Lord Buckhorn called to him as he rode off, "Stay safe. And take care of the boy."

"Cley, what do you think?" Sir Torrent asked.

"What? What was the question?" Cley focused his attention on the knights sitting around the table. He had drifted off into his own thoughts again. Despite the good company he was surrounded by, he could not help fading off. The Knights of the Barrel could spin amazing tales as they drank, and there was little that went on in the kingdom that they had not heard.

"Thurmond said he heard we are not breaking camp tomorrow." Torrent leaned toward Cley, lowering his voice so that nearby tables could not hear. "What do you make of that?"

"Maybe the Southerners are late coming to Crosstimbers," Cley guessed. "That city will have no love for Prince James if he camps outside its walls for days waiting for the southern lords to make their way up the Sands Road."

"That could be, Cley," Sir Boswell agreed. Although a young knight like Cley, he had hints of gray already showing in his short-cut black hair. "James's entourage continues to grow, and Pontifer would love to see us well and away from Pebble Creek."

"Hosting the prince and princess has been a costly affair for old Pontifer, I think," added Sir Bartlett before he took a long drink from his tankard. His curly brown hair sat upon his head like a bird's nest and shook as he spoke. "The prince probably does not want to upset the free city and its lord, who could be a great ally."

"Listen, look at what I am telling you all." Sir Thurmond raised his voice so that the knights sitting around him could hear. His bald head showed a bit of sweat as the day had grown warmer in the afternoon, and his face was as red as the mustang embroidered on his surcoat from drinking. "We are not breaking camp tomorrow because..."—Thurmond looked around to see if anyone was listening in from another table—"Lord Russ from Easton has been proclaimed king."

"Preposterous." Sir Boswell shook his head in disbelief.

"I am telling it true. A friend of mine told me this morning that he heard it from another," Sir Thurmond insisted. "Plus, why else would the Sorrow show up if there wasn't the chance that some killing might need to be done to claim the crown?"

Cley leaned back in his chair. The smirk he normally wore when gossiping with his friends disappeared at the mention of the Dark Sorrow.

"Sorry, Cley," Sir Torrent said quietly as he put his

strong hand on Cley's shoulder. "I meant to tell you, but you were so busy with your squire this morning. I didn't want to bother you with it. Crowe rode in last night."

Cley thought for a moment about Sir Finis Crowe, and he began to grind his teeth together.

"Here is a juicier question," Sir Boswell said, breaking the silence. "When is the wedding, Cley?"

"What wedding?" Cley replied, dragged back out of his thoughts.

"Your wedding with Lady Day. We heard you were dancing with her again last night," Sir Bartlett added excitedly.

"Oh no, Lady Day only has eyes for you, Bartlett," Cley responded, smiling.

"That's not what I heard," Sir Choate scoffed, returning with six more full tankards of ale. "It's been two years since old Lord Day died of the Sickness. Alba Day is ready to re-marry, and she is after one young knight."

The Knights of the Barrel all looked around at each other, then their eyes all fell on Cley.

"No, no, no...that's not me. She is twenty years my senior," Cley protested.

"But look at what I am telling you. She is the Lady of High Meadow, one of the richest towns of the West. You would be a lord," Sir Thurmond added.

"Good sirs, I think it is time for me to depart. I have some errands to run this day." Sir Cley stood from the bench at their table. "I would love to stay here, drinking away the day, but I have better things to do."

Sir Cley nodded to his friends. The Knights of the Barrel whistled and made kissing noises that pursued Cley from the drinking tent.

12
JORY V

Jory fidgeted. The urge to scratch his leg was driving him mad. The hose that Sir Cley borrowed for him were tight and itchy on his skin.

Don't itch.

Jory stood behind Sir Cley, waiting for someone to raise their cup.

It's not fair. None of the other squires in the melee have to serve as cupbearers at the banquet.

The other page boys serving their lords or knights at the banquet were all small boys.

The woman sitting to Sir Cley's right held up her cup, and Jory stepped forward to pour for her, being sure to pour from the pitcher in his left hand—the one with wine. The pitcher in Jory's right hand was for Sir Cley only.

"You are Sir Jonas's son," the woman said. "Jory, is it?"

"Y-yes, My Lady," Jory answered.

The woman looped her arm around Jory's waist to hold him and studied his face.

"I can see it in your face and eyes now. Handsome like your father. I knew Sir Jonas. It is a shame that your mother and stepfather could not make it here for the engagement."

"Lady Day, you are embarrassing the boy," Sir Cley said, coming to Jory's rescue.

Jory stepped back in line with the other cupbearers and waited for the next cup to be raised. He tried not to think about his mother nor his stepfather. He tried not to think about scratching his itchy legs. He concentrated on the food at the table, but that made him hungry.

Jory's mouth watered looking at the food on the lower table. There was goose as well as roast beef, and the bread smelled fresh and warm. His stomach rumbled. If he wanted to, he would get to eat in the kitchen with the other boys later, but he wanted to get back to camp so he could go see the woods witch with the girl from the healer's tent. When he wasn't thinking about his itchy legs or the food in front of him, his thoughts turned to Emily.

Emily is really pretty and not like other girls. Why am I thinking about her so much?

The engagement banquet took up the entire courtyard of the castle at Pebble Creek. Lord Pontifer was a rich lord, but there were few castles in Terros that could seat so many people. Tables were set up in the courtyard with benches in rows running away from the high table raised up on a platform.

At the high table sat Prince James and his mother. Next to the prince's mother was Lord Pontifer and his wife. Seated to the prince's left was Princess Rebecca and her mother and father, Lord Fowler. The Fowler twins sat next to their father, feeding their faces with roasted pig. Jory could spit looking at the boys.

A young woman sitting to Sir Cley's left raised her cup. Jory again stepped forward to fill it without spilling a single drop. He stepped back into line with the other cupbearers.

Sir Cley was seated about midway to the high table. He was the guest of Lady Day of High Meadow, who sat to his right. The tables closest to the prince and princess were filled with the other lords and ladies who gathered for the engagement ceremony. Lord Harroldson, his wife, and his three sons sat right in front of the high table.

Jory looked away in embarrassment as the sons of the attending lords came into the feast following their parents. They were all dressed in fine clothes, looking like lords themselves. Jory, in contrast, wore a silly-looking dark-blue shirt with ruffles on the sleeves and collar. The shirt hung down over his lower trunk and was cinched with a black belt. His breeches were not actually breeches but green hose that were tight on his skin and itched him in between his legs. On top of his head was a floppy green hat with a white feather stuck out of it like all the other cupbearers. When Jory first put on the clothes, he kept pulling the shirt down in the front to cover himself, as the tights left little for the imagination. But now that he held a pitcher in each hand, he had to give up that battle.

I am not itchy. Do not scratch.

Time crept by, and Jory's feet began to hurt. In front of the high table, a bard finished a song that he claimed he composed himself, which received some polite clapping from the prince and princess. The other nobles followed the royals' lead and offered their own lukewarm approval of the song.

"Sing something we have heard of, bard," called a knight from the back.

The bard lowered his lute. "What is it the fair lords and ladies would like to hear as they dine?"

"Sing 'Berren's Lament,'" a woman said.

"Let's have 'The Song of Ivar,'" a nobleman suggested.

"Play 'Freybird,'" called some drunken knight holding up a candle from the table.

The bard began to strum his lute and sing 'Berren's

Lament,' a popular song among the nobility. Jory heard it at every castle or tournament he and Sir Cley had visited over the last two years. A sad song about two lovers who met their untimely ends. Jory did not care for it. It was slow and boring.

As Jory stood feeling the weight of the pitchers in his hands, his shoulder began to ache again.

Maybe that potion the healer gave me is wearing off.

The love song in the background sounded sweet to Jory's ears. This bard was good. His playing was above average, and his singing voice was like a new bell ringing out. Jory noticed Lady Day setting her hand on top of Sir Cley's arm as she spoke with him. She kept touching him every time she spoke.

How can Sir Cley stand having her constantly touching him? It took me everything I have to sit still when that woman touched my arm and ribs. But when Emily wrapped my arm, it felt different.

The bard finished his song, and several men called out their next requests. Some wanted rowdy songs that were good for drinking and singing along. The bard ignored them and turned to the high table to address the princess.

"Princess Rebecca, what would you like to hear?" the bard asked, lowering his head with a slight bow. "My voice and lute are yours to command."

The princess thought for a moment. "I would like to hear a song from the West, I think. I need to learn more about my future husband and king, and the place where he grew up. I need to know what songs he likes." She looked at Prince James and took his hand in hers.

The prince cleared his throat and smiled at his princess. "I would have you sing 'When the Mountain Breaks.' Do you know it?" Prince James asked.

"That song...yes, My Prince. I know that song," the bard replied.

The bard sat down on a bench and softly plucked the strings on his lute. Jory could feel the people turning their attention to the bard and the music.

The song retold the story of the Battle of Falling Stone. Every man and woman of the West knew the words and melody.

The bard's lute playing began slow and quiet, then he added his voice softly.

> *The women of the West look out to the horizon;*
> *they wait by their windows;*
> *their candles burn.*
> *The women of the West sing for their brothers,*
> *their husbands, their sons...*

Slowly, the bard let his voice and lute grow in volume and tempo. The verses told of the bravery of the men of the West and the sacrifice they made. In the middle, the song became loud and rowdy, like a drinking song. The men and ladies at the banquet banged their fists on the tables and stomped their feet on the floor. At the end, the playing and singing became sadly slow and softer again, and the bard's voice faltered in emotion as he finished the song.

> *The mountain was laid low, and the tower remains broken;*
> *the women of the West tend to their fields;*
> *they watch their flocks and mend their nets.*
> *Their candles have burned low, the lights that were lost...*
> *The women of the West look up to the horizon,*
> *and they weep for their brothers, their husbands, their sons...*

Everyone at the banquet applauded the bard. A few of the women wiped tears from their eyes, as did a few of the older lords and knights. There were few people in the West who did not lose someone they knew at the Battle of Falling Stone.

Some lost more than others.

The bard bowed to the crowd and turned to bow to the high table. A minstrel group at the back of the courtyard took up playing music as other serving men moved about and began to take down the tables and move the benches to the sides to make room for dancing.

Jory knew his time serving as page boy was over. He could set the pitchers down and run back to the kitchen and eat before the other boys grabbed the table leavings. Instead, he stood there thinking about the song. He had heard it many times before.

The song always ends the same way. My father dies a hero. What am I?

Jory ran from the castle courtyard, having been released from duty by Sir Cley. He made his way back to their pavilion, squeezing the five copper pieces Sir Cley gave him in his hand. He needed to change into his regular clothes. He did not want Emily to see him dressed like a page boy, and Theo would be relentless in his mockery if he showed up dressed like one. He hoped Theo had not noticed him at the banquet.

Near the ale tent, Jory spotted an old woman peddling roses for men trying to impress the women who had joined them for the evening. Jory went over, gave the old woman a copper, and walked away with a single red rose.

"Who's the rose for?"

Aiden stepped out of the shadows from behind the ale tent.

"Oh, uh, n-nobody. What are you doing behind the ale tent?" Jory asked, hiding the rose behind his back.

"I was having a piss. So do you always get a rose for no-body?" Aiden asked again, smiling. "Come on, out with it."

"It's for the g-girl from the healer's tent. She wr-wrapped my shoulder," Jory answered and began to walk away.

"Nice. Well, where are you going in such a hurry?" Aiden walked to catch up to Jory.

If Aiden is with me, Theo and the Bull might be nicer.

"We are going to see the w-woods witch. Wanna come?" Jory asked.

"A witch? Hmm, I heard some people say there was one camped nearby."

Aiden thought for a moment, then continued, "Sure, why not. What's up with the page boy outfit?"

"I had to serve as cupbearer for Sir Cley tonight at the banquet. I look like a fool, don't I?"

"Don't worry about it. I hated having to wear hose. They constantly itched."

"Exactly." Jory smiled at Aiden. "When we get back to our tent, remind me to give you back your ribbons."

The two boys headed off, walking side by side as the crowd inside the ale tent roared in laughter and song.

13

THE GOLDEN KNIGHT V

The banquet was a disappointing affair, as far as the food went. The goose was too greasy, and the roast beef was tough like leather. Sir Cley drank a full pitcher of water trying to choke down his meal. It was poor fare for the engagement banquet of the future king and queen. The feast at the harvest tournament in Amberfield last fall had been much better. Two weeks of hosting the lords and ladies of the East and West, along with their knights, soldiers, squires, and other camp followers put a strain on the town of Pebble Creek.

Lord Pontifer will be glad to see us go.

The bard entertaining the lords was good. He possessed a strong voice, and his lute playing was mesmerizing. But when he began to sing "When the Mountain Breaks," Cley closed his ears. He let his mind drift off so as not to hear the lyrics of the ballad. The light touch of Lady Day on his hand brought him back to the song. He closed his eyes and tried to think of anything else. When the bard mercifully finished, Lady Day gave Cley's hand a squeeze.

The serving men and women began clearing the plates off the high table, signifying the meager feast was over. Jory stood behind him holding the two pitchers in his ridiculous page boy's uniform.

I am going to owe the boy for this.

"Jory, you can go now. You can set the pitchers down here by me," Cley said as the nobles around him wiped their eyes, sniffed, and applauded the bard. "You better go to the kitchen before the other boys—or the dogs—get what's left."

The boy came over and set the pitchers down next to him, then took off in the direction of the kitchen.

Lady Day moved closer to Cley so that her leg was pressed against him on the bench. Cley decided to play the game. He touched her hand and asked if she would like to dance.

When he stood, Cley saw Jory walking back to him.

"Not hungry, Jory?" Cley asked.

"Umm, Sir, I wanted to know if it w-would be alright..." Jory stammered.

"Come on, Jory. Relax. Take your time."

"I was invited to see a woods witch with some others after the banquet. C-can I go?"

Cley stepped back in surprise. Jory never wanted to go anywhere with anyone else. The boy went everywhere with him.

"Who is going on this grand adventure?"

"Th-Theo Harroldson and the boy they c-called the Bull." Jory took a breath. "And two girls, I think. The girl from the healer's tent, Emily, asked if I w-wanted to go."

"Look at you." Cley reached into the coin purse on his belt and knelt in front of Jory. "Making friends. And a girl. You must have made an impression on her. Here, take these. Have fun. Don't be out too late." Cley pressed five copper pieces into Jory's hand.

The boy thanked Cley and ran off into the darkness surrounding the courtyard.

• • •

Cley rejoined Lady Alba Day and her two grown children. Her son, Sir Michael, who stood to inherit High Meadow, was the same age as Cley. The daughter, Monica, was a pretty girl of seventeen with many suitors.

I should be dancing with your daughter, Lady Day, not you.

Cley took Lady Day's hand and led her onto the dance floor. The pair danced well together, moving about the dancing area. Cley nodded to the other lords and wealthy landed knights who were invited to the banquet.

Let them see you being charming and dashing.

"You know, Sir Cley, I could get used to this," Lady Day said.

"Yes, you are quite the dancer, My Lady."

Cley turned from Lady Day and noticed Prince James leaving the banquet. Lord Fowler and Lord Harroldson were leaving as well.

"No, I mean, us...together. It would be nice, don't you think?"

"Yes, My Lady, it would be nice."

Cley turned his partner in a circle with nimble feet. He knew how this dance would end. It always ended the same. There were always girls and women who were interested in him—daughters of minor lords or wealthy nobles or merchants. They all expressed interest, and he would be polite and play his part in the social game that was matchmaking, but he always found an excuse not to get too close or attached to them. Lately, he often used Jory as his reason for moving on to the next tournament or town.

I have a promise to keep.

Lady Day squeezed Cley's lead hand tighter and pressed

her body closer as they danced. Cley purposely stubbed his toe and stumbled.

"Beg your pardon, My Lady. I think the wine has finally made it to my head," Sir Cley apologized.

"It's quite alright."

Cley stepped on Lady Day's toe as they turned. He smiled to himself thinking back to all the times Jory had stepped on his foot when he tried to teach the boy how to dance.

Lady Day put some space again between herself and Sir Cley.

"I do think that apologetic smile belies that you enjoy stepping on me, Sir."

"No, My Lady. I was thinking of how I am as clumsy as my squire at this dance. I have tried to teach him the basic steps, but his feet constantly find mine," Sir Cley explained.

"You should have him visit my tent. I would be happy to teach him. After all, I have instructed my son and my daughter in the finer steps."

"I will. Thank you kindly, My Lady."

Cley thought of the greater debt he would owe Jory. First the silly page boy uniform and now dancing lessons with Lady Day. Jory was already a fine dancer for his age. As soon as Cley explained to the boy that swordplay involved footwork much like a dance, the boy took to his dance lessons immediately. Now he would need to explain to Jory that he would have to feign learning the steps all over again.

"You know, you made quite the stir today introducing your squire," Lady Day said.

"I did? How so?"

"A boy thought dead by some is brought forth and announced as Sir Jonas's son. So dramatic. My daughter could speak of nothing else with her companions who attended the melee." Lady Day smiled. "I for one am ashamed of not recognizing the boy. And of course there are the stories and rumors."

"I hardly kept the boy hidden, Lady Day. The men of Buckton all know who he is. The tournament purses in the East are richer, and the jousting season continues into the winter in the South," Cley explained. His jaw tensed, and he thought of dispelling some of the rumors he knew were being told about the boy and himself, but instead he put on his easy smile. "I suppose when you are out of sight, people either forget you or come up with their own stories as to your circumstances."

"We certainly heard plenty of news of the great Sir Cley Woods and all of his tournament victories." Lady Day moved closer to Cley again. "There was never a mention of his squire being the son of one of the greatest heroes of Terros."

Cley did not respond.

"But never mind that. When all these matters of weddings and coronations are over, you need to visit us in High Meadow. Bring your squire, of course. It would be nice to have a young boy around the keep again. A boy should have a place he considers his home, not a tent pitched at some tournament."

"You are too kind with your offer, My Lady. We will be sure to visit your fair town."

Sir Cley and Lady Day made their way around the dancing area again when a tap on his shoulder caused Cley to turn. Before him was one of the maids-in-waiting for the princess. Cley stopped his dance with Lady Day to properly face the girl.

"Excuse me, Lady Day," the girl began with a curtsy to Lady Day, "the princess has asked that Sir Cley be her partner in the next dance." Cley recognized her as the same girl who had accepted the flower from Jory at the melee that morning.

"I cannot refuse the future queen, can I?" Cley replied.

He turned back to Lady Day and excused himself. Lady Day gave him a kiss on the cheek.

"Do advise the princess to be wary of Sir Cley's feet. We do not need her limping to her wedding," Lady Day said to the girl. She leaned closer to Cley's ear, whispering, "We will finish this dance later."

Cley walked over to where the princess was seated and was introduced by her maid. He bowed and held out his hand.

"Princess Rebecca, it would be my honor if you were to join me in this dance."

The princess took his hand, and Cley led her out amongst the other couples and began the dance. The two were a striking pair of opposites. When partnered together, the prince and princess were a matched pair with the same dark eyes and curly brown hair. The princess, dressed in her red gown, matched the prince's own attire. The prince was not quite full grown and filled out as a man, so the princess did not look small in his arms. But in the arms of Sir Cley, she appeared as a girl.

Cley's clothing clashed with the princess's dress. His tunic was green with yellow edges, and his breeches were black. Where her hair was dark, he was blond. Where she was small and willowy, he was tall and athletic.

They danced about the grounds, putting the other couples to shame.

This girl has a wonderful dance instructor.

The princess slowed them down on the third round about the courtyard.

"Sir Cley, I have been wanting to meet you," she said, looking up at him.

"You have?"

"Yes, I was in the crowd when you won the joust at Dimbury two seasons ago. You ran through those knights like they were mere boys at their first tilt. I have kept track, noting any stories of you. You are the most famous knight in all of Terros. I even had my father bring me with him to the festival in Amberfield when I heard you would be there."

"I am sure those stories are all untrue, My Princess." Cley gave her a sly smile.

"I hope they are not all untrue. Imagine how disappointed I was when I did not get to congratulate you with my favor after the joust here. Instead, I was saddled with the task of applauding Sir Blake Pontifer."

Sir Cley stopped their dancing. They were on the edge of the courtyard.

"I am sorry for your disappointment. I did not mean to offend. It was not my day, and Sir Blake was the better knight. If I can make amends, I am your servant," Cley said, bowing to the princess.

"You may make amends. However, I am not the one in need of your service. My future husband—and your future king—is going to need help. I have made inquiries about you. You are not the womanizing lush the camp rumors say you are."

Sir Cley's eyes widened with a bit of surprise.

So young and already playing the game.

"When James is king, he will call for you to be a member of his court. He will need a man experienced in battle, a man who has been across Terros—a man who does not have loyalty to others," the princess said in a voice that hinted there would be no further discussion. "Thank you for the lovely dance. You are quite good."

Princess Rebecca turned and walked back to her maids-in-waiting, then left the courtyard quietly with her guards.

Cley surveyed the dance floor to see if anyone had witnessed the exchange. No one had taken notice of the princess's departure.

Cley searched through the crowd of dancers and spotted Lady Day dancing with her son. He decided now was an opportune time to flee since she was distracted. He could produce a story about feeling drunk and staggering back to his tent with some kitchen girl.

Cley slipped off into the darkness and returned to his pavilion. The early summer night was cool, and the moon was full, illuminating the creek that gurgled below. He walked in the moonlight thinking about Lady Day and Princess Rebecca, then climbed down the creek bank toward the calming sound of the water.

He sat down on a large rock that overlooked the creek, listening to the frogs peep and croak. Cley took his boots off and let his toes and feet kiss the water. He stared up into the sky, spying through the trees to find the stars above, soon spotting the bright star of the North. Feeling the cool water on his tired feet, Sir Cley relaxed and drifted.

Watching his squire, Cley stood next to a creek that flowed into Shadow Woods.

"Balance, Jory. Keep your shield up and sword back. Bend your knees. Straighten your back."

The boy balanced himself on a log on its side in the creek, the icy water flowing on either side of it.

"But the shield and s-sword are too heavy for me," Jory complained.

"The shield and sword are as heavy as they need to be. You need to get stronger if you want to be a knight. Now, shield, parry, shield, thrust. You must keep the shield up when you thrust, or you will expose yourself to the attacker."

Jory followed the instructions, fighting an imaginary warrior in front of him on the narrow log.

"When you move, you must keep your feet apart, or you will lose your balance. Again."

Jory lifted the wooden shield up and thrust his wooden sword underneath it as he stepped forward on the fallen tree. He whacked one of the tree's branches in frustration, and it sprang back, striking Jory in the face. He stepped back and lost his footing. Jory flailed his arms, slipped, and fell into the water.

Cley let out a loud laugh. The boy looked like a soaked scarecrow as he stood up from the creek. His hair was still short from Maggy's sheering, and the clothes Lord Buckhorn found for him were too big, hanging from him like wet clothes set on a small tree to dry.

Cley lent Jory a hand and pulled the boy out of the water and up the bank.

"Don't worry. You will get it. I fell into the water a hundred times when I was your age. Before you catch a cold, grab that bucket over there and fill it with water. I think a nice warm bath would feel good right now."

"But I am already w-wet." Jory shivered and held out his arms as his tunic dripped.

"The bath is for me." Cley walked away from the boy and headed toward the small keep. "Oh, you will need to get a fire going too. I think ten buckets should do. Better hurry, it's getting dark."

"What's wrong, Sir Cley? The banquet over so soon? You could not find some serving girl to be with?" A voice coming from behind disrupted Cley's thoughts. The voice was familiar, but it was older now, more mature.

Alyss stood above him on the bank, the full moon glowing behind her. She wore a simple dress that the moonlight revealed to be dark blue. It was a vast improvement from the harsh gray dress and apron she wore in the healer's tent. She was beautiful, the way Cley remembered her.

"Cat got your tongue? The Knight of the Tall Tree's speechless? That's something new." Alyss made her way down the bank to the rock where Cley dangled his feet in the water. "Have your friends in the ale tent learned of this new affliction?"

"Hi, Alyss. Out for a walk?" Cley asked softly.

"I thought I would get some fresh air, but I forgot that all types of vermin are often drawn to water too. I will head down the other way." She began to walk away from Cley.

"You don't have to go, you know," Cley said.

Stupid. Why did you say that? She was leaving. Let her go.

Alyss turned and walked back to the rock.

"What? No witty banter or rude remarks?" Alyss asked.

"No, not tonight, Alyss. I am not up to the task of jousting with you," Cley said, wiggling his toes in the water.

Alyss sat down by him. She slipped her shoes off and dipped her toes in the water alongside Cley's feet.

"It is a beautiful night," Alyss said after a minute of sitting next to the silent knight.

Cley heard her but made no response. He gazed up at the sky and stars.

"How is your squire? The boy? Is his shoulder doing well?"

"Jory? He is a good boy. It's going to take a lot more than a few blows from a wooden sword to stop that one."

"Yes, a good boy who should be at home."

Sir Cley was not going to take the bait. He sighed and turned back to swirling his feet in the black water.

Let Alyss think what she wants. Let them all think what they want. I know the truth.

"Seeing that boy today in the tent made me think of you when we first met. Do you remember?"

"Yes, I remember," he answered quietly.

"What happened to you? Where did that boy go when he went off to war with his knight?" Alyss turned to face him. "I can see you now in my mind, holding Sir Jonas's banner, proudly riding alongside him at the front of the foot soldiers. When the war was over, the men of Buckton and Seadrift came home, yet you were not amongst them. I waited for you for two years, Cley. When you did finally return, you were no longer that smiling boy who liked to laugh."

Cley sat and listened. He remembered playing in the waves on the beach and kissing the girl in the tower as the sun set over the Western Ocean. He remembered a promise he had once made.

"Then you disappear for almost three years with this boy. You have become some womanizing drunkard who plays to the crowds," Alyss went on. "If Sir Jonas could see what you have become—"

Anger flared in Cley's stomach.

If he could see me? If he could see me, Sir Jonas would be alive, and nothing that has happened in my life since Falling Stone would have occurred.

"My Lady, I need to excuse myself and turn in," Cley interrupted her. He pulled his boots on and stood. "Do you need an escort back to your tent? It is unsafe for a woman to walk through a camp unattended."

"I can manage myself, Sir."

"Tomorrow, we start off for Crosstimbers. I mean to get

an early start. If you and Maggy need help loading up, you know where I am." Cley climbed back up the bank, leaving the girl behind.

119

14
EMILY III

Saph and Emily sat outside the healer's tent, waiting impatiently.

"Women are supposed to keep men waiting, not the other way around," Emily said and crossed her arms.

"What do you want to ask? From the witch, I mean," asked Saph. "I'm askin' for what kind of man my husband will be and how many children we will have."

"Oh, I want to know that too, but I think I want to know if any adventures are before us. Will we travel? Will we have a good life? Is there any misfortune that will befall me?" Emily replied.

"That would be good to know too, I guess." Saph nodded.

The healer told Emily to ask for more than whom she would marry or if she would become rich. "A good witch can see what will come of us. Of course, some are frauds and know nothing. Either way, you children have fun," Maggy had told her before she left to wait outside the tent.

Emily peered down the row of soldiers' tents that lined the lane separating the Tidehaven and Buckton camps. Two figures approached, one figure taller than her, and the other a large, dark figure. As they walked closer, she could see in the flickering light from the cookfires that it was Theo and the Bull.

"Ladies, good evening to you," Theo said, dripping courtly courtesy as he greeted the two common girls. "Lady Emily, you remember my friend Draven, of course. But I do not believe I have met your acquaintance." Theo gave a brief bow to Saph. "I am Theo Harroldson of Tidehaven."

"And this is Saph of Tidehaven also. You two should have so much in common to talk about." Emily laughed to herself knowing that Saph, a wash girl, and Theo, the son of a lord, would have nothing in common as far as he was concerned.

Emily was happy though that Theo had shown up, and he had taken the time to dress up too. He wore a fine dark-blue cape that was clasped by a silver chain around his neck. Gold thread embroidered around the edges formed a design like waves. Theo also wore a clean white shirt and black breeches that matched his black leather boots. A small sword hung from his side, making him look gallant.

"Let's be off. If we leave now, we will have the moon's light to guide us. Maybe we can stop by Maiden's Bridge," Theo suggested.

Yes, Maiden's Bridge.

Emily knew the local legend of the old stone bridge that crossed Pebble Creek, linking the town to Shadow Woods. The tale went that a young man could tell if his future bride was still a maiden if he were to kiss her on the bridge. If she were a pure maiden, a stone would fall from the bridge into the creek. Of course, the joke in the taverns of the town was that the bridge had stood solid for over four hundred years.

"We must wait for Jory. I invited him to come with us," Emily said.

"He probably forgot," Draven spoke up. "If we go now,

we will beat any of the drunken knights to the witch and have our fortunes told first."

"Come on, Emily. Let's go. Jory can catch up if he is coming," Saph added.

The group set off down the lane as it led to the edge of camp where they could cross the creek without having to walk all the way to the bridge. Theo walked closely next to Emily, with Draven and Saph walking as a pair behind them. As they turned down the last row of tents, Emily spotted Jory walking and talking with another boy she did not recognize.

"There's Jory now," Emily said, excited to have spotted him.

"That's just great," Theo replied with a sigh.

"Jory, we waited for you," Emily called as he walked up to the group with the other boy.

Jory was dressed simply in contrast to Theo. He had a hooded black cloak pulled over himself with dirty-looking boots.

"I had to go ch-change. You know we are going to be w-walking in the woods, not going to a ball." Jory glanced at Theo before refocusing on her. "Plus, I stopped to get this for y-you because you, um, brought my shirt to me." Jory brought his left hand out from under his cloak, producing a simple red rose.

"How sweet," Saph gushed.

"Thank you, Jory. You are truly kind." Emily stepped toward Jory to take the rose from him, then leaned down and gave him a light kiss on the cheek.

"So, who's your friend, another rat?" Theo said, scowling at the taller boy behind Jory.

"I'm Aiden." He stepped around Jory.

"Yeah, this is A-Aiden. I asked if he wanted to come see

the w-witch too," Jory said. "You might remember him from the melee."

"I certainly remember the big one," Aiden said, glaring at the Bull.

Emily watched Aiden walk toward Draven and Saph. The boy was handsome. He was like Theo but with blond hair instead of black, and he wore it tied back from his face in a small knot behind his head. He and Theo were of similar height and size. His face was fair to look upon, but there was a hardness in his jawline and chin that was missing in Theo's. It made Aiden look more mature. His most striking feature Emily noticed were his gray eyes, which glowed in the moonlight and sparkled as they caught the light from the campfires.

"Hello there, Aiden," Saph said, stepping between Draven and Aiden. "I'm Saph."

"Yes, well, whatever. I'm Theo, that's the Bull, that's the bay rat. Can we get moving please? The whole stinking camp will join us if we don't leave." Theo's voice squeaked in agitation.

Theo surprised Emily by taking her hand in his and resuming the walk toward the woods. Emily turned to see that Draven was following them, while Saph walked with Aiden and Jory a few strides behind. She noticed Jory had a frown as he watched her walking with Theo.

The group found the witch's wagon in a clearing off a hunter's path in the woods. The wagon was ornamented with lit lanterns hanging from the front and back. The lights revealed that the roof of the wagon was painted dark purple with the trim painted gold. The wagon's sides were dark brown, as were the steps in the back that led up to a door the color of the night sky with symbols of moons and stars painted in silver.

Theo stopped at the stairs, waiting for the others to catch up. Emily stood next to him, staring up at the door. None of the others moved to take the first step up the stairs to knock on the door. A horse nickered nearby. Emily turned toward the noise to see an old horse tied up to a tree where it was chewing on some grass.

The door to the wagon swung open, surprising them, and a woman stepped into the doorway, gazing upon the group standing outside. Emily found herself squeezing Theo's hand in hers.

The woman at the door possessed long black hair that was tangled about her in flowing curls. She wore a dark-red robe with long sleeves. Her skin was an exotic dark color that gave her the appearance of being from a place other than Terros.

If this is a witch, all the stories I have ever heard about them are false. She is beautiful.

"Come in, children. I have been waiting for you, although there are more than I expected," the witch said as she beckoned them up the stairs.

"You have been waiting for us?" Draven croaked.

The witch looked him up and down.

"Why, yes. I have been expecting you. Madam Lucient knows all," the witch replied as she turned and walked back into the small wagon, leaving the door open.

Theo squeezed Emily's hand, and they stepped up the creaking stairs, passing through the door into the wagon together. Draven grabbed Saph by the wrist and pulled her up after them. Jory and Aiden followed, coming up the rickety stairs last.

Inside with the door closed, the six children crowded

around a small table with two chairs seated at it. There was a mixture of aromas in the room. A sweet scent of perfume, smelling of lilacs, hung heavily in the air, mixing with the spice of incense burning in a small censer in the corner. Emily thought it might be cinnamon, but under the perfume and incense, there was something else. A fetidness. Decay. Emily thought it might be the wood of the wagon itself, but in the back of her mind she knew it smelled of death.

The tiny flames of small candles flickered and danced, barely illuminating the interior of the wagon. The table in the middle was covered with a dark-blue cloth embroidered with silver runes. The walls inside the wagon were covered in heavy black drapes to the left and right, though the wall directly behind Madam Lucient featured a sinister-looking tapestry that displayed snakes of silver, blue, orange, red, green, and gold entangled on it. The serpents writhed and twisted as the candlelight and shadows danced across the tapestry. Madam Lucient sat down in the chair across from the children, placing her hands flat on the table in front of her and giving them a gentle smile.

The witch studied them.

"Which one of you shall be first?"

Emily was not sure if it was her palm that was sweating or Theo's, but she could sense the boy next to her was nervous.

"I'll go," Draven said.

The big squire stepped around Theo and Emily and squeezed into the chair.

"Do you have my price, young man?" the witch asked.

Her voice was soothing yet commanding. Draven pulled out his coin pouch and set it on the table.

"How much is it?" Draven asked.

The witch scanned the children crowded in front of her as if she were counting the coins they all had hidden away.

"There is a cost for knowing one's future, my boy. What one is willing to pay can reveal much," the witch replied.

Draven sat there silently, looking puzzled.

"It is four coppers to know what the future holds for you, my young Bull," the witch stated finally.

Draven counted out four copper coins for her, sliding them across the cloth. The witch picked up the coins from the table slowly, then took one of Draven's hands in hers. She flipped his hand over, running the fingers of her opposite hand over his palm. The witch closed her eyes and began to speak in an ethereal voice.

"Yes, I can see you will be a warrior. You will be on a battlefield, which is where you will find your true love. Your love will be dressed in red. She will kiss you light as a feather. You will beg for her in the end," the witch spoke with her eyes still closed. She never once looked at his palm, Emily noticed.

"That's it? What about riches? Will I have my own castle some day?" Draven protested.

The woman slowly opened her eyelids. "That is all Madam Lucient sees...for four coppers. Gold or silver helps my vision, and copper does not buy castles," the witch replied with a slight sneer.

Draven pulled his wrist away from the witch and stood in a huff, pushing the others aside to clear room for himself.

The witch motioned to Emily.

"Sit down, young lady. Let me tell you your future."

Emily sat down in the chair and set four copper coins on the table for the witch, who slid the coins off into her opposite sleeve where they disappeared. She took both of Emily's wrists in her hands, turning them over to see the palms and the backs of her hands. The witch stared at Emily's fingers and turned her hands back over so they were palm up on the table. The witch's fingers glided over the veins in her wrists as she traced them up her forearm.

"You are strong, girl. You are a nurturer, not a destroyer. You will give life to many."

"How many children?" Emily asked excitedly. "What about their father? Can you tell me about him?"

The witch closed her eyes now, grasping Emily's wrists tightly.

"Your husband, I cannot see. I see nothing but mist about him. There is danger on your path. A choice you will have to make."

Heat rose between the witch's fingers and Emily's wrists. Emily felt pain and sorrow emanating from the witch, and the heat grew until the witch released her, pulling her hands back. The witch opened her eyes as her face contorted from pain to relief. Emily stood quickly from her chair and returned to Theo's side.

The witch gestured for Saph to sit down after she took a moment.

"The next young lady, please."

Saph sat down in the chair and reached into her coin pouch, digging around for her copper coins. When she could only find three, she untied the pouch from her belt and shook the empty bag above the table.

"I know I had four coppers when we left," Saph said frantically.

The witch gave Saph a hard look.

"No coin? That does not bode well for your future, young woman."

Saph continued to shake the coin pouch, looking to be on the verge of tears. "Please, a moment, I know I had enough."

"Here, take one of my c-coins." Jory squeezed between

Emily and the wall. He placed a copper coin on the table next to the other three, then retreated to his spot pressed up against the back wall next to Aiden.

The witch took the coppers off the table, smiling at the girl. Saph set her hands on the table palm up, and the witch covered Saph's hands with hers, closed her eyes, and began to speak.

"Your path is clear, young woman. You will marry a handsome man of your age. You will have five children who will grow. Your life will be long and full of laughter. There will be sad times, but those will be outnumbered by days of joyfulness." The witch removed her hands from Saph's.

"Have I met my husband yet?" Saph asked.

The witch smiled mischievously.

"Yes, you have already met him, although he might not know it yet."

Saph nodded, turned to Emily with a happy smile, and glanced over at Draven.

"Who will be next?" the witch asked softly, bringing her attention to Theo.

Emily did not realize it, but during Saph's reading, Theo's hand had found its way back into hers, like it belonged. She thought she could feel Theo's heartbeat and a sense of doubt coming from him. She gave his hand a confident squeeze. Theo released her hand and moved to sit in the chair in front of the witch.

The witch watched from across the table as Theo set a silver coin before her. She grinned at his offering and reached ahead, taking his hands in hers. She closed her eyes and was silent for a long time.

Emily began to feel a tightness in her breathing as she watched the witch holding Theo's hands. Emily closed her eyes as the heartbeats of everyone in the small wagon thumped and pounded in her ears. Emotions swirled around her—anger, love, jealousy, hatred, and fear. Her head swam, and her knees began to buckle.

Emily opened her eyes. On the tapestry behind the witch, the serpents were moving in a writhing pile. No one else reacted. Emily closed her eyes hard, reopened them, and looked again at the tapestry. It was like before. The snakes were all intertwined, but they were not moving.

I am seeing things. It's being in this small wagon with all the fragrances.

"Young lord," the witch finally began, "you will ride before a vast host and lead them into battle. Storms will surround you, and waves will break upon your shield. Others will try to strike you down, yet you will rise."

Theo smiled and leaned forward, intently listening to the prophecy of the witch.

"They will call you the Lord of Tides, and you will be the lord of the White City in the West."

Theo violently pulled his hands away from the witch and snatched his silver coin off the table.

"Liar!" he yelled, standing up. He pushed Draven out of his way to make room. "You think I am going to let you cheat me out of my silver with your tricks? Anyone can see that I am dressed like a lord's son. You were snooping around camp and heard gossip. You think you know who I am."

The witch smirked at the boy.

"I see what I can see, young lord. You will be the lord of the White City." The witch calmly folded her hands. "I am rarely wrong."

"What a load of shit," Theo cursed at her. "I am the second son of Lord Harroldson, not the first. I will not inherit Tidehaven, and I will never be called the Lord of Tides."

Theo grabbed Emily by the arm and pulled her toward

the door. He let her go as he pushed past Aiden and banged the door open, letting the cool night air into the wagon. Emily chased after Theo down the stairs until she caught him by the wrist on the path that led back to the camps. He was breathing hard and flushed with anger.

"How dare she try to trick us. She took your coins," Theo complained. "A blind man can see that Draven is going to be a knight someday. She probably heard the crowds calling him the Bull at the melee. And you, your hands are the hands of someone who heals. It was all tricks." Theo was almost in tears.

"It doesn't matter what she said, Theo." Emily took him by both wrists and stood directly in front of him. "Seers and witches make guesses. You're right, you know. She could tell something about each one of us by looking at the way we are dressed or the roughness of our hands."

Draven caught up to them on the path, holding on to Saph by her arm. Emily let go of Theo's wrists, stepping to his side.

"That witch knew nothing. She looked like no witch I ever heard of anyway." Draven peered down the path. "Now where's that bridge you were talking about earlier?"

Theo took Emily's hand in his and turned to walk back up the path toward Maiden's Bridge. Emily walked next to him but glanced back at the witch's wagon. Aiden stepped out of the door and stormed down the stairs. The door slammed shut as if the wind had forced it, but the night air was calm. Aiden looked toward their group, but instead of trying to catch up to them or waiting for Jory, he headed off into the woods in the opposite direction from them, alone. Jory was nowhere to be seen.

Theo tugged Emily's hand.

"Come on, the bridge is not far from here."

15

JORY VI

Jory's fist clenched as he watched Theo take Emily by her arm and pull her to the door of the witch's wagon. The stupid Bull followed, with Saph pushing past him and Aiden. Jory thought of the future the witch told to Draven.

That was supposed to be my future. I am supposed to be a great warrior. I am the one who is the son of a famous knight.

"That leaves you two," the witch said. "Who will be first?"

Jory and Aiden glanced at each other, then Aiden stepped forward. The witch gazed upon his face in the candlelight, then reeled back in revulsion.

"No...Omrau!" The witch spat on the floor.

Jory did not understand what she was saying.

"Get out...Omrau. Get out!"

Aiden turned and stormed out of the wagon without even looking at Jory.

Jory tried to follow him outside, but the door to the wagon slammed shut. He pushed on the door with his shoulder, but it would not open.

"Come, boy. Sit down. Let Madam Lucient tell you what she sees," the witch purred.

"I don't have enough, and my f-friends have left." Jory pressed himself against the back wall, trying to get as far from the witch as possible.

"If they left you, they were not your friends. Check your belt. I think you might have enough coins."

Jory searched under his belt, finding the three coppers he had left. He put them on the table in front of the witch.

"Check again. Maybe you forgot one." She leaned back in her seat with an amused smile.

His fingers found a small coin under his belt where there had not been one before. He set it down on the table next to the three coppers. It was a small golden coin with markings on it that Jory had never seen before. A man's head wearing a crown of leaves was imprinted on one side, looking up at Jory. The witch leaned forward and flipped the coin over. On the other side, there was an etching of a tree with three stars above it.

The witch smiled wickedly at Jory and took the strange coin, leaving the three coppers on the table.

"See, I told you, boy. I knew Madam Lucient would be giving you a reading. Sit and give me your hands." She leaned forward and put her elbows on the table, offering her hands palm up for Jory to take hold of.

Jory sat down and nervously put his hands in hers. He wished Aiden had stayed, or Emily, or even Theo. But he was alone, feeling trapped.

"Relax, you are too tense," the witch said softly.

Madam Lucient closed her eyes. Her soft, warm fingers closed about his smaller hands, and her palms rubbed against the callouses he had worked up from all the sword and archery practice with Sir Cley.

"Ah, yes, I see it now. A soldier you will be."

The witch went silent, and after waiting a moment, Jory

decided she was done. He pulled his hands back and stood to leave, but the witch jumped forward in her chair and grasped his wrists. Her hands were like vises locking him in place. Heat emanated from her skin and increased like a growing fire. The witch's eyes opened and widened as her voice whispered in his head.

"I see blood about you, boy. It crashes about you as waves pound a sea rock. Villages will burn in your wake. There is a tower that is surrounded by many who are false. I see lonely paths where you walk with shadows. Your world will be washed in black. I see the wound that does not heal, and the revenge that you seek..."

Jory's wrists hurt where the witch grasped him, and he struggled to get out of her grip. The tapestry behind her came alive as the snakes rolled and writhed against each other.

The witch finally released him, falling back into her chair. She appeared to be asleep. The tapestry returned to looking as it had before. Jory jumped out of his seat and burst through the wagon door. He tripped and stumbled down the stairs in his haste and landed face down on the ground. As he pushed himself up, Jory spotted the small flower he had given Emily trampled in the dirt. Cutting through the night, he heard the howling of what sounded like a young wolf.

The howl was angry.

Jory struggled in the darkness to find his way back to camp, his ears burning to the echoes of Draven's voice calling him "bay rat." The vision of Emily and Theo holding hands made his fists clench. Aiden had left him alone with the witch. Everyone had left him.

I wouldn't have left them.

Campfires flickered through the forest. The tiny lights guided Jory to the tournament grounds, and he made his way to Sir Cley's camp. He found Sir Cley already sleeping when he entered the tent. Jory peeled off his boots and clothes quietly. Sir Cley rolled over and mumbled something in his sleep.

On his bedroll, Jory stared up at the darkness above him. He felt the sharp edges of the shark tooth necklace he wore around his neck and started to think about his father and mother. His father's image began to fade, and his mother's face changed into the woods witch. Her prophecy churned in his head.

What does she know? There is no blood around me or burning villages. I am going to be a famous knight someday. I'll show her. I'll show everybody.

16
THE PRINCE II

James opened the door to his chamber and stepped into the hall. The guard outside stood at attention.

"My Prince, is there something I can get for you?" the guard asked.

"No, no, I am going to retire. The banquet tired me. Please do not let anyone disturb me."

James would not be sneaking out this door. His mother had seen to that when she learned of his plans to enter the Squires' Joust in secret.

James could still hear her admonish him: "It is unbecoming of a king. What if you lose? What will people think of you?"

James closed his door and noticed the small window in the wall. He might fit through it. He carried a chair over to the wall and stood on it. He stretched his arms above his head but could not reach the window. He examined the room and spotted the dresser. If he could push it under the window, he would easily reach the opening.

The dresser creaked and groaned as James pushed it across the stone floor.

The guard outside knocked.

"My Prince, are you alright?"

"Yes, everything is fine. I am rearranging some furniture to more of my liking. Thank you."

James stood on the chair again and stepped onto the dresser, then he looked down at the small room he had been given at the Pebble Creek castle. His mother had taken the better guest room with the larger windows. James reached up to the window and opened the shutter. The cool night air of early summer entered the room.

James hopped up into the window and squeezed his shoulders through. He pulled his legs up under himself and squatted in the alcove on the outside wall. There he met the next obstacle. It was at least fifteen feet to the ground, but there was a tree with a large limb a few feet from the wall that might hold him, if he could make the jump. He took a deep breath and sprang forward. His hands caught the branch, and he was able to hold on despite being scratched on the arms and face by the smaller limbs of the tree.

James climbed down the tree to the ground, wondering how he would get back into his room. Those worries were quickly replaced by thoughts of Rebecca. He could not wait to see her. Seeing the princess made him feel better. He smiled, thinking about how he had protested the arranged marriage with Lord Fowler's daughter. If he were to be king, he thought he should be allowed to choose his own queen. But his mother insisted the match be made to ensure the East did not declare its own independent kingdom centered in Greyport as it had in the days before the Forging.

The first time James met Rebecca, he changed his attitude, as he found her to be the most beautiful girl he could imagine. Her long curly brown hair with her deep-brown eyes gave her a beauty that no other girl could match. But the best thing about her was that she was pleasant to be around. She liked music, dancing, riding, and games. Rebecca was interested in him and asked questions about his likes and opinions. She already sensed his moods. As soon as they had a quiet moment at the banquet, she asked him what was troubling him. It surprised James that she agreed with his mother on the point that he needed new advisors.

"But they truly need to be your men, James," Rebecca whispered to him as they sat at the high table, "not advisors your mother has chosen. They will be loyal to her, not you. You need to have a mix of people—older, experienced advisors along with younger, energetic ones closer to our age. Men and even women from all parts of Terros. A true council to help rule the kingdom."

To his shame, James did not tell her about his uncle, Ivan, declaring himself king. That made him and Rebecca traitors now.

Outlaws. Rebels to be hanged.

He shuddered to think of it.

James walked into the castle's courtyard and found Rebecca sitting on the bench under the flower trellis like she said. His heart leaped in his chest, and he ran across the yard. She stood, and he took her in his arms in an awkward embrace.

"You waited...I came as soon as I could," he whispered in her ear.

Rebecca leaned back from his embrace and gazed into his eyes.

"Of course I waited. What happened to your face?" She reached up and touched a scratch on his cheek.

"Mother placed a guard at my door. I had to fight a tree to reach you, but it was worth it."

James heard footsteps coming. He and Rebecca stepped

deeper into the shadow of the trellis and watched a castle guard walk by on the other side of the courtyard. Rebecca took James by the hand.

"Come with me. I know of a place with fewer eyes."

They walked a short distance from the castle and town until they found a path that led to a bridge. On the other side of the bridge, the path led into the woods. She guided him down to the bank where they found a soft patch of grass to sit on close to the creek.

Rebecca moved herself closer to James so that they were touching. "The locals call this Maiden's Bridge. One of my maids showed it to me. It is beautiful, don't you think?"

"Yes, it's nice here. You know you were right," James said.

"Right about what?"

"Right about my mother. She picked a council without me, men who will answer to her."

"Was that why you were called away from the banquet?" Rebecca asked.

His throat tightened. He wanted to tell her of his uncle's betrayal. She had the right to know. James stared down at his feet, swallowed hard, and took a deep breath.

"My uncle has proclaimed himself king. There was a meeting to plan our next move. Your father was there along with my mother and some other lords. There might be war."

"I see," Rebecca said as she slid her arm around James. He turned his head to face her and found her lips there to meet his.

His first kiss with Rebecca transported James to another world. Her lips were soft and tasted of sweet strawberries. James found himself reaching for her as their kiss continued. His hand found her hair and the soft skin of her neck. Every problem in his life melted away in their embrace.

Rebecca ended the kiss, pulling her lips from his.

"And what kind of plan did they come up with?"

James sighed and stretched himself out in the grass. "Your father is calling for his entire army to meet us at Crosstimbers. Lord Harroldson is sending for his army to join us there too. The rest of the western lords will march on Kingstown down Western Road. We will surround the capital."

"The plan sounds good. I am sure my father and the other lords know what they are doing."

"But they didn't even ask me what I thought. Mother and the other lords treated me like I was some little crown prince."

Rebecca leaned over James, pressing herself over his chest. She stroked his smooth face and played with the loose curls of hair that had fallen over his eyes. She lowered her head and gave James a light kiss on his nose and another on his lips, which he eagerly raised his head to accept. James gave her the look of a disappointed puppy when she pulled her lips away.

"It will be alright. Someday, when we are old, the stories will tell of how King James fought for his crown alongside his wife, Queen Rebecca. It will make for a beautiful story."

"I wish I had power like the old kings had in the stories. If I had King George's war hammer, there would be no doubt as to my claim. Or if I had the sword Dragon's Bane, no one would dare stand before me."

"Those are stories. A hammer or a sword does not make a king. It's what is inside his heart and how he leads."

James's heart pounded as Rebecca put her hand on his chest, tracing small circles over his shirt with her fingertips. He rose up to try to kiss her again.

The voices of a small group of people standing on the bridge interrupted the royal couple.

"So this is Maiden's Bridge. Betcha I can throw a rock all the way down to that tree stump, Draven."

James and Rebecca sat up and listened. A couple of splashes disturbed the water. Two young males were competing to see who could throw stones the farthest into the creek.

James sighed in frustration and stood.

"Let's go before we get pelted by a rock."

James kissed Rebecca and held her close in the darkness of the courtyard. He wished the kiss and embrace could last forever, but Rebecca pulled away from him finally.

"We should get back to our rooms."

James took a deep breath.

"Yeah. How am I going to get back into my room?"

"Do what I do. Simply walk in. You're the prince. You went for a walk. If the guard says anything, he will get in trouble for letting you out, right?"

"That's true. I didn't think of that."

Rebecca leaned back into James and gave him a quick kiss on the lips.

"Good night, sweet Prince."

James floated down the hall that led to his chambers. He could still taste Rebecca's lips on his, and the scent of her hair was etched in his memory. The big grin he wore was starting to hurt his facial muscles. The guard outside his chamber door stood at attention and said nothing as he walked past.

It's good to be king.

James pushed open his door and was surprised by the light inside.

"Back from your stroll, I see."

His mother sat in a straight-backed chair near his bed.

"Mother, I—"

"Sit down, James," she said sternly.

James walked to his bed and sat.

"You are to be king. You know that. To wander off late at night is dangerous. There are people out there who want to hurt you. There are people in this castle who want to hurt you. We can trust no one, James."

"But I was with Rebecca..."

"Ah, yes, the beautiful princess. You think you can trust her? That one is like her mother."

"What do you mean?"

"Look at her twin brothers. One looks like Lord Fowler, the other like Lady Fowler's personal guard. You're no fool. How do you think that happened?"

"Rebecca is different. She loves me," James choked.

"Of course she loves you. You are about to be king. She is no different from her mother, I am afraid."

"You're wrong."

"Am I? Your princess was seen dancing with Sir Cley Woods after you left the banquet. They apparently had quite the conversation and were seen to be shockingly close. How was it put? Yes, I was told the princess was draped over him like some cheap tablecloth."

James turned away from his mother. He bit his bottom lip and thought of Rebecca and Sir Cley embracing one another.

His mother stood from the chair and looked down at James.

"It should not surprise you that she would be interested in Sir Cley. He is handsome and famous. You are still a boy in her eyes, a plaything she thinks she will manipulate when she is queen. I will make sure that does not happen. You are lucky also that Sir Cley will lose interest in her as soon as he gets what he wants. Rumors say he is not satisfied with one woman."

James sat on the bed in misery. His head pounded with his heartbeat, and his stomach rolled in knots. He wanted to cry. He heard his mother close his chamber door.

It can't be true. I have to show everyone I can be king—Mother, the lords, Rebecca. I need to show them all.

17
JORY VII

Jory struggled in the man's arms as waves broke around them. He thrashed his legs and kicked at the man holding him from behind but could not get free.

The man put his hands on his shoulders and tried to push him under the surface. Jory lowered his head and bit the man's hand hard. The man howled in pain.

"Stupid brat!" the man shouted, plunging Jory's head under the water as the waves rolled in. He held Jory under with his hand grasped around the back of the boy's neck. Jory struggled and kicked again.

"Let him up, Carter," a man called from the beach.

Carter pulled Jory's head up from under the water and lifted him out of the surf by his neck to face his stepfather.

"Next time I want something, it won't be you out here in the water," Lord Wells said.

Carter dropped Jory back into the foaming surf. Jory crawled in the wet sand as the tide pulled back and watched Carter and the man he was supposed to call his father walk toward the manor.

Jory woke with a gasp, his skin damp with sweat and heart hammering in his chest. Another nightmare. Across the tent,

Sir Cley breathed deeply in sleep. Jory wiped his forehead with his hand and felt his hair plastered to his brow. He got up and stepped out of the tent into the cool morning air.

The sun had yet to appear on the horizon, but the sky was starting to lighten up. The sound of the rippling water drew Jory down to the creek. He took off the old shirt he slept in, knelt on the edge, and splashed cool water on his face.

I should have known I was going to have one of those dreams. That stupid witch...and Emily...and stupid Theo.

"You there, boy. Look alive now, eh."

The harsh voice brought Jory out of his thoughts.

He peered across the creek. A large man stood watching him as he washed his own face and upper body. The man had long, greasy black hair that hung down to his shoulders, and he wore a beard of unshaved black stubble. With his shirt off, Jory could see the man's chest and arms were covered in coarse black hair. His skin was pale like the underbelly of a shark. Pink scars slashed across his left shoulder and on his left side like thick worms.

"I thought you might fall into the creek asleep, eh." The man's voice was rough like a wheel pulled over gravel.

He pulled off his breeches and stepped out into the creek naked. He walked about halfway across until the water was above his waist, then continued washing himself while keeping an eye on the boy. His eyes paused at the shark tooth Jory wore around his neck, and Jory's muscles tensed. He was exposed and vulnerable sitting there in only his underclothes. He glanced over his shoulder to see how far it was to Sir Cley's tent. He could run up the riverbank. Jory's hand drifted up to the carved tooth, feeling its serrated edges between his fingers.

This man oozes danger.

The man turned his back to Jory and dunked his head

underwater. A tattoo of a black bird with spread wings covered his upper back from shoulder to shoulder. Jory thought about bolting back to the safety of Sir Cley's tent, but his body froze. The man came back up and tossed his wet hair back out of his face and turned to face Jory again.

"You're the Turner boy, aren't ya?" It sounded like it was more of a statement to himself than it was a question to Jory. "I saw you in that melee yesterday, eh."

Jory nodded.

The man stepped closer to Jory's side of the creek.

"Them Fowler twins beat ya."

"They cheated," Jory snapped. He was tricked by the Fowler twins, and now this man was intimidating him. "I had them b-beat."

"Were they dead?"

"No."

The man scoffed, "Then they weren't beat."

Jory again judged the distance between the man and himself. He scanned the bank to see if there was a rock or stick nearby.

"There you are, Jory. I thought I heard voices."

Sir Cley walked to the edge of the creek bed. The knight froze, standing at the top of the bank wearing only his breeches. Jory turned back to the man standing in the creek who stared daggers into Sir Cley.

"Cley," the man said, nodding to the knight.

"Fin," Sir Cley replied, returning the nod.

There was a gap of silence bigger than the Western Ocean as the young knight and man stared at each other. There could not have been a greater difference between the two. Where the man in the creek had unkempt black hair, Cley's was blond and tied back neatly. The man's eyes were dark, as were his brows. His nose appeared to have been broken and healed wrong. Cley's eyes were blue, and his face was clean. The man had large muscles that made him look thicker and heavier than the lean and athletic Sir Cley.

"Come on, Jory. We need to get something to eat before we start to pack," Sir Cley said.

Jory stood and climbed up the bank of the creek, then turned, remembering he had left his old shirt below. The man Sir Cley had called Fin stood in the middle of the creek looking up at them. His gaze went right through Jory to Sir Cley. Jory decided to leave the shirt.

"Who-who was that?" Jory asked, catching up to Cley outside the pavilion.

"Finis Crowe," Cley answered, entering the tent. He turned away from Jory and lowered his voice as he said, "The Dark Sorrow."

18

THE GILDED KNIGHT

Sir Cley stepped into his tent and tried to look busy. There was much to be done to prepare for the march to Crosstimbers, and he knew Jory would have questions about the Sorrow.

"W-who is he? Why do they call him the Dark Sorrow?" Jory asked all at once.

"Finis Crow is a knight with a bad reputation, much of it well deserved." Cley searched around the tent for his tunic. "He is ill news. It would be better if he were not here."

"You know him?"

"He fought in the Pirate King's Rebellion." Cley sat down in his camp chair, feeling like he had not slept a wink.

"He fought for the Pirate King? Why was he not kept as a prisoner for being a traitor?"

"He was sent to prison for a time, but not for being a traitor. The Sorrow fought for King Edward."

Cley sat for a moment, wondering what he should tell Jory of Sir Finis Crowe. Outside, the sky grew brighter as the sun began to rise. Cley decided that what he knew could wait for a different day and a different place to share with the boy.

"Jory, go ahead and get dressed. We will have a cold

breakfast this morning. When we are done, we will start to pack for the march. Oh, remind me to get up to the castle to ransom Thunder."

Jory stood, looking as if he had a thousand more questions to ask.

Cley gave Jory plenty of chores to do around the tent to keep him busy as they prepared to break camp. Cley was loading the folded camp chairs and table into the small cart when he heard Sir Torrent coming up the row.

"Cley, quit packing and come with me. Lord Buckhorn wants a word," Torrent said between heavy breaths. "Something has happened. We are not leaving for Crosstimbers."

"What has happened?" Cley asked.

"Not sure. The Old Buck will tell us what's going on. Maybe what Sir Thurmond said is true."

Jory walked out of the tent with a large bag of their foodstuffs to put in the wagon.

"Jory, hold off packing anything else until I get back. Sir Torrent and I are going to speak with Lord Buckhorn. Stay here," Cley ordered the boy.

Jory nodded, and the two knights headed down to the Lord of Buckton's pavilion.

When Cley and Torrent entered the tent, Lord Buckhorn was standing and talking to three other knights of his manor. His eldest son, Ethan, was noticeably absent.

"Good." Lord Buckhorn nodded in greetings. "Cley, Torrent, plans have changed. Lord Russ of Easton has decided to call himself king. The West will see to it that James takes the throne instead." Lord Buckhorn surveyed the men in his pavilion. "I sent Ethan back to Buckton. He will raise my swords to march east along Western Road. Ethan will command my forces and be joined by Lord Storm from Turtle Bay and soldiers from High Meadow. Storm and Lady

Day's eldest son left camp last night as soon as we were given word. It will be war for sure. I can feel it."

Lord Buckhorn was a plain speaker. Cley had never known him to mince his words or to flower them up. His thoughts turned to Lord Buckhorn's eldest son. Ethan Buckhorn was a good man but not much of a fighter. He was more at ease with a book in his hand than a sword.

"My Lord, send me to catch up with your son. I can assist him in whatever he needs," Cley said.

"Cley, we will remain here with Prince James. It must not look like we are abandoning James or trying to mount opposition against Russ. The northern lords have not declared their allegiance yet. They must be shown the strength that supports the prince. We will wait here at Pebble Creek for three more days to give Tidehaven the chance to muster its forces. They will catch up with us on the road to Crosstimbers. Prince James needs every good sword that surrounds him now."

Lord Buckhorn's voice grew softer, but he spoke with no less authority.

"Gentlemen, Prince James has gathered about himself favor seekers and parade knights. We are men of the West. We are men of Buckton, and we will defend our future king. Be armed from here on around camp and be ready. Sir Tice, I charge you with finding extra provisions. We will not starve during this campaign. Sir Reaves you are to assist him. Sir Torrent and Sir Halford you need to organize my house guards."

"And what of me, My Lord?" Cley asked.

"Sir Cley, you are to go about as if nothing is amiss. Do what you do. Stay close to the knights of the East and listen to them. They will speak openly in your presence, especially with a few tankards of ale in them. We must make sure there are no traitors about."

Cley nodded. His assignment was not pleasant, nor

honorable. Spying. He would rather be leading the Buckton forces down Western Road.

"That is all. Plan to be on the move in three days."

Lord Buckhorn sat down heavily in his chair as the five knights left his pavilion. Sir Cley stopped at the entrance and turned to face his lord.

"The Sorrow is in camp, My Lord," Cley said.

"I know. It will be alright. Fin will be needed now, I am afraid."

"If you knew he was in camp, why not send me to Buckton with Ethan to lead your swords?"

"Sir Raymond will be bringing the men of Seadrift and marching alongside my son." Lord Buckhorn let Cley contemplate this.

Cley clenched his fists at the mention of Sir Raymond Wells. The vision of his hands wrapped around the bastard's fat neck and pinning him to the floor flashed in his memory.

"It is the lesser of two evils. You are the best knight here, Cley. You need to stay close to your future king. He needs us here. Remember, you are a Knight of the Realm. Your duty is to defend the realm and its king."

Cley left the pavilion and headed back to his tent with Lord Buckhorn's voice echoing in his head.

My duty. Defend the realm... A Knight of the Realm... I am the best knight. No one would argue against Lord Buckhorn on that, no one except for the Sorrow.

Arriving back at his campsite, Sir Cley spotted his charger, Thunder, tied alongside his other horses. The jousting saddle and his armor were sitting in the small wagon outside his tent. Cley did not see Jory anywhere.

This is not good.

Cley stepped inside his tent—still no sign of Jory, but there was a purse sitting on the small camp table. A bag of gold left open.

The gold can wait to be counted. I need to find Jory and find out what happened.

Cley walked down to the creek and followed it until he found Jory sitting on the large rock that Cley himself had been sitting on the night before. The boy had his knees pulled up to his chin with his arms wrapped around them tightly.

The boy raised his head to Sir Cley. His eyes were reddened as if he had been sobbing.

"Why did you do it?" Jory asked.

"What happened, Jory? Who brought Thunder back?" Sir Cley walked over to the boy and sat against the large rock. He had a feeling he already knew the answer.

"Sir Blake, h-he brought Thunder, the saddle, and the bag of coins. He said next time he meets you in a joust, he w-won't need his father's gold to put you on your back," Jory said bitterly.

Lord Pontifer must have revealed that he paid for his son's victory. Next time I see Sir Blake, I will make sure he remembers who the better knight is.

"W-why did you fall in the joust? He said his father paid you to lose."

Cley stood in silence, thinking. The water babbling in the creek seemed to question him.

"Look, Jory, I was going to tell you about it when you got older, like your father taught me." Cley tried to look Jory in the eye but found he could not. "I am a knight without land. I have no income other than the prizes I win at tournaments. I... We need coin to survive, to buy the things we need—

armor, saddles, horses, food. It all costs gold, and sometimes I can make more than the prize if I lose. Lord Pontifer offered me this tournament's prize plus another half if I were to lose to his son. The gold I won is enough to buy you a pony to train on."

"B-but it's not honorable. It's against the knight's code you taught me. Y-you said that a knight always is ready and works hard and does his b-best, even if it is j-just practice." Jory let his legs go and wiped his eyes with the back of his hand. He was stuttering more, Cley noticed.

"I agree. It's not honorable, but sometimes a knight must do things to survive that might not be honorable," Cley reasoned. "Is it honorable for a man to steal bread for his starving family?"

"Maybe he c-could ask for the bread instead of stealing it."

"But that would be begging. Begging is almost as dishonorable as stealing. I lost on purpose. I got paid to do it. No one got hurt."

"B-but what about the people who bet on you? People lost c-coins because they knew you could beat him."

"If those people could not afford to lose, they should not have been playing the game. Jory, I am not the only knight to fall off his horse on purpose," Cley said, rationalizing it in his own head. "Your father taught me how to fall without hurting myself."

"M-my father cheated?" Jory asked in a quiet voice. It was the same voice Jory's father had used when seeking the truth.

"It's not really cheating, Jory. It's just not... And, yes, your father lost when he could have won and got paid."

Jory stood and walked away from Cley.

19
EMILY IV

Emily entwined her fingers with Theo's as they walked down the dirt road that ran the length of Pebble Creek. Warm candlelight lit up the windows of the shops and merchant's homes above.

"Alyss said that some other lord was declared king," Emily said.

"Lord Russ of Easton. He is going to have to fight the entire kingdom to hold the throne," Theo answered.

"But I thought Lord Fowler was lord paramount of the East."

"He is. Lord Russ is cousin to the late King Edward, so he thinks he has a better claim."

The couple continued their walk under the night sky. Fireflies blinked in the darkness ahead of them at the temple's garden. Theo stepped through the small gate and led Emily to a carved stone bench by a small well on the grounds.

"With my father's army and the Army of the East coming after him, Lord Russ will run home. Plus, the southern army will be joining us," Theo said, sitting down next to Emily. "Right now, I am glad we are still here, me with you."

Theo tilted his head and leaned toward Emily. Their lips

met in a soft kiss. This second kiss was much better than the first, which had been on Maiden's Bridge. It was not at all what Emily imagined her first real kiss would be like. They bumped their lips awkwardly, and Theo was clumsy. It was as if he were trying too hard, like he was trying to prove something to himself. He might have still been angry about the fortune he had been given. Perhaps with Draven nearby with Saph, he thought he had to show off for his friend.

This time, warmth washed over her as her lips touched Theo's. After the kiss, they sat on the edge of the well. Theo listened as she described the types of flowers and plants in the garden and what they were named after or used for. They talked well into the night.

Emily gave Theo another longer kiss when he escorted her back to the tent she shared with Maggy and Alyss. As she lay awake on her bedroll, all she could think about was her time with Theo. She could not stop smiling.

The next day, everything appeared better and more special. The sky and sun were brighter, and fluffy white clouds floated above like the big ships she had seen at Tidehaven. Even the dusty, smelly camp felt like a better place.

Emily sat with Saph that afternoon at the washing tent and spoke of the rumors and gossip swirling around the camp.

"I heard Lord Harroldson will be sending his wife and two youngest back to Tidehaven," Saph said.

"I had not heard that," replied Emily.

Theo would tell me he was leaving, wouldn't he?

"Either way, we will be following the army all the way to Kingstown. It will be quite an adventure." Saph smiled.

"And I can try to see that boy Draven again. Did you hear about the princess? I heard from a serving girl at the castle that she was dancing with Sir Cley at the banquet. It upset the prince, and he left without her."

"No, I had not heard that either."

Emily tried to think of any gossip that Saph had not already mentioned when she spotted Jory walking through camp. She thought of the rose he had given her. She meant to visit him to find out what had happened at the witch's wagon after she left. Jory walked by taking no notice of the girls. He appeared to be daydreaming as children with no concerns tended to do. Maybe he was on his way to meet his friend, Aiden. Emily pictured Aiden with his pretty eyes. There was a quiet strength and determination in him.

I wonder what Aiden's lips would feel like.

That evening, Emily and Theo walked back to Maiden's Bridge and kissed again. Theo placed his hands on her hips and held her close. Emily found herself wrapping her arms over Theo's shoulders, and her fingers tousled his thick hair.

"Will you be going back to Tidehaven with your mother?" Emily asked after they found a log to sit on along the creek.

"No, my mother will be going back with my younger brother and some of the other noble women with a small guard after my father's army arrives," Theo answered. "Father says I will ride with him. If there is a battle, I might even get to be in it."

"Aren't you afraid of riding into battle?"

"Never. A knight does not ride into battle hounded by fears. I will ride alongside my father and act as his squire. I will probably win my knighthood. My older brother did not earn his knighthood until he was sixteen. I will beat him by two years."

"Oh, that will be nice for you."

It occurred to her that this relationship was pointless. A noble like Theo Harroldson could never be serious about a girl like herself. She was an amusement to him. When this journey was over, when Theo had his knighthood, what would she have?

Theo leaned in to kiss her again, but Emily backed away from him.

"Theo, what will you do when James is made king?"

"I hope to be named to the royal guard and stay in Kingstown," Theo replied without much thought. "James will need to choose his own personal guard. When I have my knighthood, I will have shown my worth to him."

He leaned in to try to kiss Emily yet again.

"What about us? Will you find some noble girl? Am I simply a plaything for you at camp?"

Theo took Emily's hand in his. "No, it's not like that. I admit, at first I only wanted to kiss you, but I do like you. You are not like some of the noble girls I have met before. You are interesting...and more beautiful."

Emily held Theo's hand in her own, and she sensed he was being sincere.

"I feel better around you. I...I don't know why, but I feel calmer and even stronger when we are together."

"But someone of your standing could never be serious about me. I am a poor commoner. Your parents would never allow it."

"I am a second son. It's my brother who must marry well, not me. A second son has more choices." Theo smiled, looking into Emily's eyes. He drew closer. This time, Emily did not pull away. She met him as their lips touched softly. Theo kept a hold of her hand in his, and Emily connected with him. Theo's thoughts, doubts, and fears as well as his dreams came to her, and she was in them.

In the early morning, Emily poked the small fire, placing some dry wood on it to make it grow as it had almost died out. She was thinking about her night with Theo by the creek when the town bell began to toll. The large bell rang at a continuous pace—a sound that invoked urgency in the listener.

Not long after, one of Lord Buckhorn's men rode his horse through camp yelling, "To arms! To arms! The enemy approaches from the east! They are forming up across the creek!"

Those men and women who were out of their tents slowly walked about, not quite realizing what was going on. The sun was rising, and most of the camp had fallen into the habit of drinking late into the evening and rising at mid-morning. Only the men in the Buckton camp seemed to be prepared.

Above the din of the iron bell, Emily heard horns being blown. The sound was carrying over from the east, she thought, from across the creek. This was it, a real-life battle. Emily's heart raced, and she held her breath.

Men ran to arm themselves, putting on what armor they had with them at camp. Emily noticed the older men were more meticulous. They took their time, and they were confident as they prepared outside their tents and pavilions. The younger men and boys forgot shields, spears, and even swords. They had to run back to their tents to retrieve the forgotten equipment. Slowly, the soldiers began to form up in lines and proceeded to march east toward the Pebble Creek bridge.

"Emily, we need to prepare. Get that fire going hot and pack a bag in case we must make a run for the castle. Things could get dangerous. Stay near me. Do you understand?" Alyss ordered in a frantic voice. "Set a pot of water to boil over the fire. Fill another pot with the wine we brought to boil next to it. We may need it to cleanse wounds. This will not be some joust or melee. You will hear and see things that a young girl should not, but we need to concentrate on our duties for the sake of any wounded who come back to us."

Emily stoked the fire with more purpose. It was growing, and she left it to fill up one of the pots with water to boil. She passed a line of thirty men with long bows in the purple and white colors of Pebble Creek marching down to the creek. A group of knights rode their horses down the lane in the opposite direction. They had to slow their horses as they drew near the company of archers who blocked the way ahead. After much cursing and shouting, the archers parted, and the knights rode through. The bell continued to ring as the camp turned into a giant ant hill that had been stirred up.

Some of these ants might die, and Theo could be one of them.

20
JORY VIII

Jory stood next to Thunder as the horse's nostrils flared and snorted. The charger shook his mane and stamped his feet on the ground in anticipation.

Thunder knows something is coming, but this isn't a joust.

Thunder was a good horse, fearless and strong, but he had never actually been in battle.

Sir Cley had.

Across the bridge, a line of foot soldiers took up positions on a hill in front of the woods. From Jory's position, he could not make out the colors they were wearing or the banners that were waving behind them. There might have been a hundred soldiers at the most. Behind them, Jory counted five knights riding on horseback.

Between the hill and the creek were close to two hundred yards of open field split by Crossing Road. The road ran right up to the Pebble Creek bridge, which was wide enough for two carts to ride side by side. The Tolar Kings insisted on building bridges and roads to link the cities and towns of Terros together to build trade and unity in the kingdom. Today, the bridge would be used for something other than unity.

"Let them come," Sir Cley said to no one in particular.

Jory guessed he might be talking to himself, or maybe Thunder. They had not spoken the last few days. After that morning when he had found out Sir Cley was a cheater, Jory had left to wander in the woods for a while, hot tears staining his cheeks.

My father was a great knight, not some cheater. All the stories and songs say so. Cley is the cheater and liar.

Jory wandered through camp the rest of that day and into the night. He wanted to leave Pebble Creek.

But to where? Where can I go? Home? I have no home. That man was there.

He could go back to Shadow Tower. No one was there, so he could live there alone. He was alone now, so what difference did it make? He couldn't find Aiden anywhere in camp, and every time he thought of Emily, all he could picture was her holding Theo's hand.

Jory thought he could go to the blacksmith's shop in the village and learn that trade. He had seen lots of blacksmiths before in other towns and camps. He watched how they worked the bellows and forge. The blacksmith at Pebble Creek was a nice man, but all he wanted to do was talk about Sir Cley or tell the story of how he had shoed his father's horse during the Pirate King's Rebellion.

Late that night, Jory, feeling tired and hungry, had found his way back to Sir Cley's tent. There was no "Welcome back," or "Where have you been?" Only Sir Cley lightly snoring. The knight had made no mention of it the next day. Jory was not about to end the cold silence. Sir Cley was supposedly the best knight in the land, and he was his squire.

The sooner I earn my knighthood, the better. I will be different. I will be honorable.

When Jory looked at Sir Cley, all he saw was a liar. Sir Cley was supposed to be his friend. He even thought of him sometimes as a father. There was a lot Jory wanted to say to Cley.

But to be the first one to break the silence would be like forgiving him.

When the bell started to toll that morning, Sir Cley began talking again. He kept it to a minimum and was calm and workmanlike. Jory helped Cley put on his armor and helped saddle Thunder. Sir Cley talked Jory through the process of checking the straps and buckles of his armor. Cley did not wear his full armor like he did for jousting in tournaments. He said if he were knocked from Thunder, he would need to be free to move around and not weighed down by too much armor.

Throoom!

The sound shook Jory from his thoughts as he stood next to Thunder, holding Sir Cley's shield and lance. He heard the sound echo through the trees across the creek, and a large object appeared in the sky. The rising sun in the east blinded Jory as he looked up into the sky to follow the object. Shortly, a huge boulder crashed into the side of the Pebble Creek castle wall behind them.

"They have a trebuchet," Sir Cley stated calmly.

The soldiers of Buckton stood in straight lines, armed with shields and short swords. They were lightly armored. Most of the men only donned padded leather armor. The march to Kingstown was supposed to have been a parade, not a battle.

The other knights of Buckton paced on horseback in front of the soldiers. Sir Torrent, mounted on his horse in his orange and green colors, was by far the largest of all the knights. He kept talking to the men below him on foot, telling them there was glory to be won today. The men cheered, calling back loudly to Sir Torrent in fearless voices.

The other three knights from Buckton began to trot up and down the line with their swords drawn.

Sir Cley sat still upon Thunder.

Jory heard a horse riding up behind him and stopping.

"Damned Tidehaven fool…"

Jory turned his head to see that it was Lord Buckhorn himself, fully armored and mounted on his warhorse. The lord rode his horse alongside Sir Cley, and the other four knights circled around.

"The Lord of Tidehaven has read in a book somewhere that King George the First defeated an army of foot soldiers by driving his horse in a single column and attacking head-on. He wants to charge up that small rise and put an end to this. Lord Pontifer is demanding a charge to protect his town and castle, but he will not even field his own knights. He has them hidden up in the castle." Lord Buckhorn spat on the ground. "We don't even know who that is up on the hill or how many more of them might be hidden in the woods behind them."

Throoom!

A second boulder soared into the air and crashed into the castle walls with a crunching of rock striking rock.

"My Lord, let me take a few men through the woods to the north of here. I know a place where we can ford the creek. We will come up behind them and disable their trebuchet if it is not well guarded," Sir Cley offered.

Lord Buckhorn mulled the idea over in his head.

"Cley, pick ten men from these soldiers. The rest of us will advance with Tidehaven and the rabble to the right. I will try to delay Lord Harroldson's folly for as long as I can to give you more time. If you cannot disable the trebuchet or discover that this enemy outnumbers us, send the signal."

Cley nodded. He rode Thunder over to the line of

Buckton soldiers, picked ten men out of the ranks, and rode back to Jory.

"I will not be needing the lance after all, but I will take my shield," Cley said, leaning down for Jory to hand it to him. Jory handed Cley his shield with its freshly painted white cedar tree on a green field.

"Jory, when I get back, we need to talk. Agreed?"

Jory looked up at Sir Cley, reading in his face a look of someone who was sorry about a million things. He had never seen that look in any grown person's face before.

Jory nodded to Sir Cley.

"Stay on this side of the creek. If the fighting goes bad, get back to our pavilion, grab what you can, and make for our safe place. Right?"

Jory nodded again and croaked, "Yes, Sir."

"You're a good boy, Jory Turner." Sir Cley smiled at him, leaned over in his saddle, and patted him on the head. Cley sat back up straight. He nodded to Sir Torrent and Lord Buckton, turned on Thunder, and led the ten men into the woods.

21
THE PRINCE III

"Why are they doing nothing? My castle will be rubble. We will be defenseless if we do not strike now. Where is Lord Harroldson? Why do we delay?"

Lord Pontifer's whining was incessant, his voice sounding like the constant cawing of seagulls. James tried to ignore him.

If I were lord of this castle, I would have already sent out a sortie to feel out the strengths of this enemy, not hide behind these walls trapped like some poor animal.

Lord Pontifer paced the tower, peering through the crenulations at the gap that was growing on his eastern curtain wall. The fifth boulder to strike the wall created a space large enough for a mounted knight to charge through. Lord Fowler offered no advice or encouragement. An amused smirk appeared on his lips, as if enjoying Lord Pontifer's misery.

"Father, let me lead our men. The knights of Pebble Creek will end this siege," Sir Blake offered.

"No! You are needed here," Lord Pontifer said. "I need you here to command my garrison in the castle if it should come to that."

"What good are allies if they choose not to act?" Lady Tolar asked no one, and no one replied.

"Lady Tolar, maybe you would be more comfortable below in the castle with the other noble women. You and the prince could bring much encouragement to the others who have taken refuge in the receiving hall," Lord Fowler offered.

"Ha! You would love to hear of me cowering below, wouldn't you? I think not." She gave Lord Fowler a sneer. "I notice you and your forces have not bothered to take the field."

These are my friends, allies, and advisors. Not even an arrow shot or sword drawn and already they argue and bicker.

"Look, Father...at the bridge," Sir Blake said and pointed at the bridge, where Lord Harroldson led the cavalry across, followed by the foot soldiers from Tidehaven.

"Thank the Four." Pontifer raised his eyes to the sky. "Finally, the Lord of Tides has roused himself."

The main body of the prince's allies in the middle of the field was impressive. The large blue and silver banner of Tidehaven waved in the breeze. Riding beneath it was Lord Harroldson himself with his household knights. James could make out the banners of many of the western knights formed up in the vanguard. The force was bolstered by the journeymen knights who had come to Pebble Creek. Their smaller banners were tied to their lances and fluttered in the morning breeze, and their armor and colors gleamed in the morning light. The only eastern knight's banner James spotted was Sir Lucas's white owl.

James puffed out his chest a bit as he looked down at the forces that were in support of his claim. There had to be at least thirty knights in the Tidehaven ranks. They would surely slice through the small enemy line.

A smaller force from Buckton followed Tidehaven, taking up position on the left flank. On the right, a ragtag group of poorly armed men on foot walked in disorder behind a single mounted knight.

"Who is that in the black riding before the militia?" James asked, looking through his spyglass.

"That, My Prince, is the Dark Sorrow, Sir Finis Crowe," Sir Blake answered. "Be glad he takes the field on our side."

A cheer rose from the Tidehaven forces, and the cavalry began to move forward, a slow trot at first. The first hundred yards, the single column progressed at an even pace. A horn sounded, and it began to pick up speed.

A hail of arrows shot up from the woods. The cavalry kept charging forward as the arrow heads glittered in the morning sunlight like scales on a fish. The arrows began to rain down on the horsemen, and several knights fell before even reaching the small hill.

The enemy line of soldiers at the top of the hill parted, and pikemen came racing out from behind them. They advanced down the hill, setting their pikes into the ground as the charge grew closer.

The knights broke into full charge. The lead horses in the vanguard smashed into the pikeman's line. Several of the knights were unhorsed by the long polearms, but the charge penetrated the enemy's defensive square. The foot soldiers were only halfway across the field, too far to offer any support to the cavalry.

James watched from his spyglass as the Buckton unit circled around the small hill and disappeared into the woods. On the right, the Sorrow slowly led the militia along the road. There they met some pikemen, who were pushed back by the greater militia numbers.

A black plume of smoke arose from the woods in the east. In minutes, a great black column of smoke billowed into the sky.

The hill became a massive battlefield. James could not distinguish between who was on which side, as men turned to face their foes. The hail of arrows coming from the woods stopped. A space in the enemy's defenses to the right of the hill opened as the black knight worked his way amongst the common foot soldiers. The Sorrow rode in behind the enemy, cutting them down where they stood, creating a circle of dead and fleeing men around him. Enemy soldiers dropped their weapons and ran for the road, only to be taken by the militia.

Arrrooooooo!

A horn sounded from the woods, where a small group of men charged out. Their battle cry could be heard across the field all the way to the castle. At the head of the line was a knight holding a shield of green with a white tree painted on it. Only five knights rode beside him, followed by men on foot, but the sound and fury of their charge caused the enemy to lose heart. The enemy knights dropped their weapons to surrender, and the knights of Tidehaven took them as prisoners. The enemy foot soldiers also tried to surrender. Some were lucky enough to be near the men of Buckton, who rounded them up. Others were less lucky, as their raised empty hands were met with sword, pike, and pitchfork from the Army of the West.

"Well done. Of course, it should have been done earlier, then maybe my curtain wall would still be intact," Lord Pontifer whined.

James scanned the battlefield. There were men lying on the ground unmoving. Riderless horses wandered across the field.

Men died because of me today. Some were for me. Some were against me. Some had no idea who I am. How many more will die? What will be the price of my throne?

22
EMILY V

lyss was right. The battle had been horrible. Men were injured, and many died on the battlefield. Worse, Alyss said this was only a skirmish, not a full-scale battle.

The men who could move on their own were the first to arrive back at the healer's tent, followed by the injured men with friends who helped them back to camp. Emily organized the washerwomen into groups to help wrap or stitch up cuts and wounds that were not life-threatening. Maggy sorted the men as they arrived. She calmly said what aid the men needed as they passed by her. Alyss had gone to the battlefield to help those who could not make it back.

The arrival of Lord Harroldson slumped over his horse surprised Emily. A knight rode on either side, holding him up in his saddle. When the knights dismounted, they pulled their lord down from his charger and carried him to the nearest table, where some common soldier hopped off at their approach.

"Come quick, old woman!" one of the knights shouted at Maggy. "Lord Harroldson has been wounded."

Maggy moved over to the table where Lord Harroldson was laid out. Emily moved closer to have a look for herself.

"Take his helmet off, kind Sir," Maggy said.

The knight removed Lord Harroldson's helmet. From what Emily could see, there appeared to be no injury, but the man's eyes were rolled back to show only the whites, and he was sweating profusely. Maggy searched the back of his head with her fingers, then clacked her tongue, unsatisfied with whatever she found.

"The rest of his armor, remove it from him," Maggy ordered.

The knights removed their lord's armor, and Maggy pulled Lord Harroldson's collar open. There was a small cut on the lower part of his neck where it met his collarbone. The cut was not bleeding, but the skin around it was a red and yellowish color with tiny veins of black spreading from it.

"Poison... Emily, fetch me the purple vial from my bag, and hurry."

Emily ran to the back of the tent and found the vial in a bag Maggy kept near her sleeping area. It was small and only half full. She checked the bag to be sure this was the only purple vial inside.

In that moment of rest, kneeling at Maggy's cot, a pressure began pushing down on Emily—despair, pain, anger. It was like a heavy pack had been set upon her shoulders. A soldier was on the ground near her, unmoving and breathless. His face was swollen, and his skin was red with black veins bulging under it.

Emily forced herself to get up and walk back to Maggy. Cries and moans for help echoed in every direction. A black-vein-covered arm of an injured knight reached out for her and grabbed her by her skirt.

"Help me..." the knight gasped, white foam bubbling on his lips. The washerwoman who had been tending the wound on his arm stood back from him in horror.

"It spread through his arm, like it was alive," the woman said.

The knight released Emily's skirt as his arm went limp. She stepped away, her head pounding with her heartbeat. The volume of voices from all the injured rose like a flood. Her shoulders slumped as the weight on them doubled. Emily staggered, about to fall.

"There you are. Come with me now."

Maggy appeared by Emily's side and took her by the arm with a surprisingly strong grip. Emily steadied herself.

"Think calm thoughts. Healing. Warmth. A mother's warm hug. Strength." Maggy's voice was soothing, and the calls of pain and anguish receded to the back of Emily's head. She found herself walking with the healer back to where Lord Harroldson was.

The black veins spread from the cut on his neck toward his right cheek. His breathing came in rasps. Maggy uncorked the purple vial and held it above Lord Harroldson's open mouth, letting a few drops of the liquid drop onto his tongue. The man's breathing slowly returned to normal, and he slumped back onto the table as if asleep.

"What kind of sorcery is this?" the knight next to Lord Harroldson exclaimed.

"It's not magic. It's poison. Widow's Root, I would guess," replied Alyss, who had returned to the healer's tent. "Men are dying of it all over the field. Any man with an arrow wound was overtaken by the poison. I found an arrowhead smeared with some tar-like substance."

"Yes, Widow's Root would be my guess also. A cruel tactic." Maggy handed the vial to Alyss. "No more than two drops to the wounded. I am afraid there will not be enough for all who may have suffered an arrow wound."

Alyss made her way amongst the tables and men on the

ground around the healer's tent, dispensing the elixir to the injured.

"Emily, there are others to tend to. Go help the other women. Remember, soothing thoughts, healing and strength," Maggy instructed.

Emily had never been so tired. It was getting close to midday. Her hands and feet hurt from working all morning, and her legs and back ached from bending over the wounded.

"Where is he? My father, where is he?" a loud, commanding voice called out.

Emily raised her eyes up from the injured farmer's arm she was sewing up to see Sir Tristan Harroldson walking through the injured men outside the tent. Theo and the Bull were behind him.

"Here," Emily called to them, "follow me."

Lord Harroldson had been brought inside the tent and put on a cot. He was still asleep, but the black veins that had covered his neck were gone, and his skin had returned to its natural color. The cut on his neck appeared to be no more dangerous than a scratch.

"Will he be alright?" Sir Tristan asked the knight standing over his father. The knight shrugged, and Tristan turned to look at Emily.

"Yes, the healer says he will sleep until the elixir has completely rid him of the poison," Emily answered.

Theo moved close to his father, and Emily sensed he was afraid to touch him.

"It's alright if you touch him. It is safe."

Theo's face turned pale, and he stepped back from his father.

"Maybe some fresh air." Emily took Theo by the hand and led him outside.

"I...I have never seen my father look so still, like he was dead," Theo said softly.

"He is going to be fine. It was only the poison. He will recover," Emily reassured him.

"He would not let me or Tristan ride with him into battle. Tristan was furious. I felt relieved, but I am not a coward. I am going to be a knight."

Emily squeezed Theo's hand in hers. "I know you will. You will be a great knight."

"There you are," Draven said as he joined the couple. "Did you see the battle, Emm? It was glorious."

Emily took a closer look at the Bull. His doublet was splattered with blood, as were the leggings he wore. He still had red droplets dotting his neck and face.

"Draven, are you hurt? The blood on you—"

"Some poor foot soldier from Kingstown. He met the end of my sword. Or maybe it was the pikeman I slammed into on the charge up the hill. I was right beside Sir Lennon when we broke through their lines. You will love it when you get into your first battle, Theo. Your sword slips in easily if you find the right spot. I was nervous at first, but you forget about everything else, and it's you and the man in front of you. It's either you die or he dies. It was the best thing I have ever experienced. I cannot wait till we storm the capital and cut down Lord Russ."

Theo stared at Draven blankly, like he was not hearing him. Draven's face flushed with passion as he spoke excitedly about how he had killed four men in the battle and helped Sir Lennon capture one of the knights that led the enemy forces.

Sir Tristan emerged from the tent and headed to their horses.

"Theo, let's go to the castle. Prince James will be passing judgment, and Tidehaven needs to be present."

Theo turned back to Emily.

"I will be back to visit my father. Thank you."

Theo gave Emily a small kiss and squeezed her hand before he let it go, leaving her at the healer's tent.

23

THE PRINCE IV

The sun was at its height as all the knights, soldiers, and villagers crowded into the courtyard of the castle at Pebble Creek. Benches were brought out for the lords to sit on. Lord Pontifer's own chair was brought out for Prince James to preside over the judgments.

James sat uneasily, surrounded by the standing presence of his mother and Lord Pontifer to each side of him. They pressed in on him like the silver circlet of a crown he wore about his head. Lord Fowler sat on a bench to his right with his household knights behind him. To his left sat Sir Tristan Harroldson, representing his father and Tidehaven. The presence of his childhood friend gave James courage.

I know what I must do. I have been ignored and talked over. This court will be different. I will show them I can be king.

Four knights of Kingstown with their hands bound together were brought before James, led by Sir Lennon of Tidehaven. The knights were older men and had the hammer sigil of House Tolar engraved on their armor, signifying them as members of the King's Army.

"My Prince, I bring before you these four traitors, commanders of the rebels," Sir Lennon said.

"Only four knights, Sir Lennon? Surely there were more sent against us than four elderly knights," Lady Tolar inquired before James could speak.

"Yes, My Lady, three were killed in the woods protecting the trebuchet by Sir Woods and the men of Buckton. Three more were struck down by Sir Crowe," Sir Lennon said with disdain in his voice.

James scanned the crowd of knights and spotted Sir Cley Woods standing behind his liege, Lord Buckhorn. There were other knights at court as well, but none dressed in the black that James had seen Sir Crowe wearing in battle.

"These knights are prisoners of Pebble Creek. I will hold them here and ransom them back to their families," Lord Pontifer proclaimed.

"The knights of Tidehaven fought in the battle, Lord Pontifer. Tidehaven should get the ransoms," Lady Tolar argued over the prince's head.

There was a brief pause as the court awaited judgment. James raised his hand to silence his mother and Lord Pontifer before they could continue their bickering. He sat up straight in his chair.

"I will hear these knights of the King's Army speak first."

"My Lord, we were only following orders from the commander general," began one of the captive knights. "We were ordered to attack the castle at Pebble Creek. We were told that Lord Pontifer had taken you captive and had you executed."

"You will address your future king as 'My Prince,' Sir Knight," Lady Tolar corrected from behind James.

James raised his hand again to silence his mother.

"He tells it true, My Prince," another captive knight spoke. "We were ordered to raze the castle and to bring Lord Pontifer and his son to the capital for judgment by King...by Lord Russ."

"These men lie. It is plain they are making up this story," one of James's new councilors said, one of his mother's cronies.

James sat in silence for a moment.

"These men are traitors, and as such—" James's mother began.

"As you can see," James interrupted his mother, "I am not dead, nor am I being held prisoner here by Lord Pontifer. I sit in his chair, and he stands to serve me. If you men swear allegiance to me as your future king, you will be ransomed back to your families. When I take my rightful throne as king, I will restore you to your ranks in the King's Army. Those ransoms shall be given to the knights whom you yielded to on the battlefield."

Lady Tolar leaned forward to argue with her son.

"I have spoken."

"My Prince, what of the common soldiers whom we led?" another of the prisoners asked. "They believed they were fighting for your vengeance."

"They will swear a similar oath to me and be allowed to march with us in our ranks to Crosstimbers and on to the capital."

"But, My Prince, who will repair my walls?" Lord Pontifer protested. "It is common for prisoners to be used to repair the damage they inflicted."

"You shall repair your own walls, Lord Pontifer. The prisoners will only be a burden on you, but they will be a welcome addition to my army. I have decided we will leave here in three days. We cannot sit here in Pebble Creek while Lord Russ takes hold of the kingdom."

The knights were unbound, and each took a knee before James, swearing their oaths of loyalty. James could not help but notice that the normally placid Lord Fowler had an amused look on his face as the judgments were made despite the objections of his mother and Lord Pontifer.

Next, a soldier brought a priest of the temple dressed in a shabby robe before James. The bald priest looked as if he could use a shave and a meal.

"My Prince, this man claims to be a priest of the temple. He was seized by the militia trying to escape."

The man in the temple robes rushed forward and fell to his knees at James's feet. The quick motion caused one of the knights near him to grab the hilt of his sword and step forward to protect the prince. James turned to see that it was Sir Cley who had responded so quickly. The other knights at court had barely moved.

"My Prince, I assure you that I too believed the story told to us by Lord Russ," the priest began. "The temple plays no part in the ruling of Terros. We are simply servants of the Four, and of course servants of the Crown. I was traveling alone to the west when I joined the detachment sent from Kingstown. I wanted to see for myself if it were true that you had been murdered here."

"He is a priest of the temple. The poor state of his robes marks him as a traveling priest, My Prince," one of the councilors spoke. "It is ill luck to punish a member of the temple."

"You may go, but you will do me a service," James began. "You will preach to every town and village you go to that I am alive, that Lord Russ has spread lies to take the throne, and that I am the true king of Terros."

"Yes...yes, My Prince. I will spread the word, but if it pleases you, may I travel with your host back to Kingstown? I will tell all we encounter of your wisdom and mercy here this day."

"Where you travel is your own business. I will not hinder you."

The priest stood and bowed again to James before being led away.

"Are there any other petitions to bring before the future king?" Lady Tolar said in a raised voice like she had overseen the entire proceeding.

"Yes, we have one."

A young woman stepped through the knights and men who stood at the back of the courtyard. Holding on to her arm for support was an old woman who could barely walk on her own.

The young woman slowly led the elderly woman until they stood before James. The younger woman performed a graceful curtsy.

"My Prince, I would curtsy if it were not for my frail body," the old woman said with a smile, revealing she had few of her teeth left. "I am Maggy the healer, a loyal servant from Buckton, and this is my assistant, Alyss."

Lord Buckhorn stood and walked over to Maggy and Alyss. "It's true, My Prince. These women are of my fief."

"How can I help you?" James asked.

"The injured men we treated today—lords, noblemen, knights, soldiers, and even common village folk—were afflicted with a poison called Widow's Root. When smeared on a blade or arrowhead, it is deadly with just a minor cut or scratch," Maggy explained.

James turned in a fury to the knights he had pardoned.

"What of this? You claim to be knights of the King's Army, yet you used poison on your blades!"

"My Prince, I swear to you our blades were not tainted," one of the pardoned knights spoke up. "We fought honorably as did the pikemen and foot soldiers under our command. I do not know of this poison this old woman accuses us of using."

"What of the archers in your ranks?" James asked. "Are there no survivors? Bring them forward to answer for this."

"I saw no archers coming from the forest with the other prisoners, My Prince," one of the other pardoned knights said. "Sir Green oversaw the archers. There were only twenty of them. Green was brought down by the Sorrow."

"Not one archer survived or was taken prisoner?" James turned his head with a look of disappointment back to the two women before him. He took a deep breath before continuing.

"It looks as if I will not find any answers from them. How may I help you?"

"My Prince, we need more ingredients for the antidote to Widow's Root. We used what we had on the men whom we could save. But twenty-two men have fallen victim to this poison," Alyss stated sadly.

"We need to find you more of the ingredients. I will pay any expense for what you need," James offered.

"The cost will not be in coins or gold, My Prince," Maggy said. "What we need is free for the taking—the nectar from a plant known as the demon's pitcher. It is plentiful enough in the swampy areas in Shadow Woods to the north."

"We will send as many people as we can to gather this plant," Lady Tolar said, forcing herself into the decision-making.

"My Lady, only someone trained to extract the juice can gather it. A large party will only trample the plant. My assistant, Alyss, and my apprentice shall go, but they will need an escort for protection."

Sir Tristan jumped up before anyone could speak and took a knee in front of James.

"My Prince, send me. The healer used this elixir she

speaks of to save my father and many of the men of Tidehaven. Put me in charge of this escort. I owe it to these women to help."

James surveyed the court to see if there were any objections. Lord Buckhorn opened his mouth as if he were about to say something, but James noticed the old woman placing her hand on his arm as he was raising it. Buckhorn stood in silence.

"Very well, Sir Tristan, you will form a small party to escort these women to find this plant," James decided.

"My Prince," Maggy said, "this party will need a guide, someone who knows these woods and knows where to find the swampy areas where the plant grows. I believe Sir Cley should serve."

"I agree with Maggy, My Prince," Lord Buckhorn added. "The swamps are in the northern parts of Shadow Woods. No one knows that area better than Sir Cley."

James thought for a moment.

Yes, send Sir Cley away from camp, away from Rebecca.

"It is settled. Sir Cley will join the party as a guide," James pronounced. "Tris...Sir Tristan, you can pick whomever you need to fill out your party, but you need to move fast, as I remind you that I plan to leave for Crosstimbers in three days."

"We will depart before sundown today," Sir Tristan replied as he bowed before him.

"This judgment is concluded." James stood and walked back toward the castle. The lords and knights present bowed or took knees as he walked past them. James was not sure where he was going, but he certainly could not turn around to see if anyone was following.

I will be king. They will all follow.

24

THE GUIDE I

"**I** think we should be able to ride a few more miles before darkness overtakes us," Sir Tristan Harroldson announced, breaking the quiet that hung over the gloomy forest.

"I believe you are correct, My Lord," replied Sir Lennon Wooten after no one else in the party responded. "A few more miles will get us closer to our goal and closer to getting back to Pebble Creek. What say you, Sir Cley?"

Cley rode upon his horse, mulling over how he had been snared into this little adventure.

Maggy.

The old healer had recommended him as guide. Lord Buckhorn added his own endorsement. It had not been more than a few days ago that old Buckhorn said his place was with the future king.

Maggy.

She insisted his squire should make the trip also, leaving his own camp unattended.

Sir Tristan rode up alongside Cley.

"What do you think, Sir Cley?"

"We need to be looking for a suitable site to set up camp

before the light fails us," Cley answered. "Darkness comes suddenly in these woods. It would be better to set up camp and tie up the horses while we can still see."

For the past mile or so, Cley had been scanning the forest for an area where they could make camp—a small hill or outcropping of rock that the party could put their backs against and risk a small campfire.

"We need to get farther into the woods, I think. We can use our lanterns and torches to set up camp," Sir Tristan said.

It sounded more like a command than a suggestion to Sir Cley. From the start, Sir Tristan showed his eagerness to assume command. At eighteen, Cley knew he had little experience outside of Tidehaven. This very morning, his own father ordered him to remain in camp during the battle at Pebble Creek. At tournaments, Sir Tristan never made much of an impression. He was never a champion, but the son of a great lord was put in command of this expedition by his friend, the future king. Cley knew his duty was to see their goal was accomplished and that no one got hurt.

Cley had to hold in the urge to laugh when he and Jory arrived at Maiden's Bridge to meet with Sir Tristan and the others. Alyss and the girl, Emily, dressed and packed sensibly. Light riding pants, dark hooded cloaks, walking boots, and bedrolls were all they brought besides the shoulder bags to carry the vials needed for the juice from the plant they sought. Sir Tristan and Sir Lennon, on the other hand, dressed as if they were off to war in full armor and mounted on heavy chargers. They brought pack mules carrying tents, lances, and spare arms. Tristan even had his younger brother, Theo, along as his squire bearing the Tidehaven banner.

"I don't think the banner will be necessary, Sir Tristan," Cley said upon seeing Sir Tristan and Sir Lennon ride up with their two squires. "The squirrels and deer will be plenty impressed with your fine armor."

"We need to be prepared for anything, Sir Woods," Sir Tristan shot back. "An unprepared knight is a foolish knight."

Sir Lennon nodded in agreement with Sir Tristan.

"That is true enough, but a knight also needs to know what he is preparing for. All your gear is going to slow us down. The name of the game here is speed and stealth. Get these women to the plants they need and get back here as quickly as we can without being seen."

With the heir to Tidehaven persuaded to leave the pack mules and banner behind, the party set out from Pebble Creek, crossing Maiden's Bridge into Shadow Woods. There were many paths that crisscrossed the woods—trails made by villagers foraging for firewood and game trails left by animals and those hunting them. Cley led the group from the front, deftly picking trails that led to the northeast where Shadow Swamp waited. There they would find the plant called the demon's pitcher.

Sir Tristan followed behind Cley with Theo alongside him. Alyss and Emily rode next in line, followed by Jory and Sir Lennon's squire, Draven. Sir Lennon brought up the rear.

The party set off a few hours before sunset in high spirits as if on some grand adventure. Cley listened to Theo and Tristan talk to Alyss and Emily as they rode. Theo and Emily spoke to each other as if they were already well acquainted. Cley suppressed a chuckle as he listened to Tristan talk about Tidehaven and his father as if that would impress Alyss.

As the party traveled, sinking deeper into the woods, the trees grew closer, taller, and thicker. Some were ancient looking. The trails now appeared as if no human had tread upon them. The shadows lengthened, and a dark gloominess engulfed the woods. The air grew stale, and the scent of decay crept in amongst the party. Travel became slower as gnarled roots reached up and tripped the horses. In some areas, the undergrowth was damp and sucked at the horses' hooves as they walked. The heavy chargers of Sir Tristan and Sir Lennon struggled the most.

"The sun is setting. We need to find a camping spot now. We are still heading northeast, and the sun is going down behind us," Cley said, turning to Tristan.

"I know our direction. Anyone can know that by looking at the moss growing on the trees," Tristan replied curtly. "Tell me something I don't know."

"Jory...tell the future lord of Tidehaven something he doesn't know," Cley said, raising his voice.

Sir Tristan checked behind him to where Cley's squire had been riding, but the boy was not there. He turned back to Cley and opened his mouth to say something when the young squire stepped out of the woods ahead of them on the trail, leading his horse on foot.

"We're being followed," Jory said.

A dark figure on foot was all Jory could tell him. The boy tried to get a better look, but he said every time he stopped, the hooded figure stopped too. Whoever it was, they were moving quickly. Of course, it was not difficult to keep up. The heavy chargers that Tristan and Sir Lennon insisted on riding brought the party to a snail's pace in the denser woods, as Cley predicted.

Flat amongst the leaves, Cley had his dagger already unsheathed. Across the path, behind a tree, Sir Tristan hid as best he could. Up in a tree down the path, Jory waited with his bow already nocked with an arrow. Sir Lennon led the others down the trail as it wrapped around a small hill. Cley did not even think of suggesting that Tristan should go ahead with the others. He did not want that argument. It was already bad enough that the group stopped. Whoever or whatever was following them would be suspicious of the party stopping for no reason.

The faint sound of footsteps coming down the path was the first indication that there was in fact someone or something following them. Whatever it was halted to check the trail. The heavy hoofprints of the two war horses left no doubt that the party had passed this way.

Cley spotted a shadowy figure on the trail at the top of a rise—someone, not something. Cley relaxed. Legends spoke of monsters and other strange creatures that lived deep in Shadow Woods.

A human. I can deal with a human.

As their pursuer got closer, Cley could see it was not a large person. He or she was slender, about the height of an average woman. Their stalker wore soft leather boots that were tied up with leather straps. A dark-gray cloak wrapped around the figure with a hood pulled up over its head. Cley could not see if the stalker carried a sword, but there was a small bow with a quiver of arrows.

The stalker slowed down in between Cley and Sir Tristan's hiding spots. Cley held his breath, waiting for the hooded figure to turn away from him. The stalker drew out a dagger and turned toward the tree where Sir Tristan hid, taking a step forward. Cley sprang from his hiding spot under the leaves and tackled the stalker to the ground from behind.

The stalker was light. Cley heard a soft grunt like a boy's

as they tumbled to the ground. Cley pinned the stalker's hand above him on the ground and took away his dagger.

"Let me go!" the stalker exclaimed. "I was trying to catch up to you."

Cley rolled their follower over, pulling its hood back. He could see that indeed it was a boy who had been stalking them. His blond hair at the top of his shaved head was tied into a knot in the back. The boy's face and hands were covered in grayish-green mud to keep them hidden.

"Who are you, and why are you following us?" Cley asked.

Sir Tristan stepped out from his hiding spot and walked to where Cley had the boy pinned to the ground, straddling him.

"Yes, why are you following us?" Tristan demanded, pointing his sword at the boy's neck.

The boy's eyes grew defiant. He closed his mouth, tightening his lips as if he were about to be beaten. Cley brushed Tristan's sword away.

"There is no need for that, I think," Cley said to Tristan before readdressing their intruder. "Why were you following us?"

The boy's eyes left Sir Tristan and went back to the knight pinning him to the ground.

"I was only following you. I wanted to help go on an adventure," the boy said.

Cley picked up the curved dagger next to the boy's hand.

"What's your name? And where did you get a dagger like this? This is not the knife of some village boy."

"It's mine. I traded for it for some work I did."

"What's your name, sneak?" Sir Tristan demanded again, pointing his sword back at the boy's cheek.

"It's Aiden," Jory answered.

• • •

They caught up with the rest of the party as Sir Lennon had made little progress leading the others. Cley suggested they make camp next to a small hollow between two hills. The dense trees would shelter them from any rain, and the hills would block any wind coming from the north.

Cley noticed Jory had an extra hop in his step now that Aiden was with the party. The two boys walked together along the path, leading Jory's horse. Sir Tristan was rather put out by the fact that the boy joined them, while Cley kept pondering how Aiden had left his knight to join them.

"Jory and Aiden, come with me so we can gather some firewood," Cley ordered. "Bring your bows in case we see a rabbit or a squirrel."

The two boys ran to fetch their bows and quivers. They followed Cley up the slope, fanning out to Cley's left and right to find wood that might be drier than the damp wood that littered the hollow.

When they were away from camp, Cley stopped and sat down on a large rock at the top of the hill. He motioned for the two boys to come to him.

"Aiden, tell me again, you left the knight you serve to join us? You know you will be punished when we get back to camp. Who is this knight?"

Aiden lowered his head.

"I am not truly a squire, Sir. I am in service to no one."

"But you were in the Squires' Melee with me," Jory said, confused.

"Where are you from, Aiden?" Cley continued. "You are certainly not from Pebble Creek."

"I grew up in a village west of Riverdale. I heard there

was going to be a tournament for the new king and queen, so I tagged along with some knights who traveled to Pebble Creek, but I wasn't squire to any of them."

"Who taught you to fight with the sword? You were quite skilled in the ring, if I remember right," Cley inquired.

"My father taught me some things. He fought in the last war. But he and my mother died of the Sickness. I didn't have anyone else. I hoped that maybe a knight would take notice of me and take me on as their squire."

"I cannot send you back, so you can stay with us for now, but stay close and obey my orders," Cley said.

"Yes, Sir," Aiden replied with a hint of a smile.

The party was in good spirits that evening. The boys caught three hares in the woods, and everyone enjoyed the roasted meat that Cley and Alyss put together along with the bread they had packed. Following the small dinner, the party sat close around the fire. Alyss was the first to tell a story after Emily hounded her. It was the story of the third moon. Alyss told it well, but on a moonless night the story lacked its importance. Sir Tristan told the old story of how King George the First cleansed the forest of the Skriatoc, a race of evil manlike monsters that roamed Terros in ancient days. They were driven off the land, retreating into the mountains and woods. Only King George's bravery and magic hammer could put an end to them. The younger members of the party listened as Tristan described the decisive battle between King George and the Skriatoc chief.

"It's your turn. Let us have a story, Sir Cley," Sir Lennon said as he leaned back against his saddle. "I am sure with all your travels you have heard plenty of tales."

"Yes, tell us about the Pirate King's Rebellion, Sir Cley," Draven added excitedly. "You were there. Tell us about the Battle of Falling Stone. How many men did you kill?"

Cley looked into the fire. The flames danced around the branches the boys had gathered. Cley's mind drifted as he thought about Falling Stone. His chest tightened, and the trees closed in on him like walls. He could still smell the flames that chased after him in the tunnel. Sir Jonah's voice echoed in his ears: "Run, boy. Run. Get out while you can." The voice gave way to screaming and shouting. Outside the tunnel, there were men moaning, trapped under rock and stone. Women and children were screaming and crying. A small child's lifeless arm stuck out from under the rubble, and a woman in a tattered dress tried to lift the stones off the child. "Help me...Sir Knight, help me..." she begged as Cley staggered past her and her dead child.

"Well, Sir Cley? Do you have a story or not?" Sir Tristan asked.

Cley blinked, shaking himself out of the nightmare that haunted him. He stared at Tristan blankly, then he turned his head toward Alyss and met her gaze.

"No...I do not have a story."

"I think I remember one," Sir Lennon announced. "A legend of this place, Shadow Woods. In the days when there were dragons, these woods were infested with giant fire rats. They could breathe fire and had the strength of twenty men. If a man were brave enough and could slay one of these fearsome creatures, he could make a fortune in gold. But if he were to capture it alive, the beast would grant him a wish. This story involves a young farm boy who wanted to make his mark in the world..."

Sir Lennon's voice drifted into the background. The boys and the apprentice girl, Emily, intently listened to the older knight as he weaved his story. The flames from the campfire died down, and the air became cold and damp.

"We should set a watch," Cley announced when the story was over. The hero had lived happily ever after with his fair maiden. "I will take the first watch. Sir Lennon, I will wake you when it is your turn. We need to be up before first light to be on our way. The swamps are still over a day's travel."

Cley stood and walked into the darkness.

25
JORY IX

"Boy... You there, wake up."

The rough hand shook Jory's shoulder again. He began to ball himself up at the feel of the man's rough hand. Waking from his sleep, he recognized it was Sir Lennon.

"Cley told me to wake you. You have the third watch. Cley said to wake him for the next watch. Don't fall back to sleep," the older knight instructed. "Do you understand what I am telling you, boy?"

Jory sat up and nodded. The knight from Tidehaven walked over to where he had made his sleeping area. Jory stood and shook his arms and legs, trying to work out the stiffness in his limbs. Despite being fully clothed, as Sir Cley taught him when they traveled, the damp coldness of the woods hung on him. Next to him, Aiden slept curled into a ball under the blanket they shared together. Jory straightened the blanket and laid it over his friend.

My friend.

Jory walked toward the edge of camp thinking about this. He had not had a true friend since he left Seadrift. It was always him and Sir Cley traveling together. Occasionally, they traveled in company with a few of Cley's knight companions on their way to this tournament or that festival, but never for long. Cley insisted it was to protect Jory. "People ask questions. People talk about things that are none of their concern," Sir Cley had said.

Maybe Aiden is my friend.

Jory was happy Aiden was there with them now. Theo and Emily rode next to each other and talked when they first set out, leaving Jory out of the conversation. All Draven wanted to talk about were the men he killed at Pebble Creek and how he couldn't wait for the next battle. Aiden smiled at Jory and clapped him on the shoulder when Sir Cley had let him up off the ground. They were inseparable after that. They had tied the horses up, gathered wood, and hunted those hares together. When it was time to sleep, Aiden had picked a spot next to him. Having Aiden around made Jory feel like he was important and gave him confidence.

Maybe that is what a friend does.

The sound of footsteps, steady and light, broke the quiet night. Jory heard them coming from in front of him. He pulled his dagger from under his cloak and stepped behind a tree. The footsteps grew closer then stopped.

"Jory…"

The sound of Sir Cley's voice allowed Jory to exhale. He stepped from behind the tree and saw Sir Cley standing before him.

"I thought you were asleep," Jory said.

"I think we are not the only ones in the woods tonight," Sir Cley said in a whisper. "I saw fires in the distance from on top of the hill."

"Maybe they are hunters or those fire rats Sir Lennon told us about."

"Possibly, but the rats are old tales, and hunters would not be this far into the woods." Sir Cley sat down on the ground, leaning against a giant oak, and motioned for Jory to sit with him. "Jory, you remember our safe place, right?"

Jory nodded. "Yes, Sir."

"If anything should happen, or if we get separated, head north to the edge of the woods and then west until you get there."

The tone in Sir Cley's voice told Jory this was important. He nodded again.

"We are going to have to get the others up soon. We can lead the horses in the dark until we get some better light. I want to get away from this place." Sir Cley stared into the darkness of the woods. "I am sorry about what I did in the tournament, Jory. I promise not to fall on purpose from now on. Your father...Sir Jonah was a great knight and was an even better man. He loved you and your mother and sister. He was like my father, and I loved him. I wish every day that he was still with us. A lot of things might be different if..."

"Were all the tournaments fake?" Jory asked, thinking back to all the victories.

"Not that I know of. I only fell one other time on purpose. That was at the joust in Fynotans, but that was out of necessity. We might not have made it out alive if I had won."

Sir Cley still had his hood pulled up over his head, yet his face appeared as Jory had never seen it. It looked older and sad.

"You are a good boy, Jory," Sir Cley went on. "Someday, you will be a good knight, if that is what you want. But it is better to be a good man. There is more to being a knight than winning tournaments or fighting in battles. It is about helping people, being courageous, and being honest."

"When you went into the forest at Pebble Creek, did you have to kill anyone?" Jory asked.

"Yes," Sir Cley replied, tired.

"How many…I mean, did you have to kill a lot of soldiers?"

"Yes, I don't like doing it. I prefer to be a tournament knight, but sometimes a knight is called to do his duty for his lord and his king. Killing another man is horrible, even if that man is attacking you. To know I am ending the life of a person who might be a father, husband, or son is something that haunts me. Your father didn't care for battle either. He always said it was better to talk than to fight. Your father could settle disputes between rival lords without spilling a drop of blood. Some knights enjoy the killing. They love battle and blood. Your friend, Sir Lennon's squire, I think he will be one of those."

"Draven is not my friend," Jory said quietly.

"But Aiden…he's your friend, right?"

"I think so."

"It is important to have friends, Jory. I know some of my friends appear to be sots and loafers. But they are good men and would be there for me if I ever needed help. Surround yourself with good people. Their friendship will support you when times are hard."

Jory thought about this. He pictured Sir Torrent and the other knights with whom Sir Cley would often talk. They were good men, and they were always happy to see Sir Cley when they arrived at a tournament.

Jory watched Sir Cley as he sighed deeply and stared up into the trees. He followed Sir Cley's gaze and thought he could see that the sky was not as dark as before.

"Let's get the others up. I am ready to be away from this place."

It was the second time Sir Cley said he wanted to be away from there, and Jory began to feel like he wanted to get moving too.

The going was slow that morning. Leading the horses on foot in the darkness, the party picked their way around fallen branches and stones that littered the forest floor. It was as if the roots from the trees wanted to slow them down. Sir Cley risked holding a torch for the others to follow while the woods were still dark. Jory slid to the end of the line like he had the day before, but this time Aiden kept him company. Sir Lennon nodded to the two boys as he passed them in line.

He took no notice of me when I disappeared into the forest the day before.

"Sir Cley thinks there might be someone else in the woods," Jory said to Aiden when Sir Lennon was far enough ahead not to hear. "He said he saw fires way off."

Aiden scanned around them.

"It's probably hunters camping in the woods."

"That's what I said. Or maybe those fire rats."

"If I found one of those fire rats, I would capture it and make a wish," Aiden said.

"What would you wish for?"

"That's a secret. If you tell someone your wish, it will never come true. But mine will...someday."

Jory thought about what he would wish for. Gold, a grand castle, to be a lord—those things were silly. He would never be a lord or live in some fancy castle. He could wish to be a knight, but he knew he would be one someday anyway and didn't need to waste a wish on that. He could wish his father were still alive. He tried to picture him. It had been almost six years since his father left for war. It saddened him that his memories of him were fading. What else would he forget? He pictured his mother and sister. Playing games and running on the beaches with his friends from Seadrift. Then Jory pictured that man, Sir Raymond Wells.

I know what I would wish for.

26
THE GUIDE II

Sir Cley's eyes tried to pierce through the tree canopy that formed the ceiling above the party. It had to be midmorning by now, but the woods were dark and dreary. The trees pushed up against the game trail they were following. It was like walking in a cave. The smaller trees were bare and struggling to survive on the forest floor as the older, taller trees hoarded all the sunlight for themselves.

Ahead of the party, a rocky hill pushed up through the trees into the sky. Cley decided to climb it to look around. Sir Tristan insisted on coming with him.

The hill turned out to be an outcropping of rock, a giant stone finger sticking out from the dense woods. When Cley reached the top, the air smelled clean, and he could see miles in any direction. The only thing to see, however, were the tops of trees. Dense clouds concealed the sun. A fine mist coming down from the sky covered Cley's face.

"There...that's where we are headed." Cley pointed to a sunken area in the woods. The canopy of trees there was a dark-green color, almost black.

"That is the only place this plant can be found?" Sir Tristan asked.

"Demon's pitcher grows in swamps and some wetlands. So here we are. At least we know we are headed in the right direction. I have not gotten us lost in these woods."

"Not yet anyway."

The voice came from behind them. It was Alyss.

"I was hoping to see a little sunshine, but even the skies are dark above the trees."

"You should have stayed back with the others," Cley said. "You could have fallen climbing up here."

"You worry too much, Sir Cley," Alyss replied. "I needed to see the sky. The woods are so close and dark. And the smell... I didn't know the forest could have such a foul odor."

"What do you make of this, Sir Cley? You're an expert on these woods." Sir Tristan crouched over the edge, looking at something on the solid rock. "It looks like something or someone made giant cuts into the rock."

Cley crouched alongside Sir Tristan. Giant scratch marks covered the sides of the outcropping, and the other side of the rock had the same carvings as well. Cley recalled a book about dragons he had found in the small collection at Shadow Tower, which featured an illustration of a dragon sitting on top of a mountain with its claws dug deep into the rock. The book was old and rare and outlawed by the temple.

"Not sure what these marks could be," Cley said and straightened up. "Maybe the legends of dragons and giant fire rats are not so fanciful after all."

Sir Tristan rolled his eyes, stood, and started back down to the forest floor.

"After you, M'lady," Cley said to Alyss before he took another look over the sprawling woods.

If I were a dragon, this is exactly where I would sit, the king of all I see.

"Are you coming, Cley?" Alyss asked.

"Yes...it's time to fly."

The day did not get much brighter in the woods. Cley tried to find paths that were open, but in places where the branches grew close to the trails, the party was forced to dismount. The reek in the woods turned rotten like spoiled eggs. Cley guessed the odor meant they were getting closer to the swamps.

When they made camp that evening, the exhausted party was quiet. Cley found a clearing in the trees bordered by a small stream of water trickling along until it joined with a pool in the swamps. The stream would eventually meander south until it widened and deepened and turned into Pebble Creek.

"No fire tonight," Cley announced in a voice that suggested there should be no argument. "Jory and Aiden, find a patch of grass to tie the horses up, but not too far from camp."

The rest of the party went about setting up camp.

The easy banter that had brightened camp the night before was missing. When Jory came back from feeding the horses, he was quiet and sat away from the others as they ate their cold dinner of cheese and bread with salted beef.

The boy is brooding about something.

"Come on, Jory. How 'bout a rematch?" Aiden tossed a long stick at Jory and took a swordsman's stance in front of him.

Jory sat on the ground with his hood pulled up over his head.

Aiden poked Jory with his stick. "That's one strike for me already."

Jory stood and sulked off to sit under a tree near the small stream with his elbows on his knees.

"I'll take you on," Draven challenged.

Draven grabbed the stick on the ground and began to make several cuts and stabs at Aiden, who dodged and ducked the Bull's attempts. He poked Draven several times as he maneuvered around the plodding squire. Emily and Alyss watched, and Tristan and Theo called advice to Draven as he became frustrated. After he was disarmed a second time, Draven threw his stick to the ground.

"If this were a real fight with swords, you would be dead like the five men I gutted in the battle." Draven stormed off into the woods. Sir Lennon displayed little concern for his squire's attitude.

No stories were told as the party sat quietly after the stick duel. Tristan reclined against a fallen tree and yawned in boredom as he listened to Emily talk with Theo about how carefully the nectar of the demon's pitcher must be extracted from the plant.

"The plants grow individually, not in clusters," Emily instructed. "To make things more difficult, they do not grow near each other. They spread themselves out like lords in charge of their little fiefs in the swamp. They are small and hard to spot."

Theo looked to be completely enthralled by the girl, as if each word she said was music to his ears.

Draven sat sharpening his sword with a scowl on his face. Sir Lennon was already sleeping in anticipation of his turn at watch. Aiden sat next to Alyss, both listening to Emily. Jory was already asleep under the tree he picked away from everyone else.

"We should reach the swamps tomorrow. The earlier, the better. That means an early start like this morning. Get some sleep," Cley announced to everyone. "I will take first watch like before. Sir Lennon, I will wake you for your turn."

Sir Lennon rolled to his side in reply.

Cley tossed and turned after his watch was over. He kept thinking about what might be following them. Maybe it was his imagination, but he was certain there were three fires on different hilltops last night. But if someone were following them, they certainly would not make a fire on top of a hill and risk being spotted.

When Cley did manage to fall asleep, he dreamt he was a giant green dragon gliding over the forest. He soared into the clouds above and dove down toward the woods. The trees turned into soldiers, and he flew toward them. The soldiers dropped their weapons and ran from him. He thought he could see the walls of Kingstown in the distance. The wind raced under his wings, then a storm of arrows came from the walls of Kingstown. The arrows pierced his wings, and one struck him in the neck. Cley felt himself falling.

Cley awoke with a jolt just before he struck the ground. He found he had moved over a root from a tree that was jabbing him in the neck. Cley sat up from his bedroll and rubbed his neck with a grin. He surveyed the camp, noting the others were sleeping, though Jory was missing from the area where he and Aiden slept.

Must be third watch already.

Cley rose stiffly and went to check on the boy.

He found Jory sitting against a large elm tree. Cley sat across from the boy, but Jory made no movement or sound to greet him.

"Any noises or giant fire rats?" Cley asked.

"No," Jory answered in a sullen voice.

"Jory, what's wrong? Why are you in a foul mood? You have been upset since we made camp."

"It's n-nothing."

The stutter was gone last night when we talked alone, but now it's back.

"Come on, you can tell me, or else it will get worse. Did you and one of the boys have an argument? Did Aiden say something to you?"

"No."

Cley could see in the dark that the boy had pulled his hood up over his head so that his face was hidden from view.

"So, what? You are clearly upset about something. Did I do something again?"

"No."

Cley heard Jory sniff. It could have been caused by the cold dampness of the woods, but more likely it was the result of being upset. Cley moved over to sit next to the boy and leaned against his shoulder a little to let Jory know he was there for him.

"Did my mother tr-trade me for a horse?" Jory finally asked.

The question caught Cley off guard.

Where is this coming from?

"You know why you are with me. People hear stories and make up what they don't know. We have been over this."

"D-do you think my mother st-still loves me?"

"I know she does. Your sister too. They have not forgotten you." Cley glanced up into the darkness of the trees that loomed over them. "What happened today, Jory? Why the questions about your mother? Who was talking about it?"

"I heard them talking and saw her k-kissing him..."

"Your mother?"

"No...n-never mind."

"Who? Who was kissing whom?" Cley thought for a moment.

Not his mother. Alyss? Who would Alyss be kissing? Certainly not Tristan. And there was no chance of her kissing Sir Lennon Wooten. Why would Jory care if she kissed someone? Would I even care if I saw her kiss someone?

The answer came to him.

Theo and the girl, Emily. The boy likes her.

"I know it hurts," Cley said quietly, staring straight ahead into the blackness of the deep woods around them. "Do you like her? The girl?"

"Sh-she gave me a kiss when I gave her a rose. I thought sh-she liked me."

"That can happen. She was friendly to you. She helped wrap your shoulder after the melee. She likes you, but not the way you might want her to."

"But why Th-Theo? He's such a fool."

"They look to be about the same age, so he has that going for him. She probably doesn't see you as old enough for her. There will be lots of other girls your age."

"Wh-when I am around her, I feel different, like I forget about other things and only think about her."

"Women can do that," Cley said. He had figured Jory was still too young to start being interested in girls in that way. A distraction was what Jory needed.

"How did it go at the woods witch? We never talked about it," Cley said. "Did you get your fortune told?"

"No, Sir..." Jory swallowed. "What does 'omrau' mean?"

That made Cley sit up straight. He had not heard it spoken since his childhood in the North, and then only by old women and men.

"The witch called you that? *Omrau?*" Cley asked.

"No, she called A-Aiden that. It sounded like a curse. It made him mad, and he ran off."

"I have never heard it before. Some old word from across the Eastern Ocean. It probably means stinky or smelly," Cley said with as much cheer as he could. "It's going to be time to get the others up soon. You can go back to sleep if you want. I will finish your watch."

Jory did not get up to leave. Instead, he leaned against Cley's back and shoulder.

Cley thought about getting this mission over and getting out of these woods. Thoughts flowed in and out of his head as he stared into the darkness with his squire at his side. He envisioned Prince James entering Kingstown in triumph. He recalled winning the tournament at Amberfield last fall with the crowd cheering for him. He remembered teaching Jory how to hold a sword properly. Having his first kiss in the Broken Tower with the sun setting over the Western Ocean. He pictured Alyss kissing Sir Tristan and frowned. Cley remembered the surprised expressions on the faces of the three knights guarding the trebuchet at Pebble Creek. He looked at his hands resting on his knees, and they were covered in red. He squeezed his eyelids shut to drive out the image.

In the quiet darkness, Cley's thoughts turned to Aiden.

The *omrau.*

The *evil boy.*

27
THE PRINCE V

"It still puzzles me," Prince James said, turning to Lord Buckhorn. The yellow light of the second moon glowed above the men on horseback as they rode through camp.

"What is that, My Prince?" Lord Buckhorn asked.

"Why would Russ send such a small force against us? Surely, he had to know our numbers. And the men were older and entirely from Kingstown. Not one is from the East."

Lord Buckhorn rubbed his shaggy beard as he rode alongside the prince. Five knights of his household flanked them, along with the knight known as the White Owl, Sir Lucas Bardas. Lord Buckhorn insisted that Sir Lucas be at the prince's side from now on as his personal bodyguard. Buckhorn rode with the knight known as the Great Tor. The horse bearing the huge warrior sagged pitiably. Although surrounded by guards, James enjoyed his new freedom. With his mother confined to her chambers, feeling poorly since that afternoon at court, he was out of her reach.

"Don't you feel it is odd?" James asked.

"It does feel off, My Prince," Buckhorn offered. "What say the other lords?"

"They are concerned about other matters. Fowler thinks three days is too long to wait to move to Crosstimbers. Pontifer is only concerned about the minor damage done to his wall. They do not listen to me. Lord Storm is not even here to consult."

"It is good to think of these questions. It's a sign you are thoughtful. It will serve you well when you are king. The soldiers like you. Your prayers at the Temple of the Four last night endeared you to the people. You spoke well."

"I meant what I said. When I become king, I will help the maimed soldiers, widows, and orphans."

James glanced at the Lord of Buckton riding next to him. The old knight's armor and dress were plain, his hair and beard shaggy. The Buckhorns rarely attended festivals or ceremonies held at Tidehaven, but his respect for Lord Buckhorn grew as James learned that he had been a leader in the King's Army during the Defiance of Frostmark and the Pirate King's Rebellion. The men from Buckton were serious warriors. When Lord Buckton spoke, he was often gruff and plain-spoken, but he gave good advice.

The prince's entourage rode through the Tidehaven camp and up to the pavilion of Lord Harroldson.

"Harroldson is not happy that his sons went off into Shadow Woods in search of some flower," Lord Buckhorn said. "He will be a prickly host."

"But Tristan pleaded to go."

"He did. We all saw that. But Harroldson will not see it that way. He will act coldly. A warning, My Prince. Tidehaven is the key to your claim as king. If you have his support and the support of the West, you have a claim. We cannot be seen as divided by Lord Fowler or any of the Free Cities. Lord Harroldson needs to lead his army at your command."

Entering the tent, James was greeted by Lord Harroldson, who was seated in a chair behind a small table. He brought his eyes up from something he was writing and feigned to be surprised that James was in his tent, but James had been announced by one of the Tidehaven guards.

An actor.

"Lord Harroldson, it is good to see you sitting up and working," James said, trying to sound joyous.

I can act as well.

Lord Harroldson tried to stand. He pushed up on the arms of his chair and struggled to rise.

"My Prince..."

"Do not strain yourself, Sir. Please remain seated."

"My Prince, I am honored by your presence. I wish there were another chair to offer you."

James noted the lack of any other chairs in the large pavilion, though there were spaces around a table where there had obviously been chairs before. He assumed Lord Harroldson had them stacked up behind the pavilion.

An actor and a petty man.

"Lord Harroldson, it is not a problem for me to stand. I will not trouble you for long. I wanted to see you in person to confer with you on our plans."

"Yes, those plans... It is my understanding that you plan to leave Pebble Creek soon. Who will be your escort?"

"I was hoping your levies from Tidehaven would make up the bulk of my army, along with smaller units from Pebble Creek and some of the traveling knights and mercenaries."

"That is impossible with me recovering from this wound. Besides, my main force has yet to arrive. Who would lead this force you plan to go with?"

"Well, I would," James said uneasily.

"Lord Harroldson," Lord Buckhorn interrupted, "you spoke only two days ago of the urgency that we get to Crosstimbers to maintain an open road for our armies and the armies of the South. The skirmish here only proves that you were correct. Lord Russ is on the move."

"We soundly defeated him, Lord Buckhorn," Harroldson replied. "Things have changed. We need to wait for reinforcements."

"I disagree, Sir," James spoke confidently again. "To move now would show the rest of the kingdom that we are resolved and united. To wait might show others who have not declared their allegiance that we are weak and uncertain of my claim to the throne."

He noticed Lord Harroldson's polished armor hung on a mannequin nearby. His sword and shield were similarly displayed. The sigil of Lord Harroldson was everywhere. The white tower on fields of silver and blue was engraved or embroidered on everything.

The man is vain.

"Lord Harroldson, if you need to rest here for a longer period to recoup from your wounds, remain in Pebble Creek. No one in the kingdom would blame you. Once your main force from Tidehaven arrives, and you feel you can ride, you can catch up to us. We will wait for you at Crosstimbers after we have secured their allegiance."

Lord Harroldson remained silent. James could see the man was trying to think of his next step.

"What of my sons? They are somewhere out in Shadow Woods. We have no idea where they might be or when they will return."

"Lord Harroldson, we know they went to the swampy areas of the woods," Lord Buckhorn said. "Sir Woods is their guide. He said it would take three days to get there. Cley spent a year living at Shadow Tower. No one knows those woods better. They will rejoin us in Crosstimbers."

"Plus, one of your own knights, Sir Lennon, is in the party," James added. "They were well armed and well provisioned."

"Very well, we will leave the day after tomorrow," Harroldson said. "Do not trouble yourself with the planning, My Prince. I will oversee the organization and orders. It will not be said that a Harroldson licked his wounds while there was more fighting to be done."

James and Lord Buckhorn left the pavilion together, then Buckhorn clapped James on the back.

"Nicely played, My Prince. Nicely played."

28
EMILY VI

Emily bent over the beautiful demon's pitcher flower, concentrating as she gently tilted the plant to transfer the nectar into the small glass vial in her other hand. Theo stepped closer to her.

"Be careful where you step, Theo," Emily said.

"Give the girl some room, Theo. You're practically on top of her," Sir Tristan said and laughed.

"Shut up, Tris. At least I am trying to help and not sitting around like a bump on a log."

"Quit bothering the girl and let her do her job. If you are looking for something to do, fetch me an apple out of my pack, squire," Sir Tristan ordered as he reclined against a fallen tree.

"Get it yourself. You have legs," Theo shot back.

Emily held back a giggle, listening to the brothers bickering back and forth, then refocused on the task before her. The thick red liquid slowly poured from the flower.

Emily noted the others trying to look occupied. Sir Lennon posted himself at one end of the path picking dirt from his nails with a dagger. Draven sat at the opposite end of the path sharpening the blade of his sword. Jory stood at the edge of the clearing they were in, carving a mark into a tree with his knife.

The decision to split the party when they reached the swamp late on the third morning was obvious. It would take days to gather enough nectar from the plant if they stayed in one group, and the likelihood of trampling the demon's pitcher was high if they remained together. Sir Cley, Alyss, and Aiden took the path that headed east, while Emily and the others headed northeast. They were to work until twilight before heading back to camp where they left their horses and packs.

"Can I help hold the vial?" Theo asked, kneeling next to Emily. "Maybe that would speed things up."

"Thank you, but no..." Emily replied. "The poison would burn through your gloves if it were to touch them. You would lose your hand for sure."

Theo pulled his hands back away from the plant, smiling uneasily.

"Oh, I guess I will keep watch like the others."

As Theo stood up to walk away, an arrow whizzed over Emily's head and planted itself in an old willow tree. Four more arrows followed.

"There...the arrows came from there," called Tristan.

"No, this direction over here," Sir Lennon answered, pointing in the opposite direction.

Emily ducked her head low and stopped up the vial she was filling.

Five men in dark-green clothes appeared from behind the trees in front of the party and ran forward with drawn swords.

Emily froze as the men got closer. Jory ran up next to her, grabbing her bag of vials from the ground. He took her by the hand and pulled her to her feet.

"Follow me," Jory said.

Sir Lennon drew his sword. "Behind me, children. Tristan, Draven, form a line."

Emily ran behind Sir Lennon to Theo as the men rushed forward. Draven, grinning with his sword drawn, pushed past Emily to line up next to Sir Lennon.

"Theo, come on! Come with us!" Emily yelled. She grabbed Theo's arm when he did not move and pulled him in the direction Jory was pulling her. But Theo pulled his arm away and drew his sword to stand next to his brother.

Another volley of arrows hissed through the air around Emily. She let go of Jory's hand and stopped, turning around. One of the arrows sank into Sir Lennon's arm. The knight cursed at the men. Four more men with swords ran out from behind the bushes. One of them chased after Jory into the woods. Cries like the howls of wolves came from the woods around them.

"All of you, run! Tristan, get them back to camp. I will slow them," Sir Lennon ordered.

More men came running at them from behind trees. Theo grabbed Emily by the arm and pulled her with him. A man came out from behind a tree and lunged at them. Theo swung his sword at the man who reached for Emily, putting a gash in his arm near the shoulder. Blood from the wound sprayed out over her cloak.

"Run!" Theo shouted.

Emily ran through the woods alone. She tried to find Jory, but he had vanished into the woods. Howls from the men continued, and howls in the distance answered back.

Emily stopped and hid behind a tree. Her heart pounded, and she tried to gather her breath. The clashing of swords rang in the woods until she heard it no more. Despite her fear, she crawled back to where she thought she had heard the fighting. She risked running from tree to tree, staying low until she rested beside an old oak tree. Men were talking, but she could not make out what they were saying.

Emily peeked from behind her hiding space and saw a large willow closer to the voices and a dark figure lying on the ground by it. It looked like Theo's cloak covered in leaves and mud. Emily held her breath. The figure moved slowly, like it was trying to peer over the gnarled roots of the tree. It had to be Theo. He was alive. Emily pushed herself up off the ground and ran as quietly as she could to the willow. Every twig and leaf she stepped on screamed her presence, but Theo did not turn. She slid onto the ground next to him. He gasped in surprise and gave her a weak smile. Emily held up a finger to her lips for silence.

"I am Sir Lennon Wooten. I surrender and yield myself for ransom," Sir Lennon announced, kneeling on the ground. A man tied his hands together behind his back, and another tied his feet. Next to Sir Lennon knelt Tristan, already bound. There were only ten men surrounding them.

I thought there had been twenty or thirty men. Where are Draven and Jory?

"The ropes are not necessary, as we are unarmed and have yielded to you. The rules of battle clearly—"

Sir Lennon was cut short as a large man in a black cloak stepped up to him and punched him in the mouth, knocking the knight to the ground. The man's face was wrapped in rags, his eyes dark and sunken.

"Your rules of battle will not serve you here, Sir Whatever," the man growled as he kicked Sir Lennon in the gut.

"I am Tristan Harroldson, son of Lord Harroldson of Tidehaven. My ransom will be high. You will all be rich men," Sir Tristan said in a panic.

"The son of Lord Harroldson, you say," the man in black replied.

"Yes, I am the heir to Tidehaven..."

The man in black walked up to Sir Tristan. He drew a cruel-looking dagger from his belt and plunged it into Tristan's chest near his heart. The dagger glowed a ghostly blue color when the man pulled it out. The blade absorbed Tristan's blood before it could drip to the ground.

"Now you are the heir to nothing."

Tristan's body collapsed to the forest floor, motionless. Theo gasped and moved to push himself up from the ground. Emily climbed on top of his back to hold him down and wrapped her hand around his mouth to keep him quiet.

Calm. Quiet.

She could feel the boy tensing, then shuddering in grief.

Snap!

A tree branch cracked somewhere behind them.

Footsteps of someone doing a poor job sneaking in the woods.

Emily looked to her left. Draven walked in between some bushes and tall grass trying to make his way to their willow tree. She wanted to hold her hand up to stop him from coming closer, but she feared Theo might make a noise.

Snap!

Another loud crack rang out in the forest from a branch under Draven's heavy boots.

"Over there, I see one of them." Another man in the group surrounding Sir Lennon and Tristan pointed his sword right at the big squire. Draven ran toward the willow tree, while Emily stood to run. Emily's eyes caught the notice of the man in black. Their eyes met, and a chill rolled through her. The men came running after them. One of the men in front suddenly dropped to the ground with an arrow lodged in his eye. The other men kept coming.

"Here! This way...quick!" Jory called from behind her.

He had his bow nocked with another arrow ready to shoot. Emily grabbed Theo by the arm and pulled the boy to his feet.

"Come on, Theo. We have to go," Emily pleaded and pulled on his hand.

Theo stood in a daze, tears streaming down his cheeks. His face had gone pale, and his hand was cold and clammy.

"Go, Theo!" Draven yelled as he finally reached them. He pushed Theo hard, and they all hurried in Jory's direction.

Jory let loose another arrow, and Emily thought she heard a man grunt and fall behind them. He let off yet another arrow, turned, and ran into the swampy woods off the trail. Emily and the others followed him. She did not dare turn to see how many men pursued.

Emily's legs screamed, and her lungs burned. She bled from several scratches on her cheeks and hands from trees that had thorns. She stopped running only when she heard Draven call out that he needed a rest.

"We have to keep moving," Jory implored quietly.

"Where are you leading us?" Draven asked, gasping for breath.

"Away from them," Jory whispered angrily.

Emily could hear the men calling to each other behind them.

Why are they chasing us?

Emily turned to Theo, who looked lost and was wheezing in pain. His face was a blank slate of disbelief, sweat, and blood. He said nothing as he sat on the ground.

The pursuers' shouts sounded like they were getting closer.

"You are getting us lost in these woods. We should circle back to Sir Lennon and the others," Draven ordered.

"The others may be gone," Jory said. "We are heading to a safe place I know."

"You would have us hide in these woods when the rest of our party might need our help. You're a coward." Draven's voice rose in anger.

"If Sir Cley needs help—"

A man with a pox-marked face burst through the bushes surrounding them. He pointed his sword at the four of them.

"Here they are!" he called out loudly. "And the girl is with them!"

Draven rushed at the man, brandishing his sword. The man deftly dodged Draven's swing and sliced at the boy with a knife he pulled from his belt. Draven lunged again, stumbling as the man delivered another cut. Draven fell to the ground.

The man turned around, but not soon enough to see that Theo was standing, his bright steel sword in hand. Theo's blade plunged into the man's belly. He fell to the ground holding his insides in his hands.

"Get up, Draven. Come help me, Jory," Theo ordered.

Jory and Theo got to each side of Draven and helped him to his feet. There was blood on his cloak, and it was soaking through his shirt.

The group of four headed away from the shouting voices behind them. They moved slower now, having to assist Draven. Emily replaced Jory on one side of Draven. She was taller, and Jory needed to lead the way. Emily and Theo held Draven up as best they could, but he was heavy. His footsteps were plodding, and he began to moan in discomfort.

"Please, we must stop. It hurts," Draven moaned.

Emily took a good look at Draven's face. It was growing pale, and sweat rolled from his brow.

After they made some distance, Jory found a small clearing surrounded by trees.

"Let's stop so I can tend to his wound," Emily suggested.

Theo agreed with her and stopped to lower Draven to the leaf-covered ground. Jory, turning to see that they had stopped, sighed.

"I have to tend to his wound or else he will bleed to death," Emily said as she pulled off Draven's cloak.

Draven's shirt was soaked red with blood and sweat. He had a large gash on his lower neck below the collar, and another cut on his upper arm below his shoulder. The wound on his neck was turning black. Dark tendrils like roots formed under his skin and branched up his throat toward his face.

"It hurts. Please make it stop." Draven grabbed Emily by the arm and squeezed in pain. "Please..."

The wound on his neck rotted before Emily's eyes.

"Theo, cut a strip of cloth from Draven's cloak. I will wrap the wound and try to stanch the blood flow."

Emily put her hand on the wound, putting pressure on it. Dark blood seeped between her fingers.

"Help me. Make it stop," the boy begged. Blood gurgled out of his mouth in bubbles as he spoke and gasped.

"Here, hurry," Theo said, handing Emily the cloth strip he cut from Draven's cloak.

Emily held the cloth to Draven's neck and wrapped it around the wound. She stopped and leaned back on her heels. The boy let go of her arm and stopped breathing. His skin turned cold and pale except where the black veins bulged. Draven appeared younger now, lying there silently like the boy he truly was.

Theo knelt next to Emily and took Draven's hand in his. Emily felt his sorrow and grief. Tears ran down his cheeks as he hung over his dead friend.

"We...we have to get moving again," Jory said from behind them.

"What? We can't leave him out here," Theo argued.

"And we cannot c-carry him out of here either," Jory answered. "We will remember this place and come back when we can for him and your—"

"Yes, we will come back," Emily interrupted. "There is no way we can carry him."

"But we should at least bury him, you know, to keep the animals away," Theo cried.

The shouting of the men drew closer.

"There's no time, Theo. Come on," Emily encouraged.

The three ran off into the woods, leaving Draven's body behind.

29
THE GUIDE III

"Be careful where you walk," Alyss ordered Cley. "You're going to step on the plant, but more likely it's going to be on something that either bites or stings."

Cley stopped in his tracks. Alyss bent down to look under a small shrub, then came up disappointed.

"You too, Aiden," Alyss said to the boy carrying her vials. "The swamp is full of adders and insects with enough poison to bring down a bull."

Aiden froze where he was standing. Alyss continued to look under the dense leaves. She had only collected five vials of its nectar, and it was getting close to dark.

Hopefully the apprentice girl will have more success. We need to head back to Pebble Creek tomorrow. Five vials and whatever Emily gathers will have to be enough.

"Aiden, tell me about that dagger on your belt," Cley said. "Where did you get one made like that?"

"I found it, Sir," Aiden replied as he watched where stepped.

"Found it? I should think the man who lost that would still be searching for it."

"Maybe it was a woman's," Alyss suggested.

Cley glanced at Alyss. He knew she had a dagger hidden in her right boot.

"I doubt a woman would know what to do with a dagger," Cley jested.

Alyss stood and turned toward Cley.

"Women know what to do—"

She suddenly collapsed to the ground with an arrow lodged in the back of her leg. Several more arrows hissed into the clearing, barely missing Cley. Alyss clutched her leg and writhed on the ground, an arrow tip protruding from her pants.

"Aiden, down!" Cley ordered, but the boy had already found refuge behind a large tree.

Cley made his way over to where Alyss was on the ground to look at her wound. There was a crashing in the bushes near them, and two men pushed themselves into the clearing brandishing short swords. Cley stood, drawing his sword as the two men charged him. He dodged the first man's strike, going low and tripping the man as he lunged at him. The second man tried to stab Cley with his short sword, but Cley's longer reach and sword made quick work of him. He turned back to the first man, who scrambled back to his feet. The man came at him again. This time, Cley's blade caught the man's blow. Cley stepped close to the man, pulling a dagger from his belt and stabbing the man with it.

Three more men stepped out of the bushes. They surrounded Cley, looking for an opening, but none wanted to make the first move and join the dead men on the ground. Cley panted and glanced down to check that Alyss was not harmed further. The attackers stood menacingly with swords drawn to each side of him.

Awwooooooo!

Distant howls came from the forest. Cley knew they were

not the calls of a wolf or dog. The three attackers turned and made a break for the woods in the direction of the howling.

Cley gave chase. He threw the dagger in his hand at the nearest man but missed his mark. The men disappeared deeper into the swamp as the howling got louder in the distance.

Cley ran back to where he left Alyss. Aiden was helping her by pulling the arrow out of her leg and wrapping it.

"Bandits out here in the swamp?" Alyss grimaced.

"Maybe," Cley answered. "We have to get you back to camp and find the others."

Cley carried Alyss back to their camp, while Aiden carried her bag and the rest of their gear. The horses were still at camp along with their supplies.

These were not thieves, or else they would have taken the horses and food.

Cley left Aiden to watch over Alyss at camp. He ran up the path the others had taken and found the notches on the tree trunks he taught Jory to make when hiking. Eventually he found a trail of heavy footprints on the soft forest floor. The trail led to a clearing in the woods and Sir Lennon.

Cley found Lennon injured and bound hand and foot, lying next to the dead body of Tristan Harroldson, the young man he was sworn to defend. As Cley cut Lennon free from his ropes, the knight began to sob as he spoke of what had happened and how the bandits chased the others farther into the woods.

Cley left Sir Lennon and headed into the woods in the direction Lennon said the men had gone.

The others are alive. I've got to find them.

Close to the clearing, Cley found two dead men shot through with arrows, and he bent over their bodies to examine them. The men wore clothing with no markings.

Nothing was found to identify who they were or where they were from. Cley checked the arrows sticking out of the corpses. The fletching was Jory's work.

Smaller foot tracks indicated the children had headed northwest.

Jory will head to Shadow Tower if he thinks he cannot make it back to camp.

Cley weighed his options. It was getting dark. Lennon needed aid with Tristan's body, and Alyss was wounded.

Cley stared into the darkening woods.

I will find you, Jory. Gods protect them.

He took a deep breath and headed back to camp.

30
EMILY VII

Darkness descended on the forest. Every step Emily took made her feet and legs hurt. She twisted her ankle on a tree root sticking out of the ground, but she got up and continued trying to keep up with the boys. Theo came back to help her.

She thought they had lost Jory, but when she limped out of the woods into a clearing, the full summer moon revealed him standing in front of a bog surrounded by tall grass and reeds. The bog stretched in front of them, blocking their way. They would be seen trying to cross it. Jory scanned the woods on the other side.

"Now what?" asked Theo.

"I...I don't know. We have to get to the other side. Maybe they will not spot us in the dark," Jory said.

Emily heard voices behind them in the woods shouting that they had picked up their trail again.

"It's too risky," Theo said, looking at Emily. "We will be sitting ducks out there."

"Look over there." Jory pointed across the bog. "I see a flame over there."

"I don't see anything," Emily said.

"Neither do I," Theo added. "It could be more men over there."

"It might be Sir Cley," Jory said hopefully.

Jory bolted and ran off through the tall grass in the direction he claimed to have seen a flame. Emily looked at Theo in complete exhaustion.

"Come on, Theo. We have to stay together."

Behind her, Emily heard a man crashing through the forest. She gritted her teeth and ran as fast as she could on her turned ankle. She was halfway across the bog when Theo halted in front of her. He turned with his sword drawn. Emily stopped. There were three men not far behind. An arrow landed near Theo.

"No, Theo, run!" Emily said breathlessly.

Emily lost sight of Jory but had an idea of where he had re-entered the woods on the other side. She and Theo ran for the edge of the woods, staying apart and weaving in and out of the tall grass.

Jory appeared at the edge of the woods on top of a small rise.

"Here, over here."

Emily and Theo reached the bottom of the earthen embankment. Theo scrambled up easily. It was only about five feet high, but to Emily it might as well have been a mountain. Her body ached, and her ankle throbbed. Theo and Jory helped pull her up and into the woods. The men were right behind them.

Jory led the way deeper into the woods. The trees in this area allowed pale moonlight to trickle to the forest floor. Theo held on to Emily around the waist, and she put her arm around his shoulders to support herself. They walked that way until they both stumbled over some tree roots and fell to the ground.

"Even in this moonlight, we still cannot see where we are going. We're never getting out of this," Theo complained.

Jory titled his head as if he were listening for something. He ran back toward the bog. Theo helped Emily sit up on the ground, then he rose and paced in front of her. Jory returned shortly and stood in front of Emily and Theo, catching his breath.

"I don't know what has happened, but I don't think we are being followed anymore," Jory said quietly. "I cannot hear them, and there is no sign of them behind us."

"Well, they snuck up easily enough on us in your swamp," Theo snapped at Jory.

"Where are we, Jory?" Emily asked.

"I'm not sure. I thought we were heading northwest. We should be close to Shadow Tower, but I don't remember that bog ever being there," Jory replied. "I thought I saw someone over here with a torch or flame."

"You stupid bay rat! You've gotten us lost in the woods," Theo barked. "We should have circled back around them like Draven said. We should have stayed together. But now Draven's gone, Tristan's gone, and everyone else too. No one knows we're here, and it's your fault!"

Theo's face twisted with anger, and he charged at Jory, punching him hard in the face. Jory dropped to the ground in a heap.

Emily struggled to stand up on her injured ankle. She pushed herself between Theo and Jory lying on the ground. "Shut up, Theo. Leave him alone. It's not his fault. He did his best. He probably saved us."

Emily watched the boys. Theo's gloved hands stretched and balled into fists over and over, his breathing coming in gasps. Jory sat up slowly, wrapping his arms around his knees. He pulled his hood over his head to hide his face.

"We need to keep moving, in any case. I can walk a bit without help. Running is out, but we cannot run in the dark anyway." She touched Theo on his shoulder and could feel the tension in his body. "Come on, Theo. We need to keep moving."

Theo relaxed his shoulders and stepped forward.

"Okay," he said, subdued.

Jory remained on the ground, holding his knees tight to his body and keeping his head down.

Emily limped over to Jory and knelt beside him with some effort.

"Come on, Jory. We need you to lead us out of these woods. We cannot stay here. Those men may come back."

Emily put her hand on Jory's shoulder. She could feel his hurt and anger.

"Please, Jory, we need to get moving again."

Jory stood slowly. In the dim light of the moon, Emily took a good look at the boy who had been leading them through the woods. He still carried her pack with the vials of precious nectar she collected slung over his shoulder. Only one arrow remained in his quiver. There were rips in his cloak and pants from where thorns and branches tore at him as he blazed the trail for the rest of them. There were dark spots on his clothes that were either blood or mud. Jory walked to a large oak, staying out of Theo's reach, and checked the bark.

"I-I think we have to go this way," Jory finally said.

"Okay, I'm right behind you. Theo, you're behind me."

Emily and the two boys walked in the woods in silence for the rest of the night. The sounds of birds and other animals announced the coming of the morning. Emily spotted squir-rels in the trees, as well as rabbits and deer on the ground. It had been so long since she had seen or heard birds, and the chirping and singing were a welcome break from the silence.

Jory stopped ahead of Emily, motioning for her and Theo to stop. He looked around as if he were listening to something. The woods seemed different. Over the ambient sounds came a voice talking, or maybe it was singing. It sounded like it was getting closer. Theo drew his sword, while Jory motioned for everyone to hide behind a tree.

As the voice grew closer, Emily could make out that it was a child's. No other voice replied. Theo grabbed Emily's wrist and pulled her behind him.

A lone boy came out from behind a tree. Theo stepped out in front of him with his sword drawn, and Jory stepped up behind the boy with his dagger bared. The boy's eyes widened in surprise.

"Oh, you're here. I thought you would still be at the bog."

The boy showed little concern that he was surrounded by others with weapons. Emily guessed he was about nine or ten years old. He had dirty-blond hair that he wore long about his ears and collar. He stood there barefoot wearing a clean red vest over a tan-colored shirt and a pair of short black pants that stopped at his knees.

"Follow me. He is waiting for you." The boy turned around to head back the way he had come.

"Wait, who are you? Who is waiting for us?" Emily asked.

"I'm Alistar, and Marwyn is waiting for you," he replied as if the answers were obvious. "He told me to help you find him and to tell you that you will be safe here."

"Who is Marwyn?" Theo asked before Emily could speak.

"Marwyn is a wizard. It's not far, and breakfast is waiting. Let's go."

Emily had not thought of food since yesterday morning at camp. Her stomach growled.

"I have never heard of this Marwyn," Jory said.

"He's a secret," the boy replied over his shoulder as he headed back into the woods.

Emily turned to Theo and Jory to see what they were going to do. The boys hesitated. Emily decided for herself and stepped forward to follow the younger boy somewhere into the woods.

Alistar was right. It was not far to get to where he lived. After a few minutes, the forest opened to a grove with neatly planted trees that lined a path to a house made of stone. The trees had apples, pears, plums, and other fruits that were foreign to Emily. The stone house had three simple glass windows in the front and an inviting red door.

Alistar ran up to one of the trees on the path, then jumped up to a low branch and picked a pear.

"Grab what you like," he called back to the others. "They are all ripe today."

Emily watched as Theo went and picked two red apples, then brought one back for her. She walked alongside Theo, noticing that her ankle no longer hurt, almost like she had never twisted it. She bit into the apple and found it to be the best-tasting, sweetest apple ever. Emily checked behind her to see if Jory was still there. He had not spoken since they followed after Alistar. He must not have been hungry since he did not bother to pick any of the fruit.

When Alistar opened the door to the house, the aroma

of baked bread lured Emily inside. The scent reminded her of home and her mother back in Buckton. The interior of the house was larger than Emily expected. Tapestries hung from the walls, and a large carpet covered the floor. A long wooden table occupied the middle of the room, its legs carved in the likeness of different animals walking around tree trunks. A massive hearth took up most of the wall to Emily's right, and an old man sat in a chair stirring something in a pot over the cook fire.

"We're back, Marwyn," Alistar announced.

"Yes, I see that," the man replied. "Get them something to drink, and some fresh bread and cheese too, I think. Children, come here before me so I can have a look at you."

Alistar exited the main room through a doorway to the left. Emily hesitantly walked toward the man.

I have never met a wizard before. Are they even real?

As Emily drew closer to the wizard, she could see he had long gray hair peppered with black. A mustache and long white beard that went down to his waist matched his white hair. Deep wrinkles lined his face. His eyes, however, drew Emily's attention. They were gray, not cold gray but lively, almost fiery. Emily tried to straighten her hair and clothes.

Theo stepped up next to her in front of the wizard. His face quietly expressed the horrible events in the woods. Emily felt Theo's apprehension.

"I am Marwyn, and this is my house. You shall be my guests." The man's voice was warm and friendly, like a deep, slow-moving river. "You have met Alistar. He is my student. There is a woman here also, Veranice, who cooks and keeps the home. Now, what is your name, girl, and where are you from?"

"My name is Emily. I am from Buckton, sir," Emily replied courteously.

"Welcome, Emily, my dear. And you, young man, what is your name?"

"I am Theo Harroldson from Tidehaven. I am the son of Lord Harroldson."

Marwyn smiled at Theo. "I thought so, by the look of you. I knew Lord Harroldson. Bright man. Same curly black hair and nose like you." The old man was pleased he recalled Theo's family, feeling like he had won at some guessing game.

Emily thought for a second.

Theo does not look much like his father. He has thick black hair like his father, but Theo's hair is curly, and his nose is common looking—snub and upturned—whereas his father's is larger and noble looking. Maybe as a young man, Lord Harroldson appeared more like his son.

"And you, boy, come closer so I can see you," Marwyn called to Jory, who remained in the doorway.

Jory walked closer to the fire. Emily sensed his fear.

Marwyn seems nice enough and harmless. Why does Jory act like he is afraid?

"Pull back your hood so I may look upon your face," Marwyn requested.

Jory obeyed, revealing his swollen red eye where Theo had struck him.

"What is your name, boy? And where are you from?" Marwyn asked kindly.

Jory's eyes darted around the room, as if he were trying to avoid the wizard's gaze.

"I'm J-Jory."

"It is good to meet you, Jory." Marwyn kept his eyes on the boy, studying him.

The room was silent for a moment.

"His full name is Jory Turner, sir. He is from Seadrift.

His father was the great Knight of the Broken Tower, like in the song," Emily blurted out. Her hands went to cover her mouth.

Why did I say all that? It was as if I couldn't control myself.

"I see..." Marwyn turned his attention to Alistar, who reappeared carrying a tray with cups and a pitcher along with some bread and cheese. He barely made it to the table with the heavy tray.

"You are safe here. You will not be troubled by the men who were hunting you in the forest. Grab something to eat and drink. We will talk more after we have had some sleep. It has been a long night for us all, I think. Alistar, show young Lord Harroldson and Jory to the rooms we have prepared for them. Come back for Emily when you have them settled."

"Yes, sir," answered Alistar.

"I will have Veranice bring something to your room for that swollen eye, Jory," Marwyn said. "It looks like you took quite a hit from one of those men."

Jory made no reply, and neither did Theo, who walked over to the table and took a cup that Alistar poured for him. He picked up some of the bread and slices of cheese on the tray. Jory scanned the table and took nothing.

"Follow me, please," Alistar said in a childish voice that sounded like he was playing at being proper and courteous.

Emily went to the table and picked up a cup. It contained some thin brown liquid with a citrusy smell to it. She guessed it was tea, but the smell was different. After her first taste, Emily had another drink.

This tastes amazing, sweet but a little sour too.

"That is tea, Emily, with dragon fruit. I do not suppose you have ever seen a dragon fruit before," Marwyn said.

"No, sir," Emily replied as she took a piece of bread and cheese.

"Come back over here near me," he suggested.

Emily walked back toward Marwyn. The presence of Theo and Jory had given her confidence earlier, but now she was alone with this man she did not know.

"Do not be afraid, Emily, and please turn it down a bit for me."

"Turn it down? Sir?" Emily asked.

"The emoting. I am an old man. You need not charm me."

"Emoting? I don't understand."

"You, child, are an emoter. Some people might call you a charmer or enchantress. Who is your teacher?"

"I don't have a teacher. I am an apprentice for Maggy the healer. I don't know anything about charming people."

"Ah, Maggy... Yes, Maggy always liked to bring her apprentices along slowly. So you are not aware of your ability?"

"No, sir, are you sure?"

"Quite sure. It is one of my talents. I can spot a Drasani when I see one," Marwyn explained.

"A Drasani? What is that?"

"More commonly called a mage. I am surprised Maggy never told you. She is a good teacher, although set in her ways."

Marwyn's gaze wandered around the room until it came back to Emily. She stood silently waiting for Marwyn to explain everything he had told her. But his eyes narrowed, and he leaned forward, looking at her like he was seeing her for the first time.

"Who are you? Who sent you here?"

Emily stepped back from Marwyn in fear. Anger boiled in his eyes. The twinkling gray disappeared, and now they were mean and suspicious. The wizard stiffened defensively in his chair, his hands squeezing the armrests.

"Marwyn, it is time for you to rest."

Emily turned when she heard the voice. A short older woman wearing a clean gray apron over a black dress stood at the entryway to the kitchen.

"You were up all night. You need some sleep."

The woman smiled at Emily as she walked past her to Marwyn's seat. At the woman's touch, the anger melted from the wizard's eyes. She helped the frail man stand up. Alistar returned to the main room from the other doorway. There was a small ball of fire spinning in the palm of his hand. The fireball changed color from orange to red to yellow to green.

"Alistar, put that out, and quit playing around. Help this girl to the room we prepared for her. I will take Master Marwyn to his room. Don't dawdle. You have other chores to get done this morning."

"Yes, ma'am." The fireball turned from green to blue then disappeared from Alistar's hand. He came over to Emily and pulled on her arm. "Follow me, please. We have a nice room for you."

31
THE PRINCE VI

"Lo, I say unto you that the time of the Four has come, a storm to wash away the evil and corruption that has festered in the hearts of men..."

The priest on top of the stacked boxes thrust his arms into the air and pointed down at the raptured crowd gathered to listen to him. His bald head was burnt from the sun, and his scraggly beard had spots where no hair grew. The temple robe he wore was torn and faded to the point that it was hard to see what colors it had been. The priest went barefoot, a penance. He stood atop a large crate before a crowd of nearly three hundred people in the southern market of Crosstimbers.

"We have suffered the Great Sickness, suffered the filth that lands on our shores from across the Eastern Ocean, and now the corrupt Lord Russ claims the throne for which there is a rightful heir, a live heir. Prince James Tolar, the favorite nephew of King Edward, is alive and healthy, I tell you. He is camped out to the west of this city with a host of knights and men. He shall cleanse this nation and reforge it in the righteousness of the Four. It is time for you, for all people of Terros, to go back to the Temple and pray for our prince, to ask for forgiveness, so that the rightful heir shall take his throne by the grace of the Four."

The priest thundered on. Prince James heard him plainly from the back of the square.

I think I can even see the crazed eyes of the Beggar.

The Beggar was what James and some of his guards had taken to calling the priest, who had indeed followed James and his army east to Crosstimbers. He begged for food, clothing, shoes, and money along the way. It was rumored he drank all night, and when he was not drinking, he caroused with the women who were following the Army of the West.

The excited crowd cheered during the pauses in the priest's sermon. They chanted James's name, and some called for the head of Lord Russ. James stood in the back of the large crowd with Sir Lucas Bardas, both dressed in commoner's clothes as they watched the throng. He liked Sir Lucas's company. The knight had a way of getting him out of camp without anyone knowing it.

"What do you think of him?" James asked Sir Lucas.

Sir Lucas peered at James from under his hooded cloak.

"Not bad. The Beggar drew a bigger crowd today. I would guess it is double the size of last night's. He is quite a talker. I believe he added some new material this afternoon."

"What's with the part about the filth from across the Eastern Ocean?" The oversized straw hat James wore slid down over his eyes so that he had to tilt his head back to see Sir Lucas.

"You will find that as we move east and north there will be more dislike for the elves that have been landing on the northern shores. The people are ignorant. Most have never even seen an elf. Do you want me to say something to the Beggar about it?"

"Yes, I think so. I will wait to decide how to handle that

matter after I know what is going on in the North. Let's get back to camp."

James and Sir Lucas walked through the narrow streets of Crosstimbers unnoticed. As he gazed over the river at the raised bridge and the white stone citadel, James recalled the legend that told of how the giant, Naynub, felled two giant redwoods in the west and dragged them to this spot to create a crossing so that he would not have to get his feet wet when traveling north. The dragging of the trees smoothed and cleared the land, creating the Crossing Road that ran from Greyport to Tidehaven. Over the years, proper bridges were built and a village sprang up around them. That village became an urban sprawl on both sides of the Grey, as the locals called the river. A center of commerce and trade, Crosstimbers attracted merchants and tradesmen. The city became wealthy.

I need this city to support my claim as king. When King George the First came, the elders of Crosstimbers would not even meet with him.

James and Sir Lucas made their way down along a river path back to camp on the south side of the river. James glanced at the northern bank where an army from Kingstown was encamped.

At least Crosstimbers is denying Lord Russ as well.

Arriving back at camp, James found his mother inside his pavilion sitting at his camp table.

"Back from your little dress-up game? Did you find Crosstimbers to your liking?" Lady Tolar remained seated.

She glared disapprovingly at James and Sir Lucas in the common clothes they were wearing.

"We went to the city to see what support I have, Mother," James replied. "Hundreds were there in the square chanting my name. The city elders will have to open the bridge to us."

"I am sure it was great fun to hear your name chanted by the unwashed rabble." Lady Tolar picked at some spot on the table with her fingernail. "While you were gone, Sir Cley rode into camp. His appearance was very rough, I heard."

"They found the flower they sought?"

"I believe so, but talk is that Sir Cley returned only with his squire, the young healer, and Sir Lennon, who was injured."

"Where was Tristan and the others?"

"Dead apparently, my dear," Lady Tolar said coldly.

"Sir Lucas, find Sir Cley. I want to know everything!" James yelled at Sir Lucas, who was already leaving the tent.

"You might want to look for him at Lord Harroldson's pavilion. Sir Cley rode straight through camp to give Lord Harroldson the news himself," Lady Tolar called after Sir Lucas in mock concern.

"James, you need better knights around you than Sir Lucas. He is from petty stock. His family are up-jumped merchants from Safe Harbor—hardly nobility," Lady Tolar lectured.

James removed his floppy straw hat and ran his fingers through his hair in disbelief.

"I fear that Lord Harroldson will take his army and go home now," his mother continued. "The loss of his two eldest sons will be crushing for him. You must listen to me now. We need to take command of the army from Tidehaven ourselves. Attack Crosstimbers, burn it to the ground if we must. We will show them you are the king and will not be disrespected. The city elders will open the bridges with a show of force."

James gaped at his mother in amazement.

How could she suggest killing innocent people? What kind of king would do that?

"Also, there is the matter of Princess Rebecca."

"What? What about the princess?" James seethed at his mother's guessing games.

"Lord Fowler has sent his daughter back to Greyport for safekeeping, at least until you can march into Kingstown and sit on the throne."

The news stung James like an arrow to the heart.

Rebecca would be against this. She wanted to be by my side. She said it would make an amazing tale someday that the two of us had faced danger together to become king and queen.

"I shall let you get out of those rags. You will have guests soon, no doubt." Lady Tolar stood and walked past James to the pavilion's entrance. "You should look like a proper prince and not some farmhand."

James sat down, trying to think of what to do next, but the only thoughts he had were of Rebecca.

32
EMILY VIII

"I'm a coward. When it was time to fight, I froze. I did nothing. I saw my brother get killed and did nothing. I watched Draven fight that man alone."

Emily stroked Theo's back as another violent wave of sobs made the boy shake.

"It's okay, Theo. You did your best. There was nothing any of us could do to stop what happened. You could have been killed."

"I could have done something, but I was craven." Theo buried his face in his hands. "I could not even think straight enough to take charge and order that bay rat to lead us back to camp. Instead, I allowed him to get us lost."

Theo fell back on the bed on his side. Emily curled herself around him, stroking his arm and hair until the boy's sobs stopped and he fell asleep. She stood, pulled a blanket over him, and left his room.

The light of the moon filled the long hallway that led to the bedrooms in the stone house. Emily's room was not as lavish as Theo's, only containing a small wardrobe, a bookshelf, a table, and a small bed. Upon opening the door to her room, Emily found someone had placed two large books and a lit candle on the table.

Marwyn?

The wizard had been absent at dinner. The three visitors sat with Alistar and the woman who ran the house, Veranice. Emily dug into the roasted chicken ravenously. Theo nibbled at his dinner. Jory ate nothing. There had been little talk.

Emily picked up the first book. Stamped in the leather cover was the title *The Flowers and Fauna of Terros*. Opening it, Emily found the author was none other than Marwyn himself. The second book was a history of Terros entitled *The Forging of a Kingdom*, written by a scholar named Martin the Elder. It was a thick tome bound in red leather. Emily flipped through the book, finding several blank pages at the back, as it appeared to be unfinished. Someone left a bookmark at a chapter called "The Purge of Dragons and Magic."

Under the history book, Emily found a thin leatherbound journal, which she opened. She read the first lines.

This is the journal of Cyril the Bold. Cyril the Soother. Cyril the voice of the king. Cyril, the greatest of Drasani.

I am not sure when I learned of my gifts, but I always had them...and used them. From getting attention from my parents to the detriment of my brother and sisters, to talking my friends into escapades they dared not think of. The first time I used my gift consciously was at the age of five when I committed my first theft.

Despite Emily's weariness, she sat at the table and read into the night of Cyril's exploits and schemes. He wrote of how every person and even animals had an aura that was given off by their emotions. Cyril could touch that aura and control their emotions and desires. When the sun rose that morning, Emily awoke, sitting at the table with Cyril's journal in her hands.

Marwyn's gardens contained every conceivable plant, even ones Emily had only seen described or drawn in books. There were plants and trees that should not even have been growing in this part of Terros, but here they were.

"This plant is black nightshade. Ground up and dried, the powder you make from it will remedy certain illnesses of the lungs, nose, and head," Marwyn instructed Emily as they walked. "That next to it is thistle. Of course, you know what to do with thistle. The king's grief... Pardon me, Emily." Marwyn shouted across the gardens at Allister as he shot three firebolts at a stone column set amongst some bushes. "Alistar! Control the size of the bolts, not the number!"

The wizard turned back to her. "Did you by chance get to look at any of the books I left for you?"

"Yes, thank you. I spent most of the night reading Cyril's journal. He was an interesting man, even though he was a thief."

"An interesting man is an understatement," Marwyn said and chuckled. "Cyril was a thief, but only when he was younger. King George the First put Cyril's talent to better use."

"Cyril could control people's emotions? He wrote that he could negotiate peace treaties and get lords to agree to anything."

"Yes, Cyril thought highly of himself. He was good. King George would have had a much more challenging time forging Terros into one kingdom without him. This plant here is kale," Marwyn pointed out, interrupting himself.

"Oh, I know kale. It is common enough. It can be used for digestive troubles."

"Yes, yes, but did you know that kale is the bane of Alistar's existence?"

"Will it kill him or take his fire powers away?"

"No, nothing as serious as that. The boy hates the taste of it." Marwyn smiled. "Here, let's have an experiment. Alistar! Come here, please!"

The boy shot a yellow fireball into the air, where it disappeared in the clouds, and came running at Marwyn's call.

"Here, Alistar. Try this kale and tell us if you think it is ripe." Marwyn held a leaf out to the boy.

"Yuck!" Alistar said as he backed away, scrunching up his nose.

Marwyn passed the leaf to Emily.

"I bet if Emily asked you to try it, you would."

"Kale is gross. It tastes bitter," Alistar said.

"Please, Alistar. Try it," Emily said, holding out the kale to the boy.

Again, Alistar backed away from it.

"Emily, concentrate. Think good thoughts, agreeable thoughts. Think of something that tastes good and how that makes you feel. Now add that feeling to the kale," Marwyn instructed.

Emily concentrated. The natural colors around her faded, and a red glow surrounded Alistar. Her own hands emitted a violet hue. She thought about peach cobbler, her favorite dessert. She concentrated on Alistar and reached out with her color and touched his. She thought about eating kale and how sweet it tasted.

"This kale is good though, Alistar," Emily said.

Alistar took the small leaf of kale. He put it in his mouth, chewed, and swallowed. "Hey, that was pretty good. Is there more?"

"That is enough for now, Alistar. Go back to your practice. Remember to control the heat," Marwyn instructed.

"Yes, Marwyn." Alistar ran back to the blackened stone pillar.

"That was amazing," Emily said. "I could see colors from Alistar and myself."

"An aura, I think Cyril called it," Marwyn said. "It works even better if you touch the person you are trying to emote to. Emily, you have a talent, but talents are like a double-bladed knife. They can cut both ways. You can give comfort to those who are in need—soothe an angry man or animal, persuade people to do things they might not normally do—but it is dangerous to trifle with people's emotions."

Emily nodded to Marwyn as they continued to walk through the garden. Marwyn stopped at a small plant with a white flower. He knelt and plucked the flower off, holding it up for Emily to have a better look. It appeared much like a clover's flower.

"This is fool's bane. It grows mostly in the North. A person who ingests this in great quantities will begin to hallucinate. He could be controlled by an experienced emoter from a distance. Cyril once put fool's bane in the food at a feast. He was able to get the lords and ladies in attendance to hand him all their valuables without a fuss, including their fine clothes and robes. He left that province a rich man, and the nobility...quite exposed."

"I have not read that far into the journal yet," Emily said and giggled.

"Oh, it becomes more interesting the further you read. His tales may sound like those of a braggart, and Cyril does love to brag, but I checked on his adventures, and they are true for the most part. He did have a crew that helped him. He rarely acted alone, but it was his emoting that was at the heart of the schemes."

Marwyn stopped when they reached the end of the

garden. A stone pillar stood amongst three burned fir trees. Emily stopped, assuming Marwyn would turn around to head back toward the stone house, but he gazed down into her eyes with a grave expression.

"Emily, you must learn to control your emoting. It can be dangerous. There are some emotions that are too dangerous to try to control," Marwyn said. "An emoter's feelings are often reflected or copied by others. For instance, you emote that you like kale, which persuades Alistar to think he likes kale. He felt the way you wanted him to feel. If you want someone to love you, they will love you."

Marwyn said the last bit slowly. Emily stepped back from him, a look of horror creeping over her as she realized what he might be saying.

"No, I never..." Emily's voice shook.

"No, not intentionally, but I have seen how the boys look after you and act around you." Marwyn put a hand on Emily's shoulder to ease her. "Love is the most volatile of all the emotions. Love can cause people to act with the best of intentions, but also the worst."

"But I do love Theo. How will I know if he genuinely loves me in return?"

"I wish I knew the answer, my dear. I am not an emoter like you. No emoter I ever met talked about it," Marwyn said with a hint of sadness.

Were Theo and Jory only nice to me because I caused them to be that way? Is Theo only reflecting my emotions? I need to read further into Cyril's journal to see if he mentions anything about love.

"I would like to do one more test with you, before we head back. It's a thought I have. Go to that burned fir tree over there. Put your hand on the trunk."

Emily walked over to the tree. Putting her hand on it, she

could feel the brittle, charred bark underneath, but there was something else too. Life.

"Now concentrate. Think about healing and growth," Marwyn instructed.

Emily pressed her hand against the tree, slowly feeling a warming sensation. On the ground, new green shoots of grass pushed up through the scorched earth around the fir. New green needles appeared on the lowest limbs of the tree. Emily's legs buckled, and she pulled away from the tree.

"Good, Emily. Good." Marwyn came and patted her on the shoulder.

"What did I do?"

"You are a healer on top of being an emoter. One talent is rare. Two is extraordinary in Drasani," Marwyn explained.

"Are there many Drasani?" Emily asked.

"No, the Purge made sure of that," Marwyn answered. "I will let you read about it. There may only be a few remaining in the world. Alistar is one. He is a Firecaster."

"What other types are there?"

"Windcallers, Summoners, Dragontalkers, Dreamwalkers, and others."

"And what are you?"

"Me? I am simply an old man who has seen too much and needs some dinner."

Emily spent that evening in her room reading. Sometime during the early morning hours, she skipped to the end of Cyril's journal. The man was a thief and a scoundrel. Though he never married, he had a devoted woman in each of the major cities of Terros. No matter where he traveled, he had a place to call home. Near the end of the journal,

Cyril's writings were less about his exploits and heists and became more reflective. He wrote about calming his emotions. He learned to use breathing techniques to enhance or dampen his talent.

Emily dropped the journal to the table upon reading the last entry, which was written in another person's handwriting.

This was the journal of Cyril the Bold, Cyril the Soother, Cyril the Trickster, Cyril the Coldhearted. He met his death because of a love that could not be shared. A fire that he stoked and could not control. A flame that flared too hot and burned him in the end.

When Emily finally slept, she dreamt of running from the wagon of the woods witch. The witch turned into a mass of black smoke that chased her and her friends in the woods. She took Saph and Aiden, their screams echoing through the trees. Draven stumbled and begged for help as the smoke swallowed him. Theo was next. He stood unmoving and silent as the witch engulfed him. Jory ran ahead, and Emily lost sight of him. In the rustle of the leaves, she thought she heard a boy crying, then the sound of laughter came to her ears, sharp and crackling. The witch was coming for her. Emily was lost in the woods...alone.

Emily woke in a panic, scanning around to see that she was safe in her room at the stone house. She sat up and began to count her breaths, blocking out her thoughts and emotions. She breathed in and out slowly, as Cyril described in his journal, beginning to gain control.

33

JORY X

The bushes and trees that scratched at Jory turned into dead cold hands that clawed and grasped at his arms and legs from the darkness as he ran through the woods. His legs churned, but he went nowhere. Voices surrounded him, calling and howling like a pack of wolves on the hunt.

Jory stumbled and fell. He heard footsteps behind him, and a man in a green cloak stepped out of the gloom. He had an arrow lodged in his eye.

"Here he is! Here's the bay rat! The murderer!"

Jory struggled to get to his feet. Every time he tried to get up, his legs tangled with the tree roots that rose from the ground and held him down.

Jory jolted up in his bed. In the darkness, he could see his legs and lower body tangled with his blanket.

A bad dream.

But it was real enough. His heart raced, and he was wet with sweat like he had been running. His shark tooth necklace twisted tightly around his neck.

Jory's mind was still in a haze when a large shadow moved from the corner of the room. The shadow walked over to the chair near the bed and sat down.

"You killed a man, eh. More than one by the looks of it."

Jory's bow and quiver were against the wall near the shadow. He had fired off all but one of his arrows in the woods, saving the last one for an emergency.

"No worries, eh. We all do it...eventually. Even your precious knight. At least you know they won't be back."

The voice sounded familiar, but Jory could not place it. He reached under the mattress where he had his dagger hidden, then sat up quickly with it in hand, but the chair was empty. The shadow was gone.

Another dream?

Jory rubbed his eyes, then stood and walked to the small window of this strange house. A pool with colorful fish shimmered in the moonlight under his window. Looking at the pool and watching the fish was the only thing Jory liked about this place. It was going on three days since they had arrived. Jory did not like it. That first night, he had spent a sleepless night lying in the small bed, staring at the ceiling. He could not talk to the others about it. Theo only left his room to eat dinner. Emily spent most of her time speaking with Marwyn or visiting Theo in his room. Jory chafed at the thought that she might be kissing him behind the closed door.

On the second day, Emily spent the whole afternoon speaking with Marwyn. Jory tagged along with them as Marwyn showed Emily his garden and orchard. He explained the different plants and their uses. It bored Jory, so he walked off and found the pool with the fish. It was peaceful. The colorful fish were large with big fins that waved in the water like veils in the wind as they swam. Jory spent most of the afternoon watching them, eventually falling asleep in the soft grass. He only woke when Alistar came to fetch him for dinner.

Jory's stomach growled. He was hungry. He had eaten

the last apple in his pack yesterday, and there was no jerky left. He avoided eating any of the food from the stone house. He drank some of the water last night and still felt healthy. The others were eating the food here and they didn't get sick, so he guessed he could risk eating something for breakfast. The woman who cooked for Marwyn appeared nice enough to be trusted. And the boy, Alistar, was friendly and had taken to following him around when he was not doing his chores or lessons. Jory was still unsure of the wizard.

It will be morning soon.

The moon hung above the treetops of the well-kept rows of trees that led to the dark forest. Jory thought of Sir Cley.

Is he still alive? Why has he not come to find us? Is he at Shadow Tower waiting?

Jory sat down on his bed in the plain room. There was a peg on the wall for his clothes, a chair, and a small bed with one blanket. It was simple but comfortable enough. His cloak was draped over the back of the chair. He tried to remember if he had hung it up on the peg when he took it off the night before.

Jory's stomach growled again, and he came to two decisions. One, he would eat something for breakfast. Two, he and the others needed to get away from this house.

"It is good to see everyone at the table this morning." Marwyn nodded to Theo, who had managed to drag himself out of bed. "And it is good to see that everyone is eating."

Marwyn did not look over at him, but Jory knew whom he was talking about. Jory took another spoonful of oatmeal with honey into his mouth. It was good, as were the fresh strawberries and blueberries on the table.

Alistar sat next to Jory at the far end of the long table, away from Marwyn, eating his oatmeal as fast as he could. Jory wondered whom the boy was racing against. Emily and Theo sat on each side of the old wizard.

"I think we should be leaving today," Theo announced. His eyes were red and puffy, and his hair was tangled. "I need to get back to my father."

Jory tried to swallow his mouthful of oatmeal to agree with Theo.

"I am afraid that is quite impossible, Theo," Marwyn said. "My agents have informed me that those men are still out there searching for you in the woods."

"Why are they searching for us?" asked Emily. "I would think bandits would have given up."

"Good question, Emily. You are a perceptive young lady. Perhaps they were not bandits at all. Maybe they were sent to get someone or something."

Emily looked over at Theo, who looked back at Marwyn. The wizard looked down the long table at Jory. Alistar let some oatmeal dribble onto his shirt.

"Who would send someone after us? Who even knew we were in the woods?" Theo asked.

"That is another good question," Marwyn said. "I am trying to find out the answers to all your questions. For now, know that you are safe here as long as you do not stray too far into the woods. They cannot find or hurt you here."

And how are you accomplishing that?

The feeling of being trapped hung about Jory. There was nothing to do at the stone house. Normally he would have some chores to do for Sir Cley or some errand to run, but here Alistar and Veranice handled the chores.

Jory walked around inside the house. He checked out the kitchen, where Veranice was cleaning up the breakfast dishes.

"Hungry again already?" she asked Jory kindly.

"Oh, no, ma'am. I w-wanted to see the kitchen," Jory replied.

"Whatever you want, be sure to ask."

Jory nodded and went back into the main room. There was a door on the far wall by the fireplace. Jory tried the door handle, but found it was locked. The doorway that led to the long hall was on his left. Jory walked down it, counting six doors. He had seen Veranice coming and going from the first door on the left and assumed that was her room.

The first door on the right was Theo's room. The door was left slightly open. Right after breakfast, Theo joined Emily for a walk in the gardens after she had begged him to come outside.

Jory stood at the door and pushed it open wider with his finger. The room was immense. A large canopied bed covered in pillows occupied the middle of the room. Rich-looking tapestries hung from each wall except the one that had a large window with dark, thick drapes. The room contained two overstuffed chairs in one corner next to the window, and several candle stands were placed throughout. A large wardrobe with fancy carved doors stood against the wall to the right. Next to the wardrobe was a rack with different-colored cloaks and hats. Near the bed was a wash table with a mirror along with some towels. The bed was made up with sheets and folded blankets at its foot. The thought of walking into the room came to Jory, but he decided he better not in case Theo and Emily returned.

The second room on the left, with the door wide open, was Emily's. Jory stood in the doorway, peering into the room, which was larger than his. A window gave a view of the gardens. There was a simple bed with two pillows. At the end of the bed, two blankets, one red and the other blue, were neatly folded. Under the window stood a table with a chair. A book was opened in the middle of the table, and three more books were stacked up on one of the corners. A large candle occupied the opposite corner. The melted wax around the base spoke of the long burning time the candle had undergone. A small bookshelf occupied the wall to Jory's right, though the books were too far away for him to be able to read the markings on their spines. On the wall to the left was an open wardrobe with two nice dresses hanging inside. Jory resisted the urge to go into the room and touch them.

Across the hall was Alistar's room. The door was closed, but Jory opened it carefully. The room was much like Emily's. The beds were the same, but Alistar only had one pillow and one blanket. There was a bookshelf with no books and a table with a candle. It did not look like Alistar had been reading much, as the candle had no melted wax about it. He also had an open wardrobe, but the clothes that were supposed to be hung up in it were scattered here and there on the floor.

Sir Cley would have tasked this boy to clean up.

There were two odd things about Alistar's room. One, there was no window. The other rooms Jory investigated all had windows. The second oddity was the scorch marks that scarred the whitewashed walls. There were even some on the ceiling. Jory noticed the room had an odor to it that reminded him of the old hearth at Shadow Tower.

Jory walked down to the end of the hall. The door to the right opened to the room he was sleeping in. The door to the left was closed. Jory had never seen it open. He figured the room was Marwyn's, but he never witnessed Marwyn walking down this hall. Jory tested the door handle. Finding it was locked, he peeped through the keyhole and under the door, but it was dark. When he got down on the floor, a draft of cold air struck Jory's face from under the door. The air smelled damp and moldy. Perplexed, he stood and tried the handle again.

Still locked.

Jory went into his small room. On his small bed with its pillow, the single gray blanket was still tangled up in the middle. His torn and dirty cloak was draped over the back of the wooden chair. Jory picked it up and hung it on the peg on the wall. He was still wearing the shirt and pants Sir Cley had bought for him for the Squires' Melee. Jory had been so proud of them. There were small tears and holes in them now along with mud and blood stains.

Feeling curious, Jory walked the hall again, measuring it with his steps. He went outside to check his measurements, which did not add up. He puzzled over how the house was bigger on the inside than it looked from the outside. He had walked around the stone house three times. The hallway that led to the rooms was forty paces long, but outside it was only twenty paces from the front to the back. He sat by the pool again and watched the fish, then fell into a dreamless sleep and did not stir until Alistar woke him for dinner.

At dinner that night, Jory's jaw dropped open when Emily came to the table wearing one of the new dresses. It was a light-green color, and the fabric seemed to shine in the candlelight. The sleeves opened up at her elbows and ended in little puffs near her shoulders. The neckline plunged down to the start of her chest, revealing the girl's smooth ivory skin. Jory could not take his eyes off Emily. She was beautiful.

Theo came to the table wearing a new shirt and pair of pants along with some leather shoes. The dinner table was set with food as good as Jory had seen at any tournament feast. There was roast chicken with vegetables and rice. All sorts of beans and greens were mixed in a bowl. There was also a large bowl of cut-up fruit. Jory found himself eating without care until he glanced down at the end of the table and Marwyn smiled at him.

"I think we should set off tomorrow morning," Theo said, picking at the food on his plate. "If we leave in the morning, maybe we could get back to Pebble Creek in two days."

"Again, I would advise against that, Theo," Marwyn answered. "Shadow Woods remains far too dangerous right now. You should rest and gather your strength. In a few days, you can set out when it is safe."

Jory remained silent. Across the table from him, Alistar concentrated on a chicken leg. The boy shrugged at Jory in response to an unasked question.

"I agree with Marwyn," Emily said confidently. "We are safe here. It is far too dangerous in the woods. Plus, we do not even have mounts to ride back. It might take four or five days without horses."

Theo balled his fingers tightly around his knife, then raised his fist and slammed it back down onto the tabletop, making the plates and cups shake.

"We need to get back!" Theo shouted. "None of you understand. None of you have ever lost anything."

Theo pushed himself up from his chair and stormed off to his room. Emily excused herself from the table to follow him. Marwyn sat calmly at the end of the table and took a drink from his cup. Alistar reached for the big bowl of fruit for another helping.

"That is enough for you, young man," Veranice said to Alistar. "Help me clear this table."

Veranice and Alistar grabbed some plates and bowls and carried them to the kitchen, leaving Jory and Marwyn alone at opposite ends of the long table.

"And what do you think, Jory?" Marwyn asked as he reclined in his high-backed chair.

Jory swallowed and cleared his throat.

"I think we sh-should go soon."

"There are dangers out there, Jory—dangers of which you have not even dreamt."

How would this old man know what I've dreamt of?

The wizard went on, "You are worried about your knight. Sir Cley is alive and well. In fact, he is already back with the others."

"A-Aiden and Alyss? H-how do you know?" Jory asked.

"I have seen it, Jory. It is one of my...talents. I know Alistar told you I was a wizard. Did you doubt him after you met me in person?" Marwyn took another drink. "I am what some people would call a conjurer...a mage. Do not underestimate others by their appearance. I am sure Sir Cley taught you this important lesson."

Sir Cley had taught this lesson. He also taught me to be cautious around strangers.

"You...you are keeping those men who were after us away from here?"

"I have been able to keep my home hidden from outsiders for years—a warding along with a simple illusory spell."

Jory was not sure what "warding" or "illusory" meant, but they sounded like magic.

"W-what about the house? It's too big inside."

"Very observant. The house is made for necessity. If I

need six rooms…"—Marwyn wiggled his fingers—"…I get six rooms. If I need ten rooms and a stable, they are here. If I need a room for a prince, the room is there."

"W-why were those men after us?" Jory asked.

"I wish I knew the answer, but I cannot see everything. Their purpose is shrouded from me. There are other mages out there. Some can mask their plans and movements."

"There are other wizards?"

"Yes, Jory, there are." Marwyn stood from his seat at the table, then moved over to the chair by the fireplace. Jory took this to mean their conversation was finished. He got up to go to the room he slept in. Passing by Theo's room, he could hear Theo speaking.

"You always take his side. You always defend him. It's his fault we are stuck here."

Jory pressed his ear up to the door.

"He led us to safety. He was trying to help us," Emily answered. "You never even talk to him. You should at least apologize for punching him in the eye."

"I saw you kiss him. You know?" Theo's voice accused.

"When? When he gave me a flower the night we went to the woods witch? It was a little kiss on the cheek, a kiss I would have given to a little brother."

Jory bit his lower lip. They were talking about him. Jory remembered that kiss and how it made him feel that night.

"I think you're in love with him…"

"I don't love him." Emily paused. "Jory is a boy. I am in love with you, Theo."

Jory doubled over like he had been punched in the stomach. His breath came in gasps as he staggered down the long hall toward his room, feeling tears welling up in his eyes. He got to his room and closed the door quietly. Getting in his bed and curling himself up, he pulled the single blanket around him.

If Emily and Theo don't want me around, I will leave tonight.

The bright moonlight woke Jory up. He was unsure of how long he had been asleep. The rising moon outside his window was still low in the sky, so it had to be early evening.

Jory got out of his bed and retrieved his cloak from the wall peg, then slipped his arms through the shoulder straps of his backpack. Next, he slung his bow over his shoulder, noticing it had been restrung. He strapped his quiver full of new arrows around his waist, then took his dagger out from under the bed mat and tucked it into his belt.

Jory quietly opened his door. Everything in the stone house was silent as he snuck down the dark hall. Only a flicker of candlelight shone from under Emily's door. Jory thought about knocking on her door and telling her he was leaving, but he remembered she would not care anyway.

When he got to the main room, it too was dark. Faint moonlight illuminated the table and chairs and other furniture. The door to the outside was ahead of him as Jory crossed the middle of the room.

"Is that it, Jonas? You are leaving already?" A frail voice drifted from the darkness near the hearth.

"Did you finish your chores? Are your lessons complete?" The voice was Marwyn's, but it was much weaker than Jory had ever heard it. "Where are you going, boy?"

Jory could barely make out Marwyn sagging in his chair by the glowing coals in the fireplace.

"Don't go silent on me again, Jonas. I know you hear me. Come closer, boy."

Jory walked slowly to the wizard. He could see by the

moonlight a withered Marwyn sitting and wringing his hands in an agitated manner.

"Ah...there you are. Good boy. You are off to the tower?"

How did Marwyn know I was going to Shadow Tower?

"Be sure you take back the books I put on your table—the one with the green binding, the one with no title. You will remember, won't you, Jonas?"

"I'm... My n-name is not Jonas," Jory said.

Marwyn leaned forward to get a better look at Jory, who thought he could hear the man sniffing the air.

"No...no, you are not Jonas," Marwyn murmured.

Marwyn put his head in his hands and began to rub his temples gently. Jory thought he could hear the man sob as he backed away from him toward the door.

Jory quietly opened the door to the stone house. A light breeze stirred the warm summer air. The moon was still rising in the east over the orchard and its ordered rows of trees. Jory headed north to the dark woods looking for Shadow Tower.

Unsure of how far he was going to have to walk, Jory picked fruit, mostly apples, from the lower branches of the trees as he walked under them and put them into his pack.

"Where are we going?"

The voice startled Jory. He turned to see Alistar walking after him. He was dressed much like Jory was, in traveling clothes, a cloak, and a backpack.

"I am leaving. I don't know where you are going."

"I'm going with you. Marwyn said I was supposed to help you."

"Help me with what?"

"With whatever. He told me to go where you go and help you. So here I am, helping you."

Jory thought for a moment. He was not sure he was heading in the right direction.

"Do you know Shadow Tower?" Jory asked.

"Yes. It's, umm, that way." Alistar pointed toward the woods, but off to the left from where Jory had been heading.

"Okay, I guess you can come, then."

The two boys walked together in silence along the rows of fruit trees under the summer moon until they entered the darkness of the forest.

34
A KNIGHT OF THE REALM I

S ir Cley's heel tapped the ground as his left leg bounced up and down nervously. Sitting by himself in his tent outside Crosstimbers, his mind raced. He took deep breaths and tried to relax, but his self-exile left him feeling trapped and alone.

Choosing a campsite away from the rest of the Army of the West was his own decision. The quiet, questioning looks he got from his fellow knights were not of his choosing. Cley could feel the hostility as he walked through the Tidehaven camp. He was asked to leave the ale tent that was set up for the soldiers. Even the small group of soldiers and knights from Buckton were quiet around him, lowering their voices and looking into their mugs or fires as Cley approached.

Sir Torrent came to visit that first night, but he had not been back since. No one liked misery, and no one wanted to be around failure. Even Lord Buckhorn suggested that Cley remain near his tent rather than be around Prince James.

Cley leaned back in the camp chair, tossing his head back. He covered his face with both hands.

How could it have been worse? The most famous knight in the land led a small party into the woods and came back with less than half of them. The first- and second-born sons of the Lord of Tides were both gone—one dead, the other presumed dead.

"It's time we left."

Lord Buckhorn's voice shook Cley out of his web of thoughts. The old warrior stood at the entrance of Cley's tent. His sword hung from his side, and he wore a dark hooded cloak. Traveling attire. Cley stood to join him outside. The two men mounted their horses and rode to the edge of the Buckton encampment, where Sir Lucas joined them.

"Sir Cley, I am sorry about our last meeting. It could not be helped. The prince wanted to hear the news from you himself," Sir Lucas explained. "I am glad you are still with us."

The three knights rode in the dark and disappeared into the woods. They rode along the ridge of a dry creek bed until Cley saw a flicker of flame down in a hollow between two hills. They made their way in silence toward the flame.

Cley could see there were two men sitting around a small fire as they rode closer. A man, old and frail, sat tending it. The man was bald with a long, shaggy beard. The skin on his head had brown age spots. The presence of the knight seated next to him surprised Cley.

Before the men could make any greetings, another rider pulled up outside the firelight. A large, hooded man dressed in black dismounted his horse. The dark figure walked over to the campfire and stood opposite the others. He pulled back his hood, revealing himself to be Sir Finis Crowe, the Dark Sorrow. He offered no greetings to the others. He pulled out a wine skin, drank from it, and spat some of the wine onto the fire.

"I am unaware of the last time a council of the Knights of the Realm was held," the old man sitting at the fire began.

"I know in my fifty-two years as an appointed knight there has never been one. I am eighty-one. This is as good a time as any. Each one of us was chosen, appointed, as a Knight of the Realm by King Edward. As such, we are sworn to defend the realm and protect its people. Tonight, we must decide what is the best way to fulfill our oaths." The old man stood with difficulty. "I am Sir Utor Nix of Felltre." The old man reached into his belt and pulled out a coin. He held it up to the firelight, illuminating a hammer and anvil stamped on one side and a compass rose on the other.

"I am Lord William Buckhorn. King Edward and I were both young men when he appointed me at Frostmark." Lord Buckhorn produced a similar coin to that of Sir Utor.

"I have the book with me also." Lord Buckhorn reached into a bag hanging at his side, then withdrew a small book and four small scrolls with wax seals. He handed each man one of the scrolls, all except for Cley. "Keep that scroll safe. You may have need of it someday." Lord Buckhorn walked closer to the campfire, then opened the book and began to read.

"Sir Baddon Teague."

"That would be me." The man who had been sitting next to Sir Utor stepped forward and showed off a well-polished coin. Cley recognized the knight before he even stood. The slicked-back black hair and well-kept mustache were legendary in the South. The Knight of the Rising Sun. He jousted with him in a tournament at Wylofam last winter. He remembered defeating Sir Baddon easily, five lances to none.

"Sir Finis Crowe," Lord Buckhorn went on.

"Aye." Sir Finis spat into the fire. He fumbled around in a pouch tied to his belt, eventually pulling out his coin to show the others.

"Sir Ulrich Veritas."

"I stand for Sir Ulrich," Sir Utor said. "He was in Winterhaven when he sent me the message that he could not make the journey."

"Sir Lucas Bardas."

"Gentlemen." Sir Lucas gave a slight bow to the other knights present and showed them his coin.

"The White Owl. I have heard of you," Sir Baddon said, returning the bow. "Why we have not met at a tournament previously is a shame. I do believe you have been avoiding me."

"I am flattered you have heard of me, Sir Baddon. I did not make any tournaments in the South last season due to family concerns. I have heard of your prowess, of course."

Sir Finis spat into the fire again.

"Sir Cley Woods."

"Here." Cley wanted to say more, something of importance. When on the victory stand or toasting at a feast, he had a quick wit and could be eloquent, but his tongue was tied in front of these men. He reached into his belt and pulled out the same coin the others had. King Edward knighted Cley after the Battle of Falling Stone, in front of his entire court. Later that night, the king made the new Sir Cley a Knight of the Realm with Lord Buckhorn as witness. The memory of it came with pride and pain.

"Sir, umm, the Black Axe," Lord Buckhorn finished.

"I stand for him too...if he is alive," Sir Utor said. "I got no reply from him. No one has seen him. Last I heard, he'd gone rogue and was pillaging up on the northwest coast near Blackwall."

Lord Buckhorn checked the book.

"His ink is not faded. He lives still."

"This is all of us?" Sir Baddon asked. "The Knights of the Realm? There are only seven of us?"

"Eight, if you count the northern brigand," Sir Finis growled, spitting into the fire again.

"Men, we must discuss how to proceed with this succession crisis," Lord Buckhorn went on. "Prince James has the better claim."

"But Lord Russ already has the throne and Kingstown," Sir Baddon argued.

"Prince James will make a better king. He is already a better man than Lord Russ. He cares for the people," Sir Lucas countered. "The East will unite with the West when James and Rebecca Fowler are married and named king and queen."

"Who will the North support?" Lord Buckhorn asked Sir Utor.

"The North is in turmoil. Elves have attacked the Temple at Summerport. Northerners burned elven settlements in retribution. The lords of Hillsburrow and Frostmark argue over who needs to keep the peace. Russ has done nothing so far. It is only Sir Ulrich and his band of men who keep war from breaking out. The North will support whoever brings peace. Buckhorn, if you say it will be this young prince, I will take your word. Ulrich will go along too."

"And the South?" Lord Buckhorn turned to look at Sir Baddon.

"The southern lords have thrown in with Prince James, as you know," replied Sir Baddon.

"But we have yet to see their army. Scouts say they are more than ten days away," Sir Lucas said.

"They have met with travel complications. It is difficult to move an army through the Sands during the storm season. The Army of the South will be here."

"We are agreed, then. We will work to see Prince James

become king of all Terros," Lord Buckhorn said. "We need to recruit more lords and knights to his cause, promote him to any people we speak to, and defend him before and after he takes his throne."

"Aye," Sir Utor said.

"Aye," Sir Lucas said.

"Yes," Sir Baddon said.

"Aye," Sir Finis said.

"Yes," Sir Cley said.

The four Knights of the Realm rode back to camp in silence. The Knight of the Tall Tree led the way with the White Owl, followed by the Lord of Buckton. The Dark Sorrow trailed at a distance.

Before they reached the first sentinels, Sir Lucas and the Sorrow split off. Cley and Lord Buckhorn made their way through the pickets and into the Buckton camp.

"Ride with me to my tent, Cley," Lord Buckhorn said, breaking the silence between the two men. "I have some-thing for you."

Inside the sparsely furnished tent, Lord Buckhorn undid his sword belt and hung it, along with his dark cloak, over a hook on one of the tent poles.

"The scrolls I handed to the others contain the names of the last Knights of the Realm written upon them, along with their last known homes or whereabouts," Lord Buckhorn began. He unfastened the satchel at his side and pulled out the book he had read from at the meeting. He set it on the camp table in front of Cley.

"Go ahead and take it," Lord Buckhorn said. "I leave it to you now, as it was left to me eighteen years ago. I wasn't as young as you are now, but you are responsible. That is *The Knights Roll*. Every knight who has ever served in the Knights of the Realm has their name written in the book."

Cley picked up the book, which was not larger than a personal journal. The green color of the soft leather had faded with time, and the corners were bent. Cley opened the roll to the first page. Ten knights were listed. He had never heard of any of them.

"The roll and the knights go all the way back to King George the First. That book is close to four hundred years old, I believe. It was given to me by Sir Ben Perrin. Now I am giving it to you." Lord Buckhorn walked next to Sir Cley and put his hand on Cley's shoulder. "Cley, you are a great knight. Sir Jonas saw it in you, I witnessed it, and so did King Edward. You belong in the roll. Some of the others you met tonight...I am not so sure."

Cley flipped through the pages until he reached the last entries. Another ten names were listed. In faded blue ink, the second name read, "Sir Jonas Turner, Knight of the Broken Tower." The ninth, entry written in dark-green ink, read, "Sir Cley Woods, Knight of the Tall Tree." The writing of his name was in his exact hand, but his title was written the same as all the other knights.

"Lord Buckhorn, how did my name get in here? I have never seen this book or put my name in it."

"Remember when King Edward appointed you? He had you sign your name on some parchment that was tossed into a fire. Your name appeared here in the book. How? I do not know or care to know. Your name appeared soon after King Edward appointed you to the order. Your title appeared not long after. When a knight dies, his name will fade but still be legible. I am sure there is some enchantment on the book. I will be glad to be rid of it."

Sir Cley flipped back to the last page of entries. "But only eight knights?"

"King Edward only appointed fourteen knights during his reign. I fear that Sir Utor will be next to fade, and I am no youth myself." Lord Buckhorn walked over to his camp chair and sat heavily.

Cley read the names above his. "Sir Lucas Bardas, the White Owl," was written in a neat, flowing script in white ink that stood out on the parchment. Cley's own signature was chicken scratch in comparison. Sir Ulrich's name was written in purple ink, each letter of his name standing tall and upright. The Dark Sorrow's name was next. The writing in black ink was surprisingly neat, although it slanted in the wrong direction, as Sir Finis was left-handed. Sir Jonas's name stood out to Cley—a simple script of faded blue ink with straight, well-made letters.

"It will be up to you to keep track of the roll now. Keep it safe. I never carried it into battle with me. I always left it back in Buckton hidden in my library. I thought I would share it with James once he was made king, but I think you should do that. Teach him how King Edward appointed you. Encourage him to choose more worthy knights to add to the roll."

On his camp bed, Cley was unable to sleep, holding the small green leather book to his chest. Lord Buckhorn gave him the satchel to keep it in, but Cley liked the feel of the leather in his hands.

The book is enchanted, according to Buckton. That couldn't be. Magic is dead.

Cley sat up and lit his lantern, then opened the roll to the last page. He thought about the names still written in dark ink. He wished he could know if Jory were alive as easily as looking at some ink written in a book. He glanced at Sir Jonas's faded name again and thought of the promise he made to him.

Cley remembered the night the king appointed him. He did not know what it meant to be appointed to the order. He knew Sir Jonas had been a member, but that was all. That night, Cley swore to protect the defenseless, dispense justice in the name of the king, and answer should he ever be summoned to defend the realm. But those were merely words. No summons ever came from the king. He never even saw the king again in person after the night he was appointed.

Cley thought about the other surviving knights in the book. Sir Utor and Lord Buckhorn were old men. Utor's fighting days were over, and Buckhorn was getting there as well. "Sir Baddon Teague, the Knight of the Rising Sun." A vain man, a glory seeker. How he earned the honor, Cley could not begin to guess. "Sir Finis Crowe, The Dark Sorrow." Cley clenched his jaw and his muscles tensed reading that name. "Sir Ulrich Veritas, The Lightning Lord." Cley tried to picture what a knight with that title would be like. The image of a tall knight on a white charger swinging a bright sword as lightning flashed around him ran through Cley's mind. Cley thought of his own tall tree and grimaced. "Sir Lucas Bardas, The White Owl." A good knight. Honorable and skilled with the blade. A knight deserving of the order.

The final entry below Cley's own name was King Edward's last appointment to the Knights of the Realm. The ink appeared fresh. The name written down was in black but smeared with something that was the color of blood. Next to the unreadable name was the title, written in the same script as all the others, "the Black Axe."

35

JORY XI

"See, there it is!" Alistar proclaimed with excitement. "I told you I knew where it was."

Jory stepped from behind some trees along the edge of the forest. A tall, dark tower stuck out from the trees surrounding it. After two days of walking, they finally reached Shadow Tower.

Jory was glad for the company. Alistar was not too talkative, but he was not quiet either. Jory learned that Alistar was ten and had been living with Marwyn for two years, serving as the mage's apprentice. He was from a small village called Tumbledon in the foothills of the Great Mountains north of High Meadow. Jory shared with Alistar about his home in Seadrift and about seeing the Western Ocean and riding the waves. Neither boy spoke of his parents. Jory wanted to ask Alistar how he became Marwyn's apprentice but was afraid he would have to explain how he became Sir Cley's squire.

Nestled on the outskirts of the woods, Shadow Tower was not a particularly imposing fortification. Some of the trees in the woods were taller than it. The tower was only three stories high, built from rocks of all shapes and colors. The most common was black and green from the moss and lichen that grew on the surface. Creepers clung to the sides and climbed halfway up the tower on the southern side. There were three outbuildings. Sir Cley had fixed up the stable for their horses when they lived here. The other two buildings were beyond repair, he claimed.

"Race ya to the tower!" Alistar took off toward it with a head start.

Jory caught him by the time they reached the low outer wall. It was only a pile of stones that had been cleared to create a yard to practice riding and have a vegetable garden. Jory stopped when he reached the steps that led to the tower's entrance. A white cat with one black ear and black paws waited at the top step in front of the closed door.

"Sir Morris! You're still here!" Jory exclaimed, scratching the cat behind the ears.

"This is your cat?" Alistar panted as he caught up and sat on the tower steps next to the cat.

"Yes, we got him wh-when we first came here. There were lots of mice in the tower. I figured he would be gone by now. It's been over a year since we left." Jory sat on the other side of Sir Morris. The cat stood and rubbed its back and tail on Jory, then investigated Alistar and began to rub against the younger boy.

"Let's go inside."

Jory stood and pushed open the heavy wooden door, which creaked as the metal hinges moved. Sir Cley had paid a farmer to come check on the tower from time to time, but by the sound of the door, it had been a while since it was last opened.

The first floor was dark, as there were no windows, and there was a stale smell in the air. Jory and Alistar walked into the dark room flanked by Sir Morris. The main floor had a kitchen and dining room all in the same area. There was a large hearth that served as the cooking area. A narrow spiral staircase built into the wall wound its way up, connecting the main room to the second floor.

Jory left the door open to let light in. Everything was still the way they had left it. The table and chairs remained. There was a stack of firewood near the hearth. Sir Cley did not bother to furnish the tower elaborately. Most of the furniture from the previous lord was musty smelling and damaged with time, so they spent the first few days clearing everything out. To Jory, those days were a long time ago.

"So now what do we do?" Alistar asked.

"We need to find some lanterns, then light them so we c-can see."

"No, I mean, what do we do now that we are here?"

Jory thought about the question.

"We wait for Sir Cley, I think. He t-told me that if something happened to meet here."

"Wouldn't he be here by now though?"

Jory thought of what Marwyn had told him.

The wizard could be trying to trick me. How can I trust someone I don't know?

"M-maybe. He might still be looking for us in the woods."

"Or maybe he went back to Pebble Creek with those other people you were with. Maybe one of them was hurt. Or maybe he got..."

"No! He's out there."

Alistar stepped back from him, and Sir Morris scurried ahead to the spiral stairs.

Jory went to the fireplace mantle, took down a lantern, and brought it back to the table in the middle of the room.

"Can you light it, A-Alistar?"

"Do you have your tinder box?"

"I thought you said you could make fire."

"I can, but Marwyn says I am not supposed to do it away from the house. I already told you that."

"What good is being able to do magic if you cannot use it?"

Jory shrugged off his bow and backpack. Using the small tinder box from his pack, he created a flame and lit the lantern. The two boys made their way up the stairs to the second floor. The entire floor was one room that Sir Cley used as his sleeping quarters. The room had one large bed and an old cot. A table and chairs for reading and writing were near the fireplace. The wooden floor was covered by a thick carpet. A bookshelf full of old books was cut into one of the walls.

Jory picked up a chair and walked over to the bookshelf. He stood on the chair and searched through the shelves until he found a box hidden among the books. He hoped it would feel like there was something in it, but his hope faded to disappointment when he opened it to discover there was only a blank piece of parchment and a stylus inside, the way Sir Cley had left it two years ago.

"What's in the box?"

"Sir Cley said that if we were to ever get separated, I was supposed to c-come back here. He would leave me something to tell me what to do next," Jory explained with disappointment.

He sat down on one of the chairs at the table. Alistar sat across from him, resting his chin on his hands. Jory tried to think about what to do. He scanned the room. The two windows facing east were still shuttered, as were the windows facing west. There was a wooden ladder that led up to a trap door in the ceiling, giving access to the third floor, which Jory had used as his room to sleep in on warmer nights. The arrow slits in the tower wall allowed a cool breeze into the room. From the third floor, hand and footholds were cut into the wall to be used to reach the top of the tower with its crenellations and murder holes. There would be nothing to help from above.

Jory's stomach growled.

"I'm hungry too," Alistar mumbled to the table. "We have some apples left."

Apples for breakfast. Apples for lunch. Apples for dinner.

Jory was ready for something else.

"Let's see if we can catch something, like a r-rabbit. There is an old farmer not far from here. Maybe he would let us have a chicken or some eggs."

The two boys left Shadow Tower and hiked the path that led away from the woods to a small farm. The corn and hay were beginning to grow taller in the fields, but the vegetables in the garden were trampled. Jory and Alistar approached the farmhouse and could see there were no horses in the small stable, no pigs in the pen, and no chickens or cows in the yard.

"Hello? Is anyone here?"

No one answered.

"Maybe they went to town," Alistar suggested.

"The nearest town is over a day away. And they w-wouldn't take all their animals."

The sky above them was a dark reddish and black color. The setting sun reflected off smoke coming from somewhere in the distance to the north of the farm.

"Who is out there?"

Jory heard a voice coming from inside the farmhouse.

"It's me, Jory. Sir Cley's s-squire."

An elderly man came to the door holding a pitchfork defensively.

"Aye. I see... Grown some, have ya?" the farmer said, looking Jory over. "Where is Sir Cley?"

"Umm...back at the tower. He sent us to see if we c-could trade for some food."

"There is no food here, boys. Them soldiers took what we have."

"Western soldiers? But they would not steal from farmers," Jory said.

"An army takes what it needs. It don't matter which direction it comes from," the farmer stated bitterly. "This army happened to be from the East. Some of their foragers came through here two days ago. Took my good cow, the horse, all the chickens, and the pigs, not to mention everything from the garden." The old man spat and raised his eyes to the sky. "That fire been burnin' since sunrise. Some type of battle, I bet... You boys shouldn't be roamin' with all those soldiers wanderin' around. Mayhaps you get grabbed into their army, or worse."

Jory looked up to the darkening sky.

"The sky gets dark like that after a b-battle?"

"It can. Whoever won may have piled the bodies up to burn before the birds can get at them. You can stay here with me and the wife, but you would be safer with Sir Cley in the tower."

"You and your wife could come with us to the tower," Alistar suggested.

"Nah, without a horse, me and the missus cannot go that far."

Jory glanced back again at the darkening sky as smoke blocked the setting sun. "We b-better get back to the tower, before it gets too dark."

•   •   •

"What are we going to do now?" Alistar asked, leaning back in his chair.

"I don't know. I guess wait h-here at the tower."

Jory's stomach hurt. Another apple for another dinner. They would need to catch a rabbit or some fish from the creek. Maybe he could get a pheasant tomorrow. He had seen some at the border of the woods.

"Why can't we go back to Marwyn's? He has lots of food besides apples."

Jory thought about it. He could leave Sir Cley a note in the box and something to prove it was him who left it. They couldn't wait forever for Sir Cley to show up.

"Let's give him thr-three days. If he does not show up, I will leave him a message. We will then go back to Marwyn's," Jory said. "Let's get ready for bed."

The boys fit into the bed Sir Cley had used as his own. Alistar snored lightly in the dark, and Sir Morris settled himself between the two boys. Jory stared at the wooden ceiling above him. He had never been scared of living at Shadow Tower. It was not until later when he and Sir Cley began to travel to tournaments that others would tell him stories of ghosts and wraiths that haunted the place. The tale told most often was the story of the lord who murdered his prisoners and bathed in their blood in the tower's dungeon.

The scariest story was of the last lord who lived in the tower. He went mad and strangled his two sons, whom he accused of trying to kill him and his wife. He tossed his wife off the top of the tower and followed her by jumping off himself. According to the story, the ghosts of the two boys would climb up and down the stairs in the darkest hours of night.

Jory resorted to telling people that he and Sir Cley were from Buckton. No one had any stories about Buckton. Jory knew the tales could not be true because the tower did not even have a dungeon. He did remember the third floor had two small beds and some toy soldiers and horses carved out of wood. Sir Cley insisted on throwing everything out and burning it.

Jory tried closing his eyes. The vision of the man he shot in the eye with the arrow haunted him. Every noise inside and outside the tower kept Jory awake. He told himself the wind was blowing and finally drifted off to an uneasy sleep.

He dreamt of being held underwater and struggling for air. He was drowning and struggled in the darkness. The nightmare ended when Sir Morris awakened him. The cat stood on Jory's back and hissed into the darkness toward the window facing the west.

Jory climbed out of bed and walked over to the window, peeking out into the darkness through one of the gaps in the shutters. The woods surrounded the tower as if the trees were laying siege to it. A noise that sounded like metal striking stone came from below. Jory scanned the darkness until he saw a dark figure stumble into the clearing. A soldier dragging a sword on the ground hobbled toward the tower.

Did I bar the door below? I think I remembered.

The sound of galloping horses swelled in a low rumble from the forest, and three men on horse came into the clearing. The horsemen circled the limping man, cutting him off from the tower. One of the horsemen fired his crossbow at the lone soldier. The quarrel brought the limping man down to the ground. One of the men dismounted, walked over to the fallen soldier, and knelt next to him, placing a hand on the soldier. A dark glow emitted from them, and the soldier began to stand with the quarrel sticking out of his chest. The kneeling horseman motioned toward the tower. The other two horsemen dismounted, and all three walked to the door, followed by the limping soldier.

Jory hurried to the bed and shook Alistar's shoulder.

"Wake up, Alistar. We have to hide," Jory urged.

"What... What's going on?" Alistar mumbled, still half asleep.

"Soldiers outside...coming in," Jory said, trying to keep his voice low. "We can hide up above."

Jory heard the men opening the door below. He had forgotten to bar it. There was not enough time to grab their things. Jory made for the wooden ladder with Alistar behind him. He climbed the ladder to the trap door in the ceiling and pushed up, but it only opened part of the way. Something heavy weighed it down. Jory pushed again with both hands, but it was still too heavy. Alistar got on the ladder and made his way up behind Jory.

Jory turned to the stairs. He could see torchlight coming from below and hear the men talking. He pushed again on the trap door, this time using his shoulder and back. The door rose higher but not enough to slip in.

"Hurry, Jory," Alistar whispered.

"I'm trying. Something heavy is blocking it."

"What do we have here? The ghosts of Shadow Tower?"

The voice was deep and menacing. Jory turned toward the stairs to see the three horsemen were in the room holding torches. The soldier limped up the stairs behind them, the whites of his eyes glowing in the darkness.

"Come on down from there. I ain't never seen a ghost. Let's have a look at you."

The horsemen wore dark-brown cloaks over leather armor. No sigils or badges were displayed to show where they were from. Each was armed with a sword, and one of the men carried a crossbow. The soldier with the quarrel in his chest stepped into the room. The torchlight showed he was wearing a leather vest with antlers stamped on it.

A soldier from Buckton.

"Hurry up, you two. Down here, now," another of the horsemen said.

Jory nodded at Alistar to start climbing down the ladder. Jory followed him carefully down. His bow and quiver were on the table not far from where he stood.

"Only two boys. Rest of the room is clear, M'Lord," the man with the crossbow said, walking around the room.

"Are you boys here alone?" the lord asked.

"Y-yes," Jory said as Alistar stepped closer to him.

"What are you doing here? Are you runaways?"

The torchlight showed that the faces and hands of the other two horsemen were covered in dark grime or soot. The man the others called lord had a hood pulled forward, making it difficult to see his face.

"Yes...r-runaways. We live here now," Jory answered.

"Makes no matter who they are, M'Lord. All's fair in war." One of the soldiers sheathed his sword and stepped toward Jory, who bolted toward his bow on the table. The soldier blocked his path and grabbed him by his arm. Jory struggled against his grip.

"Don't touch him," Alistar called.

"Where do you think you're going?" The soldier pulled Jory toward the stairs as Jory fought to pull away from him.

"Don't touch him," Alistar said again, louder.

The lord sniffed at the air, then pulled his hood back, revealing black sunken eyes and dark rags wrapped around his face from the nose down to his throat. "I know what you are," he hissed at Alistar. "Seize that one for me."

The man with the crossbow set his weapon down and came after Alistar.

Jory dropped to the floor, causing the soldier to lose his grip on Jory's arm. He kicked at the man, trying to scramble away, but the man grabbed his foot.

"Don't touch him!" Alistar screamed.

A rush of heat boiled over Jory. Fire licked at his bare foot. The heat raged above him like an iron-smith's forge. The screams of the men behind Jory were piercing. He had never heard anything like it before. Jory covered his ears and balled himself up. The intense heat in the room caused the wooden floor to crack and splinter. He looked up at Alistar. The boy was surrounded by red, yellow, and orange flames, and more leapt from his outstretched hand toward the soldiers. Alistar's eyes were narrowed, and golden flames danced in them. The smiling boy was gone.

The screams of the men stopped, and the room cooled. The smell of burning wood and cloth hung in the air, but there was also a horrid, rank scent. Jory had never smelled burning flesh before, but he knew what a tanner's shop smelled like. The odor stung Jory's nose and made his eyes water. His stomach lurched like he was going to be sick.

Jory gathered himself and stood. He found Alistar sitting on the bed. He went over to him and sat down next to the younger boy.

"I didn't want to," Alistar said, head lowered with tears running down his cheeks.

"It's okay. I know."

Jory put his arm around Alistar. His skin was cold, and he began to shiver. Jory laid him down in the bed and covered him with the blankets they brought.

"The Summoner got away," Alistar said in a weak voice.

"The what?" Jory asked, but Alistar's eyes were already

closed, and he was asleep. Jory scanned the room. Three piles of ashes were smoldering on the floor.

The fourth man with the rags wrapped around his face.

Jory thought for a moment. He and Alistar could not stay here at the tower. More soldiers might be coming. He needed to tell someone about the battle that happened to the north. He had to get back to Marwyn's and lead the others back to Prince James's camp.

Jory got up from the bed and went to the bookshelf. He found the secret box again and wrote a note to Sir Cley on the parchment, telling him that Emily and Theo were alive, and that they were at Marwyn's in the woods. He added that there was a battle to the north of the tower, and there was a Summoner.

Maybe Sir Cley would know what that meant.

Jory folded the paper and put it back in the box. He needed to leave something in it to show that it was truly him who wrote the note. He thought of his shark tooth necklace, but he couldn't part with that. There had to be something else. Jory went to his bag and rummaged to the bottom until he found what he was looking for. He pulled out the armband with the Broken Tower sigil, then folded it and placed it in the box.

36

THE PRINCE VII

The early morning sun peeked above the trees to the east of Crosstimbers as Prince James stood alongside Sir Lucas on the banks of the Grey River. The water slowly rolled by in murky swells. James studied the far banks. He could see smoke from small fires in the distance. Only a small detachment of guards surrounded him, as the majority of the Army of the West had crossed the Grey River before dawn. Close to one thousand men had made the crossing of the wide river, mostly on fishing boats and barges.

Three days before, Lord Buckhorn had led his own men plus fifty of the soldiers from Kingstown west. The plan called for them to cross the Grey River north of Lord Russ's army to create a distraction. Spies reported that Russ's eldest son, Vasili, had arrived to take command of his father's army. Crown Prince Vasili, he called himself. Lord Buckhorn was positive that Vasili would overreact to the attack and send all his troops, leaving his rear exposed.

The plan was sound, all the lords agreed. Even James's mother said the battle plan was good, although she still called for a direct assault on the southern city. It was mostly Lord

Buckhorn's idea, but he allowed Lord Harroldson to present it as his own.

At midmorning, a clamor of bells rang from within the city. The drawbridge known as Sands Bridge slowly descended to the southern city.

"To the bridge, My Prince?" Sir Lucas asked him.

"Yes, it is time, I think."

James rode through the main street of the southern city. Fishermen, dockworkers, and warehouse men lined the streets and greeted him with cheers. Commoners leaned out their windows calling to him. Children ran up to touch his boots and spurs. Joining the procession were Sir Lucas, riding at his side, Lord Fowler, Fowler's two sons, and the small force from Greyport.

"The true king has arrived! Hail to King James the First!"

The Beggar's voice rose above all the others, proclaiming James's ascension to the throne. The priest, still dressed in his faded temple robes, stood on top of a stack of crates. The people shouted back, cheering for their new king.

The procession made its way through the southern city until they arrived at Sands Bridge. The southern span of the bridge finished its descent. Soldiers of the city guard placed smooth wooden planks down to fill the gap between the bridge and the road. Two riders rode across from the citadel to meet James. One rider bore the sigil of the city of Crosstimbers. The other rider held the banner of Tidehaven and Lord Harroldson.

"My Prince, your forces have won the day. Lord Russ's army is in retreat. Lord Harroldson sends word that it is a great victory," the knight bearing Lord Harroldson's sigil reported.

"My Prince, the elders of Crosstimbers have opened the

city to you and your men," the herald holding the banner of Crosstimbers announced with as much pomp as he could summon. The gray and black-striped banner with two golden keys crossed on it waved in the light morning breeze. "Lord Denek, the Holder of the Keys, invites you to use the engineering marvels that are our bridges to make your crossing to the northern city."

"I accept Lord Denek's invitation and thank the elders for the city's...belated hospitality," James replied. He turned his attention to the knight from Tidehaven. "My good knight, please lead me to Lord Harroldson so that he may tell me more of the battle."

The citadel's garrison of soldiers hailed James as he entered the gates. Trumpets sounded, and the bells of the city on both sides of the Grey rang out. The main keep of the citadel was made of white rock that gleamed in the sun. Ropes, chains, and pulleys hung from everywhere on the walls. The drawbridge system the city engineers had created truly was a marvel.

James noted there was no delegation of city elders to greet him, only the herald they sent. Lord Denek, the leader of the elders, did not bother to make an appearance either. The Free Cities were known to be rebellious. James knew their attitude toward the Crown was one of tolerance at best.

The commoners in the northern city lined the streets like the people of the southern town. Most cheered for their new king, but some only stood and gawked, expressing neither acceptance nor rejection. It was bothersome for James after the excited greeting he had received in the southern city.

"I am going to be their king. You would think they would be more excited," James said to Sir Lucas as they rode through the main street.

"My Prince, some of these people believed you were

dead, remember," Sir Lucas said. "The northern city is where most of the wealthy merchants and tradesmen live. The Crown means taxes to most of them."

James observed that the northern city did have nice stone buildings with cobblestone roads. A marble fountain was in the middle of a square that they rode through. The southern city had been mostly warehouses, docks, and shabby wooden homes thrown up here and there.

"We will hold court back in the southern city in the market where the Beggar spoke. I know it will require more effort, but I want the prisoners marched through the cities. I want the workers of the city to see me as king. Send word back to camp that they are to make the preparations."

In the middle of a smoke-filled battlefield, a tent was set up to house the future king.

"My Prince, we have routed the enemy for you," Lord Harroldson said, kneeling before James.

James offered his hand to help Lord Harroldson return to his feet.

"Rise, Lord Harroldson, and tell me of the battle."

"It was not much of a battle in truth, My Prince. It went as I planned. Vasili took the bait and sent his forces north to our diversion. We hit him when he turned. The most unexpected event was the defection of the Kingstown soldiers to our cause. Over half of Russ's forces joined with us. We have nearly four hundred men to add to your army."

"What of Vasili? Was he captured?"

"No, he and a small detachment of his own soldiers from Easton were able to escape. As soon as our attack came from the south, Vasili tucked his tail like the coward he is and headed back to Kingstown. Once he fled from the battlefield, the other knights and soldiers of Kingstown surrendered. Casualties on both sides were low."

"Of our casualties, how many?"

"Only some common soldiers. A few knights were injured, and of course Lord Buckhorn," Lord Harroldson added without emotion.

"Lord Buckhorn is injured?" James asked with alarm. "Take me to him."

"No, My Prince, I thought you knew. Lord Buckhorn is dead."

37
A KNIGHT OF THE REALM II

"Seven men, seven sons of the West, seven warriors of Buckton...Lord Buckhorn had been the best," Sir Torrent said as he touched his torch to the funeral pyre. The fire spread and engulfed the men who gave their lives for their prince.

Torrent led the men gathered in a song and offered another drink to their fallen brothers and lord. Cley stepped forward to speak. His throat was tight.

"To the Old Buck," Cley said. It was all he could manage. His hand clenched at his chest near his heart.

The sky grew dark and full of smoke. The hot coals of the funeral pyre smoldered on the ground. The surviving men of Buckton had their fill of drink and went back to their camp, while Cley sat on the ground near the pyre alone. He waved off Sir Torrent when the knight offered to sit with him.

Lord Buckhorn had meant everything to Cley after Sir Jonas died. It was Buckhorn who made sure King Edward knighted him and named him to the Knights of the Realm. It was Buckhorn who told him what happened at Falling Stone was not his fault. It was Buckhorn who supplied him and sponsored him in the tournaments. And it was Buckhorn who put Jory and him together.

Lord Buckhorn's sword rested across Cley's knees. He had been a man of simple tastes, but his sword was a work of art. Deer antlers made of silver, jagged and dangerous, formed the pommel. In close quarters, those antlers could do more damage than the blade itself. The blade was forged of the finest steel in Terros with etchings of leaves decorating it. Cley planned to give it to Lord Buckhorn's son when he arrived at Kingstown with the rest of the western lords.

Cley thought back to the battle. They had split into three units to disorient Russ's army, attacking in waves and withdrawing to make it look like there were more numbers in their force. Cley heard stories of other knights and soldiers from Tidehaven offering no quarter in retaliation for the deaths of Lord Harroldson's two sons. Sir Lennon's tale of what happened in Shadow Woods angered the men of the West. The carnage was the worst with the Sorrow's group. He took no prisoners. It was his unit that drove Vasili off the field in retreat. The Sorrow needed no excuses of revenge to claim the lives of knights and soldiers who opposed him, even if they were on their knees in surrender.

Cley turned the coin he had removed from Lord Buckhorn's belt between his fingers.

The hammer and anvil. How long would this war last?

Cley surprised himself by considering this conflict a war after two small battles, but battles and wars had always been the way of Terros. The soldiers and knights were the hammer, constantly beating against the anvil, never getting anywhere. Terros was the anvil, unmoving and solid. The people were caught between the two forces. The smith was whoever was in charge, whether it be a king or a lord. Some smiths liked to pound the hammer. Create, destroy, and create again.

Others had a lighter touch, crafting something nice, beautiful, delicate. Cley knew which type of smith he would be.

"There you are."

The voice was sweet, yet it was not the voice Cley wanted to hear. He did not bother to look up as Alyss limped over and sat down next to him.

"I am sorry for your loss, Cley. I know how much Lord Buckhorn meant to you. He was a good warrior, I have been told, but I knew him as an even better lord. Everyone in Buckton loved the man."

Cley raised his eyes to Alyss.

"Yes, he was a good lord, always fair. He will be missed sorely."

"So will the men and knights go back to Buckton?" Alyss asked.

Cley took a deep breath.

"No, we will be folded into Lord Harroldson's forces now, marching under Tidehaven's banner. He has already let it be known that we will march on Kingstown in two days. He is spoiling for a fight with Lord Russ to avenge his son."

"His sons, you mean."

"Only Tristan is known for sure to be dead. The younger one, Theo, was with the others, remember. I must believe he is still alive with Jory and the other two."

Sir Cley gazed up into the night sky. The weight of Lord Buckhorn's sword pressed on his knees. He thought of the sword he carried in his pack but still refused to wield. He looked down at the coin in his hands again, turning it over between his fingers. The compass rose on the back side of the coin pointed to the west. He rose to his feet and began to walk away.

"Whatever you hear, I did not desert," Cley said, turning back to Alyss.

"Where are you going?" Alyss called to him as he walked into the night.

"To find them."

The top of Shadow Tower stuck out amongst the trees of the forest like a rock on the edge of a murky puddle. Cley exhaled heavily in his saddle, relieved to be at his destination. He led his horse along the tree line. The past three days, he rode around the woods, making his way while looking for signs of Jory and the others. He questioned farmers, hunters, and woodsmen who lived on the outskirts of the woods, though they claimed they had not seen any travelers.

He knew Jory would make for the tower if he and the others were still alive. Only death or being taken prisoner would have kept Jory from arriving. Cley prayed for the latter.

Between speaking with farmers, Cley thought about what might be going on back at Crosstimbers. Lord Harroldson would be furious that he left. Torrent and the other Knights of the Barrel would think he had finally lost his head. The soldiers would see him as a deserter. He was unsure how Prince James would take his sudden departure.

Cley tried to shut these thoughts off. They were not helping but kept creeping back.

The Knight of the Tall Tree coming down with battle fatigue. The great Sir Cley Woods, the Deserter. Sir Cley the Traitor.

The soldiers and other knights were looking at Sir Cley in a different light already. "Just a tournament knight," they would say in their cups. "The knight who lost half his party in the woods, including his own squire."

Cley rounded the bend of trees that formed the border of Shadow Woods. The tower stood as he remembered it. The outbuildings still needed repair and tall grass was overtaking the courtyard again. He watched for signs of visitors to the tower as he rode toward it, finding six apple cores littering the waste pile outside the old rock wall.

Someone has been here recently, and they cared enough to take out the rubbish.

Cley rode into the courtyard and dismounted his horse. There were hoofprints in the dirt, and some of the tall grass was trampled down near the steps to the tower. Cley drew his dagger and walked to the entrance.

A lounging cat at the door picked its head up as Cley approached, standing at attention as if it recognized Cley and moving out of the doorway.

What is the cat's name?

The hinges on the heavy wooden door complained as Cley pushed it open. The cat scurried between Cley's legs, making for the spiral staircase's fifth step and watching Cley move about the room. Cley noted that dust had been wiped off the table and two of the chairs. Inside the tower, there was a strange scent in the air—a cross between brimstone and dampness.

"Has Jory been here?" Cley asked the cat. "Would you tell me if he had?"

The lamp sitting on the table had been lit recently, maybe only a few days ago. He lit it himself then climbed the stairs to the second floor, the cat bounding up in front of him.

At the top of the stairs, the scent of burnt leather and wood overwhelmed him. The table and chairs in the room had black scorch marks on them. The rug he had shipped down from Buckton was singed and held three piles of ashes upon it. The tapestries on the walls were in burnt tatters, but the books on the shelves in the wall behind the bed looked unscathed. The bed sheets were pulled back as if someone had slept in them.

Cley watched the cat stroll across the carpet.

Sir Morris, that's what Jory called you.

"What happened here, Sir Morris?" Cley asked. The cat moved over to the ladder leading up to the third floor.

Cley climbed the ladder and pushed on the trap door with his hand. It would not open. He pushed harder, and the door opened a little bit. Something was on top of it. He put both hands on the door and pushed up with his arms and legs. The door rose heavily until whatever was on top of it slid off. Cley found the third floor empty. A part of the wall had fallen in to cover the trap door. Cley cleared the debris from the door and went over to the hole in the wall. The woods to the south spread over the land like a dark veil.

"Where are you, Jory?" Someone had been here recently, and by the looks of the footprints and hoofprints in the courtyard, there had been at least two people.

But where did Jory get horses from?

Cley descended the ladder to the bedroom, then went over to the bookshelves and searched through the books.

"There you are," he said when he found the black leather-bound book. It was not truly a book but a box designed to look like a book when placed on the shelf. Cley took the box off the shelf and placed it on the table. His hopes rose when he observed there was not much dust covering it. Inside, he found the parchment and stylus. The handwriting was Jory's. He had seen it enough when he had made the boy practice his writing at night by copying from the books on the shelves. But to leave no doubt he had been here, Jory left the armband Cley had given him before the melee back in Pebble Creek.

Cley opened the note and read.

> *Sir Cley, I was here. We went back to Marwyn's to get Emily and Theo and head to Crosstimbers.*
> *There was a battle to the north. Soldiers came here.*
> *A Summoner also.*
>
> *Jory*

Cley sat down in one of the chairs at the table and thought about the note. He smiled in relief, knowing they were alive, and read the note again.

Why were Jory and Sir Lennon's squire separated from the other two? Who is Marwyn? Who fought a battle north of the tower? What's a Summoner?

Cley went over to the nearest pile of ashes on the floor and poked his finger through it. He found a few metal buttons in it, but they had melted. The second pile had one button that had part of a hammer still etched into it. The third pile near the spiral stairs had a piece of metal with antlers engraved on it.

Soldiers from Kingstown and Buckton were here. Was it a battle between the West and Kingstown? Why the piles of ashes and melted metal?

Cley tossed those questions aside and thought about what he knew for sure. The children were alive and headed for Crosstimbers. He could not be sure how many days ago the note was written, nor how many days it would take them to get to the eastern border of the woods. He could not risk plunging into the woods after them. It would be like trying to find a mouse in a hayfield.

I must go back to Lord Harroldson. He will order outriders to keep watch for the children.

Resolved and sure of his plan, Cley went down the spiral staircase and out into the courtyard to his horse. He grabbed the bundle strapped to his saddle, then went back inside and up to the bedroom. He opened the bundle and removed Sir Jonas Turner's sword.

Courage, Sir Jonas called it.

Cley often thought of using it in a tournament or lately taking it into battle. But the sword was not his to use. It should be for Jory. He wrapped the boy's armband around the hilt, covered the sword back up, and took it to the bookshelf. He stood on a chair and placed the bundle out of sight on top of the books on the highest shelf.

Cley opened the pouch at his side and pulled out the journal Lord Buckhorn had given him. *The Knights Roll...* He had resisted the urge to open the book and look inside since Lord Buckhorn had died, but now he did. On the second to last page with writing on it, he found the name he was looking for above the faded name of Sir Jonas Turner. The faded brown ink read: Sir William Buckhorn, the Silent Stag.

Cley closed the journal, picked up Jory's note and read it one more time, then hurriedly wrote a few lines to Jory on the back of it in case the boy should return. He placed the box back on the shelf with the other books and slid the journal next to it. It would be safe in the tower guarded by the ghosts of the past.

38
EMILY IX

mily rolled over and stared at the ceiling. She had slept soundly for the last three nights, but tonight, the night before they were supposed to leave the stone house, sleep eluded her.

She still had so many unanswered questions. When Jory and Alistar returned from Shadow Tower, Marwyn ushered the two boys away. It was not until the next night that she saw them again, and Jory acted differently toward her. He smiled less and was less friendly. Emily tried not to emote any ideas of love around him.

Maybe that is it. The boy was normally serious and un-friendly, and it was my emoting that caused him to be friendly and possibly infatuated with me. But something happened at that tower.

Emily heard the story from Marwyn about the battle to the north and understood that was why they had to get back to Prince James, to let him know, but there was more she was not being told. She could sense it. Alistar was tight-lipped for once and avoided her. Jory's only comment was that they needed to hurry to Crosstimbers.

Theo was happy they were leaving. He never liked being

at the stone house. Despite having the nicest room, he moped about constantly. Emily tried to talk to him about the loss of his brother Tristan and his friend Draven, but their deaths weighed on him as if they were his fault. Marwyn assured her that Theo would improve. It was important that she try not to use her emoting to change or hide his true feelings as that would only lead to problems later.

Emily rolled to her side. Before her were the books sitting on the table—still so many that she wanted to read, so much knowledge she had never known was out there. She was going to take only one book with her, and she decided it would be Cyril's journal. It was small and would take up little room in her pack. Plus, a second reading might reveal more about their shared talents.

In the silence of the darkened house, Emily heard shouting from outside. She sprang from her bed and went to her window. A voice shouted again, and it was followed by a flash of white light and a clap of thunder. Several more flashes of lightning came. A storm began to rage outside.

A knock came on her door. She found Theo on the other side when she opened it.

"It's Marwyn. He's outside in his nightclothes. I think he is making it lightning."

"Wake up Veranice and the others. I will go to him."

Emily found Marwyn alone in a clearing of grass, standing against the night. Dark clouds boiled in the sky above him, blocking out the moon.

"They are coming. They will not take us," Marwyn said to Emily as she ran up to him.

"Who? Who is coming?" Emily shouted over another clap of thunder.

"The temple. The Purge is coming for us."

"Where are they?"

Marwyn spoke into the sky, using words Emily did not understand, and a bolt of lightning leapt from the clouds and struck a tree, shattering it into splinters. The ground shook as thunder roared around them. Marwyn held his arms out wide. A gale of wind came from behind them, forcing the trees in the orchard and the surrounding woods to bend and creak. Marwyn's hair and beard waved in the wind that swirled around him. His eyes were wide, and his pupils darted from side to side as he scanned the stormy sky.

Jory ran up to them against the wind. "What's going on?"

"I don't know. Marwyn says we are being attacked," Emily answered.

"Jonas, it's about time," Marwyn said, looking at Jory. "Did you bring your sword?"

Jory scanned the ground nearby and picked up a tree branch.

"Yes, sir, it's right here," the boy answered, swinging the branch into parry position.

"Good, we will need it."

Marwyn and Jory stood facing the dark woods against unseen enemies.

Is any of this real?

Marwyn spoke into the sky again. The wind changed direction and became frigid. Sleet pelted down on them from the sky, falling heavily and stinging Emily's face as it struck her.

Alistar came running from the house. He ran up next to Marwyn and grabbed his hand.

"Marwyn, it's me, Alistar. It's okay. We're safe," the boy said. He repeated it again and again until the wind died down and the heavy sleet turned into soft flakes of snow floating in the air.

"Alistar, yes...Alistar," Marwyn whispered. He stumbled

a bit and Alistar grabbed him around the waist. Jory went to the man's other side to help support him.

Veranice made her way to them with a blanket, draping it over Marwyn and helping the boys walk the wizard back to the house and to his room.

Back in her room, Emily sat and waited with her door open. She spied Jory walking past.

"Is Marwyn going to be alright?" Emily called.

Jory stopped and walked back to the open door.

"He will be fine after some rest."

"How did you know we were not being attacked?"

Jory shrugged. "He called me Jonas. His mind was mixed up. Alistar told me it happens sometimes."

"You can come in and talk for a bit, if you want."

"The sun will be up soon, and I need to pack," Jory replied before walking to his room. Emily resisted the urge to emote and make him come in and tell her everything that had happened at Shadow Tower. She got up, closed her door, and went back to her bed.

In the morning, they were all at the table eating breakfast except for Marwyn, whose chair remained empty.

"We should be leaving soon. I am going to gather my pack and gear," Theo said. It was the happiest he had appeared since they kissed in the swamp while the others set up camp.

Jory and Alistar both got up at the same time and ran down the hall toward their rooms.

"I am sorry for the scare I gave you last night, my dear."

Emily turned to see Marwyn sitting near the large hearth. She walked over to him and sat on a stool at his feet.

"Are you alright, Marwyn?"

"Yes, I am healthy, but my mind is growing old, I am afraid. I forget things more than I used to. Sometimes I become confused and relive events from the past, like last night. As I told you, our talents are like a double-bladed sword. There are costs when we use them. The cost is different for each Drasani."

Emily put her hand on Marwyn's knee. "Maybe I should stay. I could help you, and you could train me. Plus, I would like to read from your library some more."

"No, you must go with your friends for now. Veranice can keep watch over me, and Alistar is here." Marwyn reached out to take Emily's hand in his. His hands felt cold and weak. "I think you will return someday. The books will still be here. Until then, you need to continue to practice your talents...learn control and command."

Theo entered the main room and walked over to stand next to Emily. He was dressed for travel with his pack slung over his shoulders and his sword hanging from his belt.

"I am ready to go," Theo announced.

"I want you to take this, Theo," Marwyn said, holding out a silver coin. "May it help you in your travels. It is not for spending, but it will help you get where you want to go."

Theo took the coin and turned it over in his fingers. Emily could see there were no markings on it. The coin was a flat silver piece.

"I know we did not get to spend much time together, young man. I knew Lord Harrold. You remind me of him. He was not such a terrible king."

Theo's eyes widened in surprise. Lord Harrold, the founder of Theo's family, had been King of Terros over two hundred years ago.

"Maybe next time we will speak of him together."

Theo nodded.

"Yes, I would like that."

The three young adventurers left the stone house early that morning as the sun brightened the sky above the trees of the forest. Before they departed, Marwyn spoke with Jory in private. Alistar remained in his room, upset that he was not allowed to go. Emily had to say her goodbyes to him through his door.

Emily looked at her two companions as they walked away from the stone house. Theo displayed the colors of his house, dressed in a blue hooded cloak with silver trim and a white tunic along with brown pants made of fine cloth. He wore a silver brooch in the shape of a wave that held his cloak together near his throat. His sword was tied to his belt, and his face displayed resolve. He was starting to look like a warrior, not the boy she had first seen back in Tidehaven. But a sadness hung about Theo now, guilt for what he perceived as his failings in the woods.

Jory was outfitted in the same tattered clothes he wore the day they arrived. Emily wondered if Marwyn had even offered him new clothing like he had for Theo and herself. His bow was strapped across his back, and he wore a short sword at his side. He spoke little. Emily tried to reach out and read Jory's emotions but could not find anything. His face betrayed nothing of what he was thinking. He said simply, "We need to get going."

Emily chose to wear simple traveling clothes. She could have been mistaken for one of the boys at a distance. She carried her bag with the demon's pitcher nectar over one shoulder. On the other, she carried a pack containing Cyril's journal, a journal for herself, and one of the nice dresses left for her.

I know who I am now. I am not some helpless girl waiting for a handsome knight to come rescue me.

39

JORY XII

Shadow Woods must have been tired, exhausted from holding back the sun and obstructing the path of the three travelers. The eastward path Jory found was mostly level and free of the roots and brambles that blocked their way when they first traveled into the woods with Sir Cley.

Jory was happy to be walking, which kept his mind off the image of the man he had shot in the eye with the arrow. The sounds of the forest drowned out the screams of the burning men in the tower. The sunlight that trickled to the forest floor chased away the dark thoughts of Emily and Theo holding and kissing each other. But in the dark of night, those images and thoughts came back to him. He tried to think of something else—anything else. He tried to think of Sir Cley and the towns and cities they had been to.

Has Sir Cley always cheated? What about the jousts he won? Was it all fake?

He wished Alistar had come to keep him company. He missed the little boy already. He tried to think of home— playing on the beach, running in the surf with his friends in Seadrift. But that only darkened his thoughts as eventually he would think of that...man.

Theo took the first watch that first night back in the woods. Jory tried to sleep, but his mind raced. Every noise in the woods brought thoughts of evil men hunting for them. The man with the rags around his face haunted Jory's dreams. A Summoner. Alistar said it was a person who could call on demons and the dead to do his bidding. A Summoner could collect another person's spirit and use it. A Summoner was out there, somewhere. Marwyn said there were others out there in the world too, people who had talents to do magical things like Alistar did with fire. Drasani, he called them.

If I could do magic, I would be a great lord, and have a big castle, and no one would be sick or hungry in my land.

On the second day of their journey, Theo and Emily were quiet as they hiked through the woods. Jory liked the quiet. He could hear the woods speaking. Ravens croaked in the trees above. Doves cooed in the lower branches. Squirrels chattered down at them as they passed under their trees, and pheasants squawked in the tall grass.

It was the squawking of the pheasants and the tall grass that made Jory realize they were close to the edge of the woods. When they stepped out from the tree line, sloping plains of tall grass led off to the east, and eventually to the Grey River. He gazed over the plains in amazement. It should have taken them four or five days to walk to the eastern edge of the woods. They had done it in two.

Marwyn.

The sun was setting behind them in the west, and dark clouds were gathering overhead. There would only be a few more hours of light to walk in. A decision needed to be made.

"The Gr-Grey River should be straight east of here," Jory said, pointing. "I don't know how far, b-but it will be dark soon. We could make camp here, or do we walk some more and camp out in the grass?"

Emily searched the sky. "Those clouds look like rain. We would be better off under the cover of the woods."

Soon, the sky opened, and rain poured down. They retreated into the woods, and Jory found a dry flat spot under a huge oak tree on some higher ground inside the forest. They tied a sealskin tarp he had in his backpack to the trees with some rope to provide cover from the rain. The small tarp made the three of them crowd together under it. Jory was barely covered by their little shelter.

The three travelers ate a small meal of cheese and bread along with some jerky that Veranice packed for them. The rain came down harder, and the sound of thunder rumbled in the sky as darkness descended on the forest.

"I am not sure how I am going to face my father," Theo said, breaking the silence.

"Theo, we have talked about this. He will be so happy to see you," Emily replied.

"But what if he doesn't understand? I mean, he has never lost a battle. The first battle I was ever in, I panicked and ran away, leaving my brother behind."

"We did what we had to do to survive. Right, Jory?"

Jory sat trying to stay warm and dry with his hood pulled up over his head. He was still getting wet from the rain that was rolling off the tarp above them. He thought about the question. Emily was right, of course.

We would have died if we had stayed to fight, but what do I care about making Theo feel better about it?

"Jory? We had to run, right?" Emily repeated.

"Y-yes, we did," Jory said, lowering his eyes to the ground as the rain puddled around his boots.

The three of them fell into silence as the sound of rain pouring on the trees above grew louder. The only thing that broke up the sound was a flash of lightning and the rumble of thunder. Emily began to count the seconds between the flashes of lightning. During one of the flashes, Jory saw a dark figure walking along the edge of the woods. Jory reached for his dagger and pulled it out from under his cloak. His bow and quiver hung from a dead limb above them.

Emily's count was at four, and Theo didn't say anything. Maybe I am seeing things.

Lightning flashed again, and the figure appeared once more. Jory's muscles tensed, and he leaned forward.

"What is it?" Emily asked.

"Someone is out there. I saw them when the lightning flashed," Jory whispered. "Stay still."

Jory waited for another flash. None came, but the sound of sloshing footsteps and heavy breathing did.

"Hello there...under the tree. Mind if I join ya?" the stranger called to them through the rain.

"Go find your own tree! Gods know there's plenty in the woods," Theo shouted back. His sword rattled in its scabbard as he tried to draw it.

"No need for that now. Just lookin' for a dry place to sit. Most o' the woods is gettin' swamped. Looks like you found some high ground. I have a larger tarp. It would keep us all dry, and maybe we could have a fire."

The man was armed with a sword. Jory squeezed the dagger in his hand and leaned forward, ready to jump to defend the party.

"You may join us," Emily said.

Her voice was a crack of thunder. Jory almost fell over in disbelief at Emily's kindness to the stranger after everything they had been through.

•   •   •

The fire was low and smoldering. There was not much wood to be gathered nearby that was not already soaked. But the stranger was right. His tarp covered a large area tied between three trees. Jory stared out from under his hood across the fire at him and kept his dagger ready under his cloak. The stranger reclined against his knapsack smoking a pipe. His wet cloak hung from a limb under one of the trees. Theo told him to hang his sword with it.

"What are you children doing in these woods?" the stranger asked.

"We aren't children," Theo answered.

"We were out hunting and got caught in the rain," Emily lied.

"Hunters, are ya? Bad luck gettin' caught in the rain," the stranger said. "Any luck catchin' anything? I'm a bit hungry."

"We have some bread and cheese," Emily offered. She took some food from her pack and leaned over to hand it to the stranger.

"A girl, huh? I thought so," the stranger said after Emily handed him the food. "What's a girl doin' with a couple of boys in the woods huntin'?"

"Girls can hunt as good as any boy," Emily said.

"No offense. It's just not proper where I am from."

"And where are you from?" Theo asked sharply. "And you never told us your name."

"My apologies. Originally, I am from Duskfield, but more recently from Kingstown. I am Sir Carter Witts. Excuse me for not standing up to perform a proper bow."

"I never heard of a Sir Witts from Duskfield or Kingstown," Theo said.

"Livin' out here in the woods, my name probably didn't reach ya." Carter dug into his boot and pulled out a long knife, which he used to cut himself a slice of cheese. "You know my name. Now I'll have yours. 'Tis only fair. How 'bout you first, little lord?"

Sir Carter pointed his knife right at Theo. Jory wanted to smile when the stranger called Theo "little lord." Theo's fine cloak, silver brooch, and boots all but set a crown upon his head. But the sight of the knife with its black onyx handle made Jory hold his breath.

Carter, the same Carter from Seadrift who was always bragging about his beautiful knife, the same Carter who had worked for his stepfather, the same Carter who had held him down in the waves.

"My name is Tim, and this is my brother and sister, thank you," Theo lied.

"Is that right, Tim? Well, it's my right pleasure to meet ya."

Carter stuck his knife into the soft ground in front of him, then leaned back onto his knapsack again and ate his cheese.

"There was a story goin' round amongst the soldiers I was with down at Crosstimbers. Seems there were some lost children up this way in the woods, one o' them some lord's whelp. They say there is a nice reward for anyone who is to find the boy. You wouldn't have happened across any lost children in the woods while you were huntin' now?"

Jory gripped his dagger tighter again.

"You were in Crosstimbers?" Emily asked. "How long ago?"

"Been near a week now. We were sent to protect the king's city from those rebels. But the Lord o' Tides marched right across the Grey with his army and put it to the king's own son. We didn't stand much of a chance against the pretender's army, what with him having support of all those famous knights who kiss his arse, like the Knight o' the Trees.

Rumor went round that the Sorrow was with him too, and many a man packed up before the fight began. Most dropped their weapons and joined up with the pretender." Carter cut himself another slice of cheese. "Now, me, I says I'm done with marchin' and fightin'. I'm goin' to the coast. Find me a nice little boat and house and a nice little wife and live a nice little life. Now, if I could find those lost children...well, the reward would pay for all that maybe."

"There was a battle at Crosstimbers about six days ago?" Emily asked.

"Roughly, yes, six or seven days ago. I lose track. The pretender's scouts are only about a day behind me though. Headed to Kingstown. Don't figure they will go into the woods. Now, I don't want to look discourteous, but all my marchin' in the rain has made me weary. If you don't mind, I am going to catch some sleep."

Carter rolled over to set his head down, facing away from the others. After a few minutes, the man began to snore.

"I'll take the first watch," Theo said.

Jory decided to watch too.

In the darkness, Carter rolled over and raised up on his knees. He plucked his dagger from the ground and crawled toward the three lumps curled up before him.

"Hold there."

Carter froze in place. He peered into the gloom, turning his head until he spotted the outline of Jory's dark figure against a tree.

"The little one, huh?" Carter said quietly. "So you do talk."

Jory stood silently, holding his bow in his left hand and

an arrow in his right, ready to nock. Rain struck his cloak, and water dripped from his hood pulled down low over his head.

"I could tell you weren't with them. Tell you what, we can split the reward for the sleeping lordling over there," Carter whispered into the darkness.

Jory made no reply and stood motionless.

"The girl, is it? You want the girl? I'll hold her down for ya," Carter offered.

Jory still made no reply.

"You think you can beat me in some sword fight?" Carter challenged, louder.

Jory nocked the arrow in his bow and raised it.

"It won't be a sword fight," Jory said coolly as he pulled the bowstring back. The sound of the bow being drawn played across the distance between them.

"So, what now?" Carter asked, leaning back on his heels.

"Leave."

"Smallest one is the most dangerous. Didn't see that comin'." Carter crawled back away from the sleeping figures to the edge of the makeshift shelter. "What about my tarp and my sword over there?"

"Leave."

"Man of few words. Gotcha. Ol' Carter will be on his way, then."

Carter backed out from under the shelter and grabbed his knapsack, then paused for a moment. The muscles in Jory's arms trembled from holding the drawn bow for so long.

"Good luck to ya." Carter walked off into the forest with rain coming down all around him.

Jory relaxed his arms and lowered his bow. It was hard to tell how long it would be till sunup with the dark rain clouds in the sky. He knew they could not stay here. Carter would be back, and with others if he could manage it. Jory moved to a different tree and climbed up onto a low branch where he could see Emily and Theo sleeping next to each other under the tarp. He put his bow and arrow in his lap and leaned his back against the tree trunk. Rainwater trickled down his cloak and steadily dripped from his hood. Jory had never prayed much, but now he prayed for morning.

40
EMILY X

The chirping birds overhead woke Emily. The forest floor emitted a damp but fresh smell. A dull pain poked her in the back. She rolled over to find that she was lying on top of Theo's pack. She sat up and stretched. The muscles in her legs and back ached, and her clothes were damp. Shadow Woods was not as comfortable as the room she had at Marwyn's.

Theo stretched out to her right, his blanket moving up and down with his deep breaths. To her left, Jory slept in an unmoving lump. Across the extinguished campfire was an empty space where Sir Carter had been. His tarp was still tied above them, and his sword hung from the tree where he had left it the night before. Letting the man camp with them had been risky, but it was worth the news he told them.

Jory stepped out of the woods to her left, water dripping from his rain-soaked cloak.

"I thought you were here next to me. Where's Sir Carter?" Emily asked.

"He left," Jory replied.

"Without his tarp and sword?"

"He was in a hurry."

"That doesn't make any sense."

"We need to get to the river. There may be more soldiers searching for us," Jory said.

Jory did not smile, and he sounded tired.

There's fear in his voice.

"I'll wake Theo," Emily said.

After a light breakfast, they made their way back to the edge of the forest, but this time it was early morning. The grassy plains stretched before them to the east, the tall green grass standing almost waist-high to Jory.

"The Grey River should be straight east from here," Jory said.

"How far do you think it is?" Theo asked.

"It depends on where we came out of the woods. Maybe two days of walking, no more than three."

The prospect of walking under the open sky across the plains sounded like an easy task, but Jory and Theo debated which way to go. It was left to Emily to make the deciding vote.

"If we hike over the grass, it will be a shorter distance," Jory said.

"But it will also be the most difficult. The grass is over our knees. It will slow us down. And it will be easy for some-one to spot us in the open. There is nowhere to hide," Theo replied. "If we find a path, it will be easier on our legs, and faster in the end."

"We are more likely to run into people like Carter on a path," Jory countered.

"But more likely to be seen by my father's scouts," Theo added.

The two boys turned to Emily, waiting for her opinion. Both plans made sense.

"I think we should find a path. Fighting through this grass will be hard for me, and I don't want to slow us down," Emily said. "There might be a farm along the way where we can get more news. We need to know exactly where your father's army is, Theo. They could have left Crosstimbers already."

"We head south to head east," Theo said. He pulled the straps on his backpack tighter and began to walk. Emily followed, with Jory bringing up the rear.

Emily adjusted Sir Carter's sword at her side. Theo insisted she take it. She had never used one before and hoped she never would. It threw off her stride and kept hitting her leg.

If the boys can walk with these things, so can I.

They walked south for the entire morning along the edge of the woods. They found two trails that were too small to be paths that would go all the way to the river. The sun was at its highest point when they came across a path rutted with wheel tracks, a cart path that came directly from the east.

"Here we go," Theo said excitedly. "Now we only need a wagon and a team of horses."

Emily could feel Theo's satisfaction that he had been right. Jory remained silent in the rear.

By late afternoon, they were tired and hot under the sun, but they trudged on. The land was open with a few trees sprinkled on the rolling plains. Standing at the top of a hill, Emily saw a farm along the road below them.

"Look, a farm," Emily said, pointing. "Maybe we can get some news."

"We cannot simply go up there and knock on the door. We don't know these people," Theo said. "Jory, how much farther do you think the river is?"

"I don't know. I have never been on this r-road before," Jory said. "But I'm with you. We should avoid the farm."

Emily gave Jory a curious look. The boy never agreed with Theo.

As they walked along the road that led past the farm,

Emily kept an eye out for anyone working in the wheat fields or gardens, but the farm appeared empty.

"Riders behind us. Hide," Jory suddenly warned.

Emily checked behind her and spotted two riders on the hill. The riders began to descend on them. Theo paused as she and Jory scrambled to a tree on the side of the road.

"They could be my father's scouts," Theo said.

"Or they might be others trying to catch us," Emily countered. "Come hide with us."

Theo ran to where Emily and Jory crouched behind a tree.

"This tree will not hide the three of us," Theo said.

Emily pointed at a barn close to their hiding spot.

"Maybe we can get to the barn before they see us," she said.

"We will be trapped inside if they do," Theo replied.

"W-we should hide in the fields," Jory said.

They ran from the cover of the tree toward the fields, but two more riders dressed in brown cloaks galloped up the road from the east and blocked their escape into the fields. Emily veered away from their direction toward a hay shed.

"No, Emily, with us!" Theo yelled.

It was too late. The riders were coming in their direction. Emily continued to run to the shed near the fields. Theo and Jory followed.

Emily slammed the shed door behind the boys once they were inside.

"There was no time," she panted as she looked for something to bar the door.

Theo drew his sword and peered out the gaps between the boards of the shed.

"The others are here too," he announced.

Emily peeked outside. Three riders dressed in dark-green

cloaks dismounted in front of a fourth rider wearing a black hooded cloak.

"We know you are in there. Come out and show your-selves," the man commanded in a rough voice that Emily recognized.

Theo stiffened and pulled away from the shed's wall. Emily realized it was the same man who had killed Tristan in the swamp. She felt Theo's anger rise, and at the same time she sensed something different from Jory. Dread.

"What is it, Jory?" Emily whispered.

"It's him...the Summoner," Jory said. "He was at the tower."

"Burn them out," the Summoner ordered.

The soldiers surrounded the shed. They lit torches and tossed them onto the hay. Smoke began to fill the air inside.

"We cannot burn in here. We must go out and fight," Theo said.

Jory nodded and readied his bow. Emily drew the sword she carried. It was not as heavy as she thought it would be. She awkwardly jabbed it forward in practice.

"Ready?" Theo asked. He leaned against the door, poised to spring out.

"Use your power," Jory whispered as he walked by Emily to kneel at the entrance.

Did Marwyn tell him about my talent? And how would I use it in a fight?

Theo pushed the door open, and Jory let loose an arrow. It found its mark on the unlucky soldier standing outside the door, and he fell to one knee. Theo charged out and was at-tacked by a soldier coming from his left. Jory dropped the wounded soldier to the ground with his second shot. He fired a third arrow at the Summoner, but it passed over his head. Emily rushed past Jory with her sword in hand. A soldier jumped out at her on the right and swung his blade, knocking the sword out of her hand.

"Use it!" Jory yelled at her.

Emily concentrated on the man before her. Everything around her slowed down. Shades of color surrounded the soldier, who gave off a reddish-orange aura that she reached out to. She thought about letting go and stopping. The soldier stopped where he was, his aura changing to a lighter shade of orange. He dropped his sword and stood in place. One of Jory's arrows pierced his chest with a thump, and the man fell to the ground.

Emily collapsed. Her breathing came in gasps, and emotions bombarded her. Smoke and fire filled the air. Colors moved in waves that crashed against each other. A dark aura of blue came to her. Her eyes focused, and it was Jory.

"Are you okay?" Jory asked.

"I think so," she answered. "Where's Theo?"

"I'm here." Theo stepped through the smoke, his face and sword smeared with blood.

A voice began to chant in some language Emily had never heard before. The soldier on the ground before them began to move. Theo ran his sword into its chest, but the soldier continued to rise, dark blood drooling from its mouth. Theo backed away.

The chanting came from the Summoner. He held his hands stretched out toward the ground. The hood of his cloak fell back, exposing a skull-like face scarred with burns. The words he said sounded evil, and his lips barely moved. A soldier with two arrows stuck in his chest stood from a pool of blood and was joined by another soldier with a stab wound on his side.

"There is nowhere for you to run," the Summoner taunted.

41

JORY XIII

Jory helped Emily to her feet. The dead soldier closest to them stood upright, holding his sword, and staggered toward them. Theo attacked and landed a blow that cleaved the soldier's sword hand off. The dead man grabbed Theo by the throat with his remaining hand and raised him off the ground. Theo kicked and struggled. His cloak and sword fell to the ground as he gurgled, fighting to breathe.

"Help him!" Emily cried.

Jory jumped onto the dead man's back and tried to pry him off Theo. Jory pulled his dagger out and stabbed him in the back with no effect.

"Run!" Jory yelled.

Emily ran toward the field. The Summoner rode after her.

The dead soldier dropped Theo to the ground and threw his handless arm behind it, knocking Jory off its back. Jory dropped his dagger, and the dead thing attacked him. It pinned him to the ground and began to strangle him as it had Theo. Jory grasped with his hands, searching for anything to fight with, but all his right hand found was dirt and grass. His left hand found Theo's brooch for his cloak.

Jory stabbed the dead thing in the leg as hard as he could with the brooch's pin. It shrieked with a sound that pierced Jory's ears. The soldier turned to ash and his empty gear fell onto Jory, who scrambled to his feet. Theo was lying on the ground, unmoving. Jory could not tell whether he was breathing. The other two soldiers were getting closer to him, and Jory prepared to attack them when he heard Emily scream. He checked Theo. It would be too late to save him, he decided, so he turned and ran toward Emily's scream.

Jory ran through the smoke and haze until he came to the barn. He peered through the door and saw the Summoner standing with his back to him, leaning over Emily with a curved dagger that radiated a blue light above her head. Emily floated like a puppet on invisible strings and a strange vapor emanated from her.

Jory rushed in and jumped on the Summoner's back. The Summoner lost his balance, and they fell over in a heap. Jory held on tight, his arm squeezing its throat from behind. The Summoner pushed at him, struggling to get away. Its fingers grasped Jory around the wrist, and his skin began to crawl. The fingers were cold, but they seared into the skin. The Summoner said something Jory did not understand, and with renewed strength, tossed Jory away from him.

Jory rolled over, trying to get his bearings in the dimly lit barn. The air was cold and damp despite it being summer. He could not see where the Summoner had hidden himself, but he could hear its rasping breath. Emily was on the ground unconscious, the curved dagger next to her.

"You do not have the Firecaster with you this time, boy. You cannot win," the Summoner said from a dark corner. "Leave the girl to me, and I will give you what you want."

"No," Jory said. He went over to Emily and picked up the Summoner's dagger.

"Not even if what I offer you is...me?" The voice changed into something Jory faintly recognized. Out of the shadows stepped his father. "Come with me, Son. We will go back home. You will have me, your mother, and sister together again. We will get the vengeance you seek."

Jory froze. Sweat trickled down his back, yet he could see his breath when he exhaled. The dagger in his hand began to feel heavy. Tears traced down his cheeks.

"It is time for us to go home, Son." His father went to one knee and opened his arms to welcome him.

Jory dropped the dagger and stepped forward. He thought of his mother and sister. He thought of Emily, Theo, and Sir Cley. He stepped into his father's embrace.

As his father's arms folded around him, Jory took the silver brooch in his hand and stabbed it into the Summoner's neck, holding it there. The face in front of Jory changed from his father's back into the scarred skull-like face of the Summoner. He shrieked in a high wail and fell onto his back, clawing to get away. Jory held on, pressing the sharp pin of the brooch deep into his neck.

"This is not over, boy," the Summoner hissed at Jory. He spoke an incantation and dissolved into the ground beneath them.

Jory sprawled on top of the Summoner's cloak. The coolness in the air gave way to the heat from the fire burning outside the barn.

Emily. I have to get her out of the barn.

Jory crawled over to Emily.

"Emily, wake up." He shook her.

Emily opened her eyes.

"You have to get up. We need to get away from the fire," Jory explained.

Jory helped Emily to her feet, and they walked out of the

barn. In the haze of smoke, Jory could see two figures approaching them. His shoulders sagged as he realized the battle was not over.

The dead soldiers.

Jory searched the ground for something to fight with as the figures grew closer, still clutching the silver brooch in his hand.

"Get behind me. If they bring me down, use the pin on the brooch," he said to Emily.

The two figures kept advancing as Jory gritted his teeth and tried to stoke his courage. He could hear Emily sobbing behind him. Finally, the two figures stepped from the smoke, and Jory could see it was Theo and Sir Cley who began to run toward them.

Emily ran from behind Jory to meet Theo and hugged him around his neck.

Jory began to shake and his breathing came in gasps. He thought of everything he had been through in the woods, at the tower, and at the farm. He fell to his knees and leaned back onto his legs. The brooch slipped from his fingers, and he looked down at his bloody, scarred hands resting on his knees. He choked back a sob and tried to breathe normally as he looked back up to see Sir Cley standing before him. Tears flowed down his cheeks, cutting wet trails in the dirt and soot covering his face.

42

A KNIGHT OF THE REALM III

Sir Cley looked up from his plate and could not help but smile. His squire sat across from him at the camp table, biting into a chicken leg. He still could not believe the boy was with him again.

Lord Harroldson held a great feast earlier in the day to celebrate the return of his son. Emily and Jory were invited guests of honor. Jory said he did not want to go, so Cley grabbed some of the food in the camp kitchens so they could have their own feast.

He smiled again at his squire across the table as the boy was about to take another bite of his chicken leg.

"What? Are you always going to smile at me like that fr- from now on?" Jory asked.

"No, just tonight. Tomorrow, you need to polish my armor and sharpen my sword. Oh, and brush down Thunder. I will frown at you after you do your normal horrible job," Cley answered, smiling still.

Jory grinned and ate some of the potatoes on his plate with his fingers.

"Did you find your friend Aiden today?"

"Yes, h-he was with some other boys grooming the

320

horses. He said he was hoping to be taken on as a squire by some knight from the East. I asked him to come eat with us, but he said he had an errand to run tonight. Maybe he will stay with us tomorrow."

"It's good to have friends. You need to have someone you can trust and lean on when times get difficult."

"Do you still have any friends from when you were my age?"

"I left most of my friends behind when I became your father's squire. Losing a friend can hurt. I have lost a few, but you cannot be afraid to make friends because you might lose them. I thought I had lost you."

On his ride to and from Shadow Tower, Cley had considered what he would do if Jory never came back. A ship across the Eastern or Western Oceans was the most common thought. Get away from Terros and everything that haunted his waking thoughts and dreams. That was when he saw the smoke rising from the grass plains ahead of him. A gut feeling told him it was Jory.

"I think we missed your birthday while you were out there. You're twelve now. I guess I will have to find you a present when we get to Kingstown." Cley took a drink from his cup. "You know, Jory, you did a great thing. You did everything you could to get the others to safety. You even made your way to the tower, like I told you. You saved them at the farm. I am so proud of you. If I could, I would dub you a knight right here."

"I think that would be a fine idea."

The deep voice boomed from the open tent flap. Sir Torrent stood at the entrance. The fat knight entered, followed by several of the other Knights of the Barrel. The tent was soon full of Sir Cley's friends.

"Stand up, my boy, and take a knee in front of Sir Cley," Sir Torrent ordered.

Jory hopped up from his seat and got down on both knees in front of Sir Cley.

"Let's see, a sword for the ceremony," Torrent said, looking around the room, his own sword dangling from his hip as he turned exaggeratedly. "Ah-ha, this will do."

The Great Tor grabbed an uneaten chicken leg off a plate and handed it to Cley, who touched the chicken leg to each of Jory's shoulders.

"Do you swear to fight for justice, protect the innocent, and defend the defenseless?" Cley asked.

"I so swear," Jory replied seriously.

"In the name of the Four, I pronounce you Sir Jory Turner, the Knight of... What's a good nickname for this one?"

"Knight of the Woods," Sir Thurmond offered.

"Nah...too obvious," Torrent shot back.

"The Swamp Knight," Sir Choate said.

"No...the girls will never like that," Torrent complained.

"Knight of Shadow Tower," Sir Boswell suggested.

"Bad luck, that one," Torrent said.

"Knight of the Broken Tower," Sir Bartlett urged.

"No," Cley said bluntly, thinking for a moment. "How about the Chicken Leg Knight?"

"Yes! The Chicken Leg Knight!" the Great Tor roared. "Stand and be welcomed into the most exclusive and honorable order of knights ever assembled, the Knights of the Barrel."

The other knights cheered, slapped Jory on the back, and patted his head.

"I hate to take you away from this great feast, Cley," Torrent said, looking at the plate of chicken bones, sliced potatoes, and carrots, "but Lord Harroldson and the prince want to plan the advance to Kingstown. Maybe there is some fair maiden out there for our new hero to rescue or kiss. Hmm?"

"Jory, ignore Torrent. He hasn't kissed a girl in thirty years," Cley said, standing to leave.

"His belly is so big he can't get close enough," Sir Thurmond added, laughing.

All the knights filed out of Sir Cley's pavilion. At the entrance, Cley stopped and turned back to Jory.

"I'll be back. Don't wait up. You deserve some sleep. It's good to have you back home."

The real war council was held in Prince James's pavilion, while the lower lords and knights supporting him awaited their assignments in Lord Harroldson's huge meeting tent. The lords and knights wore their finest armor, like roosters strutting about trying to intimidate or impress each other. Sir Cley did not bother to wear more than his traveling clothes and his sword at his side.

The minor lords from the South made a spectacle of themselves wearing their shiny ringed armor. Their knights stood behind them talking and laughing.

These men have yet to shed any blood or lose a friend in this conflict.

The lords from the East also were unbloodied, having avoided the battles so far. Lord Fowler managed to keep his small unit out of any of the fighting at Pebble Creek and Crosstimbers. The army that did finally arrive from the East was a disappointment. Only Lord Elmhurst of Dimbury came forth with his meager force, along with the main force of Greyport. Fowler promised over one thousand men to join with the West and the South. The East mustered a mere seven hundred men. Lord Payne of Amberfield had yet to be heard from. He had the least distance to travel, but reports were saying he held his force in Amberfield.

A little over twenty-five-hundred men on foot and cavalry in support of the prince approached Kingstown from the south. Cley knew the forces from Kingstown were depleted. Lord Russ already lost at Pebble Creek and Crosstimbers. Defections, desertion, and death cost him over a thousand men.

The lords and knights in the room went silent as the Lords Paramount of the East, South, and West entered the pavilion. Lord Harroldson appeared healthy despite having almost died at Pebble Creek. Lord Fowler's normally expressionless face wore a frown. Lord Tew of Fynotans, the capital of the South, strolled next to Harroldson and Fowler. Dressed in a robe made of glass beads that shimmered as he walked, the man looked like one of those colorful birds Cley had seen in the menagerie at Kingstown. The three lords walked over to a long table and stood behind it.

"All rise for Prince James," a herald called from the tent's entryway.

The seated lords stood, and the knights around them straightened up. As Prince James walked by, all the lords and knights bowed their heads. Sir Lucas Bardas escorted the prince to his right. Lady Tolar trailed behind her son, walking slowly and nodding to those who still bothered to bow their heads as she passed. James joined the three lords behind the long table, where he took a seat. The Lords Paramount sat soon after him, as did the prince's mother.

"My Lords and Knights, I thank you for your support in this critical time in the history of Terros," Prince James began. "The Lords Paramount have devised a plan for the assault on Kingstown. It is my wish that we do as little damage to the city as possible and take control of it with few deaths to its people. I will let Lord Harroldson tell you of your assignments."

Lord Harroldson stood and cleared his throat. A knight of his house came over to the table and unrolled a map in front of the other lords and Prince James. Another knight came forward and placed markers on the table near Lord Harroldson.

"Russ has placed some of his forces to the south of the city. He has lines of scorpions and palisade walls constructed for defense. He does not have the manpower to defend the city," Lord Harroldson began, placing a carving of an infantry soldier on the map. "He has a smaller force of men over here guarding the western bridge that crosses the Grey. I have received word from Lord Storm that he and the rest of the western lords await on the other side. Eight hundred strong..."

Harroldson placed a carved cavalry marker on the west side of the map, and another infantry marker on the east side.

"We will strike at the heart of Russ's defenses here. The cavalry archers of the South shall advance in front of the main force of our armies. The Army of the West shall be on the left, and the Army of the East will be on the right. We will attack the center of Russ's defensive line."

Harroldson placed cavalry and infantry markers on the maps to show Prince James's forces.

"While we are pressing the attack in the middle, Sir Finis Crowe will lead a force along the levee between the Grey River and George's Lake. You will capture the bridge to allow our Western brothers to attack Russ's lines from behind. We will give you one hundred men for this task, more than enough for you, I should think."

Cley surveyed the crowd of knights in the pavilion for the Sorrow. He wanted to see his reaction, but Sir Finis was nowhere to be seen.

"Lord Tew, we will keep your mounted lancers in reserve to protect the camp and our baggage, as we discussed earlier."

Lord Harroldson placed a final cavalry marker at the bottom of the map to show where the lancers would be placed.

"When Lord Storm brings his full army across the bridge, we will have Russ cut off from the city. Retreating will be impossible. We will crush him between the hammer and the anvil." Lord Harroldson pounded his fist into his hand to make his point. "Russ will be overwhelmed. The city will welcome us and Prince James. Good lords and loyal knights, your Lords Paramount will instruct you in your individual tasks. In two days, we will be celebrating the coronation of the rightful king in the Great Hall of King George."

Sir Cley noted that Lord Harroldson had not mentioned a wedding. Princess Rebecca had not returned with Lord Fowler's main army. Fowler's two sons, the twins, were still with him, but his most prized child remained absent.

Prince James stood and left through the back of the pavilion with his mother and Sir Lucas. The other lords and knights followed, leaving only the knights of the West.

"Men, come forward and look at the map," Lord Harroldson commanded. "Sir Crowe, I will give you a hundred men from the Kingstown forces that joined us in Crosstimbers."

Crowe stepped out of a dark corner of the pavilion. He spat on the ground as he walked toward the table.

"You think a bunch of defectors can be trusted?" Crowe asked. "Give me what's left of the Buckton men. They'll do."

"That is quite impossible. Sir Cley and the Buckton men will be leading my vanguard."

"Lord Harroldson, let my force go with Sir Crowe," said Sir Blake Pontifer, stepping forward. Lord Pontifer sent only fifty soldiers with his son. It was poor support, but he was still licking his wounds from what he perceived as a slight from the prince after the Battle of Pebble Creek.

"Sir Blake, I do not doubt your courage, but I have already made your assignment," Lord Harroldson said. "Pebble Creek will be our rearguard."

"I do not wish to sit in the rear and watch the Southerners guard our baggage. It is a duty for young boys and old men," Blake said defiantly.

"With twenty good men, I'll get your bridge. Let me have the Buckton men," Crowe said again.

"I am giving you one hundred. You can pick them yourself tomorrow," Harroldson said calmly. "There will be no more discussion."

Lord Harroldson walked away from the table, followed by his knights. Sir Blake sulked off into the night. Cley stood next to Sir Torrent at the table looking over the drawn map of the proposed battlefield. The Sorrow stepped around to the other side where the western bridge was drawn. He frowned and grunted in disgust.

"The Ol' Buck would be against this," Sir Crowe growled, then spat on the ground again.

"Aye...if he were here—" Torrent began.

"But he's not here," Cley interrupted. "We do as we are ordered... It's a good plan if everything goes right."

"Things don't always go right in battle, do they, Cley?" Sir Crowe muttered, then gave Cley a hard look before walking away from the table.

"When you two finally have it out, I want a seat around that ring," Torrent said, watching the Sorrow walk out the pavilion's entrance.

"There won't be a ring," Cley replied. "Come on, I need some sleep."

•   •   •

"The defenses are shabby," Sir Lucas said, handing Sir Cley's spyglass back. "There are wide gaps in the palisade walls. The western bridge is lightly guarded. Lord Russ is not a master tactician, but even this defense is below him. The generals of the King's Army should know better."

"Do you think it is a trap?" Cley asked.

"I don't know, Cley. The spies say there are only five to six hundred soldiers left defending the city. With that few, Russ should have pulled back all his defenses to the castle. Instead, he spreads them thin across this defensive line. The message from Lord Storm said that he defeated a force of close to six hundred men north of Shadow Woods. Lord Fowler has heard nothing from Amberfield, Duskfield, or Fairhaven. To me, that is more troubling. I fear they have thrown in with Russ."

"I agree. The eastern lords have no love for Fowler or Greyport," Cley said. "I wish I had been given the chance to talk to the messenger from Lord Storm."

The two knights sat on their horses, looking out over the terrain that led up to Kingstown. The rising sun glinted off the distant castle, the city of Kingstown sprawling before it. Cley envisioned the city as he remembered it. The Old City was the heart of the capital. It had cobbled streets and was surrounded by stone walls with great wooden gates. The castle was in the middle, with the Ministry of Law to the east and the Temple of the Four to the west. Squares with fountains of fresh water and parks lined with the manses of rich merchants and nobles surrounded the castle.

Outside the Old City, Kingstown had grown wild like an unkempt garden. Houses, taverns, inns, and warehouses grew there like weeds. There was no pattern to the streets as they often ended in dead ends or cesspools. The people there were common. Many were poor and had come to the capital looking for work, or trying to get away from some cruel lord. The Sickness was rife in Kingstown. Half of the population had perished from it over the last seven years. Cley hoped those who survived the Sickness would survive this conflict as well.

Sir Lucas and Sir Cley rode their horses over to the banks of the Grey River. Fishing boats and barges moved up and down, ignoring the armies that faced each other. A levee of raised earth close to fifty yards wide divided the river from George's Lake, where fishermen trolled the wide expanse of water. Across the river, smoke rose to the sky from behind the hills to the northwest.

Lord Storm's camp. Eight hundred strong.

"What do you know of the Drasani?" Cley asked Sir Lucas.

"The Drasani?" Lucas scoffed. "Only the tales told to children to make them behave. I remember a few. In Safe Harbor we had tales of a Windcaller who would send ships off to sea with a mighty gust."

"Jory told me of a Summoner at Shadow Tower, and he was at the farm as well. I would have doubted him, but I saw the dead with my own eyes. If it had not been for the silver antlers on Lord Buckhorn's sword, I never would have defeated them."

"Did you tell the story to Prince James?"

"I cannot get close to him, but you can. Jory also told me of a wizard who lives in a magical house in the woods and a boy who can cast fire. There is magic still in this world, Lucas, some for good and some for evil. The prince must know."

Both knights sat silently for a moment. A fishing boat sailed across the lake, breaking the smooth reflection of the sunrise.

"Before Lord Buckhorn died, he gave me the book *The Knights Roll*," Cley said. "He said it was up to us to teach James about the Knights of the Realm. I never thought much about being a member of the order."

"I know. I thought it was merely an honor bestowed by the king," Sir Lucas said. "I have been thinking about the others."

"Me too... We will need to help him add deserving knights," Cley said.

"I agree. The book, is it with you?"

"I have it hidden in a safe place. You have your scroll with the names?"

"Yes," Sir Lucas answered. "It will be up to us to show Prince James the way. His mother is rash and vain. Lord Fowler is hungry for power. He will need good advice and our help. He is smart and likes to ask questions. He seeks the truth. He will make a good king."

"We will help him. Stay by his side, Sir Lucas. Trust no one."

As the sun rose higher in the morning sky, the two knights turned their horses and rode south, side by side back, to their camp.

43
JORY XIV

Jory checked the saddle straps a third time, looking for any cuts in the leather that might break. He did the same for the stirrups, the bridle, and the reins. Thunder quietly ate out of his feed bag next to the other horses at Sir Cley's pavilion.

Next, Jory checked over Sir Cley's gear—his gauntlets, helmet, breastplate, and leggings. Sir Cley preferred to wear leather armor in battle, but said he would wear some steel for this one over his leathers. Jory checked the straps for wear and cleaned any dirt off the armor. The freshly painted shield was last. A white tree on a green field for the Knight of the Tall Tree.

Earlier in the morning, while Sir Cley rode out with the White Owl, Jory went down to the horse lines and found Aiden helping the other squires check the horses for their knights. The boys there talked about the upcoming battle, although most were going to be part of the rearguard. The older boys spoke of their chances for glory and knighthood. Aiden seemed distracted by his duties and spoke little, so Jory left him to start work on his own chores for Sir Cley.

"There you are." Emily interrupted Jory's thoughts. "I have been looking all over for you."

She is not very smart if she didn't come looking here first. Where else would I be?

Jory set Sir Cley's shield down next to the rest of his armor and turned to face Emily. She looked pretty with her brown hair pulled back into a ponytail, showing off her dark eyes. She was dressed in her healer's apron and dress.

"Can we talk?" Emily asked as she sat on a stool near the campfire.

She is not going to leave until she has her talk.

Jory stopped his chores and stood near the pavilion entrance.

"Have you told Sir Cley about everything that happened in the woods?" Emily asked.

"Y-yes. Why?" Jory answered. He had told Sir Cley almost everything, but Jory told no one about recognizing Carter in the woods or seeing the Summoner as his father. He also left out the part about overhearing Emily and Theo as the reason for him to leave Marwyn's to begin with.

"You even told him about Marwyn?" Emily asked.

"Yes."

"Did you tell him about me and my...talent?"

"No."

Emily breathed a small sigh of relief. "How did you know?"

"Marwyn told me a-after I came back from the tower with Alistar."

Emily thought for a moment. "I don't know if I should tell Maggy or Alyss."

"W-why not?" Jory asked.

"Upon our return, we told everyone the story that we hid in Shadow Tower before we made our way back. I feel like I would be lying now if I told the truth."

"How is it lying if you are telling the truth?" Jory knew they had to tell their made-up story when they got back. Lord Harroldson and the rest of the camp would have laughed if they heard the truth. It was a child's tale, a magical man living in a magical house.

"Well, yes, I don't want Maggy and Alyss to think I am a liar."

"W-why are you asking me?" Jory picked up an old practice sword, sat down on the ground, and began to clean it with a cloth.

Maybe if she sees I am busy, she will go away.

Emily watched Jory clean the old sword. "I figured you would tell Sir Cley. What did he say?"

"Nothing," Jory said, not bothering to look up from his cleaning.

Emily sat and watched Jory rub the cloth on the dinted sword. "I guess you will be holding Sir Cley's banner for him tomorrow, but you won't be riding into the battle."

"Uh-huh." Jory nodded. He was still too young and small to help Sir Cley like an older squire could help a knight.

"Theo's father won't let him be a part of the charge either. He was pretty upset about it when I visited him this morning," Emily said.

"Then why don't you go kiss him and make him feel better," Jory lashed out.

Jory's own voice and flash of anger surprised him, and Emily pulled back from him in her chair like he was a growling dog. Angry, upset, and embarrassed all at the same time, Jory got up, dropping the sword and cloth on the ground, and walked away. He did not know where he was going, but he knew he could not sit there in front of Emily. His walk turned into a run as he got past the last tent in the row. He held in his breath, trying not to cry.

I am twelve now, almost a man and a knight. A knight wouldn't cry about a stupid girl.

Jory ran toward the Grey River, finding a spot in the tall grass to sit and gaze out over the water. He breathed heavily, choked back a sob, and sniffed a few times. He wished he and Sir Cley could get on one of the boats on the river and go somewhere else, be in tournaments and have adventures the way they used to.

Jory watched the river roll slowly by, its movement reminding him of the blood that flowed from the wound in Draven's neck. He wondered what happened to Draven's body. Emily and Theo had both cried over his death, Jory hearing them as they walked. He wondered if Draven's mother even knew or if anyone would tell her. Jory thought about what would happen if he were to die.

Would anyone even care? Would my mother cry?

Eventually Jory thought about the man he had shot in the eye again. Who was he?

Why couldn't it have been Carter I shot? He deserved to die.

Jory heard a horse snort and spotted a riderless black charger walking toward him along the river. Behind the charger trailed the knight they called the Dark Sorrow. Jory sat quietly as the knight walked slowly behind his horse. The man hummed a tune Jory remembered hearing back in Seadrift when he was a small boy. His mother would sing it to him before bed, and she sang it for his younger sister too.

In the song, a little turtle played in the waves along the beach with his friends until one by one they all had to leave the little turtle to go to bed. Finally, the little turtle was called home to go to sleep. It was a song for small children, not squires or knights. Sir Finis Crowe did not look like some demon of death walking alone with his horse, humming a bedtime song. The Sorrow walked past Jory and made no gesture that he was aware of the small squire sitting on the grassy bank above him.

Jory looked up at the midafternoon sun. It was time for him to get back to camp.

A real knight doesn't cry. A real knight finishes his duties.

That evening, as the sun disappeared and darkness settled in over the camp, Jory was unable to sleep. Distant sounds of men shouting and singing could be heard if he listened closely. The night before a battle and the whole camp was awake. Even Sir Cley went off with the Knights of the Barrel after he had shared a meal with Jory. At tournaments, the knights often would stay up most of the night drinking, telling stories, and chasing after women. Some knights would drink so much that they would miss their joust the next day.

Sir Cley never missed a joust.

Footsteps outside the pavilion made Jory sit up on the cushion he used for a bed. Sir Cley walked inside and found his way over to his bedding in the dark.

"What are you still doing awake?" Sir Cley asked.

"It...it was hard to sleep with everything," Jory replied.

"I found it hard to sleep before a battle when I was a squire. It's still difficult," Sir Cley admitted.

"How many battles were you in with my...my father?"

"Umm, not sure. There were many small skirmishes in the Pirate King's Rebellion. There were only three true battles. Your father was always ready, but he too found it hard to sleep the night before."

"Will it be scary to be in the vanguard?" Jory asked.

"The fighting there will be the heaviest. I would be out

of my senses if I were not a little afraid, but a knight rises above the fear of death to perform his duty and protect his lord or king or kingdom. Many men out there will meet their end tomorrow. Some men will drink and carry on like they are doing tonight as one last celebration of life."

"But your lord was Lord Buckhorn, and he is dead now."

"And so now the men of Buckton are made part of Lord Harroldson's Army. If need be, we will be under the command of the king."

"But what if the lord or king who is in charge is not good? Do you still have to follow their commands if they are bad?"

"That is a good question, and you would get many different answers from knights. For me, I would do what I believe is right for the greatest number of people. Like this battle tomorrow, I believe Prince James will be a better king for all of Terros, not only the West. I will tell you a secret your father kept from me until I was fifteen. He was a member of a group called the Knights of the Realm. Lord Buckhorn was a member, and I was appointed to the order as well. Those knights are sworn to protect the kingdom, not just the king. Before Lord Buckhorn died at Crosstimbers, the order met, and we decided Prince James is the best choice for king. James will be good for Terros, and so will Princess Rebecca. We are on the right side. We are doing the right thing by fighting for his kingdom. When you are doing something that is right, it...feels like you have more strength and courage."

Sir Cley lowered himself to his bed and reclined on the cushions. Jory settled back and stared at the pavilion cloth above him.

"Do you ever think about the other men? The men you have killed?"

"Sometimes...yes. You try not to. Remember, they are trying to kill you. If you think about them too much, it can drive you mad. We should get some sleep. Good night, Jory," Sir Cley said and yawned. Jory heard him roll over to his side.

"Do...you ever think of your home up in the North?" Jory asked quietly in the dark.

"Yes...but your home is where you make it. Home is where you are with the people you love."

Jory thought of his home as he drifted off to sleep.

The morning air smelled of horses and leather. A stiff wind made the banners held by knights and squires straighten and flap noisily. Jory stood in front of Sir Cley Woods, holding his banner with its white tree on a green field. The wind pulled at the banner, and Jory held it tight to keep it upright.

Sir Cley sat mounted on his charger, ready to lead the vanguard of Lord's Harroldson's Army of the West. Flanked on either side of him were the knights and men of Buckton. The Great Tor sat astride his horse next to Sir Cley, who had Lord Buckhorn's sword sheathed and tied to his saddle. Lord Buckhorn would be making this charge with them.

Jory scanned the line of mounted knights. Up and down the line, squires held the standards of their knights. Much like the first day of a jousting tournament, the squires bore their knights' colorful banners. The younger squires in the line were on foot. They would be part of the rearguard, assigned to protecting the camp. The older squires who were going into battle were mounted. They would carry their knights' banners into battle and act as another set of eyes to protect their knights' backs.

Off in the distance, to the left, the Dark Sorrow sat on his black charger. He had no squire holding his banner. Jory did not know if he even had a banner. Behind him on foot were a group of soldiers armed with various weapons and shields. Most were soldiers who had surrendered at Crosstimbers.

Behind him on a small hill, Prince James surveyed the army from his horse. Lord Fowler stood to his left. Sir Lucas, the White Owl, rode on his right. Jory spotted Theo Harroldson mounted on a horse next to Sir Lucas. Jory imagined Theo whining about taking part in the battle and being angered that his father assigned him to the rearguard with the other boys.

The sound of bells from Kingstown began to ring and carried across the field. As if in answer, a blare of trumpets came from the east. Jory scanned the low hills to his right. A mounted army came into view at the top of a hill.

Sir Cley held his spyglass up, looking to the east.

"It looks like Amberfield has decided to join us," Sir Cley said loudly so that the men around him could hear.

The soldiers from Greyport and Dimbury shouted to their eastern brothers. Calls could be heard coming back from the men of Amberfield. Swords pounded on shields as both forces greeted each other.

A horn from the west brought Jory's attention to his left. At a distance, another large army of mounted men moved toward the western bridge.

"What is Storm doing?" Sir Cley said to Sir Torrent. "He is supposed to wait in the hills until the bridge is taken."

Jory watched the left flank begin to move as the Sorrow spurred his horse and led his force over the levee. A trumpet sounded from behind Jory to signal the advance, and the Army of the West moved forward at a walk. To his right, the Army of the East from Greyport and Dimbury began to move alongside them, keeping pace. Jory took down Sir

Cley's banner and walked between the soldiers and horsemen, being careful not to get trampled over. When he reached the back, he turned and could see the giant wave of Prince James's supporters surging toward Kingstown.

339

44

THE PRINCE VIII

"Prince James, we are assured a victory now." Lord Fowler rocked forward in his saddle. "With the added force from Amberfield, Russ will be crushed."

The trumpets, shouting, and thumping of swords on shields across the plains drowned out the sound of the bells coming from Kingstown.

"It will be a resounding victory. I would not be surprised to see the Kingstown soldiers dropping their weapons and surrendering like they did at Crosstimbers." Lord Fowler turned to his twin sons mounted next to him. "See, boys? The power of the East, united under the leadership of Greyport."

Prince James had never seen Lord Fowler excited or even happy before, but now he sat smiling on his horse. The appearance of Lord Payne's army from Amberfield did little to alleviate James's anxiety over the battle. The history books of Terros were full of legends of knights leading a small force to victory against impossible odds. Those were the stories he liked best, but James's story would not be like that. He sat behind an army of almost three thousand knights and soldiers. His opponent, Lord Russ, commanded an army a third that size.

A horn blew in the west. James used his spyglass to search across the Grey River.

"What is Lord Storm doing?" James asked Sir Lucas in dismay. "He is moving on the bridge too early."

The left flank of the Army of the West began to move quickly. James watched from his spyglass as the small force climbed onto the levee and began to move its way toward the defenses set up on the eastern side of the bridge. The whole of the Army of the West slowly began to move forward in the center. The forces of Greyport and Dimbury pushed forward on the right.

At the front, the mounted archers of the South began at a walk, sped up to a trot, and eventually increased to a full gallop as they moved ahead of the western cavalry. It was a beautiful sight to see as they advanced their lines.

Trumpets blew in the east as Amberfield began their advance on the eastern line of defenses on the far-right flank. Across the river, Lord Storm reached the bridge and started to cross his army. James watched the reckless cavalry approach the middle of the bridge. He could barely make out the banners of Turtle Bay, High Meadow, and Buckton being carried in the front.

"Lord Storm is young and brash. But this is a major blunder, My Prince," Sir Lucas responded. "Let us hope it will not cost too many lives."

The mounted archers of the South picked up speed as they charged forward. A flight of arrows shot up from their lines toward the Kingstown defenses. A second volley of arrows quickly filled the sky. The archers broke off their attack. The lines split in two and wheeled around both sides of the advancing western army. The maneuver was a testament to the training and discipline of the southern army.

To the left, the vanguard of the Amberfield army veered toward Greyport to join them in their assault.

"If Lord Payne is not careful, his vanguard will entangle with yours, Lord Fowler," Prince James said. He leaned forward in his saddle to see Lord Harroldson's reaction as a crossbow bolt shot over his shoulder and impaled itself in the back of the head of one of his guards. A second bolt struck his horse on its side, causing the horse to rear up in panic.

More crossbow bolts whistled in the air. Sir Lucas jumped from his horse and onto the back of James's. He spurred the scared charger away from the hill. James ducked low as Sir Lucas surrounded him with his shield and body. James heard Lord Fowler yell something about a "fool" and "traitor."

The sounds of shouting and fighting came from all directions. All James could see was the ground passing by as Sir Lucas rode through the camp. The sound of another horse galloping with them turned out not to be a pursuer but Sir Lucas's own horse running alongside. Screams of women and men swirled together. James kept his head down, feeling like a coward.

"Get the prince's mother!" Sir Lucas shouted. "Get her across the river to safety."

Sir Lucas pressed the injured horse on. They rode down a slope at breakneck speed until the horse began to slow to a trot. James peered over Sir Lucas's shield. Three mounted southern knights blocked the way across the field. On the ground before them was Sir Blake Pontifer, a lance driven through the armhole of his armor. Beyond the southern knights rolled the Grey River.

"The White Owl," the knight in the middle, holding a shield emblazoned with a fiery red sun rising over a golden field, called to Sir Lucas. "What good fortune to see you again. It looks like I will get that joust after all. It would appear I have an unfair advantage, as it is three against one."

"Two," Theo said, riding up from behind and drawing his sword.

The other two knights advanced on Sir Lucas and Theo.

"Let me help," James said. "I will only be a hindrance for you. Let me fight for my kingdom."

"Grab the reins," Sir Lucas said as he dismounted and climbed back onto his own horse. "Use my shield," he added, handing James his shield. "Defend yourself."

The other two knights descended on Sir Lucas and Theo, whose horse reared and kicked at its attacker. The two horses crashed into one another. The knight made a slash at Theo, putting him off balance, and Theo crashed to the ground.

Sir Lucas evaded the knight charging him. He circled around to deliver a blow to the back of the head of the knight attacking Theo. The strike sent the knight off his horse to the ground. The second knight turned his attention to Prince James. He swung his sword in a wide arc that James caught with his shield as the knight rode past him. The third knight with the sun painted on his shield entered the fray, charging into Sir Lucas and knocking him from his horse.

James turned back to his attacker as he charged in from James's left. James caught the knight's sword swing with Sir Lucas's shield. The knight charged in again from his right side now, but James again deflected the attack. The knight rode in close and began to hammer down on James with his sword. James held Sir Lucas's shield up to catch a blow, and the knight slashed at him with a dagger in his other hand.

The two horses circled around each other as the knight continued to beat down on James. The southern horse bit James's leg and his horse's ear. The knight caught James on his helmet with a blow that sent James reeling back in his saddle. He then raised his sword to deliver another blow to the defenseless prince, when Theo crashed his horse into the southern knight headlong. The knight flew from his horse and sprawled out on the ground. Theo sprang from his charger and quickly attacked the immobile knight, driving his sword under the chainmail mask and into the knight's throat.

James turned his horse around to see the knight that Sir Lucas had knocked to the ground earlier was still down, now with a dagger sticking out of his chest. The clash of swordplay sounded behind him. James turned again to see Sir Lucas dodging a swing from the knight with the flaming sun on his shield.

"Your cause is lost, Sir Lucas. The others are dead by now. Only the northern knights live, and they can freeze, for all I care," the other knight said as he and Sir Lucas circled each other. "Join us. King Russ will pardon you. You have no dog in this fight."

"I have the word I gave," Sir Lucas replied. "The word we all gave, Sir Baddon."

Sir Baddon lunged again. Sir Lucas parried the sword thrust. The southern knight stepped away to regain his balance, then dropped his shield, pulling a stiletto from his belt. He went on the attack again. With each swing of his sword, the stiletto would slash out like a snake's tongue. Sir Lucas moved to parry the sword and step out of the way of the stiletto thrust. Another attack came, and another. Sir Lucas defended each time, but his sword began to lower under the pressure of the attacks.

"Lucas, take your shield!" James yelled as he rode toward him.

"No, stay back!" Sir Lucas warned.

Sir Baddon attacked again while Sir Lucas spoke to

James. The knight brought down a heavy smite on Sir Lucas with his sword. The White Owl caught most of the force with his sword, but it knocked him down to one knee. Sir Lucas panted as Sir Baddon stood in front of him, twirling his sword in his right hand. He rushed in to finish him, but Sir Lucas sprang up as the southern knight grew closer. He went straight into his attacker, moving to his right. Sir Lucas slashed his sword, and Baddon's hand holding the stiletto flew off in a spray of blood, landing in the grass. Sir Baddon stood, staring at where his left hand had been.

Sir Lucas came back at the knight and swung his sword against his opponent's feeble parry, knocking the southern knight's last defense away. A final forward thrust of Sir Lucas's sword under Sir Baddon's breastplate ended the duel.

The sounds of the battle around them brought Prince James out of his narrow focus. The tents and grand pavilions that made up his camp were besieged with flames. Southern lancers and soldiers fought the rearguard left by Lord Harroldson.

James looked around him at the chaos of battle. Sweat dripped into his eyes, and he reached up to wipe his brow under his helmet. When he pulled his hand back, his fingers were covered in blood. His eyes became unfocused. His vision swirled and he tumbled from his horse.

"Theo, find the healer!" Sir Lucas called, his voice fading.

Darkness engulfed Prince James.

45

JORY XV

It didn't make any sense.

Jory stood with his mouth agape on the low hill that had seen the Army of the West descend toward Kingstown. The southern mounted archers performed their charging volley, but when they broke off, they began to fire volley after volley of arrows into the ranks of the western men.

On the right flank of the battlefield, the Amberfield men crashed directly into the Greyport and Dimbury army. The initial Amberfield charge left the combined force stalled. On the left flank, Lord Storm's Army dropped their banners and came pouring across the bridge, heading straight for what remained of the West's vanguard. There was fighting on the levee, but Jory could not make out what was happening.

Behind Jory, the troop of southern lancers attacked the men from Pebble Creek. Some of the older soldiers and boys set up a defensive line, but the lancers broke through and set fire to the camp, killing whoever stood against them. A few crumpled figures were on the hill where Prince James had stationed himself to observe the battle.

Horns trumpeted from the battlefield, sounding the retreat. The rear lines began to turn, and men clashed into one another. Fighting broke out in the ranks. Soldiers from Kingstown, who had surrendered at Pebble Creek and Crosstimbers, turned and struck down the soldiers from the West whom they were marching next to.

Jory scanned the field looking for Sir Cley. He thought he saw him in a small circle in the middle of the field. Sir Cley and some other men tried to clear a path out of the pressing enemy cavalry and soldiers. A hail of arrows went up and rained down on the area, and Sir Cley fell from his horse.

Jory dropped Sir Cley's banner and grabbed the reins of a riderless horse, swinging himself up onto its saddle. His stomach churned and lurched as he charged the horse down the hill to the battlefield. Men and riders struggled back up the hill against him. Jory weaved through the tide of injured and panicked soldiers trying to retreat.

Reaching the bottom of the hill, Jory spurred the reluctant horse forward to where he thought he last saw Sir Cley. Individual battles of life and death dotted the field as men fought against each other desperately to stay alive. Jory slowed the horse down when he spotted Sir Cley's charger, Thunder, lying on the churned-up ground. Arrows riddled the horse's body. Jory's throat tightened, and tears began to well in his eyes. He swallowed hard, trying to breathe. He rode over to Thunder, searching the area for Sir Cley.

Around him, men were surrendering or dying. Other men were stripping boots and armor off the dead in the field. Jory spotted Sir Cley lying on his back without his helmet. He jumped from the saddle and ran to Sir Cley. An arrow stuck out from his neck above his shoulder armor. Blood slowly flowed out of the wound where the arrow penetrated by his collarbone, and small streams of blood trickled down Sir Cley's face from a wound on his head.

Jory jumped down onto his knees next to his knight, who sighed and smiled.

"Jory," Sir Cley wheezed.

"I will find a horse for you and get you out of here," Jory said, looking around for help.

"You need to save yourself." Cley struggled to talk and he winced in pain as Jory tried to pull him up. The knight raised his head, looking into Jory's eyes, and spoke again. "The Tower...the Roll is there... Courage... My brother..."

Jory stopped looking for a horse and concentrated on his knight. Tears rolled down Jory's cheeks and fell onto Sir Cley's face, mixing with the knight's blood and sweat. He took Sir Cley's hand in his and took off the gauntlet. Sir Cley's large hand was cold and wet as he squeezed Jory's hand.

"You're a good boy...Jory," Sir Cley whispered. "Never forget—"

"This one here might have some goods. He's got himself a little squire at his side."

The voice shook Jory. He let go of Sir Cley's hand and turned to see three men walking toward him, each man hauling a bag slung over his shoulder. Two of them were carrying pairs of boots. Jory grabbed Sir Cley's sword from the ground and jumped to his feet to defend his knight.

"Easy there now, boy. We mean no harm to you and yours," one of the men said.

They were not dressed like soldiers. They were dressed in ragged clothes and had dirty faces and hands. One of the men had a bag full of swords with ornate golden hilts and scabbards tossed across his back. Jory recognized the hilt of Lord Buckhorn's sword in the bundle. Jory held Sir Cley's sword out in front of him in a defensive stance, eyeing the three scavengers as they walked closer.

"Stay away!" Jory growled with tears pouring down his cheeks.

The men drew nearer, and when they got to within a few feet of Jory, he lunged at the man on the right holding the bag. The man swung his bag at him, but Jory ducked and thrust Sir Cley's blade into the man's belly. The man let go of his bag and dropped heavily to the ground, holding his stomach and cursing in pain. Jory spun toward the other two, but they ran off with their battlefield plunder.

Jory turned to go back to Sir Cley when he was tackled to the ground from behind. Sir Cley's sword slid in the grass away from his grasp. A large man's knee drove into his back and pinned him to the ground. The man grabbed Jory by the wrists, twisting his arms behind his back. Jory struggled until he heard a voice that made him freeze.

"Tie his hands and feet tight, then take him back to my pavilion. And make sure that one over there is dead."

The man on top of Jory bound his hands and feet, then he stood Jory up and slung him over his shoulder, carrying him to a nearby horse. Jory raised his head toward where the voice had come from. He saw the fat man mounted atop a white charger. There was no mistaking the man's voice or his face. Jory could still remember the smell of the man's breath and the coarseness of his hands and his beard... It was the man he hated, the one he was supposed to call Father, Sir Raymond Wells.

Jory watched as another soldier walked up to Sir Cley on the ground, poking him with the butt of his spear. The soldier turned and nodded to Sir Wells. The fat man sauntered his horse over to the soldier, took the soldier's spear, and drove it into the belly of the defenseless knight.

A howl boiled up in Jory's throat, but when he opened his mouth, nothing came out. Tears burned down his face. Anger and hatred hardened his heart.

46

THE PRINCE IX

Rebecca cradled the boy's head, rocking back and forth in a soothing motion. The boy heard her softly singing an unfamiliar tune. She smelled of flowers and strangely also of horses. Rebecca smiled at him and stroked his brow and cheek. The boy smiled back at her.

A bump shook James. In the darkness, there were faint voices.

"Careful now. The river is full of sandbars on its edges. We need to be farther south of here before we head east," a man said.

"East? But shouldn't we be going west?" a boy asked.

"They won't be looking for him to the east."

James slowly opened his eyes, and the vision of Rebecca faded away, a different girl's face replacing hers. She held his head in her lap and smiled down at him.

"His eyes are open again. I think he is awake," the girl said.

"Good, see if he can drink some water," the man said.

The girl held a water flask to his lips, and James felt some water pour into his mouth. He tried to swallow but instead choked and coughed. He sat up quickly, causing his head to spin briefly. As he regained his senses, James could see he was floating on a small pole boat. The man he heard speak turned out to be Sir Lucas. He manned a pole on the left side of the boat, pushing the boat along with the river's flow. Lord Harroldson's son, Theo, worked the right side. At the rear of the boat, his horse stood tied next to two other horses.

"Here, try to take another drink while you are sitting up," the girl sitting next to him said.

James turned to her, and she smiled at him again.

"We won't be calling you by your name or title for a while. Lucas said it is safer that people don't know who you are. You can call me Emily."

James smiled back at the girl. Her touch and voice were soothing, warm, and calm. James turned his head again to look behind him. Beyond where the horses stood on the pole boat, a dark sky loomed. Upriver, smoke filled the sky and blocked out the late-afternoon sun.

Smoke from my camp. My kingdom in ashes. How many men and women died because of me today?

James's head pounded, and his stomach lurched. He put his hand up to hold his head and felt a damp cloth bandage wrapped around it.

"Don't touch that," Emily said. "Lie back and rest."

James laid his head back down in the girl's lap. She smiled yet again, and James closed his eyes, replacing the girl's image with Rebecca's.

All I want is Rebecca, and I will fight to get her back.

Epilogue

The Princess

"That will be one hundred gold in ransom." The sergeant stamped the butt of his spear on the tiled floor. "Bring the next traitor forward."

A poor-looking knight was led to the front of the court

by two guards and shoved to his knees. Scrapes and dried blood covered his bald head. A sling wrapped around his shoulder, holding a heavily bandaged arm. His blue tunic was dirty with mud and blood stains that made it difficult to see the red mustang embroidered on the shirt.

"This is the traitor, Sir Bryan Thurmond, a traveling knight, My King," a clerk said from a long table set below the king and his court's seats on the dais.

"Do you swear to do your king homage and from this day forth obey his laws and commands?" the sergeant asked the kneeling knight.

"I do so swear...by the Four," the knight said meekly, bowing his head.

"One hundred gold in ransom." The butt of the spear slammed onto the marble tile.

The king began to cough, shaking as the fit racked his body. Next to him, the queen patted him on the back and handed him a handkerchief. The king held it to his mouth and spat. His face was ashen, and his cheeks sunken.

The king looked in poor health today, Princess Cirice thought.

"Bring the next traitor forth!"

How many more knights could there be?

Close to forty had been judged before the court this morning, and it was all for show. Each prisoner had already been ransomed, with the council passing judgment on the traitors.

The king began hacking and coughing again as another knight was brought before him to swear allegiance on his knees—pay a ransom, of course. Princess Cirice paid attention to the proceedings, keeping track of each knight who came forth and where they hailed from. Her brothers were notably absent.

"My King, I present to you the traitor Lord Marius Fowler of Greyport."

This should be interesting.

Lord Fowler approached the dais and went to his knees. After the formalities of swearing loyalty and fines being assessed, he struggled back up with the help of the two guards on each side of him.

"King Ivan, you have shown great mercy to me, but I ask for your pardon for my sons," Lord Fowler pleaded.

"Your sons?" King Ivan asked.

"Yes, my twin boys were taken with the other squires and boys as prisoners." Fowler gestured toward the guards that surrounded a large group of boys to the left of the court.

"Guards, bring them forth," the clerk at the table ordered.

The twins were pulled out of the filthy mass of boys. They did not look like twins. One had blond, almost white hair, while the other had a dull-looking face framed by reddish-brown hair.

"The Crown releases these boys back into your care, Lord Fowler," the clerk announced.

King Ivan assented with more coughing.

"Lord Fowler, which of the twins is to be your heir to Greyport?" the queen asked.

"That would be the first born, Daxian," Lord Fowler said, placing his hand on the twin with the reddish-brown hair.

The Minister of the Word stood from the table that seated the rest of the Grand Council. "My King, it is my recommendation that the other Fowler boy be appointed to the High Temple. In the histories of Terros, it has been noted that twins can often be, how should I say, *problematic* in matters of succession. Let him be instructed in the ways of the Four."

"I agree, Minister Hiam. The younger twin shall be sent to the High Temple and become a member of that order in due time," the queen added.

The blond twin tried to run, but one of the guards seized him by the arm and held him in place. Lord Fowler ignored the boy's pleading and walked back to his place along the wall with Daxian. Another guard came forward, grabbed the legs of the struggling twin, and the two guards carried the cursing boy from the court.

Minister Hiam remained standing. He pulled a scroll from his sleeve and began to read from it.

"'Let it be known to all present, and all of Terros, that James Tolar is named a traitor, a usurper, and a rebel. A bounty of one thousand gold coins is placed on his head. Also, Lord Harroldson of Tidehaven is named a traitor and a rebel. A bounty of five hundred gold coins is placed on his head. Any lord or knight who fled and is not present for these proceedings is also duly named a traitor and a rebel, and shall have bounties of one hundred gold coins placed on their heads. All holdings, titles, land, or property are hereby stripped of these rebels and placed under the direct control of the Crown. This is the decree of King Ivan the First.'"

Minister Hiam rolled the scroll back up and handed it to the scribe sitting at the table.

The king began another coughing fit.

"Minister Hiam, are there many remaining petitioners for the king to hear?" the queen asked.

"Yes, My Queen, there are a few more lords and knights to be heard," the minister answered.

The high priestess rose from her seat at the Grand Council's table to address the king.

"My King, it has been a long day for you. Let the council finish these proceedings. With the divine guidance of the Four, the temple will pass judgment over these lesser lords and knights."

"I agree, Ivan. Let us retire from court. The council can

finish these lesser matters," the queen said, standing. She helped the king to his feet and walked him back to the family quarters.

Cirice remained in her seat. She liked the look of the high priestess, a tall woman with long straight black hair. Her facial features were beautiful in a harsh sort of way with high cheekbones and deep-set dark eyes. Her calm, commanding voice never wavered. Cirice remembered she was one of the first officials of Kingstown to greet them when her father first arrived in the capital.

The high priestess confidently strode up the stairs of the dais and sat on the king's throne.

"Now, let us continue," she commanded.

A parade of lesser lords and knights appeared before her, each being sentenced to a ransom made payable to the High Temple. The other members of the Grand Council offered no objection to this new policy of paying the temple instead of the Crown.

Cirice considered leaving her seat until a large knight was dragged before the court. The heavy chains that shackled his arms and legs clattered along the marble floor as two guards struggled to carry the knight between them. His long black hair was matted with blood from a wound on top of his head. Mud and blood covered his clothing, hiding any sigil that might have been on it.

Another guard walked behind them holding a thick chain attached to an iron collar around the prisoner's neck, which he pulled back, forcing the prisoner's head up. The knight was not only bound but also gagged. His eyes were swollen shut and nose smashed.

"This is the traitor Sir Finis Crowe, a traveling knight, High Priestess," the sergeant announced. "His ransom is to be set at—"

"I think not," the High Priestess interrupted. "This one is far too dangerous to be ransomed. Send him to the temple prison. We will reform him in the wisdom of the Four."

Temple guards took charge of the bound knight and carried him from court.

"Are there any more petitioners?" the sergeant called out to the court.

"Yes, I have a petition for the king," a voice replied. A fat man shaped like a pear and dressed in a fine red and purple robe strode forward from the crowd of people lining the wall on the right. He dropped to his knees in front of the high priestess and addressed the court. "I am Sir Raymond Wells, Lord of Buckton. I request the return of my son, who was seized unjustly from me by temple guards on the battlefield."

Minister Hiam flipped through the pages of a great book in front of him while Lord Wells spoke. His eyes rose from the book and questioned Wells.

"Could the newly made Lord of Buckton explain why his son was on the field of battle? My records indicate that your son is only five years old," the minister inquired.

"That would be my trueborn son. I am speaking of my stepson," the lord replied. "I wish to reunite him with his mother and sister."

"Lord Wells, you have received the reward for your part in leading the western army into the ambush near High Meadow, yet Lord Storm still sits in his seat at Turtle Bay. You were to deliver him and all his forces as well as those of Buckton and High Meadow. He was able to escape with over half of those combined forces. It was only by the temple's efforts that the rebels did not discover the ruse we planned," the high priestess said in a disdainful voice. "You have been rewarded enough for a failure. The king has been overly generous with a man such as yourself."

The fat lord narrowed his eyes at the high priestess while he struggled to stand back up. His face contorted as if he were about to say something else, but instead he turned and stalked out of the court.

As soon as Lord Wells left, the high priestess stood from the king's throne and spoke for all to hear.

"The common soldiers and men who were captured shall be enlisted into the King's Army and sent west to deal with the fleeing traitors. The captured squires and boys shall be held by the temple and judged at a later time. This court is now adjourned in the name of the Four."

"Wait, wait, I want to be heard."

A voice called out from the group of squires and boys being held by the temple guards.

Princess Cirice watched as some grungy boy shouldered his way through the group of prisoners standing in the front. A guard blocked his way with a spear.

"High Priestess, wait, you promised. I seek my reward," the boy called again.

"Bring that one forward. I shall hear him," the high priestess ordered.

A guard walked the boy over to the high priestess, who peered down at him from the first step of the dais. The guard tried to push the boy to his knees, but he refused to kneel before her.

"I claim the reward for my service. I did what you said. I told you their numbers and movements. I sent you their plans as soon as I knew them. I even found one of those special people you told me about, although your men failed to catch her in the swamp," the boy said, looking up at the taller woman. Defiance shone in his eyes.

This one is not afraid of the high priestess.

The high priestess reached out and placed her long fingers under the boy's chin.

"My little outlaw prince, I wondered what became of you. Of course I shall keep my promise," the priestess purred.

She walked the boy away from the guard with her arm around his waist like a loving mother and over to the Grand Council's table, where she spoke to the scribes.

"Let it be written that Aiden, son of Olin Dhampir, the Pirate King, shall be returned to his home, reunited with his mother and sister, and named Lord of Rockport with all its rights and privileges. You will be given one hundred gold coins to assist you on your journey back to your home. A sum of one thousand gold coins shall be delivered in your name to the temple from the Crown for your service."

"His King's court is adjourned," the sergeant announced to all present.

Cirice sat on her chair on the dais wondering what other promises the high priestess had made. She watched as the boys and younger squires were led out by the temple guards. Some had their hands tied behind their backs. Some were bloodied and bruised. They looked like sheep being led off to the slaughter.

The princess watched the high priestess walk from the court, the other members of the Grand Council trailing her like ducklings following their mother.

I wonder what promises the high priestess would make to me. What would it take to be queen of all Terros?

ACKNOWLEDGEMENTS

This novel has been in the making for over five years, and I need to thank the people who helped me along with this adventure. The developmental editors Ashley Wyrick and James Abbate offered notes and encouragement to get my story out. The copy editing was done by Jason Letts who diligently and patiently smoothed out the rough edges of my writing. The cover art and book formatting was done by Daniel Pyle.

I must thank my parents who read bedtime stories to me and encouraged me to read. They never discouraged me from reading Tolkien, Lewis, or Golding or the Choose Your Own Adventure books that helped shape my imagination. My sister, Tamara, is one of the first readers of my story and was able to read a rough draft to our dad before he passed away.

Also, thanks go out to my coaching friends, Brian, Justin, Tim, and Dwayne. The real-life Knights of the Barrel. My D&D friends Arty and North, who let me take them on weekly adventures, and my other reality friends Connor, Ethan, and Colton who are huge supporters.

JOHN J. CURTA is a graduate of Iowa State University and has been a teacher and basketball coach for 30 plus years. *The Knight's Squire* is his first published novel. He lives in Port Lavaca, Texas with his dog Cinco.

www.ingramcontent.com/pod-product-compliance
Lightning Source LLC
Chambersburg PA
CBHW060516160726
47991CB00001B/59